TEEN
SAS

10/03/23

Sass, Adam

Your lonely nights are over

YOUR LONELY NIGHTS ARE OVER

ADAM SASS

VIKING

VIKING
An imprint of Penguin Random House LLC, New York

First published in the United States of America by Viking,
an imprint of Penguin Random House LLC, 2023

Visit us online at PenguinRandomHouse.com.

Library of Congress Cataloging-in-Publication Data is available.

ISBN 9780593526583 (hardcover)

10 9 8 7 6 5 4 3 2 1

ISBN 9780593690734 (international edition)

10 9 8 7 6 5 4 3 2 1

Printed in the United States of America

BVG

Edited by Kelsey Murphy
Design by Lily Qian
Text set in Calisto MT Pro

For Terry and Russell, the Coles in my life

AUTHOR'S NOTE
(WITH CONTENT WARNINGS)

THIS IS THE STORY of Frankie Dearie and Cole Cardoso, two best friends who face down a murderer and, in doing so, end up suspects themselves. However, Dearie is white and him being a suspect unfolds differently than it does for Cole, who is Latine, so be forewarned this book occasionally intersects with racism and hostile law enforcement. These characters also grapple with the realities of abusive relationships, like gaslighting, and verbal and emotional manipulation, and at times, the abuse becomes physical.

These struggles don't dominate the book and are rarely depicted on-page, but the story couldn't be told appropriately without them, so just know they are present from time to time.

Your Lonely Nights Are Over is an ode to gay friendship. Where I am closest to Dearie, Cole is a combination of my close friends Terry and Russell—queer men of color who are daily examples of fearlessness, individuality, and impeccable high standards of self-esteem. My mission in life is to be as powerful a friend to them as they've been to me. If you end up loving Cole as much as I do, the credit is theirs.

With these advisories in mind, I am very pleased to share with you the adventures of those beautiful, bitchy besties, Dearie and Cole.

The #1 streaming show in America is
YOUR LONELY NIGHTS ARE OVER:
The Search for Mr. Sandman

A terrifying docuseries based on the

bestselling true crime chiller

by Peggy Jennings

Don't frown, don't pout, don't ever cry.

If he hears your lonely heart, then you're the next to die.

From 1971 to 1975, the San Diego serial killer Mr. Sandman held the city in his grip, slaying the lovelorn and recently dumped. Any gender, any age—no one was spared. If you were crying over being stood up, if you pined over someone you couldn't be with, if your sweetheart left you for someone new, Mr. Sandman would find out. If he set his sights on you, you were as good as dead. And if you broke someone's heart, you might as well have swung the blade yourself.

Why did Mr. Sandman do it? Some say he couldn't stand self-pity. Others believed he wanted people to stop being so careless with one another. **"STAY TOGETHER"** became the rallying cry of a city who believed they could outsmart the most elusive murderer of the twentieth century. They thought they could find meaning in the mayhem.

In reality, it was a senseless, never-ending bloodbath, until one day, without warning, it ended.

Almost fifty years later, the killer has not been found or identified.

Where did he go? Why did he stop? Is he still alive—and if so, will he strike again?

Watch now and see what everyone is talking about!

PART ONE
MR. SANDMAN

CHAPTER ONE

DEARIE

I'M PROBABLY THE ONLY person in school not obsessed with that Sandman show. I can't escape it. Popular kids, nerds, teachers, janitors—since the show dropped, everyone's become an amateur detective. Yesterday, AP Bio didn't start for fifteen minutes because Mr. Kirby was theorizing about the killer's incomplete shoe print. He and my best friend, Cole Cardoso, went on and on about how modern technology could recreate the print better than seventies computers (if only the evidence still existed).

"It's a shame San Diego PD didn't keep better records before the FBI got involved." Mr. Kirby sighed.

Cole was trying to convince Kirby that Mr. Sandman knew someone in the force—a father or friend—who messed with the evidence. But Mr. Kirby just shook his head. "Never ascribe to malice what can be explained by incompetence."

Cole rolled his eyes. "Corrupt *and* incompetent, then."

Mr. Kirby clumsily tied his obsession back into the bio lesson for the day, but nobody was mad at the distraction.

For the first time in his teaching career, he had his students riveted.

Anyway, because Mr. Sandman was never found, this show has my classmates thinking he's behind every corner. But the slayings happened in San Diego, California, and this is Stone Grove, Arizona: a rusty, dusty canyon town of twenty thousand. A lonely place to live, sure, but unlikely to see the return of a famous boomer slasher. I don't blame people for gossiping. They like thinking something exciting could happen here.

But Stone Grove isn't that special.

Which is why I'm not bothered about these death threats that have been popping up. They're a prank, as simple as that. Today, Queer Club is meeting about the texting drama during free period, and I'm here to make sure they stop believing the whispers that Cole and I are behind these anonymous texts. This happens a lot—people blaming us. Looking cute and inspiring jealousy are kind of our thing. But death threats? That warrants a public denial.

Maybe we should get publicists! High school reputation publicists should be a thing, but until that day comes, I have to make my own statements. So here I am in room 208, the Queer Club's regularly reserved space—where the band and choir rehearsed before they built the new auditorium. It's a theater-in-the-round classroom with desks scattered across three levels of crescent-shaped stadium platforms. Since the auditorium opened, it's become a flex space, either for clubs or a quiet study area—which is why I'm a stranger here. I study in my own time.

Just kidding, I have extremely bad senioritis.

Actually, that's also a lie. I got early acceptance to my top-choice theater school in LA, so I don't have senioritis; it's more like *I'm ready to leave this town so I can start living my life*-itis.

"I didn't see you at the meeting last week," says a pretty, upbeat white girl with long, silvery hair. Her name is Em. She's a trans sophomore whose cheerleading social circle has never quite bumped into mine—which is a circle of just me and Cole. Em and I wait alone in the cavernous classroom, which usually hosts a dozen Queer Club members but so far is shockingly empty.

Typical. I finally come back to this damn club and everybody ditches.

"I used to come to these Queer meetings when I was a freshman, but I just wasn't a joiner," I admit, brushing on a coat of cherry ChapStick. Em nods in awkward silence at her desk atop the room's highest platform. "I'm Frankie Dearie, but everyone just calls me Dearie."

Em smiles. "I know. You're a big-boy senior now." Her brow furrows. "Boy, right?"

Chewing my lower lip, I give my outfit a cursory scan: a black cropped tank with cutouts on the sides, calf-high boots, and a sheer lilac bandanna worn tightly around my throat. I snort. "Yeah, boy, but . . . I'm figuring it out."

Em sighs into her resting palm. "I feel that."

Tick. Tock. Where is everyone? Where's Cole? He was supposed to be my buffer.

Em taps her pen against her cheek, watching me, clearly about to ask what she's wanted to since I sat down. "You know . . . It's okay if you did it as a prank—"

"JESUS," I groan. "We didn't send those threats."

Em throws up innocent palms. "Hey, I thought it was kinda funny . . ."

"Believe me, if it was us, we'd claim credit by now. Our primary goal is always attention."

Em returns to her phone, and I return to mine. No response yet from Cole to my *HELP MEEEEE, ARE YOU CLOSE?* texts. I open a saved screenshot of the reason I'm sitting here in purgatory: the death threat texted from an anonymous number to two members of Queer Club.

Your lonely nights will soon be over.

Mr. Sandman used to mail the words in a note to his victim the day before he killed them. If you saw that message, you were as dead as hamburger in twenty-four hours. On the bodies, he'd leave a second note—*Your lonely nights are over*—closing the deadly circle. That's how the news gave him the name Mr. Sandman. It's the title of a creepy 1950s song that uses that "lonely nights" lyric.

So, half a century later, two states away, and after a show glorifying the killer starts streaming, this cursed message is sent to two of the most exhausting people in school: Grover Kendall (Queer Club's secretary) and Gretchen Applebaum (treasurer). Now those two believe they're either hours away from being slaughtered or the victims of a cruel prank.

Grover, Cole, and I used to be friends years ago (all of us in Queer Club used to be, actually), but it got complicated in middle school, and by high school, Grover had such a falling-out with me and Cole that he will now never miss an opportunity to shit-talk us. Who knows what Grover has been saying privately, because the dirty looks we get in public are constant. His bad vibes for us are so well known that all he had to do was put out a TikTok saying he's the victim of bullying and the whole school jumped to us as suspects.

I thought that Cole and me showing up at Queer Club would smooth things over, or at least help everyone see the truth: we don't care enough about these people to prank them.

Yet here I am, with no Cole, no Grover, and no Gretchen. Nobody but me and Em.

"Is this the L . . . GT . . . B club?" asks a small, dark-skinned Black freshman who has wandered inside the classroom. A janitor with a bushy mustache holds the door open for him.

Em perks up. "Yep!" The boy cautiously hugs his

overstuffed backpack. "Well, it's just G and T so far." She chuckles. "I'd love a G&T."

I courtesy-laugh, and she can tell. Her face falters. "I've never had one. My mom, um . . . loves them." She groans to herself. "Ah, God, I gotta get out of this town."

"SAME," I mouth to Em.

The freshman boy has already left, in—I can only assume—fear.

The door bursts open again, and my heart lifts. Cole Cardoso, an eighteen-year-old boy with light brown skin, a swoop of inky-black hair, and a sharply handsome face, sneaks in wearing a maroon bomber jacket over a tightly fitting white tee. A gold chain drapes over the top of his muscular chest. At the sight of him, I thrust my fists in the air victoriously. Em starts compulsively brushing her hair. Cole's beauty can be debilitating.

"Thank God you're here," I moan luxuriously.

"Got behind, sorry, was running to my venting music," Cole mutters as he slips his AirPods into their case. His tone is oddly self-conscious. He eyes Em like she's an enemy combatant, which isn't surprising. I dragged him back to this club, which is probably still nothing but snippy, humorless debates or news about the latest inhuman bill from our ogre congresspeople.

"I thought there were like ten people in this club?" Cole asks.

"Right?" Em laughs. "This is my second meeting."

"Apparently, it's down to just us three," I say, hugging my bestie. He certainly smells like he's been running, and his hands are bone-cold, so he must've been outside. Even in a desert town, February gets chilly.

Cole doesn't sit. His sculpted eyebrows arch as he scans the room. "No one's here?" he asks. "Byeeeee. Dearie, let's go."

"Maybe they're running behind!" I open my phone to text Lucy, the club's vice president. "Five more minutes and then we'll go."

Cole boops my nose. "We don't need to be here. You've been manipulated. We didn't send those threats, and Grover made this a character assassination because he's a jealous FLOP." My friend sighs, as if disappointed in me. "The Flops called the shots and you came running."

I can't even look him in the eyes, that's how correct he is. "Then why did you come?"

"Every statement you make on this rolls the dice with my reputation too."

My ears get hot. I forgot again.

When you've been best friends as long as Cole and I have, it's easy to forget you're not twins. Well, it's easy for the white friend. As time has gone on, more every year, I'm reminded with a painful spasm that Cole is not my twin and this bullshit jealousy people have for us lands differently on his shoulders.

"I was gonna deny *everything*," I whisper, hooking Cole's pinky in mine.

Smiling, he takes my frail shoulders in his strong hands. "You have a soft heart, and snakey bitches can smell that. They'll tell you how scared they are. You'll apologize even though you had nothing to do with those threats. But not on my watch! If I hear one 'I'm sorry' leave your lips, I'm going to sit on your face in front of the whole club."

"Don't make promises you can't keep." I kick his shin playfully.

Em stares, wide-eyed, and my smile falters. "He's kidding!" I tell her. "We're just friends."

Em holds up *say no more* hands, but Cole says, "See, that's the stuff I'm talking about."

"What stuff?"

"*We* know we're friends who talk sexy for fun without it meaning anything. You care *so* much about how you come across!" Tsk-tsking, he slips off his jacket and gets comfortable next to me.

Chewing her pen, Em asks, "So, who do you think sent those death threats?"

"Who?" Cole asks, flipping hair from his eyes. "How about they sent them to themselves?"

"Why would they do that?"

"For the *attention*?" Cole snorts, as if he's the only rational person left on earth. "This is something everyone in

14

a so-called Queer Club should be suspicious of: attention-seeking. That's what we are. That's what we do. It's the oldest motivator in the book besides, like, money."

"I mean, that could make sense," I say. "Grover and Gretchen feel invisible."

Ever since Grover made that video where he sobbed about what he called his "death message," I've had this lump of dread in my chest. Grover's not *not* cute, and his vulnerability about feeling unloved made him . . . I don't know . . . I got this overpowering impulse to take care of him. But was that his intention? A thirst trap of guilt?

To paraphrase Ms. Spears, there are two kinds of people in the world: ones who attract through confidence and ones who attract through self-pity.

Cole is the epitome of one, Grover of the other. That's why they're perfect enemies.

Em, deep in thought, slaps her pen against her open palm. "There was no tragedy mask."

"THANK YOU." Cole thrusts his hands toward her. "Where's the tragedy mask?"

"Wait, what?" I ask.

Cole scoffs to Em, "He doesn't watch the show." She smirks, seemingly pleased to finally have an inside track on Cole that I can't access.

"Sorry I'm not a death addict like the rest of you," I say, playing with my neckerchief. "Explain the tragedy mask."

Cole takes my hands and brings them to his lips. "My sweet friend, you live on Jupiter. It's the poster for the show. The main symbol of the killer. Mr. Sandman signed all his victims' messages with a doodle of a tragedy mask. You know, the theater kind . . ." Cole scrunches his face in an exaggerated frown. "The few witnesses and survivors all saw Mr. Sandman wearing the mask. It's his thing, and it is *not* present in the fake-as-hell messages those Flops sent to themselves."

"But . . . that was in the seventies. He'd be a grandpa now. What if he can't master a phone, and this is the way he does messages now, with no doodle?" Cole's blank stare cuts me deeper than any words could. I run my hand through my mop of dark curls, embarrassed that I'm taking this circus remotely seriously. Standing, I pull on my black leather jacket that's decorated across the back with hot-pink roses. "Okay, enough scary stuff, no one's coming."

"Thank GOD!" Cole bellows. Even Em seems grateful someone finally made the decision to pack it in. She slides her notebook into a canvas tote and flings it over her shoulder.

Leaving the room how we found it—lights on and door open—the three of us step into the empty hallway. Large shafts of afternoon sun cut through the circular overhead windows, casting spotlight shapes across rows of hunter-green lockers. In the distance, a smattering of footsteps

16

squeak over the linoleum, but otherwise, for two in the afternoon, there's surprisingly little going on.

Cole and I sling our arms around each other's waists, as Em tags along two paces behind. "Ugh," Cole says, "dealing with Grover was so much easier when we were kids, and I could just titty-twister him into shutting up."

I elbow him and whisper, "I'm sure he'd love it if you did that now."

"I would jump into traffic first."

"Maybe he just needs some smooching to calm down."

Cole squints. "Dearie, guys who do the wounded sparrow thing are manipulators. If you fall for it enough times, you're gonna marry some dickhead who controls every breath you take."

"Okay, harsh!" I flick his ear and he hisses.

"I'm sorry! He's just . . . Ugh, Dearie, don't like Grover. He sucks."

"I can handle myself." I lace my cold, slender fingers into Cole's, which are warm and soft, despite all his deadlifting. Cole is sporty, but he also knows proper skin care.

We swing our arms lazily. Em is probably baffled about what our deal is. Most people are.

"Don't worry," I whisper, "I'm not marrying anybody until I'm fifty."

Cole's dimples pop. "Me, right?"

I nod. "For the taxes."

Our chortling is interrupted by a flurry of footsteps. Ms. Drake, a fortysomething white woman in a blue polka-dotted jumpsuit, rushes past, clattering her hip against the school's double exit doors before running into the parking lot. A gust of bitingly cold wind rushes in.

"Ms. Drake?" Em calls.

Ms. Drake is our librarian and the Queer Club's faculty sponsor. Whatever her reason is for not showing up today, something has her terrified. She shouts into her phone: "HELLO? We need an ambulance right away! Stone Grove High School!"

Every muscle in my body freezes.

By the time Em, Cole, and I look at each other, the screams begin.

We turn toward the sound. Students are clutching their faces as they run sobbing down the corridor—away from a place we can't quite see. "A shooter?" I whisper.

"We would've heard shots," Cole whispers back uneasily.

I can barely speak with this lump of fear in my chest. "What do we do . . . ?"

Cole's grip on my hand tightens as the three of us wait against the lockers.

My mom is a detective. If I text her, maybe she can get here faster? Slowly, with a sweating hand, I open my phone to text Mom, when Ms. Drake bolts back inside.

"They can't be dead!" Ms. Drake mutters to herself as she rushes past us.

Dead. Who?

"Get out of here," Cole says, pulling me away urgently, but I rip free and sprint after Ms. Drake, her courage contagious. I have to help. Cole yells, "Dearie, wait!" and chases me until we round the corner.

A dozen students swarm around someone on the ground whose tennis shoes stick out of the crowd like the legs of the Wicked Witch's sister under Dorothy's house. The shoes squirm on the ground, so whoever it is, they're still alive. As Ms. Drake parts the group, a young boy with thick glasses and light, tawny-brown skin runs out, sobbing incoherently. It's Benny Prince from Queer Club. A crimson streak of blood stains the shield on his Captain America shirt.

"Benito?" Cole asks, horrified, as he stops the boy. "Oh my God, you're bleeding . . ."

"Cole, he's . . ." But Benny is in too much shock to finish what he was saying. He whispers something softly in Spanish and Cole nods, his eyes laser focused.

"Then whose blood *is* it?"

Another person wrestles free of the crowd: Lucy Kahapana—a small girl with light bronze skin, a side-buzz haircut, and rumpled skater boi clothes. Her hands are stained red, and her eyes are puffy from crying.

"Lucy, what happened?" I ask, stepping into her path.

"We need an ambulance!" she shrieks as she moves to run down the hall. But almost immediately her sneaker slips, sending her hurtling backward into me. Before I can correct my balance, we both collide with the linoleum. Pain rockets through my shoulder. From my vantage point on the ground, the crime scene becomes clear: two more Queer Club members—Mike and Theo—crouch over a boy shaking uncontrollably, sitting with his back against the lockers. The shoes I saw. It's Grover—I recognize his blond hair and beefy arms. Ms. Drake shushes him. He's alive but drenched in scarlet. Barbed wire is wrapped around his neck like a noose. Puckering gashes have turned his throat into a waterfall.

It's like *Saw*. I'm breathless.

"They're coming, sweetie," Ms. Drake says. "Don't touch it. Don't touch the wire. Mike, HOLD HIS HANDS DOWN." Mike does as he's told and presses Grover's hands to the floor. Grover fights him—he very badly wants to pluck the barbs out of his neck, but Ms. Drake is right. If he dislodges them, there'll be no stopping the bleeding.

Grover blubbers in a panic: "He—he—he—had a mask."

"Don't talk," Ms. Drake says forcefully. "Your neck, remember?"

Assurance has swept over her, crowding out any fear or doubt. My fear and doubt, however, aren't going anywhere.

If someone doesn't come soon, Grover will die—twenty-four hours after getting that text.

Still on the floor, Lucy covers her face as she cries. Cole's confident hands wrap under my arms, and he lifts me . . . but not before I spy another body.

Gretchen Applebaum. The other club member who received a Mr. Sandman message. She lies next to Grover, motionless and ignored. Her eyes stare open vacantly. Her blond pigtails lie soaking in the pond of blood that seeps from the barbed wire wounds across her neck.

She's dead.

At the edge of her body is a note made from sandy-brown cardstock, which sits tented on the floor like a dinner invitation. Written in neat cursive is an unmistakable message: YOUR LONELY NIGHTS ARE OVER. Next to the handwriting is a doodle of a tragedy mask—the symbol Cole and Em said kept it from being a true Mr. Sandman message.

The texts were real. They were a threat.

The killer from TV has found our Queer Club.

CHAPTER TWO
COLE

QUEER CLUB GOT US to come to a meeting after all. After Gretchen's body was taken away and Grover was rushed to the hospital, police escorted the surviving members of Queer Club back to room 208. Almost two hours later, we're still waiting to be questioned.

It's the Slap all over again.

Back in sophomore year, our racist history teacher called the cops on me for slapping Walker Lane—Walker, who hit *first*, had a slap coming after a day of trash-talking. He was jealous I beat him out for captain of the Rattlers. But unlike me, Walker got to go home right away. I was never arrested, but the police interrogation lasted hours. *Hours* spent on a slap. Scariest day of my life—until today.

By the way, that racist teacher ended up getting the chop. Benny from Queer Club did some digging and found out that teacher had a history of aggressively racist tweets under an alt account tied to their personal email. Amateur. And Dearie helped us leak said information to the superintendent—and to the masses over at his anony-mous finsta. For a moment, Benny, Dearie, and I got our old friendship back as we took that asshole down.

Although, today, we're not talking slaps, we're talking murder.

At least this time, there's fingers pointing all around. It's not just me alone, sitting for hours, too terrified to move from my chair. Ms. Drake is being interviewed in the next room, an attached side office we discovered is tragically soundproof. Barely a murmur has escaped that door, even with our ears pressed flat against it.

"They could've at least let us wash our friends' blood off our hands," grumbles Mike Mancini, a short and cubby Italian senior with swooping black hair and a patchy half beard. He's single-handedly destroying the myth of the fashionable queer. No one responds to him. Eight students sit quietly and separately across the raised tiers with at least two desks between, each of us islands apart—except for me and Dearie. I gently pet my bestie's tangled curls, which always calms my heart. He's my pretty, smooth fawn, and after tonight, he and I might need to do our annual hookup, because I've got some seriously bad hormones I've got to release.

I think he needs it too. The more I pet Dearie's hair, the more he keeps staring through the wall at nothing.

Above us on the top tier, Em waits near Theo, a small, white nonbinary senior with short, choppy red hair and a flair for fashionable bow ties. They'll be questioned first; their parents rushed over as soon as they got the news and are being held just outside. The rest of us either have parents too poor to bounce out of work so quickly, or in mine and Dearie's cases, our parents are involved with the crime. One of my moms is a surgeon currently operating on Grover. Dearie's detective mom is questioning Ms. Drake. As for the other four members, Mike Mancini's father runs the body shop in town, so closing early is a struggle; Lucy Kahapana's divorced mom is a nature photographer, and she's been in Mooncrest Valley all day with no cell service; Benny Prince's dad runs Tío Rio's, a local restaurant and karaoke bar, and is on his way over as soon as his waitstaff can be left alone; the last Flop—er, Queer Club member—is Justin Saxby, a senior I've mistaken for Grover a million times. Blame it on white-boy-face blindness, but they're both tall and vaguely husky blondies. Only Justin is much cuter (and nicer), with a small shamrock tattooed on his upper thigh.

How do I know about such an intimately placed tattoo? How do you think? Grow up.

"I just wish we knew if Grover's okay," Lucy moans into her palms.

"Me too," Benny adds.

"He will be," Dearie says lifelessly. "Cole's mom is the best."

I clench Dearie tighter. At least he's talking again.

Dearie's compliment is muted by my worry that while my mom *is* the best, I don't know if medical science has found a cure yet for twenty throat wounds. Half of that Flop's blood was on the floor, and the other half is splattered over the rest of us. If she saves Grover—if he lives to irritate me another day—then maybe we'll have some answers about who did this.

I could've sworn those messages were bullshit.

I'm almost never wrong. I hate this.

"A successful surgery takes at least a few hours," I say, "so the longer we don't hear anything, that's good news."

"Hmm," Justin snorts viciously.

The needle breaks on my Bitch-o-Meter, and I stiffen. "What?"

"Nothing." Justin munches his nails casually. "Just funny how you're trying to care."

I stifle the urge to cuss him under his desk. It's bad enough Justin was a boring hookup (he just lay there like I was supposed to be his masseuse), but now I've got to deal with this attitude?

"I do care," I say.

Theo groans from the top tier, rolling their eyes at Em, who does not return the gesture. Good for her recognizing an asshole when she sees one. Theo is second only to Grover in being the reason why I put thirty football fields between myself and this club. Scolding, self-important closet

Republicans. Just because Dearie and I meet up with boys from other schools—and *not* for little milkshake dates—we're what's "destroying the queer community" (i.e., why they can't get a date). Same old envy-fueled slut shaming from the Pilgrim days, just with a new Pride flag filter.

"Oh, PLEASE," Mike chimes in, a hungry glint in his eye. "Don't act like you're concerned about Grover."

I raise a finger. "No one's talking to you, babe."

"I'm not your babe."

"Absolutely right you're not, sweetie."

"Not your sweetie, either!"

Dearie slowly leans back into his seat, our cuddle time over. The rest of the club awaits my response, but I just roll my eyes. "Mike," I say calmly, "I know you're like three seconds out of the closet, but this is how a lot of us talk, so you should know it really doesn't mean the flirty stuff you think it means. But I respect that you don't want to be called these names anymore, so I'll stop and go back to when you didn't register in my mind in any way."

He stares, gagged and slack-jawed. Baby's first reading.

"You're treating us how you treated Grover," Justin sneers. "Like insignificant bugs to be squashed."

"Girl, stop right there," I say with my deeper vocal register. Dad voice, but without volume. Not loud enough to draw in the doofus cops from outside, but tough enough to make these Flops go silent. Em holds her pen between her teeth. Dearie is finally alert, a strawberry hue returning to his sun-kissed white cheeks. We must sense the same thing: the club *definitely* still blames us for those messages.

"One Cardoso cuts him up, the other Cardoso sews him up," Mike grumbles.

Benny and Lucy gasp. Theo snaps their fingers in support of Mike.

My throat tightens. They can't really think I did this, right?

"Enough!" Dearie barks, his cheeks reddening. My breathing is shallow. Oh God, Dearie, maybe don't escalate right now.

But it works. Mike visibly cowers. The queer newborn has an obvious crush on my bestie, but his confidence has all the sturdiness of a baby deer crossing an icy pond. Mike licks his lips as his eyes dart around the room. "Just a joke . . ." he mutters.

"Oh, it was a knee-slapper, hon," I say. "Netflix stand-up special any day now."

"OKAY," Lucy shouts, leaping from her seat. She paces the room in some vain attempt to burn off her excess energy. "So happy I'm stuck here listening to my favorite show, a bunch of mean gays complaining!"

"Cole's the mean one," Justin mumbles.

"I'm bi," Mike scoffs.

"Don't get cute, you know what I meant," Lucy says,

jabbing her finger. After a deep cleansing breath, tears still hanging in her eyes, she smooths back the unbuzzed side of her hair: "My friend is dead. Maybe two friends." She shakes her head. "They never caught Mr. Sandman back then. And by the way? The show said his body count was so high because he probably had copycats." On the ground tier, she spins around to look at each one of us. "Did one of you feel like being a copycat tonight?"

Dearie, Mike, Justin, Em, and Benny glance away. Only the meanest ones present—me and Theo—don't blink. Lucy swallows hard, her courage plummeting the longer we stare back.

Lucy takes another breath and turns to me. "While we're here, I want to know what I was gonna ask at today's meeting," she says. "Why did you send those messages?"

Emotion cracks Lucy's tough facade.

It's difficult to feel defensive around such a brokenhearted person.

"It wasn't us," Dearie says, his throat sounding dry.

"He's right," I say. "We didn't send those messages. We were coming here to tell you the truth. Not that we should've had to."

Mike and Justin bristle at my defense, as if they blame me alone, not Dearie. Of course they do. This is going somewhere bad fast.

In the corner, Benny hides his true feelings beneath his

enormous glasses. It's hard to get a read on him from this distance. Mostly, he's been keeping to himself.

"You hated Grover," Lucy says, not breaking eye contact.

"*Hate*," I correct. "He's still alive. And you can think someone's a prick and not want them dead. 'Not liking someone' and 'murder' are two"—I make bunny ears—"different things."

Lucy snorts back tears. "So, where were you during free period?"

Smiling, I lace my fingers under my chin. "I'll save my answers for the detective."

"Seems like an easy question to answer," Theo butts in. "Unless you're hiding something."

"No," I say, flashing my dimples, "I just don't want to validate Lucy's authority to question me like I'm a criminal."

Theo's lip curls. Em giggles into her fist.

Until this is figured out, *all* of these Flops need to get it through their victimized heads that I will not be treated like a criminal.

As Lucy seethes, Dearie stands abruptly. "Cole was running track, listening to music."

"Dearie," I groan. This is everything I warned him would happen if we came to Queer Club today. They'd treat it like an inquisition, and he'd crumble under questioning because he wants to be seen as whatever their version of "good" is.

"What?" Dearie asks. "It's not a secret."

I stand up, towering over Dearie and Lucy. "I'm trying to mind my business until your mom—the actual investigator here—needs me." I turn to the others. Em is the only one not glowering in my direction. "Grover and Gretchen got death threats, and you all accused us without an ounce of proof. That is *serious*, children. Dearie and I don't need to say a thing to any of you."

Dearie shuts his eyes and exhales. "You're right."

He sits back down, and so do I. "You're goddamn right I'm right. It's serious and—given that everyone remembers how I was treated after Walker's slap—gambling with my life."

Across the room, Benny nods miserably. He gets it. The others—most of them white—look anywhere but in my direction, as if they're trying to pretend no one said anything.

Complicity does that.

Dearie plants a quick cherry-scented kiss on my knuckles. I can breathe a little easier.

With a swirl of my finger, I turn the tables on Lucy. "When *we* were here with Em—when Queer Club was supposed to start, where were you all? You're all such perfect babies, I'm amazed you weren't five minutes early. And it can't be because you already found Gretchen, or we would've heard the screams sooner. So. Explain."

So Lucy does. "Gretchen texted me and Theo to meet

her outside fifth period so we could walk over together." Her shoulders deflate. "She never showed."

Like an Agatha Christie detective on too much caffeine, my accusatory gaze shifts rapidly around the room. Each time I land on a new Flop, they confess instantly:

"Grover texted me," Justin says. "He wanted me and Mike to meet him in the cafeteria. He was nervous you were gonna be at Queer Club today and wanted emotional support."

Grover. No one acts wounded better than him. I wouldn't trust those cuts in his neck were real without putting my fingers in them.

Now it's Benny's turn. He burns holes into the classroom carpet, his jaw angrily set. "I heard Mike and Justin talking about meeting Grover," he says. "But Grover didn't ask me for any support." He holds back tears. "I felt left out. I've been Grover's friend longer than them. I don't know, whatever. I didn't feel like going to Queer Club anymore, so I went to the library. Then Ms. Drake and I heard screams."

Cool friend, Benny.

If I knew Grover was going to live, I'd have said this out loud. Benny deserves real support, not some one-sided friendship. He and I know each other better outside of school. Our parents hang out, and my other mother is their family doctor, so Benny has always been more like my cousin from the other side of town than a friend. Because I'm always with

Dearie, and Benny's on the shyer side at school, Grover probably pissed in his ear about me enough to keep our social circles separate.

But if those two are so close now, why would Grover leave Benny out from his lunch table therapy? Wouldn't he want as many sycophants gassing him up as possible?

"So." I clap my hands once. "Now we know where we all were. Dearie and Em were here on time. I was running laps to blow off steam before coming to this awful, blamey, bad-friend (apparently?)"—I glance at Benny, who cracks a smile—"club."

"And no one can alibi you," Justin says singsong-ily.

Pivoting slowly to Justin, I present him with my open palms. Clean. Unblemished. "A medical examiner will tell you that strangling someone with razor wire tends to leave a mark."

"Ever hear of gloves?" Mike asks.

"Ever hear of deodorant?"

All mouths drop open at once. Mike is speechless. Whatever goodwill I may have gained with the Flops is once again flushed—but I don't care. Sure, it was mean, but what do you call accusing me of FULL murder just because you don't like me or are jealous of how much time I spend with Dearie? Is an insult only mean when it's coming out of a popular boy's lips?

Sighing, Dearie turns softly to Mike. "Cole couldn't

have been wearing gloves. When he came into the room, his hands were freezing. He was outside, where he said he was."

We share a smile. I'm happy to be vindicated. Less happy Dearie is still taking their arguments seriously, as if they're based on merit and not jealous Floppery, but whatever.

A door opens behind us.

Benny jumps with a gasp as Ms. Drake walks out of the back office. Her graying dark hair sticks out in wild, exhausted directions, and her blue polka-dotted jumpsuit now features two scarlet streaks down the front, like tire tracks.

My heart thuds. Ugly reality returns, forcing out my petty arguments with the Flops.

"I'm sorry that took so long," Ms. Drake says weakly. "Your parents should be here—"

The door to room 208 bursts open from the hallway, and poor Benny jumps again. An older, stern-looking white man with a pearly-white beard stomps inside wearing an overcoat. While the door is briefly open, police hold back a swarm of haggard, desperate-looking families. When Ms. Drake sees the old man approaching, she sighs. "Leo, they're keeping everyone outside. Their parents aren't even—"

Ignoring her pleas, the man—Leo—wraps her in a hug, which Ms. Drake immediately squirms out of. "Is it him?" Leo asks desperately. "Tabatha, was it *him*?"

"I'm taking you home. NOW." Gripping Leo by the elbow, she shuffles him outside. She's so livid, she doesn't say goodbye.

Who is this guy? Something about him seems familiar.

"Cole, honey?" a strong but welcoming voice calls from the office. Detective Dearie, my bestie's mother, stands in the doorway. She's as short and raven-haired as her son, but where my friend is paler, she always sports a rich tan. She has impeccable nails and wears a crisp indigo pantsuit. She's compassionate, but it's her job to make us feel like whatever's happened, we'll get through it okay.

At least, that's how she makes me feel. My back finally unclenches at the thought that, with Mrs. Dearie running things, this will *not* be like the Slap incident.

With a flash of her lavender nails, Mrs. Dearie beckons me into the office, which has been vacant since our old civics teacher retired last year. When I sit, the room feels less like an office and more like an apartment someone moved out of hastily. The bookshelves are blank except for a copy of last year's student handbook. Mrs. Dearie shuts the door gently, sits behind the desk, and smiles pleasantly before asking, "How are you feeling?"

"Overwhelmed," I say with a nervous laugh.

"I know." She leaves a long silence as I dig my nails into the chair's wooden armrests. "Cole, you and Frankie are . . . schemers." She winces comically, forcing a small laugh from me. Her son and I have been partners in crime since we could form long-term memories. Before continuing, Mrs. Dearie raps her nails against the desk. "But you're harmless."

Why is she tiptoeing? Why isn't she just launching into questions about what I saw?

"Mrs. Dearie, what's wrong?"

"A girl's dead."

I nod. Gretchen, we know. My heart hasn't left my esophagus since I saw her. "Something *else* is wrong."

"Cole, you're the smartest kid I know." Mrs. Dearie laughs hollowly. "So, what I'm not gonna do is ask you where you were at two o'clock, because I'm sure you've got an answer, and I'm not gonna ask why you boys suddenly came back to this club after years of making fun of it—because I know about the text messages."

The air thickens.

Mrs. Dearie pulls on a blue surgical glove and opens Mrs. Benson's side drawer, which should be totally empty. "Because of the . . . rumors, we did a locker check of everyone in the club," she says. "I didn't want to discourage the idea because it might show bias toward Frankie. I don't even think he's been to his locker in months."

I laugh to be polite, even though I'm seconds away from peeing my pants if she doesn't get to the point.

In my mind, that ugly officer's face reappears—tattooed on my brain since the Slap. I have an intimate understanding of when a cop is playing with their food. The coyness, the patently fake ignorance. It isn't them doing me a kindness; it's aimed at unsettling, inducing stress, and getting their target to crack.

With a shiver, I realize Mrs. Dearie isn't taking my statement. I'm being interrogated.

"I assumed we'd find nothing and move on," Mrs. Dearie says, exhaling slowly and reaching into the drawer. "But when I opened Frankie's locker, I found this . . ." Finally, she pulls the mystery item from the drawer and lays it on the desk. An old flip phone—ancient model but new. A burner. Breath flies out of me as her smile falls. "Do you know the last text this phone sent?"

Your lonely nights will soon be over.

We don't need to say it. We both know it's true.

"It texted Gretchen Applebaum," Mrs. Dearie confesses, her chin quivering as she attempts to remain professional in the face of a clue that points to her son as the person who sent the death threat. A threat that has come true.

She has to know this phone was planted. She can't suspect Dearie.

Then my thoughts jump to a logical—if agonizing— conclusion. "Is that the same phone that texted Grover too?" I ask. Steeling herself, Mrs. Dearie reaches again into the drawer, pulls out an identical burner, and places it next to the one from Dearie's locker.

The phones are cute twins. Schemers. Besties.

"This is from your locker," she says.

There it is. Evidence framing Dearie and me for murder.

CHAPTER THREE
DEARIE

GROVER IS AWAKE.

After a suspense-filled day and a half, Grover survived his surgery and is talking again. According to Mom, he didn't see anything unusual until a masked man appeared and attacked Gretchen. Things became hazy for him after that, which is understandable due to the trauma.

I would never admit this to Cole, but I've been dreaming about Grover. They aren't sexy dreams—I don't think. It was just him and me in the darkened school hallway. He was upset, like a child lost in a store. He's larger than I am, but that only makes his vulnerability sweeter. A tall yellow Lab of a boy who needs help. My help. I found him, wrapped my arms around him from behind, and shushed his whimpering. "I'm sorry I didn't see your pain," I said.

Grover placed soft, grateful hands over mine.

When I wake from this dream on my living room sofa, I'm brimming with tears. I've been sneaking micronaps here and there because I haven't been sleeping through the night.

Neither has Cole. Our superintendent shifted the whole school to virtual classes until the police have finished sweeping for evidence.

Unfortunately for our nerves, the only evidence the police have found has been those burner phones. Mom assures us it's suspicious they found something this incriminating at a crime scene where they hadn't even found a stray eyelash—but still, it's not easy when this makes us the only suspects.

This has been triggering for Cole, I can tell. His texts have become short, sparse, and lacking in exclamation points. No matter how many reassuring messages or inane TikToks I send him, his energy still isn't back to normal.

"The only people who know about those phones are you, me, and my mom's team," I say in a voice memo to Cole.

He responds with his own, sounding strained and far away: "How long's that gonna last? This show is worldwide—people are gonna be *thirsty* to know the suspects of a new Sandman killing. Dearie, if they don't find other leads soon, they're probably not even gonna let your mom stay on the case. Her son's a suspect."

Lying flat on the couch, I watch my living room ceiling fan spin. I have no clue how to calm Cole's anxiety. Mine is on the rise. Finally, I respond with: "Person of interest."

Cole responds, "If you had actually watched *Your Lonely Nights Are Over*, you'd know the original investigation

RUINED the lives of several persons of interest."

Dread settles over my thoughts like a cloud of mist—like it's *Silent Hill* in my brain. The healthiest solution is to retreat to creature comforts. Perhaps a leisurely chat with a casual hookup.

Tucson High is like twenty times the size of Stone Grove, which means a much stronger stock of dates to choose from. Cole and I each have our regular, casual boys and theys over there for whenever we're feeling anxious.

shitty day over here, luv, could use some attention, I DM three different Tucson High seniors at once from my finsta. Two replies come instantly. One is Ben Wally Jones, a tall, sweet-as-pie Black nerd for whom I tried to get invested in *Dead by Daylight*, but the game was just so much work.

Sorry, poodle, he texts. I'd love to but I'm heading to Tahoe with my dad. Is it serious?

Not at all, don't worry. Stay warm out there!

The next response is from Griffin Bateman, a short, cubby, white rich kid with impeccable style. A little bland, but he's nice and has beautifully soft hands (Cole makes fun of my hands thing, but we all have our vices). He texts, Sorry to hear that. I have some attention I might be willing to part with. How bad is your day? Texting bad or in-person bad?

I wet my lower lip as I respond, in-person bad.

my parents are at golf.

My eyebrows rise. So does my tent. Well, God bless golf. When are they back?

in a few hours.

Plenty of time.

I don't know, Dearie. It might cut it close
by the time you drive into town.

Okay, Griffin wants to play hardball. I know what he needs. With a grunt of frustration, I pry off my socks and snap a picture of my bare legs. The moment the picture sends, Griffin launches in on the dirty talk. I tell him I'll be there in thirty.

Boys can be so easily puppeteered.

I'm halfway dressed when I get a text from Lucy Kahapana—she's at the hospital with Grover. He says if I come around after his parents leave this afternoon, he has something to tell me. Lucy won't confirm or deny that it's something that will exonerate Cole and me, but she coyly insists I want to hear what he has to say.

Hope returns to my body, but when I text Cole about it, he snuffs it out. "Dearie, it's another manipulation," he says as I call him on my way out. "If he's got something that will help us, make sure we're not suspects, why wouldn't he just tell your mom? And according to you, nobody but us knows we're suspects."

"Persons of interest!" I correct, running cream through my curls and slipping on a pair of raspberry-tinted glasses. "I don't know, I have a feeling. If this takes heat off us, especially off YOU, I have to try. Me and Grover used to be close, maybe, I can convince him to speak up for us."

Silence follows on the call until I'm in my car. Then Cole's voice comes: "Well, while you're in Tucson, get some D."

I smile. "Already been arranged."

Luckily for my busy schedule, Griffin is a very *quick* lover, but he's just what I needed to work out my nerves. After leaving Griffin's, I guzzle a large Dunkin' iced coffee and park at the hospital until Lucy texts to tell me Grover's parents have left. No one in the Queer Club would be getting through this grim era if it weren't for Lucy, our unofficial matriarch. Cool in every crisis, if there's news that needs to be spread, she spearheads it. If we're arranging a party, she's the planner. Her mom is gone a lot on photography assignments, so she's basically been a self-sufficient adult since middle school. The only way you could derail her is by asking her about *Doctor*

Who. She'd start in on her preferred viewing order and forget whatever she was just doing.

There's no better person to be the liaison between Grover's hospital bed and the club.

In the hospital, I weave through an ICU glutted with nurses, police, and reporters. When I get to Grover's room, Mike Mancini is already there. I never realized this before, but he looks like a dark-haired Wario version of Griffin. It's kind of working for me.

Becoming a person of interest has made me voracious.

Mike greets me more sweetly than he's ever done before. After all, I did walk in serving: tinted glasses, shirt with a plunging neckline, and hair mussed from Griffin's greedy fingers. Rustled hair always makes me think of sex, so I didn't fix it. Looking this way can only help my mission to win over Grover—and convince him to help Cole and me get out of this mess.

"Good to see you," Mike whispers outside Grover's private suite, which has multiple officers posted outside. "You look c— Uh, come in."

We sidestep the officers and walk in.

There isn't a single corner of the room not stuffed with bouquets of roses, "get well soon" cards, and handmade posters saying "you are not alone." At the center of this love shrine is Grover Kendall, the boy from my dreams, looking far less dreamy. His floppy blond hair lies wilted across his forehead, his eyes are dark-ringed and puffy, his lips are chapped and peeling, and his neck is swaddled in a foam brace. This is a boy who came within centimeters of death. Still, when he lays eyes on me, he smiles.

"You . . . came . . ." he says through a clogged, wounded throat.

I return the smile, trying not to wince at how pitiful he sounds. "I was planning to come anyway, but then I heard from Lucy."

Lucy smiles and hugs me, as if she's a totally different person from back in room 208. Without Cole present, the Flops seem more than willing to call a truce for Grover's sake.

"You okay?" she asks, petting my arm. "Have you slept?"

"Not really." I shrug and glance at Grover, who is still smiling. "I'm so glad you're all right."

His eyes water gratefully, as if he can't believe I even care. My heart sinks. This whole time, have I really been giving off the impression that I wouldn't be bothered if he *died*?

I drag a chair toward Grover's raised bed rails. The urge to take his hand—to hug him like I did in the dream—is overwhelming. "Grover," I say, "before you say anything, I want you to know you're not invisible to me."

He swallows painfully. He wants to talk, but each word must be agony.

"Neither was Gretchen," I say to Lucy, who hides her tears with her bunchy sweatshirt sleeve. I nod at Mike, who

43

is hugging his own arm. "Neither are any of you."

Grover's chin trembles over the top of his neck brace.

I gather a large breath. This might be totally deranged, but something inside me says it's the only way forward. "Cole and I didn't send you those messages," I say, rubbing cherry ChapStick onto my drying lips. "You're gonna hear something soon, but, um . . . I need you to hear it from me first."

Smiling, Grover chokes out, "It's okay . . . I know."

The floor vanishes beneath my seat. "You know what?"

"About the phones," Lucy whispers. "That's why we asked you to come."

"*How?*" I ask, my fingers tingling as I grip Grover's bed rail. "No one's supposed to—"

Lucy presses a shushing finger to her lips, but my feet won't stop tapping.

"We know it's not you," Mike whispers, nodding at Grover. "Show him before he has a heart attack!"

Too late! The room tilts around me as Grover opens his phone and searches through the camera roll. Grabbing my hand, Lucy says, "After Grover left Justin and Mike in the cafeteria, he recorded a video. He never got to post it because . . . yeah." She glances nervously at Grover, who has found what he's looking for. "We didn't show your mom yet. Grover was watching old videos in bed, and that's when he saw the . . . thing."

Lucy, Mike, and I press our cheeks together as we gather

around Grover's bedside. In the video, Grover—no idea what's coming for him—addresses the camera in front of a row of lockers. *"Hey, everyone,"* he says. *"About to go into Queer Club. Feeling pretty freaked, but I'm so lucky to have great friends who build me up. I feel like I can conquer anything."*

Next to me, Mike beams and gently rustles Grover's hair. They smile, but my stomach won't untwist. Something bad is going to happen.

In the video, Grover sighs with relief. *"I'm gonna be okay. The messages aren't real."*

Yards behind him, a shadow passes by the lockers. He doesn't see it—but I do.

A man opens a locker. His hands are gloved. He places something inside, shuts the door, and looks at the camera—at us.

Then we see his face. A tragedy mask. Mr. Sandman.

I swallow an enormous, choking gasp. Lucy and Mike grab my arms, but all I can do is stare at Grover, the real one in bed. "It wasn't . . . you guys . . ." he croaks.

I reach for Grover's hands, those soft, grateful hands from my dream—only this time, I'm the one overwhelmed with gratitude. Squeezing tightly, I promise, "We're gonna find who did this."

CHAPTER FOUR

COLE

NOT TO SOUND LIKE a Flop, but this is one big Monday of a Monday. We're back in person at school after a week of parents badgering back and forth with the school board. I'm spending my free period at the top of the outdoor stadium bleachers, freezing my ass off as I try to figure out who can give me an alibi for Gretchen's murder. You never realize how hard it is to prove your whereabouts until you suddenly *really* need to prove them.

Fortunately, it's slightly warmer than last week, when I ran laps around the track trying to work out my anger with Grover. Flecks of blue peek out from beneath the gray cloud cover, and half the school is out to soak it in. It's as if nobody feels like being inside, waiting for Mr. Sandman to step out from behind a locker.

Benny and Em huddle beside me (if I have to turn to the Flops for help, I'm starting with the nicest ones). Em's in a snowy-white hooded parka looking like Elsa, while Benny's shivering inside a thin denim jacket.

Somehow, over the weekend news finally leaked about the burner phones. My money is on someone within Detective Dearie's team. Mr. Kirby's voice rings in my ears: "*Never ascribe to malice what can be explained by incompetence.*"

Well, malice or incompetence, I'm in deep shit. Thanks to Grover's video, Dearie is in the clear, but Stone Grove's Most Hateful aren't convinced yet that I'm not Mr. Sandman.

"But Grover *said* it wasn't you or Dearie," Em says.

"Too little, too late," I grunt, scratching out another potential alibi in my notebook. "The locker in the video is Dearie's, but no one has video proof for *my* locker." I sigh. "Plus, the killer's in a mask, so Grover's current testimony is mostly nothing but vibes. I need a stronger defense. Someone who knows I wasn't inside the school."

Despite a torrent of vicious posts from randos calling for my arrest, the phone evidence isn't enough to hold me on suspicion. But my uncle Fernando is a lawyer, and he said if any more evidence turns up against me, shit can start getting real. So, for now, I'm being proactive clearing my name, if no one else is going to.

On the track, a trio of white girls walk in a tight cluster and cast dark looks up at me. I keep my eyes on my notebook. There's no time to make another scene—I've already made two today confronting nosy juniors who couldn't keep their eyes to themselves.

"I saw you on the track from the library window," Benny

says, pushing up his glasses. "I know it was just before two because Ms. Drake asked if I was coming to Queer Club. On the way over, I watched you run laps." My eyebrow jumps— *Watching me, eh, Benito?* He jerks his head away, probably realizing how leery that sounded. "Shut up. I mean, uh, I saw you. For like a minute. It was so cold, I thought it was strange you were outside. That's why I remember."

Normally, I would tease Benny about being a horny perv, but he's saving my ass, so I slap him on the shoulder and write down his details. "Thanks, Benny. I still need to cover myself for the next twenty minutes or so, but this is a start."

"I wish I knew more to help," Em groans, fiddling with her pen. "When you came into 208, I remember Dearie said your hands were cold. You looked freezing."

I'm about to thank Em for her nice (albeit probably irrelevant) testimony, but at that moment, a vile Flop comes stomping up the bleachers: Justin—in an Irish-green tracksuit.

"Are you still pressuring people to give you alibis, Cardoso?" Justin sneers, squatting on the bleacher beneath us. "Pretty soon, you're gonna run out of people who want to help because they want your D."

His flimsy taunts only stiffen my spine. "That mean you're next in line to give me an alibi?"

"You *wish*."

"Wellllll, I have texts from you that say otherwise." His color drains, and in a flash of green, he's dashing back down to the track.

"I thought you wanted to start shit!" I call after him. "Don't mess with the maestro!"

Once Justin's gone, Em excuses herself to get out of the cold, and I suggest Benny do the same. "You shouldn't be alone," Benny says.

I lock my eyes on my notebook. "Why should I be scared to be alone? I'm the killer, right?"

He fiddles with his backpack straps. "Come to the restaurant after school. Ma says you eat on the house."

It's my first genuine smile in days. Benny's mother has always been a real one. "Your family is Team Cole, then?"

"Always have been."

"Sure. I might. Thanks."

Benny leaves. Bitterly, I leaf through my notebook, which a few days ago only needed to hold physics notes. Now I have to become a detective, all because I wanted some alone time for thirty minutes.

Except, after the return of Mr. Sandman, alone time hits differently.

Em and Benny shrink down to dots in the distance as they throw open the courtyard doors to return inside. A quiet—lonely—wind surrounds me on the bleachers, flipping the pages of my notebook and tightening my shoulders.

It's like fingers grazing the back of my neck. Without thinking, my hand moves protectively to my throat.

Slowly, I turn to check behind me—nothing. I'm on the highest bleacher, my back to a metal fence, with a long way down to the student parking lot. No Sandman.

I laugh. *He's not up here, Cole.*

Finally, I exhale and do what I always do when I'm alone and don't want to be: text Paul Barnett, a white, shaggy-haired senior cutie at Tucson High who I sometimes detour out of town to have fun with. We met when his Badgers played against my Rattlers. I happened to notice what an impressively sized shoe he had—*wink wink, nudge nudge*—and the rest is history. His mom is hyper-Christian and his dad's military, so our no-strings rendezvous have to be sneaky.

Very retro vintage.

I pull up FaceTime first, thinking we'll get straight to video—but then I see my call history and want to scream. Last week, while Gretchen was being murdered, while I was blowing off steam around the track, I snuck in a video chat with Paul.

The time stamp proves it!

We only had a few minutes, so nothing happened beyond some verbal spiciness, but we both got the attention we needed. And maybe now I have an alibi.

Paul is closeted . . . But he *could* confirm I was outside after Benny saw me.

I fire off a few texts, careful to keep things casual but urgent: Hey muffin, got a q for u

As always, his responses come rapidly: Hey captain. You ok? I saw the news

Of course he did. Acid roils through my stomach, but at least I don't have to be the one to bring up the topic: It's bullshit. But . . . I could be in trouble, and you might be the only one who can help.

His typing lasts forever. It makes sense. He knows what I'm going to ask—I only fool around with smart boys: Did that murder happen while we were on the phone?

I reply: Yeah.

He replies: Jesus. No one else saw you?

I reply: This one kid, Benny, but only for a little bit. Our call has an actual time stamp. That's hard evidence. It might not need to come up, though! They might believe Benny, and that'll be it. I'm sorry. I know this puts you in a tight spot.

Paul doesn't respond. He doesn't even type. Every corner of my body feels rotten and manipulative. He's a hookup. We keep it light. Now, because of my bullshit, he's going to have to out himself in court. On the news. We'll be the sordid faces of this whole story, and while I may be cleared as the killer, the headlines will be full-blast queer-hating: BASKETBALL RIVALS EXPOSED AS SECRET WHORES IN SERIAL KILLING BOMBSHELL.

Finally, Paul responds: Cole, I'm not gonna let you go to prison just so I can keep lying to my dumbass family

No relief comes, just more regret that I've spoiled our hotness with Flopness.

Before I can type anything else, another rude sight strolls down the track. Mobs of students swarm a pair of boys. One of them is wearing a foam neck brace—Grover, soaking in all the sympathetic attention he could've dreamed of. People hug him, high-five him, ask if they can sign his brace. There's so many people around, in fact, that I can't see the boy he's with. Through the throng, I spot them holding hands.

Don't tell me this ordeal scored him a boyfriend already.

When the crowd breaks apart enough, Grover *is* holding hands with a boy—a fashionable, resting-bitch-face handsome boy who brings Grover's hand to his lips. The students around them gawk and swoon.

It's Dearie. Dearie is dating Grover.

"Oh," I say. "Well."

CHAPTER FIVE
DEARIE

TWO MONTHS LATER

IT'S LATE APRIL—A MONTH left until graduation—but there's been no movement on the hunt for Mr. Sandman. Three weeks ago, he struck again. Claude Adams, an old spy novelist from San Francisco, rented a cabin just outside town near Mooncrest Cemetery to finish his next book. Mr. Sandman finished him instead. They found two texts on Claude's phone—*Your lonely nights will soon be over*—and then, twenty-four hours later to the minute—*Your lonely nights are over.* The texts came from different burner numbers than the ones found in our lockers, which doesn't clear Cole and me, but it has Mom and me sleeping easier.

Cole too. He hasn't brought up his Paul alibi yet to Mom—not until there's no other choice—and now it's looking less urgent.

It was sad about Claude, though. Another Stone Grove attack. And another gay victim. His husband died six years ago, and the news keeps talking about how he was finally writing again, no longer held down by his grief and loneliness.

Somehow, Mr. Sandman knew he was still vulnerable. He always knows.

Following Claude's headline-making murder, the FBI sent a profiler to take over the investigation, with my mom assisting. Agent Astrid Astadourian (*an absolute queen name*) has been holed up at a local motel ever since. Mom has invited her to dinner, but she always politely declines.

Probably because Mr. Sandman's surviving victim stays here *a lot*.

Grover Kendall sprawls across my living room's leather sofa, his shaggy blond head in my lap and bare feet hanging off the armrest. My house is empty, a suburban palace of succulent plants and burnt-sienna ceramic tile. It's the perfect low-maintenance home—minimal watering, minimal cleaning—so Mom can continue being a workaholic. She'll be waist-deep in crime scene photos this weekend, so my boyfriend and I have total privacy.

Once again, Grover insisted on rewatching *Your Lonely Nights Are Over*. His therapist says it's healthy. For him, maybe. Me, every second it's on, I teleport out of my body, either to a beach or a club. Today, I'm mentally visiting an Alaskan spa, with snow everywhere and my lithe body heating up inside a steamy hot spring.

I care about Grover. All my Tucson boys got put on hold when I started seeing him. He just brings out this fierce protectiveness in me where I never want to let him out of my sight, but . . . What's next? Soon, I'm gonna graduate and move to LA. I want to take improv classes, vocal lessons, and become the quintuple threat I know I am.

Since Cole and I are big movie-heads, and he's already written four *brilliant* screenplays, our plan since freshman year has been to move to LA. Cole makes the movies, I star in them. But . . . I've been too scared to share my plans with Grover.

Unless Grover is coming to LA with me, that'll mean the end of us.

And with Mr. Sandman still around, the end of *us* could mean the end of *him*.

Loneliness kills . . .

As a familiar squall of panic batters my chest, I kiss my boyfriend's head, and it subsides. Grover moans sweetly and traces his finger across his own throat, which is marked by bumpy, off-white scars. Sandman Hickeys, he calls them. They look like hash marks. Ghosts that will never vanish, not with all the vitamin E patches in the world. I don't even think Grover wants them to heal. I catch him staring at them sometimes, almost admiringly.

I don't want to draw attention to his scars, but he likes when I kiss them. Whenever he strokes them like that, it's his cue for me to give his near-fatal owies some healing af-fection. Leaning down, I softly peck each puncture wound.

There are fourteen scars. I've counted.

Grover *mmm*s again and turns up the volume on *Lonely Nights*. In this episode, various seventysomethings are inter-viewed about their time at St. Obadiah High School, where the Mr. Sandman killings began. They lost friends. Exes. Best friends. Fifty years later, entire lifetimes have been lived since the attacks, but they still have that faraway hell in their eyes.

My insides clench with stabbing pain.

That'll be me. That dull ache. That god-awful feeling. It's never going away.

I clutch Grover tighter, and he reaches up to twirl one of my curls. He wants more than just cuddles. I'm game. Fooling around would distract me from this abysmal show. Gently, I grind into his workout sweats. He swirls his hips and then flips over on the sofa to face me. Those gray eyes always scream "Don't hurt me," as if being kissed is too much stimulation for his system to handle. Grover is more handsome than I ever gave him credit for, with a chiseled jaw and a slight beard of blond peach fuzz that he grew over the semester.

"Nice way to spend a Saturday," I whisper.

"Your mom home soon?" he asks.

"Yeah."

His face cracks into a devilish grin. "I'll be quick."

Yes, he will.

Grover is sweet, but the fooling around is . . . just okay. It's very teddy bear playhouse. Very vanilla with rainbow sprinkles.

"*Very incompatible with what you want*," Cole's voice echoes in my head.

That was the last time I ever told Cole the truth about what my sex life with Grover was like. He responded with "*Welp, time to dump him*," so from that point forward, I retreated into bland varieties of "*It's nice! Really hot*." After a while, I got so nervous to bring up Grover that I stopped sharing.

I've never not shared anything with Cole in my life.

But, I don't know . . . It's complicated now. Grover's years of childish, jealous behavior is the reason Cole has had to sleep with one eye open. Everyone knows they hate each other—so why *wouldn't* Cole be the perfect Mr. Sandman? But after that attack, Grover's been constantly telling people it wasn't Cole. He's tried to atone. If only the truth were as juicy as his mudslinging.

I don't even think I'm being a good friend for dating this boy, but it just happened, and then I was saying yes, then everyone was so happy, and then I blinked and two months had flown by. Grover is different now. I watched this boy almost bleed to death, all because he had a heartbroken face. That sweet face is a sponge that absorbs every drop of sadness in the world. I can't let him be alone.

If I ever broke up with him . . .

I feel like shit even letting the idea into my head.

Brushing back his wild hair, I ask, "What are you thinking about?"

"My scars," he whispers. I nod sympathetically. "Do you think it's okay I mentioned my attack in my college applications? Was that weird?"

"No." It's my job to stomp out his insecurities instantly. "It happened to you."

He glances away, stung. My throat closes with tension. *Dammit.* Did I not support him enough? Was my tone too casual? Chewing his lower lip, he says, "People think it's like on TV, where you find out who the murderer is at the end of the episode. They don't know how many killers just go free. How many times someone dies and you never get to find out who did it or why."

I swallow anxiously. "My mom is working really hard—"

"I just miss Gretchen," Grover continues. "I'm glad her parents moved to Florida. They deserve a fresh start."

I say nothing, opting instead to gently hum as I pet his hair. He enjoys the softness.

"I haven't gone to a Mooncrest Movie Night since she . . . We used to go every Friday and wonder how great it would be to date somebody. She never got to know what that's like."

Grover kisses me, his peach fuzz tickling my upper lip.

I can't even enjoy his kiss for how awful I feel, thinking of Gretchen, forever lonely in death. "I think she'd be happy her friend got what he wanted," I say between kisses. "She'd probably flip out knowing it was *me* you were with."

He smiles hungrily and kisses me again. "She knew how bad I had it for you."

"Yeah?" Giggling, I peck the tip of his nose.

"BAD. But I knew it was gonna happen, somehow, once you got to know me." Another kiss. "Once you stopped letting Cole tell you I was a nobody."

"Cole doesn't do that." Sometimes, the old Cole-sniping Grover returns, but I never allow it. Heartbreak spills over my boyfriend's eyes like egg yolks . . .

The front door opens on a tinkling of brass bells. Mom's home. Grover—with nerves of steel—slides off me and resumes staring blankly at the show with shocking fluidity. No hasty jerking away or stammering that we weren't doing anything. He's cool as a cucumber.

"Helloooooo, coming iiiiiiiin," Mom says, shielding her eyes as she totes an overflowing messenger bag. She's not alone. It's not Agent Double-A, it's Kevin Benetti, the local medical examiner. Kevin, unlike Astadourian, has taken my mom up on dinner invitations plenty of times. He's white, with darkly tanned skin, a shaved dome, and a salt-and-pepper beard. His dress shirt sleeves are always rolled above his elbows like he's running for governor. My sometimes-confusing feelings about Kevin were one of my earliest clues that my affections flowed in a different direction than the other boys.

"It's okay, Mom," I say. "You can look. We're just watching TV."

"Ah," she says, relieved. But when she spots what's on— the Mr. Sandman show, with an interview of the former San Diego sheriff—she looks too tired to hide her disgust. "This again."

I darken. "Mom."

"Sorry." She shakes her head, remembering too late that Grover likes to watch this show, whether or not we understand his reasons. "Grover, hon, how're you doing?"

"I'm okay, Mrs. Dearie," Grover says, cheerfully sipping iced tea while Mom quickly hugs him from above. When she pulls back, she gives him another loving shoulder squeeze. Grover surviving his attack did a lot of good for all of us. The lone bright spot in an evil era.

Kevin leans against the armchair, watching Grover and me cuddle as he sighs. "High school boyfriends. Never heard of such a thing"—he mocks in an old, withered voice—"*in my day.*"

We laugh as my boyfriend playfully pets my leg. "What?" I ask Kevin. "When you were in high school, you never took a boy out to see a silent movie?"

Kevin erupts with a warm chuckle. "I am thirty-nine, thank you, and I make the jokes around here, missy."

As our laughter dwindles, Grover sits up rigidly and lowers his voice. "You shouldn't talk like that with Mr. Sandman around." The temperature in the house plunges thirty degrees as all eyes lock on Grover. He doesn't blink. "Before dating Dearie, I used to talk down on myself. I'm just saying."

A glimmer of fear crosses Kevin's face before he shakes it away with another winning smile. "Maybe you're right." Loneliness kills, we all know that.

The crime scene flashes before my eyes.

Blood. Screams. Chaos.

Barbed wire pushed into Grover's throat.

Mr. Sandman goes after lonely people, why not Kevin? Why not any of us?

I don't breathe again until Mom's phone rings. The special, extra loud tone reserved for her work phone. She disappears into the kitchen to take the call with quiet urgency. Kevin follows without needing to be told. As he opens the swinging saloon door, Mom's terrified face appears for a moment before the door swings shut. "What? When . . . ?" she asks before I can't hear anymore. Grover and I sit alert. He takes my hand—he's already cold and clammy.

I pull him into a tight hug. "It's okay. You're safe."

But Grover is shaking like an anxious dog. I pet his hair to calm him, but his body is erupting with trauma. I breathe steadily to keep myself calm. If I stay calm, it'll be contagious.

Yet the darkened corners of my house suddenly hold many dangers.

Mr. Sandman surprised Gretchen in a fully lit school hallway. How do I know for sure he's not already in the house, waiting patiently to draw my mother away with an urgent call?

Bzzzzztttt!

Grover jumps in my arms as his phone vibrates with a message. With a trembling hand, he reads it. I hold my breath. "Who is it?" I ask quickly.

Please don't be from a burner number!

"It's Theo." But his eyes widen with fright. "They heard from their friend over at Tucson High. There's been another kill." He looks up, his eyes glistening. "Paul Barnett?"

My limbs lose all feeling. I fight to keep myself from fainting on the couch.

Cole and I have been talking about Paul for months. The closeted hookup who's going to alibi Cole. Or . . . he was.

ON THE NEXT EPISODE OF
YOUR LONELY NIGHTS ARE OVER:
THE SEARCH FOR MR. SANDMAN

The weapon was always a ring of barbed wire. To some, it was a lasso. To the Catholic students at St. Obadiah High School, the site of the first murders, it was like Jesus's crown of thorns. Only this crown missed the head and went for the throat.

Did Mr. Sandman see his victims as suffering wretches he could save?

Or did the razor necklace have no meaning other than it was a nasty way to kill someone?

How were the victims chosen? How can you tell if some-one is lonely or just happily alone? Mr. Sandman had a sixth sense for this kind of quiet pain. In 1971, when the killings started at St. Obadiah, suspicion fell on Father Bertram, the guidance counselor who intimately knew his students' spiritual troubles. But when he was found killed, with a razor necklace of his own, paranoia spread among the students.

It had to be one of them.

Continue watching?

PART TWO
THE RAZOR NECKLACE

CHAPTER SIX
COLE

AT THE GROCERY REGISTER, Dearie scans a case of ginger beer and slides it down the belt for me to bag. Ever since he started dating Grover, our nights working at the grocery store are the only times I get alone with him. Our friendship never recovered from that day.

And now I can't even enjoy this time, because I'm not really here. I'm miles away, making out with Paul Barnett in the back seat of my car, feeling those soft tufts of hair around his nipples and the sharp V of his back muscles. We never went on "dates," but taking him to Mooncrest Movie Nights came close. Out beyond Mooncrest Valley—where that writer, Claude Adams, was killed—they show old movies in a graveyard. It's private, everyone's already making out, and nobody knew Paul there, so we could be open.

I didn't go to his funeral.

How do you tell a dead closeted boy's parents that you meant something to him?

We were hookups, but we cared about each other. Good

luck explaining that to bigots when even queers and allies poop their pants thinking about it. Especially when you're the kid half the internet wants behind bars for said killings.

Was Paul being my alibi connected to his death?

All I know is the killer went to a lot of trouble to plant that phone in my locker and then slaughter one of the only people who could vouch for my whereabouts.

As Dearie pushes more groceries down the belt, I plop the ginger beer on top of a stack of cold cuts. What am I *doing*? I'm bagging groceries for a few bucks I don't need just to be closer to Dearie, who's dating the person responsible for me being in this mess? He's now the romantic possession of a bullying, racistly jealous Flop who happily let everyone believe I was sending him death threats. The killer must've seen his video and thought, "Gee! What a great way to frame someone for the murder I'm about to commit!"

Paul's blood is on more hands than mine.

"You okay, Cole Slaw?" Dearie asks, his brow furrowed as he scans a bell pepper. I don't have the energy to answer. As he slides me the pepper, he drops his voice. "You need a break?"

I scoff. "Am I allowed one in this sweatshop?"

Dearie laughs weakly and scans a box of Pop-Tarts. I brush sweaty hair from my eyes. I've been so itchy lately. I can feel every strand of my hair. I should chop it all off, no matter how much it'll make me look like a killer changing his look on the run.

Our customer—a man in a red-white-and-blue Wildcats windbreaker—holds out his club card while Dearie beeps what's left in his cart: bottled lattes and a party tray of assorted cheeses. Groans erupt from the back of the line as shoppers impatiently ditch us for another queue. I keep bagging in a thoughtless, haphazard way until Dearie turns—at last—to our helpless Wildcat. "Sorry, you're probably in a hurry to get to your party."

"Party?" the man asks. Dearie gestures to his party tray of cheese, and the man's expression crumbles. "No . . . That's for me. For the week."

"Oh," Dearie says, wincing. He lowers his voice like a doctor delivering a grim diagnosis. "You should really consider having a party or a game night. It's not safe to be solo right now."

"Thank you, Angelina of Death," I mutter, loading the last of the man's bags into his cart. "Stop trying to clock lonely people like you're gonna find the next victim."

"I'm doing this for the public good, Cole." He rests a kindhearted palm on his heart. "You should know better than anyone that isolating—"

My chest boiling hot, I drop the cheese tray. "Paul wasn't lonely! It wasn't his fault!"

The line of white, peering faces looks up, suddenly terrified that I raised my voice.

"It wasn't your fault either," Dearie says softly.

I roll my eyes. "He could've been killed to pin the blame on me. Ask your boyfriend—this all started with him and his big mouth."

Dearie tenses as our line continues staring. "Paul was in the"—he whispers, almost inaudibly—"closet. That's one of the loneliest things someone can go through."

My chest rises and falls so loudly, I don't know if I'm going to pass out or strangle someone. I can't talk about this. I just shake my head and untie my apron. "I know it is," I whisper angrily. "I gotta go."

Awkwardly, the customer asks, "Do you have a chip reader, or do I tap my card?"

Before I can stomp away, our manager, blond and impossibly tall, swoops down on us. "Frankie, change your till," she tells Dearie before spinning on me. "Break time for you two."

Our manager jumps in with a fresh cash tray as Dearie ducks out, guiltily taking off his apron. A wave of gratitude sweeps through the customers—at long last, an adult is in charge.

In painful silence, Dearie and I march through the wine aisles to the break room. Now that we're away from judgmental eyes, my fury curdles into guilt. I don't have a lot of time left with Dearie, and I have no interest in wasting what time I do have yelling. I stop him underneath a wall of Pinot Grigio and say, "I can't fight today. Not with you. It's too much. Paul died in such an awful way, and someone's after me—trying to put me in jail—and everyone's just *letting* it happen."

Dearie's eyes are teary but hopeful. "You aren't going anywhere. We're gonna find this guy."

"We *have* to."

"We will."

At long last, a smile finds me. Like I've done a million times before, I throw my arms around my little guy's shoulders and kiss the top of his head. Unfortunately, a new vibe—a bad one—greets me. Dearie's back tenses in my grip, and I release him instantly. We're so interconnected no one needs to say anything for me to understand the truth: his boyfriend is a jealous, insecure asshole.

"Is this how it's gonna be with us now?" I ask coldly.

Dearie's eyes dart up. "It makes him uncomfortable. People talk."

Rage explodes through me, burning so hot that everything becomes silent. "I know people talk. Because of him, half this town thinks I wrapped barbed wire around his neck."

"But he's telling everyone that you didn't—"

"Dearie." He shuts up, his jaw tightening with fear. "You can help get an obvious racist fired, but a quiet one? You *date* him. I don't know if Grover wants to blow me or be me, or some mix of the two, but he's been obsessed for years." I shake my head. "The drama between Grover and me? It was bullying. He let people believe I sent him a death threat, and now the FBI is here—*three people are dead*—and his bullshit could get me put away forever, or more likely killed by some scared local asshole. He has not apologized to me once. You dating him rehabilitates his image."

I can tell Dearie wants to cry so badly, but to his credit, he holds back. Hopefully, he knows that would make this situation about *his* feelings—when this is not about him.

"I didn't mean for . . ." he whispers, voice trembling. "I had always kind of liked Grover, and I thought maybe me being with him would make a statement about you, that you're so close with me, people would think it couldn't be you because . . ." For a moment, Dearie's lips move without sound. His throat has run dry. "He hurt you . . ." He trails off. "I'm sorry."

Collecting myself, I ask quietly, "How can we make change happen when Grover hasn't even acknowledged what he's done?"

"I'm gonna talk to him."

"If he hasn't already reached that moment on his own, it's never coming," I say, tugging my hair anxiously. Seriously, fuck Grover, fuck this conversation, and fuck that I had to be the one to bring it up.

My words shake Dearie. He exhales quickly.

"Cole," he says, "I'm gonna fix this."

"Dumping him is the only way to fix it," I say, laughing bitterly. "But you won't do that because that puts a target on his back, which is why you shouldn't have started dating him in the first place, which I would have *explained* to you if you'd bothered to talk to me first." As Dearie nods, I weigh saying this next part. Hell with it—I'm mad, and Dearie needs to know. "There's something I haven't told you too. I got a late acceptance to Columbia University."

Those massive brown eyes widen with surprise. "That's . . . in New York."

"Yeah. Their film school is good."

"What happened to our LA plan?"

"UCLA withdrew their acceptance when your boyfriend told the world I'm Michael Myers."

"Girl, he said you *didn't* do it." Spittle flies from his teeth. "And they didn't withdraw your acceptance. They paused it—"

I hurl my apron—*thwap!*—onto the floor. "Same difference!"

Panic spreads across his face. "Why didn't you tell me you were applying somewhere else?"

"Why didn't you tell me you were going to date my bully?" I glance away, not prepared for the agony in Dearie's face. "There wasn't a good time. You've been with Grover twenty-four seven."

Dearie swallows hard. "LA was always our plan. You make the movies, and I'm in them . . . Grover just happened. I made a mistake." He sighs heavily. "I dated him because I needed to change. I was an asshole—that's why it was so easy for people to believe that I sent those threats, that I was involved in the murder."

My shoulders slump. "You were never an asshole. You don't even love him, and thank GOD for that, but you've gotta realize you're only dating him to keep him safe from a killer. That's gonna make you both lonely as hell. I can already feel it on you. If I was Mr. Sandman, you'd be next."

His eyes pooling over, Dearie chucks his apron onto the ground next to mine and storms off to the break room. A guilty blade pierces my chest.

He's gone.

CHAPTER SEVEN
DEARIE

I NEED TO FOCUS on not getting lost. The night is too cold, wet, and murderous. I've walked to Cole's house a billion times, but still, the fear of getting lost in this dark, suburban sprawl freezes my legs. Each step is an ordeal, but I can't stop. I'm halfway to Cole, and I have to make things right with us. I haven't felt okay since leaving him at the grocery store. Even though that was only a few hours ago, I've lived a hundred lifetimes since then.

Just minutes ago, I broke up with Grover.

It happened so quickly, so unexpectedly, I didn't even realize it was happening until the words "*I'm breaking up with you*" flew out of me. It was partly because of Cole, but he was right: I've been planning my escape for a while. What planted the first seed of doubt? I'll be untangling my reasons for months, along with my memory of the breakup itself, which already feels hazy.

I've broken up with boys before, but thanks to Mr. Sandman, this one felt dangerous. My anxiety was sky high. My temples thudded so badly, I couldn't hear my own apologies to Grover. I wanted the whole thing to be over so badly, I raced through my *"It's for the best!"* breakup chatter and then hurried him into my mom's car before I could stop to think about what I was doing.

How I was dooming him.

Minutes ago, Mom pulled out of our driveway and drove him out of my life.

I can't think about that now. I have to stay focused on helping Cole.

As I slosh through pools of rain, I press my hand to my chest, commanding my racing heart to slow. Yet guilt assaults me from all sides. Betraying Cole. Dumping Grover.

The breakup was a rush. Time pressed in around me like a vacuum seal, fracturing my memory into thousands of shards. The words fly back into my head.

I told Grover about Cole's New York news, and I couldn't hide my devastation. As always, when Cole comes up, Grover made it about him.

"You NEVER believe me!" Grover shouted. "He doesn't even love you!" Grover shrieked loud enough to tear his vocal cords. "I LOVE YOU! ME! Cole didn't get your attention for five seconds, so he abandons you—his 'BEST FRIEND'—to go to New York?!"

When that got me crying, Grover hugged me to his chest. He held me so nicely. Maybe he just lost his temper. A moment later, though, he said something he couldn't take back. Something I didn't realize he still believed until tonight.

"Dearie, Cole is not your friend," Grover whispered tenderly. "He attacked me—"

"Stop." I pushed Grover away. His eyes shifted so quickly from sweet to angry, then back to hurt.

I don't know why I ever believed Grover was on our side, that he wanted to fix things with Cole, make the world believe he was innocent. But now I know—Grover lied; he believes Cole is the killer, against all reason. He's still spreading lies, risking Cole's life. Cole was right. An air pocket of courage found me, and I knew if I didn't act then, I'd never do it. No more. "I'm breaking up with you."

We need to find the truth—the real killer—and we'll never do that if people keep suspecting Cole. My relationship was officially in the way.

It had to go.

Now a Mr. Sandman–shaped target is on me too. I feel it, loneliness. My only hope of tearing it out is to find Cole. I'm only a few streets away, but now that I'm alone—now that Mr. Sandman is everywhere—the night feels homicidal. I avoid trees, light posts, anything that looks like it could conceal a tall, frowning man.

Is that how a kill would happen? A gloved hand wrapping around a tree. The grotesque, bronze frown mask appearing from around a corner. There's no one nearby to help, but even if there were, it would be too late. In my mind, the frowning man approaches—slowly, surely—with a lasso of razors and softly lowers it over my head. One squeeze, and my lonely nights without Cole would be over.

But the trees are just trees, dark pillars that don't hide anything but the monsters in my head.

As I walk, my neighborhood's suburban mini mansions scowl like villainous cartoon faces, with only a few spare windows lit. Finally exiting the subdivision, I cross under the stone archway into River Run, a luxury community for Stone Grove's elite. Sprawling eight-room estates sit between each other with plenty of first-class breathing room. Their lawns are lovingly manicured and dotted with purple cacti.

Along the street, a sedan is parked with its lights off. Inside are the shadows of two men. Even though my heart has been racing for minutes, this sudden image doesn't terrify me. I know them. I wave, and the shadows wave back. They're plainclothes detectives my mom posted outside Cole's home—whether it's for his protection or his surveillance, I don't want to know.

The Cardoso home boasts the least amount of exterior décor in River Run, but that's only because Cole's moms are hyper-busy doctors who don't care about keeping up with the neighbors. They do what needs to be done to meet the minimum beautification requirements of the community. Everything else—especially inside—is as chaotic as a dorm room. Every light is on in the home as I ascend their porch and knock.

"Who is it?" Frederica Cardoso—Grover's surgeon—hollers. Sounds of video game explosions bleed through the walls.

"Dearie!" I shout over the game.

"Door's open!"

Two beeps later, their electronic locks undo themselves, and I help myself inside. Sounds of war shake the walls of the Cardosos' great room, where Frederica and her wife, Monica, battle each other in a PS5 game. The surround sound is cranked to full blast, so it sounds like a SWAT team is opening fire inside the room. Frederica is Portuguese, lighter-skinned, and larger, where Monica—Cole's birth mother—is Mexican American, darker-skinned, and smaller. They wear matching sweatshirts emblazoned with a neon, Southwestern-style logo for Miraval, a bougie local vacation spot. Monica lies on the sofa, her feet on a coffee table littered with dozens of empty hard seltzers. Frederica stands four feet from the TV so she can see better, her knees crouched slightly like she's sitting in an invisible chair. Neither of them look at me.

"How're you, sweetie?" Frederica asks, hypnotized. "Cole's in his room."

"Good, thanks," I squeak and dash up their carpeted spiral staircase.

"You're in for a shock," Monica says, slamming her thumb onto the controller. I turn back, confused, but she just winks. "You'll see."

Across the second-story landing from Cole's room, the video game sounds die off, replaced by the soothing trippiness of Cole's dream-pop mixes. His door is closed. I knock. I've never knocked on his door in eighteen years, so why do I feel like being formal now?

Because I messed up and I need to fix it.

When the door opens, a stranger answers: a shirtless, muscular man with light brown skin and shorn, bleached-blond hair. A damp towel is wrapped around his shoulders to catch the flecks of hair dye that have dripped off. Does Cole have somebody over?

No—it *is* Cole. He went blond, just like he always wanted, even though we always said we'd do it together.

He did it without me. He's moving on without me.

Holy hell, I feel so much worse.

My shoulders bounce as tears take me over. Smirking, he asks, "Does it look that bad?" When my tears don't stop, Cole's face falls. He rushes his arms around me. That lovely scent of icy body wash. Powerful arms rock me like a baby. "Hey? What is it? Why didn't you text?"

I bury my face in his chest and moan, "I don't want you to go. Everything was gonna be perfect, we were finally gonna get out of this town together, and then all this shit happened and took it away. I was a shitty friend and didn't understand. I'm sorry."

"You're spiraling." He strokes my hair and begins to

sniffle himself. "Listen, New York, like, famously spits people out. Maybe I'll be back before you know it."

"No!" I crane up, deadly serious. "You're Cole. Whatever you do, you crush. You're gonna be amazing there."

A tear finally leaves him, blending with the hair bleach dripping down his cheek. He tries to laugh it off. "Well, then, come with me."

"It's too late to apply anywhere."

Nodding, his face scrunches as it holds back a thousand sad songs. "I was so mad at you, I just . . . applied and accepted. I can't believe I didn't tell you. I messed up."

"*I* messed up. You were right. Grover was . . ." I trail off, needing a breath before I continue. I can't even think. I get it out. "I pitied him, so I dated him. I just didn't want anyone else to die." I take quick, sharp, lung-stabbing breaths. "I dumped him."

Once again, my shoulders do the bouncy-cry thing, but Cole doesn't speak. He tightens his hug, which squeezes more emotional pus out of me. "I am so proud of you."

"You shouldn't be." My body isn't built to handle compliments tonight.

Sniffing again, I stare hypnotically into his soothing moonglow desk lamp. More shards from my breakup fly through my mind like shattered windshield pieces in a crash:

Grover's gray eyes. Heartbroken. Betrayed. Terrified.

He clutched at his scarred neck and ran out. I begged my mom to run after him and drive him home safely.

She didn't have to ask why. She'd heard it all.

"I'm going to find out who's doing this," I whisper, lost in the lamp's glow. Cole doesn't respond. He just rocks me against his chest as my body quakes. "I'm gonna kill him."

Cole pries me off his chest, wipes my tears, and smiles. "*We* are gonna kill him."

Laughter forces out every miserable thought. The moonglow lamp illuminates a gilded halo behind his newly brightened hair. "I can't believe you finally went blond, without me. You look really hot." I giggle, mopping back more tears. "Fuck you."

With nothing else to say but to let loose the laughter of old friends, we kiss. Because that's how Cole and I do friendship. I don't know how much longer we have together—I don't know how much longer *any* of us have, with Mr. Sandman still roaming free—but whatever time we have, we're going to be ourselves.

Later that night, I fall asleep in Cole's bed, with me as the big spoon (because sometimes, that's also how Cole and I do friendship). When the big spoon is as small as I am, they call that a jetpack. Either way, Cole moans pleasantly as I clutch him tightly. I hope his dreams are peaceful.

Mine are not.

In my dreams, Grover looks up at me with shattered

eyes. He begs me to take back what I said about breaking up. I refuse.

Then he begs me to stop. That's when I realize I'm strangling him with a razor necklace.

Funnily enough, it doesn't shock me. As I kill Grover, I wonder why I feel so free.

CHAPTER EIGHT
COLE

I START MY MORNING with renewed optimism, a charcoal face scrub, and Grover dramatically exiting our Queer Club group chat. The chat was another ill-conceived attempt from Dearie to magically make us all friends again like it's sixth grade. I've barely engaged, but this morning, I couldn't be more thrilled to still be in it. Without explanation or warning, Grover bounced.

Grover Kendall has left the conversation.

You're damn right he's left the conversation. He'll never be part of my conversations again!

Sometime before I woke up, Dearie returned home, rejuvenated after unburdening himself of the boy who needed serious dumping. Just wanted to clear the air before school, Dearie texted the group. Grover and I broke up. My mom is giving him heightened security. I know he's upset, but it's really for the best.

The chat reacts predictably. Em and Justin send non-committal hearts. Lucy supports Dearie, even though she's probably side-texting Grover about what a dick he is. Mike goes overboard reassuring Dearie he's still their friend, too, and that he's there for him if he needs anything. *Like what, Mancini? A nice back rub? Maybe a comfort cuddle? Transparent bitch!* Benny doesn't respond, but he usually ghosts the chat because he gets overwhelmed by notifications. Theo says something politically pleasant and cold, but then suggests the chat might need to disband so Grover can heal.

"BYE, BABES," I snort, rinsing off my scrub.

After flipping my phone facedown, I stand quietly on my bathroom rug, naked as the day I was born, and a little smile sneaks inside my heart. I bite my lower lip as a tsunami of emotions rise without warning. *Dearie.* He's back. This entire year belongs in the bottom of the deepest dumpster, but if Dearie is back in my life—really, truly back—then I have a strong ally in my corner to beat these allegations. And our friendship can withstand anything. Even college distance. We're not going to be one of those friendships that peters out and then every three years, we get together for a happy hour and realize, "Oh, wait, it's been FIVE years since we did this happy hour." The kind my moms have with their med school friends.

Forget that.

Dearie and I will stay besties for life. Mr. Sandman—and everything with Grover—doesn't get to take that away too.

Running my hand over my newly bleached, buzzed head, I know I made the right choice. People will say I'm trying to disguise myself. They'll say I gave myself a gay-crisis makeover. Let them. I'm a gay in crisis, but this isn't a gay-crisis bleach. I've been wanting to do it, so I did it.

I'm sick up to my neck of not being in control of my life. That changes today.

I dress in my hottest look: a pec-hugging top, exposed chain, five-inch inseam shorts, and Cartier sunglasses. If I know Grover, he's already accusing me and Dearie of hooking up, as if that's why he's single again. Let it be. I don't dodge phony rumors, I accelerate into them.

Before leaving to pick up Dearie, I flip on *Your Lonely Nights Are Over*, my ritual rewatch since Paul died. *Died*—my heart squeezes painfully at the wrong word. *Murdered. Slain. His beautiful, stubbly throat shredded.* Maybe there's a detail in the show I missed. When I first watched it, Mr. Sandman was a silly, retro myth. The second time I watched, I was at the center of a police investigation. This time, I have a boy to avenge—a sweet, sexy boy whose family will never know him.

"Very noble, mijo, but the truth is gonna come out eventually," Uncle Fernando says on speakerphone while I watch *Lonely Nights* on mute. My mother Monica's brother—my godfather—is an attorney who has spent the past two months poring over this case to see how he'll tackle it if the police eventually descend on his beloved nephew. He tends to be a traditional old suit, but my wit and charm always win him over, so he forgets to be judgmental that I live a life with many pretty boys running in and out of my bedroom.

Other than Dearie, Uncle Nando is the only one who knows about my connection with Paul.

"Tío, I just need more time," I say, oscillating between the show's interviews and a picture of Paul on a Mr. Sandman article I pulled up. It's Paul's official basketball photo. That shaggy, chestnut-brown hair . . . He's gone.

"Legally, you're in the clear," Uncle Nando says, sighing. "They don't have cause to subpoena Paul's text messages other than the ones sent from Mr. Sandman. As far as everyone else knows, he's not connected to the case in any other way. No one knows he was in a position to give an alibi to a person of interest on another murder." He pauses. "But you see what I'm getting at? You and I know his death is connected. That could be seen as . . ." He sighs again. "It's not good. Every day—every hour—you don't share this information, it can be used against you."

I stare deeper into Paul's picture. He'll never be older than this moment. "I can't out him."

"You gotta get real. He's dead. You're not. What if this information helps find the killer?"

I let Uncle Nando's words wash over me. Paul's gone for

good. And I could go to prison forever if people keep thinking I'm behind all of this. Or that I'm hiding something.

Uncle Nando is right. This has to stop.

I'm sorry, Paul. When I pick up Dearie, I'll tell his mom my alibi.

After we hang up, I pause the documentary on an archival interview with Leo Townsend, a bearded professor who was a student at St. Obadiah, where the Sandman killings originated. He was briefly a suspect—and he talks about his world pretty much being turned inside out when folks accused him of the killings—but his alibis were tight and ultimately people moved on. Most of the interviews in *Your Lonely Nights Are Over* are from last year, but with some of the original survivors, they had to go back to the early eighties archives, because not everybody wanted to answer their questions again. I can see why a former suspect might not want to reemerge from the shadows.

Something about Leo is so familiar. He's white, handsome, dark-bearded, and in his thirties in this interview. His face itches the back of my brain, like I've seen him somewhere before.

But I'm out of time to pick up Dearie.

I lock the house from my app—since my parents are already at work—and wave good morning to the plainclothes detectives who have been parked outside my house for months. The men—one white and heavyset, the other scrawny with dark brown skin—raise their 7-Eleven coffees to me without a smile. We've never spoken, and it says a lot about how pissed my moms are that they've never once introduced themselves or offered them dinner, because they do that for literally anybody.

With my morning ritual completed, I jog down the driveway to Julieta, my Corvette, but stop halfway. Jagged, wicked letters are keyed into the passenger door. Across her otherwise spotless, cherry-red coat, a single word appears etched in gleaming silver:

CHEATER.

Rage sweeps over me, so powerful it's calm. I don't move. I squeeze my phone like a stress ball. My babygirl Julieta, what happened to your face?

I don't need to wonder.

Grover.

At least it doesn't say KILLER.

I growl, "That. Jealous. Pathetic. FLOP."

Slowly, I open my phone to text that rat. *I'm blocked.* I jump to his Instagram. *Blocked.* His TikTok. *Blocked.* Well, well. Mr. Kendall didn't waste any time.

In under thirty seconds, I'm at Dearie's doorstep, my poor, scarred Julieta parked in a slant across his driveway. Frustration boiling over, I slap Dearie's door instead of knocking. When Dearie greets me, it's clear he followed my same "revenge dress" style prompt: ass-hugging black jeans, a black tank with exposed lats, and jeweled Bulgari sunglasses. Even though I can't see his eyes, I can tell he's fuming. We shout our bad news at the same time:

"Grover blocked me!" he says.

"Grover keyed Julieta!" I say. My news causes him to jolt backward. "I win!"

Dearie inhales the largest gasp in history as he follows me to the driveway to behold his ex's handiwork. His mouth hangs open as he brushes the hideous scratches. "I'm so sorr—"

"Nope, not your fault."

Dearie looks at me fearfully. "What are you gonna—?"

"Do? Don't worry. I don't have to lay hands on that boy to destroy him. Every day he doesn't leave school emotionally devastated is because I ALLOW IT."

I cannot believe how efficiently this Flop has unraveled my life, but here we are.

After a moment of angry silence, Dearie's mother descends the driveway. As she approaches, I stiffen. Dearie gets weird whenever his mom and I are in the same room, which hasn't been often since the week after Gretchen's murder, when the media *somehow* found out about the planted cell phones. It was supposed to be an airtight secret for our protection—*hello, minors!*—but in my soul, I know someone in that department made up their mind about me and got the ball rolling on that news.

It's another reason I don't feel safe sharing details of Paul with her.

The sight of Mrs. Dearie's badge and holstered gun curdles my blood like old milk. I practically grew up in her house, but ever since she threw a surprise interrogation on me, my trust in her has disappeared.

"What's wrong?" she asks, toting a thermos. Then she sees the scratches. Her mouth falls open. "Cole! When did this happen?"

I shrug, wanting to say as little as possible. "Sometime last night after Dearie came over."

"Do you know who did it?"

I roll my eyes. "Yeah, it's a real mystery, Poirot."

As she shifts uncomfortably, Dearie says, "It was Grover, Mom."

"That's awful!" She swigs back her coffee. "Your house has a Ring door camera, right?"

"We took ours out," I say. "That shit is for cops."

Her uncomfortable smile stiffens. "That's a shame." She pauses, thinking. "I gave him an escort home last night, and we posted two cars outside, so it'll be tough to prove he went out at night to do this."

With every word out of Mrs. Dearie's lips, my pulse doubles.

"We can't do anything about this," Dearie says, snapping off his sunglasses. He's pissed. "Grover wants this to escalate. He wants to keep pushing Cole until he does something, to make himself look like the victim. Thanks to someone on your team, the whole town is gonna light up if Cole even breathes the wrong way at Grover." He slips his sunglasses back on and growls, "Can't *believe* I dated this scumbag."

As Dearie's body clenches like a fist, mine relaxes. Bestie finally gets it.

Grinning, I say, "I second all of that."

Mrs. Dearie studies us. She suddenly looks like she hasn't slept in weeks. "I'm sorry about your car, angel. I'll cover the repairs." She opens her own car door but then turns back, eyes glistening. "And Cole, from the bottom of my heart, I have no idea how that evidence leaked. I'm mortified." She walks back up to me. "And I'm scared. You're my second son, and I believe you're being targeted. I have people on my team who believe us, who I trust. They're the ones watching your house. They're not there to spy on you. They're for *your* protection. You have friends."

Mrs. Dearie wraps a hug around me, her thermos clinking against my back, and I let my anger seep away for now. I think I trust her, but I wish I could trust her judgment about her team. Points for trying, at least. One gold star earned back, after losing twenty during that interrogation.

As she returns to her car, the truth about Paul floats to

the tip of my tongue . . . But before I can get it out, an image bursts into my thoughts.

Mrs. Dearie's interrogation. Before I went in, Ms. Drake walked out of her interview. Her jumpsuit was smeared with blood, and then . . . That guy walked in.

Forgetting Paul, I pull Dearie inside Julieta and wish his mother a good day.

Right away, Dearie senses my intensity. "What?" he asks.

I don't respond. I pull up *Your Lonely Nights Are Over* on my phone, fresh from the pause point where I left it: Leo Townsend, the bearded professor, the face I knew I'd seen somewhere before.

"*Leo, stop!*" Ms. Drake said to the white-bearded man who barged in after her interview.

Leo. His name was Leo.

It's him. The same man. A man who was around during the original Sandman killings lives *here*, used to be a *suspect*, and knows Ms. Drake.

CHAPTER NINE
DEARIE

COLE'S SHOCKER ABOUT LEO Townsend delays us enough that we barely make it to first period on time. This turns out to be lucky—no one sees us pull into the parking lot in a CHEATER-branded car, and for now, we're spared the judgmental looks. Just like Grover, the rest of our school always thought Cole and I were more than friends, so good luck unringing that bell once they see Julieta's new face-lift.

Before Cole and I split up for the morning, he whispers, "Meet me in the parking lot at free period. We'll ask Ms. Drake about her mystery man!"

I know we're both eager to find a new suspect, but we don't even know how Leo is involved! Or *if* he's involved. We have a trillion questions, but they need to be asked *suavely*. In case this guy is bad . . . like, bad bad, and we could be putting ourselves at risk by asking.

When I reach first period, AP English, a ghoulish weight pummels me: Grover's desk is empty. He didn't come to school. Mom put two cars outside his home, but is that enough? What if Mr. Sandman is already inside Grover's house, hiding in a closet somewhere, waiting until his heartbreak is loud enough to strike? Grover's parents have gone out of state for at least a month for work; his parents felt safe working away from home because he was dating me.

But now he's alone.

Once again, a flash of our breakup pops into my head.

"What about Mr. Sandman?" Grover asks, terrified.

He places something in my hand—what was it?—*and says, "If Mr. Sandman finds me again, he won't be nice about it."*

My feet—which minutes ago felt so cute in my Cuban-heeled boots—turn cold and limp.

"Excuse me," I whimper, clutching back tears as I run into the empty halls. My fingers trace along the cool lockers, memories of my time here assaulting me like breaking waves, one after the other.

I'm not gonna see anyone anymore. Not the way I used to.

Cole. Mom. The Flops. Even Grover.

The motion of the universe is pulling me away from everything I used to be and know. Still, sick as it's making me, I'd break Grover's heart all over again. There's fear in letting go, but also freedom. Frankie Dearie of Stone Grove is wasting away until the new LA Dearie can be born. Maybe that's why Cole is going to New York and leaving everyone, even me.

Maybe we all just need to walk away from this mess.

I head toward the restrooms to splash some water on

my neck, but that takes me down the Murder Hallway. They cleaned it up, but the speckled tan color of the linoleum plays tricks on my eyes. Rivers of blood—stained brown with time—grow larger against the morning shadows cast on the floor. I shut my eyes—just for a moment, like a very slow blink. When they open, the brown remains, but it's just the brown of an old floor. Thousands of shoe prints made that stain, not Gretchen's open throat.

Why kill Gretchen Applebaum? After fifty years of hibernation, what was so objectionable about her loneliness that it brought Mr. Sandman out of retirement?

According to *Your Lonely Nights Are Over*, I'm getting caught in the same mistake the last detectives made about the killer—trying to assign meaning to the victims. He just started killing. There was no victim pattern in the 1970s and there's no pattern today, other than he's developed a taste for the gays. Three new victims, all queer, all different brands of queer loneliness: the dateless wonder, the sad widower, the closet case.

The sound of my own footsteps follows me down the hallway. I stop, and the sound stops.

Everyone's in class. I'm alone.

So why do I feel eyes on me? There's *weight* on the back of my neck.

I turn around—but there's no one. I keep going. My footsteps continue echoing.

Ka-thunk—ka-thunk. I stop. It's not just me. There's a second set of footsteps.

I turn around again—this time, a yellow mop cart turns the corner at the end of the hall. A janitor appears. My brain allows me to breathe again as we wave to each other.

Enough wasting time. Ms. Drake knows something, and I can't wait for Cole to go talk to her.

After splashing my neck with cold water, I skip second period entirely and head straight to the library, which is minuscule. A modest school in a modest town needs not a grand library—just a dozen stacks and a dozen computer desks surrounding a long conference table for study groups. The place is empty except for a few students and Ms. Drake, who looks more energetic than usual, but maybe that's because of her sherbet-orange jumpsuit.

Instantly (sadistically), I think of prison.

If she knows Leo well, and he's got something to do with it, that orange jumpsuit could be permanent. But I'll try to be impartial. I'm just here for facts.

Ms. Drake stands behind her semicircular desk, with a NO BULLYING ZONE poster behind her, and checks out several massive, ancient-looking textbooks for Theo. They wear a different bow tie every day, and today's features red-and-black card suits: hearts, diamonds, spades, and clubs. They ruffle their choppy, shock-red hair and laugh politely with Ms. Drake, who appears to be only half listening.

"Guess you could call these books pre-*pre*-law," Theo chuckles. Ms. Drake smiles weakly. "Stanford gets me as soon as summer hits, but I want to observe the campsite rule for this library. You know, leave it better than I found it? If you have a wish list of books that the school board has been too"—they drop into a whisper—"*stingy* to fund, give it to me, and it'll be my father's graduation gift, since you've been so uplifting to me."

Ms. Drake blinks, shocked. "Oh. That's . . . very generous, Theo."

Theo happily shrugs. "Let's say fifty to a hundred titles? STEM, law, memoir. Fiction's fine, but just a little. Nothing controversial. I hate giving into these outrage cretins, but I don't want to see these books get tossed in the dumpster after all that trouble, right?"

Sometimes, queer confidence is a mistake.

Ms. Drake nods patiently through more of Theo's back-handed compliments about this *little* library and the *little* people in it, all the *little* lives they want to bring a *little* hope to.

Theo better hope they're not talking to a Mr. Sandman associate right now because if so, CHOP. Although with each passing second, the likelihood that Ms. Drake has anything to do with this mayhem seems laughable. She's normie to the max.

Without looking, I snatch the closest book off the shelf and join Theo at Ms. Drake's desk. Ms. Drake, grateful to have someone new to talk to, turns with a genuine smile. Theo, however, appraises me coolly.

"Dearie, how are you holding up?" Theo asks.

"Fine!" I say, praying this is enough interaction for them to leave me alone.

"Oh, what happened?" Ms. Drake asks.

Before I can even breathe, Theo—life's permanent protagonist—takes it upon themself to spill my business. "He dumped Grover last night."

Ms. Drake stifles a gasp. Sucking my teeth, I stomp down the urge to rant and instead say, "Not the wording I would've used, but yeah." Robotically, I retreat to my prepared talking points. "He's under police protection. It's better this way."

Theo scoffs. "I FaceTimed Grover earlier, and you're minimizing it, Dearie." One of my eyebrows arches at the taunt. "He was in no condition to come to school. I told him to take a mental health day."

There aren't enough mental health days in the *world* for that boy.

Theo glances me up and down, judgment spreading across their face. "You look okay, though. I'd say you were 'glowing.'"

I don't shrink from the insinuation. Theo wants me feeling self-conscious about my intentionally sexy outfit—they would've preferred it if I'd crawled in here wearing stained pajamas. Luckily, Ms. Drake isn't having it. "Theo," she warns, "breakups look different on everyone."

"Oh, I'm just complimenting Dearie!" Theo replies defensively. "If you get me your wish list by next Friday, that timing works best."

I smile fakely. "Really cool of you to get those books for the library."

"I was born fortunate, so it's my responsibility. Cole could learn something about that, but I guess spending money on a Corvette is fine too."

As usual, Theo is comfortable being an open hypocrite. Their dad has an entire garage of rare vintage cars. They even have their own motorcycle!

My entire aura darkens as I step closer. "So, you *do* know what Grover did to Julieta."

"I don't know what you're talking about." On an obnoxiously sweet giggle, Theo glides away, the door closing loudly behind them.

Now there's no one left but me and Ms. Drake. She reaches out for me. "Getting that book?" I hand her the book I randomly grabbed, and her eyes widen. "Train engineering?" She shows me the book cover: an old, faded picture of a railroad crossing a desert.

"Yeah," I stammer. "Uh, I'm so into high-speed rail right now. Our country needs it badly."

Laughing to herself, Ms. Drake looks over the yellowing

book. "I agree, but you won't find any of that in here. This was written in the Bronze Age."

Smirking, I tap a legal pad on her desk. "Put an updated copy on Theo's wish list, then."

Ms. Drake rolls her eyes. "Please." Her expression hardens. "Frankie, I don't like to get involved, but don't take anything Theo said to heart. People have no idea how hard it is to break up with someone. Most people can't do it. They let their relationships get worse, thinking it'll get so bad, the other person will end it for them." She exhales on a shuddering breath. "If things weren't working with Grover, you wouldn't be doing him any favors staying together."

I want to believe her, but my memory of that whole breakup is so foggy. Fiddling with my sunglasses, I say, "If Mr. Sandman finds Grover again . . . I'll never get over it."

Ms. Drake winces with understanding. "Before Gretchen died, before Mr. Sandman came back . . . I got divorced." She holds up her hand—absent a wedding ring. "After the murder, my ex—Leo—begged me to come back. He was scared. Mr. Sandman could target us next. But I wouldn't take him back. If I had, I'd feel trapped and lonelier than ever." Smiling, she shakes her shoulders, as if to toss off the sad story. "Stick to your guns, Frankie. It'll be hard, but people like us can take it."

"Yeah!" I say with false brightness, but deep inside, I'm chilled to the bone.

Ms. Drake dumped Leo—the guy mysteriously connected to the original Mr. Sandman—and then suddenly, someone starts killing her students.

Could it be that simple?

Ms. Drake asks if she can hug me, which is surprisingly just what I need, and then I run back to the bathrooms, where I lock myself in a stall to catch my breath. My heart racing, I order myself not to faint.

Does Mom know about Ms. Drake's connection to Leo, or of Leo's to the original Mr. Sandman? Are Cole and I going to solve this after all?

As I comprehend the possibility of this horror ending soon, I spy a doodle on the toilet stall door: a tragedy mask. Mr. Sandman's calling card, with the words STAY TOGETHER written beneath the mask.

Stay together. A threat *and* advice Ms. Drake and I didn't take.

CHAPTER TEN

COLE

A SCHOOL DAY HAS never felt more meaningless in my life. All day, people have been staring, and I can no longer tell if it's because they think I'm a killer, a cheater, hot, dressed too hoochie for school, or all of the above. But it's Friday, and the weekend has arrived with blessings.

Because Dearie might have found our murderer.

Ms. Drake dumped her ex, Leo—a guy who went to the original Sandman school—and suddenly her sad students start getting killed. Could Mr. Sandman not handle his own loneliness?

Hidden in a brick-walled alcove outside the school parking lot, Dearie and I confer notes over a vape. Behind us, dozens of students race to their cars as Dearie takes a long drag, wafting clouds of weed vapor over me. He hands me the pen, and I inhale deeply. I rarely do this, but this is an emergency.

"Have you noticed anything funny about the straights lately?" I ask on an exhale.

"Other than them being straight?" he asks, taking the pen back.

"They've been extra amorous." I watch student after student leave. Each one of them proves my theory: hand-holding, ass-grabbing, kissing each other against cars.

"You think they're worried about Mr. Sandman too?"

Coughing, I refuse his vape pen on the next round. "So far, it's been gays only, but everyone thinks Paul was straight, so *now* they're all keyed up. *Now* they need to pair up or die."

Dearie nods, biting his pen in thought. "You wanna date me?"

Snorting, I grab the pen back. "Romance is for straights. Queers get to bicker with each other about petty bullshit while we get killed one by one, you know that."

Dearie giggles until he winces with shock. "Shit, put it away!" he whispers, chucking the vape into the grass as a flood of teachers exit into the parking lot.

While Dearie waves to Ms. Drake amid the horde of other faculty, I remember what's really important: Leo. I didn't have time all day, so now that we're alone, I pull out my phone and search "Leo Townsend Stone Grove." Thanks to *Lonely Nights*, I already know about his San Diego days, but what's he been up to here? Right away, the first hit is a publicity page for Mooncrest Cemetery. On Fridays, they show classic films outside. Dearie and I have gone dozens of times. So did Paul and I. So did

Grover and Gretchen. I scroll down the page, looking for info—Leo's name, somewhere. Then I see it: his photo and bio.

Mooncrest Movie Nights are funded by retired hedge fund manager Leo Townsend.

Leo's headshot stares back at me, his blue eyes newly sharklike with my dark knowledge.

Claude Adams, victim number two, was killed just outside Mooncrest.

All the victims, both dead and framed, have been to Leo's movies.

Like a roller coaster, my mood plunges as quickly as it rose. I've seen *Lonely Nights* enough to remember the details. Leo is a tragic character, even though he has a smaller role. His life was turned inside out by his being accused of being the murderer—without evidence. Everyone in that school made up their minds it was him—just like me. Is everyone wrong, just like they are about me?

I need to be careful how I go about this.

Leo's relationship with Ms. Drake gave him access to knowledge about Grover and me beefing, maybe even ways to get into our lockers. It's a lead, but I need to know more.

I hand Dearie my phone showing Leo's Mooncrest page. His eyes pop.

"Want to go to the movies with me tonight?" I ask, sliding on my sunglasses.

Grinning, Dearie pulls on his sunglasses. "Great minds, Cole Slaw."

For the first time since that burner phone was found in my locker, I feel like Dearie and I are unstoppable again! He leaves to walk home and clear his head (promising me to stick to busy areas), and I return to the parking lot for Julieta. When I arrive, hordes of students cruise slowly past Julieta for a look at Grover's masterpiece of keying. Some of them must need reading lessons because they have to mouth the word "cheater."

"Nasty scratches you got there, Cardoso," Mike Mancini says with a slick smile, sauntering by in a rumpled black tee. "My dad's shop could get her looking good as new, buuuuuut we're a little backed up. Might be a few weeks before we can squeeze you in. I'd hate to see you have to show up to prom driving this around."

Rage erupts out of every pore, my high only intensifying the injustice licking my skin like flames. Grover can cut up my whole car, and the school mourns his mental health. But with my current reputation, if I even walked near Mike with anger in my eyes, I'd be tackled to the ground.

I don't yell. I replace my anger with a smile.

Mike's smile drops. My bitchy handsomeness frightens mere mortals.

"You think those scratches bother me?" I ask. "I'm keeping them."

"Huh?"

"I couldn't have bought this kind of bad PR for Grover. No one wants to date a boy who cuts up cars when he's mad."

In a blink, Mike's demeanor shifts into that of a wide-eyed, bashful puppy. I glance up and down this disheveled boy. Another queer cutie led astray into obnoxiousness by proximity to Grover. With Mike, it almost wasn't fair. Just a few minutes out of the closet before Grover pounced with his Queer Rulebook for who to trust and who to hate.

"Guess you're right," he says, shamed. "I don't approve of it, or, er"—he smacks his head—"I don't know for sure *who* did it, but, uh, I would never support something like that. Um . . . How's Dearie holding up?"

Oh my God, if I were Mr. Sandman, I'd garrote this kid right now just to put him out of his misery. But I will give him points on understanding that the way to get closer to Dearie is to be nice to me. A lesson Grover never embraced.

"He's on top of the world, Mikey, but me and him gotta get ready for Mooncrest."

"Ah, I'll see you both there!" Hopping in place, Mike tosses a truly embarrassing thumbs-up. "Gonna change into something nicer."

"Mmm, something washed?" I ask, slugging back my water bottle.

Laughing nervously, Mike leaves without another word.

Let him hate me, but if he wants to bag Dearie, he'll need to dress the part (which is to say, with a drop of effort).

With Mike cleared out and the other gawkers dissipating, there's only one nearby onlooker remaining: Benny, my unofficial MexAm cousin from House Flop, in crooked glasses and a Pym Technologies shirt. He gazes at Julieta with awe. He always does. It would probably give him a boner just to sit in the passenger seat.

I like him, but I'm tired of seeing Grover's friends huddle around Julieta, and this Flop picked the wrong day to play both sides.

"Benito," I call out, walking quickly toward the boy half my size. He skips backward in frightened jumps. "Come to see what your boy did to my babygirl?" I ask in a fierce whisper. "You want to be a real friend to me, tell your other friend not to key other people's shit."

Benny gasps, his back hunched in fear. "We didn't know Grover was gonna do that."

I wag my finger. "Just 'cause you're nerds doesn't mean you can go around hurting people. Grover hurt me, okay? I'm sorry Gretchen isn't here anymore, but I didn't have shit to do with that. You tell him I'm SICK of this shit."

"He doesn't listen to me," Benny insists, shaking his head.

As swiftly as anger crashed into my thoughts, clarity moves back in.

Oh my God. I just took out all my baggage on this harmless boy who likes me.

"I'm sorry," I say, backing away. "I've had a shitty day."

Shitty year, more like.

Slowly, Benny uncurls his back and squeaks, "It's okay."

"It's not."

"I believe you didn't do it," Benny says. "I always have."

I toss my head back to laugh. "I do like your family's free meals. If I ever get out of this shit, I'm gonna have to go back to paying full price at Tío Rio's, so maybe I should enjoy the suspicion while it lasts."

His eyes find mine. "No, it's free for life. I'm going over there now to catch up on homework before Mooncrest. Want to drive me? I get a spin in Julieta, you get some free apps?"

My jaw finally unclenches. My hunger *is* gargantuan.

"Hop in," I say. "Your mom better warn her customers they're gonna see a serial killer attack those apps like they're my next victim."

Benny's cheerful giggle tells me everything I need to know: he really believes I didn't do it.

ON THE NEXT EPISODE OF
YOUR LONELY NIGHTS ARE OVER:
THE SEARCH FOR MR. SANDMAN

After a year of slaughter and panic, graduation day came for the students of St. Obadiah High School, and also for Mr. Sandman. The summer of 1972 saw his victim pool grow from St. Obadiah to greater San Diego, all but confirming the killer was a student who'd since graduated. Yet each of these graduates had flawless alibis, leaving authorities backed into a corner with no leads.

Being single was now a death sentence anywhere in the city.

"STAY TOGETHER." people chanted, convinced that by saying it enough, they'd be protected. Even after all these years, few couples will admit these killings kept their failing relationships together. After all, why admit you wish you had stayed single when Mr. Sandman could still be out there hunting for his next victim?

Continue watching?

PART THREE
STAY TOGETHER

CHAPTER ELEVEN
DEARIE

THAT NIGHT, COLE AND I almost don't make it out the door. Mom isn't happy about us going out so late—but it's not like we can tell her we're investigating a suspect. If we confirm anything useful about Leo, we'll tell her.

We hop in Julieta, and Cole drives me beyond the town limits, through darkened desert, and bullets down Mooncrest Highway, all the way to the graveyard. The road is oddly lonely—no headlights ahead or behind. Mooncrest Movie Nights usually see a caravan of people all heading in one direction, but both of us have been so scattered today we're running late.

On the winding desert road, Cole hooks his Corvette around a sharp pivot, flipping my insides like pancakes. We're overdriving the headlights. The double solid yellow lines blur as blacktop rushes forward into darkness, but Cole anticipates every bend without blinking. As our speed climbs, I settle back into Julieta's amber-colored leather seat and exhale dense weed clouds into the car. Cole enjoys a deep secondhand inhale.

For the third time since we started driving, an Imagine Dragons song comes on the radio. I slap it off. "Never heard so much of the same shit in my whole life."

"Fire up your playlist, then," Cole says.

"Trying." I tap uselessly at my phone. "I can't get signal, and Apple locked my account 'cuz I keep forgetting my password." The screen to reset my password refuses to load, held up by a signal that is unable to penetrate the ring of dark mountains surrounding us. Once you leave the confines of Stone Grove, you drive headfirst into oblivion. I flick my phone's display screen and, miraculously, the reset page loads with security questions.

"What's the name of your childhood best friend?" I read aloud.

"Is it moi?" Cole asks in a Miss Piggy voice, flipping imaginary long hair.

"It's my very best friend," I say, sickeningly sweet, and type: C-O-L-E.

Best friends forever, I think with stabbing pain.

Cole brushes more imaginary hair behind his ear, this time actually forgetting he chopped his black mane for a bleached buzz cut. I usually hate when guys abandon good hair for this dystopian look, but—*Surprise!*—Cole looks stunning, especially in his wine-dark bomber jacket. Contrary to what Cole might say, I'm not jealous. His scrappy Pedro Pascal vibe works for him. Me, I'm in head-to-toe Audrey

Hepburn black: slim, sweet, simple, and sharp.

Cole is a scuffed-up fist. I'm a glistening dagger.

No wonder people think we're dangerous.

Finally, I'm allowed to change my password, and my play-list fills Julieta with high-energy, deep-cut dance tracks. Cole and I vibe together as the last stretch of Mooncrest Highway narrows into an unpaved, single-lane access road. Through the moonless desert, Cole's headlights catch an aging ply-wood sign nailed to a monstrous-limbed cactus: DEAD AHEAD.

One cactus later, another sign comes: MOVIES WITH THE DEAD. GRINS ONLY!

As we pass the sign, the Sandman rhyme pops into my head: *Don't frown, don't pout, don't ever cry. If he hears your lonely heart, then you're the next to die.*

Breath seeps slowly into my lungs—too slowly—like smoke trapped behind a door. Mr. Sandman is close. I just have a feeling. Cole's eyes flit back and forth. His shoulders hunch as if a great, dark chill has fallen over the car.

For both of us, it has. Cole used to come here with Paul.

"Maybe this was a bad idea?" I ask, brushing on cherry ChapStick. Cole glances over, his heavy brow furrowed. "It's okay, don't answer that." I laugh, petting his jacket. The expensive smoothness of the leather slows the vibration of my nerves.

"Let's just keep our eyes open," Cole says. "It could be Leo. But maybe it's not."

I exhale more vapor. "Either way, we'll have fun. Grins only."

"Grins only." Cole pulls off-road onto the sprawling cemetery property. The desert solitude and pitch-black night give way to a crackling eruption of light and people. Outside a hillside of grave markers, upward of fifty cars park in haphazard lines under enormous stadium lamps. Nearly every one of the giggling teenagers sprinting out of their cars with picnic baskets is a classmate.

Resting at the foot of a mile-wide mesa, the cemetery hails back to the days of the Wild West: nothing but cacti and grave markers—some elegantly carved stone, some so slipshod they're barely more than a nailed-together cross jammed into the silt. The graves lie clumped in two batches connected by an open Astroturf arena (where we'll park our blankets and chairs), all leading to a grand mausoleum—the back of which will be our movie screen. Surrounding the cemetery is a wrought-iron gate. It was built as a precaution to keep out marauding animals.

Once you're inside Mooncrest, stay inside. Death stalks the perimeter.

The cemetery sits alone for miles in every direction. During the day, the mesa beyond the mausoleum is straight out of an American postcard: rust-colored, sun-kissed, and brilliant. At night, as the movies play, the mesa becomes shadow.

I usually love it—it heightens the movie mood. But now, after Mr. Sandman and my breakup, the uncertainty only tightens the grip of fear in my chest.

Tons of people have already congregated in the picnic arena, their blankets lying catty-corner to each other, filling every available speck of lawn. As expected, the moment we emerge, dozens of eyes clock that I have arrived not with my ex, but with Cole. The best friend they always suspected was something more.

Just as I thought, SLUTS, their eyes say with a twinge of satisfaction.

"Ready?" Cole asks, slinging two small beach chairs over his shoulder.

"Everyone's staring," I whisper.

"I don't care. Why do you?" Cole crinkles his nose, as if devastated his lifelong coconspirator is devolving into a Flop before his very eyes. "Grover and you are OVER. You can't spell 'Grover' without O-V-E-R. Anyone who cares about you knows I had nothing to do with it."

"You're right." I hug the blanket tighter as a desert chill clenches my shoulders. April days can be blazing, but at night, the temperature plunges. Cole hands me his black-and-yellow varsity jacket—a serpent sewn onto each arm, and on the back, the number 17: CARDOSO. The victory jacket of the Stone Grove Rattlers' power forward (and power other things). He drapes the jacket over my shoulders like an elegant mink coat, heavy and swaddling, and instantly, my shivering stops.

"Cole . . ." I protest weakly.

"You never wear enough layers," he scolds. "And the best way to get a new boyfriend is to already have a boy-friend. So, let them think I'm with you. Maybe you'll get lucky tonight—catch the killer and catch some D."

I smile, settling confidently into the large jacket, my palms barely emerging out of the arms. "You're such pond scum."

"That's my girl." He winks, and we descend into the crowd with our blankets and chairs. It takes some ma-neuvering, but with Cole confidently leading the way, the other picnickers disperse before us, particularly the quar-tet of Flops along the outer rim: Benny, Theo, Lucy, and Mike—*no Grover.* It makes sense. Grover couldn't come to school, so why would he face Mooncrest alone after losing Gretchen, his Movie Night bestie?

At least I don't have to tangle with my ex tonight, and now that I know about Leo, it's better that Grover stay far away from this place.

"WORK, HONEYS," Lucy hollers as we pass. She's dressed impeccably for spring in a lilac sweater set. Benny and Cole wave to each other, but as Cole barrels past him, he accidentally tips a half-drunk VitaminWater onto their quilt.

Theo catches it and snarls, "Excuse you!"

Bundled like a skier in his red puffer jacket, Mike sweetly calls out, "Ooh, watch your step, Dearie!" We leave the Flops in our rearview as Lucy narrates us like we're runway models:

"WALK, WALK, WALK IN LATE. WALK, WALK, SPILL THAT DRINK."

As Cole and I search the arena for an open space, black-and-white sci-fi trailers from the fifties play across the high mausoleum wall. Half the crowd pays no attention—laughing, hollering, lobbing popcorn at each other—while the other half sits enraptured by the retro schlock.

"*EARTH HORROR MEETS SPACE TERROR!*" shouts the trailer's narrator. "*FRANKENSTEIN MEETS THE SPACE MONSTER!*"

Cole and I worship this crud so much, we both almost lose our balance staring at the trailers.

We haven't even graduated yet, but I'm already overwhelmed by nostalgia for what I'm losing. *Best friends forever.* After stuffing away my feelings, I push through the crowd. My head stays on a swivel for Leo's white beard, but everyone around us is too young. Em—huddled under a blanket with four cheerleader friends—catches my eye. We wave to each other. It's nice to see a friendly face.

The same can't be said for the next face we stumble across: Agent Astrid Astadourian. A high-cheekboned woman with dark olive skin and long, shimmering black hair, Agent Astadourian appears to be here on pleasure, not business. She's in jeans, a T-shirt, and a gorgeous suede jacket. A young man I don't recognize, with light brown skin and a thick mustache, shares a picnic with her.

"Frankie, Cole," she greets us with a reserved friendliness.

Cole and I share a rapid glance before plastering on smiles. "Agent Astadourian," I say, giving a quick, silly salute. "Your first Mooncrest movie?"

She smiles. "Your mom told me I had to experience it at least once. Ray Fletcher's supposed to be quite a character."

Leo's the money behind Mooncrest, but Ray Fletcher curates and introduces the films. He's a beloved local icon—like a nonfamous Tom Hanks—and the Movie Nights get their flavor from Ray's showmanship. Last year, he invited us to hang out in his projector booth talking movies. He's the first person Cole and I ever told about our plan to make movies in LA.

It still could be the plan. Cole's just taking a little detour to New York first.

Cole and I mumble pleasantries to Astadourian and excuse ourselves out of there. If Leo is really Mr. Sandman, he'll have to make his move with an FBI agent hanging around. But Mr. Sandman has slipped past the FBI for half a century. Double-A has her work cut out for her.

Soon, the movie will begin, and it'll be too dark to see. We need to find a base camp so we can start looking for Leo.

"I'm starving," Cole mutters ominously, as if his hunger portends some imminent threat.

As Cole's self-appointed fourth mother (following my mom as third), I'm powerless against my desire to nourish my child. Just beyond the next few campsites, I spot the rows of string lights that mark the refreshments tent. "I'll grab you popcorn," I say. "Let's just find a spot."

"What a sweet little housewife you are, Dearie," a cold voice calls from the ground.

My heart stops.

No. No goddamn way is Grover here too.

But there he is, sneering. On the ground, Grover sprawls glamorously sideways on his picnic blanket like a kitten. His eyes narrow as he sips from a travel bottle of Fireball whiskey.

"Um, does your security know where you are?" I ask, horrified they let him go out.

Grover snorts. "Your *mommy's* people? Yeah, they know. They're around back. Not that I trust them or your mommy to do anything."

Another kick to my chest. It's shocking to hear him speak this harshly. He wasn't always . . . like this. Especially when we were dating. Except—the thought pops into my head—during the breakup I'm still trying to piece together.

Maybe this is the side of Grover he showed to Cole when I wasn't around.

It's hideous.

I cinch Cole's jacket tighter around me and summon another polite smile. "I'm glad you got out of the house, Grover. And I'm extra glad your security is here."

"The hell do you care?" Grover sneers, sipping again from the Fireball. He looks past me to Cole, and a shadow passes over his smile. "You changed your hair. Don't love it."

"Oh no, I was worried what you were gonna think," Cole blurts.

"We're out of here," I say, narrowing my eyes at Grover and yanking Cole away from an almost-guaranteed altercation. Unfortunately, an incoming flow of foot traffic stops us, led by Justin Saxby. Bro'd out in an emerald-green hoodie and backward cap, he balances two paper cups, each filled with a steaming drink.

"Here, honey!" Grover calls. Cole and I share stunned glances as Justin delivers one of the cups to Grover before curling beside him. "Cider for you," Justin says brightly. Grover kisses him and empties the rest of the Fireball into his cup.

"I thought you were leaving?" Grover asks me, sipping. "Anyway, you both know my new boyfriend?"

Justin grins smugly, but I glow with fiery humiliation. New boyfriend? I've been kicking my own ass all day, thinking Grover's too depressed to leave the house, thinking he's Sandman bait, and he's already shacked up with his no-face boyfriend twin?

"Hello" is all I can stammer.

"New boyfriend already?" Cole snorts. "That was fake—I mean, fast."

A loud "HA!" explodes from my chest. Grover rises from his blanket, shaking with rage—he's noticed my jacket—Cole's jacket. "You're wearing *his* varsity jacket?" he scoffs at me, as if I'm the last person who deserves to wear it.

I clasp the coat tighter and find excuses rushing to my lips: "Well, it was cold—"

"Cheater, I knew it!" Grover's heart-shattered gaze grills into me. Fire rushes up my chest—not this shit again. All around us, heads turn to gawk as Grover's lip quivers. "After what *he* did to me. And Gretchen."

I'm breathless. Grover is accusing Cole of being his attacker—*a murderer*—in plain sight of everyone here . . . when he *knows* Cole had nothing to do with it. When he *knows* it could get Cole jailed or worse. This little sack of shit.

"You LYING—" I start, but Cole is already leaping on Grover.

My ex is a dirty fighter, though. Claws out, slaps dealt. Even Justin gets into the mix, trying to pull Grover away, push Cole back. But Cole is a quick dodge. I step back, terrified. I don't want Cole to get hurt, but part of me doesn't want to stop the fight. Part of me wants to see Cole maul this jerk who willingly allowed the police, the FBI, and half of Stone Grove to treat my bestie like the Night Stalker. But Grover is a famous survivor, and everyone knows Cole is a person of interest, so this is bad all around. It just looks like Cole is attacking his victim again. I look around for help, but people are only staring uselessly, just like me. My body refuses to move.

Grover and Justin get a few more good swipes in, scratching at any part of Cole they can reach, as Cole fights back—*I'll get you, you mutherfuuuuggggg, you cut my car!*—before I jump in to finally pull Cole from the fracas.

"Stop it, he's not worth it!" I shriek. Every eye in the cemetery falls on us. Grover dissolves into sobs and presses his hand to a scratch on his cheek. While Justin fusses over him, Cole's chest rises and falls on thunderous breaths. "Cole, are you okay—?" I ask.

"Don't," he warns, backing away. "Just—I need to be alone."

Once again, the crowd parts for Cole, but out of fear. Of what he might do. Nobody knows the truth, that Grover is the aggressor.

My heart feels split as I let my friend go. But when an extrovert like Cole says he needs to be alone, he needs to be alone.

Overflowing with anger, I storm toward my ex, who is still lost in his manipulatively wounded performance. Seeing my rage, Justin shuffles backward, and Grover ditches his feigned tears.

"I'm happy you're on a date," I say. "I'm happy because I don't have to be responsible for you anymore." I point at Justin, who is mid–cider sip. "I want Justin to enjoy his night with you, with the asterisk that I don't think you're in a condition to be dating anyone right now. You need to deal with your shit. Mr. Sandman doesn't give you a free pass."

I burn holes into Grover's wounded, unblinking eyes. "You know what? I feel so *free* now," I say, the words pouring out. "And I felt guilty for feeling free, but I didn't need to. You're . . . fine. You just want attention, like Cole said." My lip trembles—this rage is overwhelming. "I did the right thing. I broke up with you face-to-face. I could've ghosted you in the hallway and pretended you weren't even there. I didn't. My only crime was that I just didn't want to be with you anymore."

No sadness finds me. Only strength.

Grover can't summon the bravery to look at me as his smug face collapses into a mask of pain—almost like a tragedy mask. "It's not your only crime," he whispers, so sinister it stops my breath. He shows me a text on his phone. "You got me killed."

On his screen is a message—dated last night—from an unknown number.

The words freeze my blood: YOUR LONELY NIGHTS WILL SOON BE OVER.

CHAPTER TWELVE

COLE

HIGH SCHOOL NIMRODS! I swear, I'm supposed to be thirty, but I'm trapped being eighteen.

These endless, meaningless high school entanglements. The smallness of it all.

If Grover keeps escalating with me, he's going to be a problem. There's no predicting how far that immature homo is willing to go.

Sweeping through the Mooncrest crowd, I clutch a raw scratch screaming across my forearm. It's not too deep, but Grover still drew blood. I should've known he would with me someday.

After a calming breath, I'm still not in the mood to settle in for the movie. We came to snoop on Leo Townsend, not guzzle cider, so I seek out the one person here who will know where to find Leo *and* have zero interest in the woes of Grover Kendall: Ray Fletcher, the long-reigning manager of Mooncrest.

Near the back of the arena, inside the projection booth,

I watch Ray fiddle with tonight's film print. It's more of a projection apartment than a booth, with plyboard walls smothered in framed posters of old car chase movies like *Vanishing Point*—which Dearie and I worship, despite the disco-era gay caricatures that had us roaring with laughter.

Ray has a knack for choosing movies that treat gays like buffoons.

Or maybe that's just a thriller thing.

Ray is a friendly Mr. Rogers–type white man in a gray, unkempt suit. Last year, he gave Dearie and me permission to pop in anytime, which we often take him up on.

When Dearie started dating Grover—and my irritation with my bestie grew exponentially—I would come here alone. Ray was my refuge from the Mr. Sandman suspicion and high school drama. For a while, he was the only person besides my parents who knew about my secret New York plans.

I hated keeping secrets from Dearie, but it just felt nice to be an adult and imagine a future free from all of this bullshit.

"No Frankie again today?" Ray asks, waving me over to an empty chair beneath a poster of Ennio Morricone conducting a film score.

"He's here," I say, sitting. "Just . . . busy with some drama."

Ray chuckles but happily asks no follow-up questions

as he pulls on white film-handling gloves. "Move those papers out of the way, would you?" An untidy man, Ray's worktable is smothered with flyers, newspapers, and scrap paper. I scoop them up, and he shuffles them over to his desk. "Excuse the mess! It's been a while since anyone's visited. Where've you been?"

"Dealing," I say, holding back a mountain of TMI. "Trying to keep my mind off Sandman."

Ray moans with understanding as he works. Using gloves, he tenderly loads a vintage film print into his ancient projector. This palace of moviemaking fills my veins with energy; when I'm here, I can visualize my new life. The movies I'll make. The craft I'll use to create them. I'll be miles away from this town and the mean little faces of the people in it. And maybe, with luck, Dearie and I will reunite and become the unstoppable creative collaborators we were always meant to be.

Soon. When we catch Mr. Sandman.

A second, digital projector continues to play 1950s sci-fi trailers while guests outside dig into charcuterie plates. "Got a treat for you tonight, blondie," Ray says, locking the first reel into place. I clasp my hands and lean over to spy the writing on the reel canisters: *Blue Stalker*. I gasp. He cranes out from behind the projector and winks. "These kids aren't gonna know what hit 'em."

"They totally aren't!" I yelp, bouncing in my chair.

Blue Stalker is a top-five film for me. Definitely my favorite thriller. 2003. Catherine Zeta-Jones and Brittany Murphy (*RIP, queen!*) are lovers. CZJ is a bitch-in-the-boardroom, bored-in-the-bedroom type who's stuck with this boring husband and nasty stepson. Then she meets free spirit Brittany Murphy (unfortunately, an era-problematic manic pixie dream girl, but who Murphy turns into something way more nuanced). Long story short, CZJ thinks it's a fling, Murphy thinks it's love, and then a much more intense remake of *Fatal Attraction* unfolds where Murphy stalks everyone within an inch of their lives.

I've never been able to convince Dearie to watch this peak of early queer cinema, and now my boy is trapped! This night is already turning around.

"You doing okay, tough guy?" Ray asks, pulling up a chair next to me. Without realizing, I've been massaging the shallow red scratches on my forearm where Grover clawed me. When I pull my sleeve down to cover them, Ray tilts his head. "How'd those happen?"

I shrug. "Just . . ." But Ray emanates such a calm, nonjudgmental energy, lying isn't necessary. "Grover Kendall."

His eyebrows shoot up. "Oh no, you're a Were-Grover now."

I sputter laughing. "Yeah, next full moon, I'll turn into a crybaby." I glance away—that came out sounding meaner than I wanted.

"He's been crying? Before or after he scratched you?" Ray smiles, but there's an edge there. He doesn't want either of us to get hurt.

I groan. *Dammit.* I really didn't want to get into it. "He's fine, don't worry."

"Well, I worry when I hear you've been fighting with the boy you could go to jail for trying to kill." Protests start spitting out of my lips, but Ray holds up a calm hand. "You had nothing to do with that, that's not what I meant. I just want to make sure you're being careful. I've lived in Stone Grove my whole life, and these people catch ugly ideas like they're catching cold."

Once again, a relieved laugh comes. "Don't get me started." I glance around at this small-but-fantastic world Ray Fletcher has created for himself. I've never seen him with a partner or anything. How has he escaped the Sandman frenzy? "Do you ever get lonely?"

"Ah, you think I'm next?" He winks and sips his coffee. "No. I was married once. Briefly. I got over it. I like my life now. I'm doing what I love. I want Mooncrest to be a place where you leave your troubles outside. Life is too short to worry about loneliness."

Energized, I sit straighter. "I agree! I know it's crappy to say, but sometimes I just wish some people could be stronger. You know?"

Ray nods with a hint of sadness. "I do. Not everyone

could go through the public hell you did and still come out here to have a good time."

"Yeah," I groan, petting my clawed-up arm and wishing I had a pepperoni pizza to smother these awful feelings with.

Behind me, the projection booth's flimsy door opens with a sharp whine. My spine goes rigid. The white-bearded Leo Townsend clomps inside to join Ray at his table. Where Ray's suit is gray and rumpled, Leo's is khaki and sharply ironed. Leo slumps into the chair with so much heaviness, I feel the impact tremor under my feet.

"Cole, do you know my friend Leo?" Ray asks. "His wife"—as Leo sneers, Ray corrects himself—"*ex*-wife works at your school."

My voice jumps three octaves. "Ms. Drake! I saw you the day"—my heart stops as they both stare, knowing full well what day I mean—"the, uh, the day the police were at school."

Looking stung, Leo turns his attention to his paper cup of coffee. "Sorry about your friends. I know how it feels."

I smile awkwardly. What do I say to that? *I know you know! Did you do it?* Although, something in his face looks so hurt and . . . tired. He was briefly a suspect. *I know how it feels.* Does he mean that even more literally? Does he know who I am and what I've been blamed for? Fifty years from now, if I'm still dealing with Mr. Sandman, will I look this exhausted?

"How do you guys know each other?" I ask, playing innocent.

"Leo runs Mooncrest with me," Ray says, clapping Leo's shoulder like an old friend. "And, small world, Tabatha—Ms. Drake to you—is my daughter."

Okay, *that* I didn't know.

"Huh?" I ask. "I've been coming to your booth this whole time, you never said anything."

"She and I don't talk much anymore. She took her mom's name." Ray chuckles carelessly, as if being estranged from your child is just another of silly ol' life's unpredictable roller coaster loops. He knocks Leo on his shoulder. "Now we've got even more in common."

The two men laugh bitterly. It makes my skin itch. It's like me and Dearie in fifty years, if we just keep collecting bad shit happening to us.

Staring into his coffee, Leo whispers, as if he were the only one in the room, "It was supposed to be over. It's starting again, and I'm losing everything . . ."

Have you ever seen an old man weep? It's REAL.

Leo disappears into quiet spasms of grief, his trembling hand spilling his coffee to the floor. I retreat wordlessly to the door as Ray kneels to wrap a hug around his friend. On a pained gasp, Leo's pink eyes look up at me. "I know it's not you," he moans. "It's never the one they say it is."

"Leo, let's get you lying down," Ray says before turning to me. "Party's over, Cole."

But I can't move.

Leo is staring into me, into my soul, seeing me and all the lonely nights that Grover and Mr. Sandman put me through.

"Don't trust anyone," Leo yells. "Whoever he is, he's already in your life. You have to be so careful." Tears retake him. "I was so careful . . ."

"Leo, *stop*," Ray says, shaking his friend's shoulders. "Cole has been through enough." He turns to me. "I'm sorry. He'll get worse. You need to go."

Excusing myself, I scramble outside into the cool night breeze and breathe again.

"*THE AMAZING COLOSSAL MAN!*" shouts the sci-fi trailer's narrator.

"*I don't want to grow ANYMORE!*" bellows a giant, as tall as a building.

Jesus Christ. Good going, Cole. Now I'm more scared than ever.

I text Dearie that I found Leo. His sobbing—it just feels like it can't be him. But my signal is too weak and the text doesn't go through.

Is Leo another Mr. Sandman dead end? Or was it a performance for my benefit from the grand master of manipulation and showmanship?

If that was fake, it was Oscar-worthy.

I have to sit down. Grunting, I stuff my phone away, scoop up my picnic blanket and chairs, and wade into the

132

masses. I circle around the outside of the suffocating crowd. An endless line of people waits to use the portable toilets—among them is Theo, wearing a bow tie lit up with rainbow LED strips, and Em, who shivers underneath a red blanket draped over her shoulders.

While they wait, they play Celebrity Who Am I. Em holds her phone to her forehead, which reads "Rachel McAdams." Theo and Em descend into giggles as Theo apparently fails—again—to give proper clues. "I don't know what other movies she's been in!" they say.

A bathroom door opens, and it's Em's turn. She pulls off her blanket, revealing a sparkly low-cut top and miniskirt. "Hold this until I'm back?"

Theo happily accepts her blanket, and as Em leaves, they check her out. That thirsty Flop.

While Theo waits, they rehearse asking out Em: "You busy after? Anything cool tomorrow?"

Smirking, I march past the bathroom line, pausing by Theo to whisper, "Em likes jerks."

Theo lets out a startled yelp. Their eyes burst with relief the moment they clock it's me, not a tragedy mask. "And how would you know that?" they ask.

"Because she flirted with me, and I'm a jerk. From one Mean to another, just be your awful, bossy self, and you'll get a yes." I wink. "Or maybe she's looking to date rich."

"It's tacky to call yourself rich."

"It's *tacky* to act like you're not."

Theo snarls sourly, but they can't deny I'm right. In the Before Times, when the Queer Club was closer friends, Theo had us over to their home for huge block parties. They were clearly desperate for friends—so much so they actually thought it would be great friend PR to tell people their mom was on Senator Sinema's staff, speaking of Dreadful Queers. Half the class didn't know her, and the half who did dropped the Galligans like a hot rock. Me and Dearie, we played along being their friend and enjoyed the Galligans' vintage car collection and ample charcuterie platters. And while Grover poisoned them against us over time, I could never hate Theo. They just were so . . . bad at making friends, I couldn't help but be swallowed in pity.

Their overeager smile whenever we showed up to a party, like they could finally breathe, like they didn't have to try so hard anymore. Surely, Dearie and I would lay our blessing of coolness upon them, and their hunt for friends could rest.

My general disdain for the president of Floppitania aside, I hope they get their yes from Em.

That's how I win my innocence—good deeds for Flops who are not named Grover Kendall.

As I cut through the center of the crowd, another familiar face reappears walking the opposite direction: Benny. Gripping a near-empty bag of zebra Popcornopolis, he sees me, halts, and waves.

"Hey, Benny," I say sweetly. Despite Benny's bumpy acne and nervous laugh that could rattle windows, he's pretty cute. His and his family's kindness has been such a refuge, but something about Benny just hurts my heart. His entire being radiates sadness (or loneliness?) I can almost touch. He wears the same baggy Marvel shirts for days at a time, and sometimes I spot unfortunate dandruff flakes in his black, curly hair. Maybe all those free meals at his restaurant can be exchanged for my style services. Another good deed!

"I didn't say it earlier, but I like your new blond," Benny says timidly. Laughing, I run my fingers through my short cut, which feels oddly weightless after so many years of a flowing mane. He tries to smile. "You look like . . . a man. Where's Dearie?"

Not wanting to utter Grover's name, I shrug. "He's around. Just about to go looking for him. I thought you were with the Flo—the—the others."

"I'm getting snacks."

"Me too! I'm starving! I should've asked for a second round of your mom's guac." A switch flips in my brain, and a two-birds-with-one-stone idea comes to me: a way to quiet my stomach and fix my karma for yelling at Benny. "Hey, since you're hungry too, you want to ride with me to pick up burgers from Stu's Diner? It's only a minute away! You'll get a second spin in Julieta?"

Benny's mouth drops open. "Twice in one day? Luxurious."

"Sorry, you want to get back to your friends," I say. Benny was probably ordered by his Flop King Grover to not go anywhere alone with me, a filthy murderer!

Yet Benny jumps in a breathless way I can only describe as a swoon. "Forget them, let's go!"

"You're sure?"

Benny bites his lower lip. "You're not gonna kill me, right?"

"I didn't before."

Benny smiles. "Now it's dark."

"Well." I draw closer, tapping his waist. "Only one way to find out."

CHAPTER THIRTEEN

DEARIE

JULIETA ISN'T IN THE Mooncrest parking lot anymore. Cole is gone.

The only thing that stops me fainting from stress is the all-consuming knowledge that I'm probably the only person who can stop the next Mr. Sandman killing. I try dialing my mom yet again—since this is the only place around here to get a signal—but it doesn't go through. I crane my neck, searching for Agent Astadourian—but I can't see her now that the stadium lights are dimmed.

Grover's death message—my greatest fear—arrived last night. We are literally in the twenty-fourth hour since it was sent. Mr. Sandman hasn't missed a twenty-four mark yet. The next killing could come any minute.

Mr. Sandman's here.

After showing me the text, Grover refused to leave the cemetery, saying being around so many people made him feel safer. He demanded that I leave him alone while Justin sneered that he could protect him better than I could. I'm a scrawny little Wednesday Addams, and he's a buff ol' Boston transplant. Too horrified to scold Justin about his masc-fem biases, I badgered Grover to leave until my ex delivered a fatal blow:

"You had your chance to save me, and you blew it."

If anything happens to Grover tonight, I'll remember those words forever.

But nothing will happen—I won't let it.

Finally, when a weak signal returns, a multitude of texts from Cole pop up:

Feeling better. Went to Ray's booth and met you-know-who. I don't think it's him. He had a complete meltdown when he saw me. He was freaked out that all of this was starting again. Also, did you know Ray is Ms. Drake's dad?

Ran into Benny. We're picking up burgers from Stu's. Back in a minute! Want anything?

Hope you're ok. Grover will be fine. He's Shamrock's problem now.

Growling to myself, I rapid-fire text him back about Grover's Mr. Sandman message and to get back here ASAP. Forget the burgers! Mr. Sandman stuff is literally going down now, and I need Cole here—not for protection, but I need him in full view of dozens of people in case something *does* happen. Maybe Benny will be a strong alibi, but I'd rather dozens of people be witnesses.

But nothing is going to happen. We're stopping this.

As I dial Mom again, my fingers tremble so much, I can barely hold the phone.

This time, she answers. "Find Astadourian," she says after I explain. Her voice is forcibly calm.

"I tried looking, but it's so dark with the movie playing," I say. "Mom, you gotta come now. It's been almost twenty-four hours since Grover got that text. Call Grover's security. He said they're here, but I can't find anyone."

Mom sighs heavily. "Frankie, Grover lied. He snuck out. I just heard from his security. They're still at his house—they're nowhere near Mooncrest."

Stomach. Into. Lead. "Shit . . ."

"You kids are killing me. You *had* to go to Mooncrest tonight. Okay, I'm gonna tell you something for your protection, but tell *no one*. There's a man at the cemetery—"

Guilt pulverizes my chest, but I confess anyway: "Leo. I know. Cole does too."

"Frankie."

"We thought we could help—"

"I'm in the car, coming to you." She doesn't even sound angry, she's terrified. "Don't go near Leo. Don't go looking for Grover. Find Asta . . ." The rest of her sentence chops up under Mooncrest's lack of signal.

"I can't just leave Grover!"

"If you . . . look . . . Grover . . . both die!"

The call ends. My bars are gone. The silence of the cemetery parking lot crashes down on me. I can barely hear everyone's laughter as a trailer for next week's feature starts, *This Island Earth*—another explosion of 1950s sci-fi.

"*A PLANET DOOMED TO DESTRUCTION,*" hollers the trailer narrator. "*WHILE CAPTIVE EARTH PEOPLE FIGHT FOR THEIR LIVES!*"

I shut my eyes to settle my insides. *Gretchen—dead. That writer—killed so close to Mooncrest. Paul—killed before he could help Cole.* Now Grover's next. Mr. Sandman is swimming closer, ready to feast again. The fear is overwhelming, but I open my eyes with a clear mission: *Astadourian—find her.*

My feet whirl forward, independent of my brain, which has gone cold and blank. I barely reach the outer rim of the arena when a tall, green blur whizzes past me. *Justin!* His green hoodie and backward cap bolt out of the main gate like someone's chasing him. He sprints so quickly, I only have time to watch him send a trail of desert soil into the air as he hunts for his car.

Grover's alone.

"JUSTIN!" I shout, waving my arms inside Cole's too-big jacket. "Where's Grover?!"

Justin's headlights ignite on his black 4x4, and he throws it into reverse without slowing or stopping. In under three seconds, he's hurtling down Mooncrest Highway back to Stone Grove.

"WHAT A MAN!" I scream, hopping in a *proudly* fem display of fury.

Unbelievable bravery tonight from Queer Club's masc finest. Justin escapes so fast he leaves tire tracks. And since Cole already vanished to enjoy a night of devouring burgers (and probably devouring Benny), it's up to the girlies, as per usj.

My head on a swivel for Agent Double-A, I weave back through the crowd, trampling people's picnics as Ray Fletcher mounts the stage to introduce the movie. Plates and blankets, forks and knives. Everything must be trodden over.

Then, out of nowhere, two strong hands grab me by my elbows.

I scream. He screams. A girl nearby screams.

In the dark, the boy in red keeps me from falling. "Sorry, Dearie, but you were gonna ram into us!" Mike whispers, bundled to his neck in a red puffer jacket.

I moan with relief. It's just the Flops.

"You okay, babe?" Lucy whispers, hugging her lilac sweater tightly. They both carry cartons of fresh popcorn from the refreshments stand.

"I'm—I'm okay," I stammer. *But please get out of my way!* I want to screech, but then I think better of it. Strength in numbers. "Come with me," I whisper. Mike leans closer, enraptured. "The killer is here."

Mike turns pale. "Grover," Lucy whispers, frightened.

I shake my head. "Not yet. But the FBI agent's here. Help me find her."

My search party expanded, the three of us shuffle through the crowd as *Blue Stalker*'s credits unfold. We pass the group of cheerleaders, already caught up in the movie, but they're all dark-haired. No sign of Em's silver hair. Without the stadium lights on, the vast darkness of Mooncrest Valley engulfs the arena, and the mesa in the distance vanishes into oblivion. But I know it's still out there—looming.

Like Mr. Sandman. Always there. Always watching.

Speak of the devil . . .

A silvery-white Santa beard appears in the dark, three blankets behind us. Leo Townsend, in a tailored suit, leans against the projection booth. A cigarette glow illuminates his features—sallow and craggy—and then extinguishes into a curtain of smoke.

Cole doesn't think it's him, but holy HELL, does he look like a killer.

As Mom instructed, I avoid Leo, taking a sharp right toward the middle of the arena. I can't stop moving, or I'll melt down in front of Mike and Lucy. Grunts and irritated mumblings from guests pester us until we reach freedom. We catch our breath just outside the picnic perimeter, the protective iron fence still a few yards ahead, and come face-to-face with an aging headstone: HARROW, 1899. The whole stone has rotted, like a cookie nibbled around the edges. Now that my breath is back, the fear returns.

"Your mom's on her way, right?" Mike asks, catching his breath.

Clutching my curls in frustration, I grunt, "Yeah, but we can't wait for her. She said to find Agent Astadourian."

"So she knew she was already here?" Lucy asks, leaning on the Harrow headstone.

Her question clicks in my mind—Astadourian wasn't here on a date. She was watching Leo. If Leo *is* the killer—and Astadourian's watching him—then he can't move on Grover!

We should find Grover first.

"Follow me," I say. No one needs to be told twice. Finally outside the glutted picnic arena, we sweep briskly through open space toward the refreshments tent, which isn't far from Grover's campsite. Yards ahead, the refreshments area's warm string lights beckon us. A circus tent, lined with yellow streamers, has been pronged into the red earth around a sleek silver food truck. The scent of warm butter is everywhere, and inside, a popcorn machine bubbles over with another popping cycle.

The light from the tent should be strong enough to help us find a good entry point back into the crowd, so I walk farther up toward the brightest spot, directly under the string lights. The refreshments tent's serving window is open . . . but with no one inside.

My shoes plant to the ground, refusing to budge. Lucy bumps into me. Mike hovers nearby—he's short, large, and eager to protect.

"What is it?" Lucy whispers.

I don't answer. The weight of eyes, out there in the dark beyond the perimeter fence, fall on me. Nearby, an unseen woman's voice squeaks, "Oh, uhhhh . . ."

"Hello?" I call out.

A startled yelp comes from behind the tent, followed by a *pop* and a *splash*. Mike and Lucy cover their gasps. A red Coca-Cola cup rolls out from the source of the scream, the soda emptying onto the ruddy soil. "Crap . . ." the voice comes again, and a young woman chases after the cup in a vain attempt to salvage her drink. She wears a candy-striped top over patched blue jeans—the casual uniform of Mooncrest's refreshment employees.

"Are you okay?" I ask, my throat dry from fear. She shuffles backward, white-lipped.

"My friend . . . she . . . went to get help," the girl says.

"Who went for help?" Lucy asks.

"My coworker . . . We found him."

No. No. No. Please no.

An unseen force pushes me closer, and I close Cole's oversize varsity jacket across my chest—yet nothing will erase this chill.

Behind the refreshments tent, barely visible under the string lights, two feet splay outward along the ground—their owner shrouded in the dark, open desert that stretches beyond the confines of the graveyard. The girl runs away screaming, as if she were waiting for us to arrive before she'd let herself panic. The rest of us don't scream. We step closer, and the body takes shape. A wicked spool of wire is coiled around the victim's pale throat. His head lies against a flat stone at such an absurd angle, such an objectively awful angle, that he must be dead.

It's Grover.

Dead.

Those gray, heartbroken eyes I've gazed into dozens of times are open but lifeless. The rest of his face is a bloody mess of shattered teeth and open, sucking wounds.

He mutilated him. Sandman got angry.

Breath catches in my throat, but I make no noise. Death doesn't shake me—my mom taught me how to stomach it. What *does* shake me is the note: sandy-brown card stock, lying on top of my ex's chest like a dinner invitation. Mike turns on his phone flashlight, and the message, drawn in black calligraphy, appears:

YOUR LONELY NIGHTS ARE OVER. Next to the words, a doodle of a tragedy mask.

Mr. Sandman's calling card. I'm too late.

Now we scream.

CHAPTER FOURTEEN

COLE

BEEF BLOOD AND SPECIAL sauce run down my chin as my jaws close around the quarter-pound cheeseburger, bibbed in the Stu's Diner's signature pink wrapper. Ultra-rare. Not how I normally order one, but I'm feeling particularly blood-thirsty after my fight with Grover.

Their indoor seating closed early, so Benny and I snatched one of the outdoor picnic tables by the walk-up window. Surrounded by black desert, just off the lonely highway, little Benny Prince sits under the icy blue lighting of Stu's patio and watches me silently maul this burger. On my next bite, I tragically taste something sour, objectionable, and all too familiar.

"I said *no* pickles," I mutter, removing four quarter-size pickle slices and plopping the hateful things onto a pile of napkins. "Even when you take 'em out, they still leave a taste."

"I'll take those," Benny says, twiddling his fingers before shotgunning my sauce-drenched slices into his mouth. "Eating your pickles. So intimate."

Benny says this with such a devilish smile, I have to set my burger down. "Benito? You got a crush on me?"

He smiles again, this time toward the table. "Everyone's got a crush on you."

Snorting, I take another messy bite. "Not Grover."

"Grover needs a brain transplant."

Benny's derision of Grover—unblemished by Stone Grove's usual fake-ass sympathy for him—instantly makes him three notches cuter. He's shy, yet comfortable in his skin. He's anxious around me, but he's not letting it cause him to overcompensate by hurling insults.

On another chomp, I smirk and say, "You keep pretty questionable company for someone who once called me 'white adjacent.'"

Benny gasp-laughs into his fries. "Did I say that?" I nod. "When?"

"Seventh-grade sleepover. Your house. You were speaking Spanish, and I couldn't keep up."

A twinkle shines in Benny's eyes behind those thick lenses. "Cool boy, look at you, holding on to baggage from five years ago." My cheeks get warm as he chuckles. "Cole, picking on you got you to notice me. I liked you, but you gave all your attention to Dearie."

"You think I didn't know that? I know you. I see you." Casually, I slip out of my shoe and graze my toes along Benny's bare calf. His shoulders go rigid, and he moves his leg away.

"Nuh-uh. You gotta take me out first."

I gesture to our plates. "What do you call this?"

"A roadside burger. I'm not one of your Tucson girlies."

"You want, like, a fancy, romantic date? For couples? Do you know who I am?"

"Do you know who *I* am?"

Beneath the picnic table, I have become mortifyingly hard. Benny Prince, nerd of nerds, is sitting across from me, not even blinking as he stands up for himself. It is rare, if not nonexistent, that a homo hasn't been all in once I make my first move.

This is excitingly new territory we're in.

"All right, I can get with that," I say, slipping back into my shoe and praying my pants de-tighten soon. A change of subject—a nonsexy subject—is needed. And quickly, my mind turns back to Mr. Sandman, to something that has been nagging me. "The day Gretchen died, did you ever find out why Grover invited Mike and Justin to the cafeteria but not you?"

Benny munches a fry slowly. "It never felt like the right time to bring it up, but it did bug me. I talked to Mike, and he thinks it's because Grover knows that I, whatever, think you're cool, like maybe I'd be too biased, since he was looking for help on how to deal with you."

I lick my fingertips clean. "If Grover was so convinced I was sending him death threats, you'd think he'd be eager to turn you against me."

Benny puts another fry to his lips but doesn't eat. "Could never happen."

Oh, this Flop has *moves*.

Of all the shocking things to occur in this year of our Lord of shocking occurrences, am I going to get with this suave twerp before school's over? I've been with nerdy boys before, and they always got a little freak going on. Overthinking can be potent.

Across the table, under the blue lights casting harsh shadows, and with Patsy Cline playing on the speakers, Benny Prince starts to look a bit . . . dangerous.

Whoever he is, he's already in your life. Leo's warning returns with a ghoulish echo.

I think back to the first attack. How long was Benny in the library before he found Gretchen and Grover? Did Ms. Drake actually leave the library with him? Could Benny have it in him to wrap that noose around his friends' necks? Killing without a trace requires a cool head and detailed planning. Nerds can craft detailed plans with the patience of a snake. Why not him?

An angry gust of wind blows our stack of napkins, but Benny manages to save a few. As he scrambles for the rest, my eyes never leave him. I'm a fool. We're surrounded by darkness. Cell service is nonexistent. This boy *could* be a suspect, and I'm out here almost totally alone with him?

Leo was right. I need to be so careful.

"We should get back," I say. Benny's expression falters. "I left Dearie alone with Grover. That's not gonna be good for anybody."

Quickly, I gather our spent wrappers and dump them in the trash. When I turn back, Benny is right there, almost a foot shorter than me, just like Dearie. I stop myself from gasping. His glasses have slipped down his nose, so when his shimmering brown eyes stare up at me, his vulnerability is overwhelming.

"We don't *gotta* go," he says. "Maybe Dearie and Grover made up."

I laugh, unlocking Julieta. "Don't talk evil. The devil's listening."

"Which part's evil?" He grins. "Grover and Dearie? Or hanging out more with me?"

This Flop has my palms actually sweating. I never sweat.

When I climb into my car, I try texting Dearie, but before I can type, a slew of texts from him pop up one by one, each more frantic than the last. Until the last one arrives and my heart drops:

Cole. He's dead.

CHAPTER FIFTEEN
DEARIE

TO PARAPHRASE MS. SPEARS, Grover's loneliness won't be killing him anymore. Once is enough.

What happened to my ex is too enormous to let inside my gay brain, which is supposed to be a receptacle for pop music and societal trauma—not *murder* trauma—so I'm gonna sit here and think of Britney until I'm ready for reality.

After news (and panic) spread about Grover's death, Mooncrest Cemetery reverted back to an empty graveyard in a shockingly brief amount of time. As agents—led by Astadourian—rush around me, I sit alone on the rear bumper of an open ambulance.

Grover is dead. Gone. Yet I'm feeling strangely empty . . . and free. Literally, why? I was all spun up about saving him. I've been making no damn sense lately.

I suppose one reason it's a relief is Cole will finally be rid of his unrelenting tormentor.

Still, I, personally, feel free.

Grover became unpleasant near the end, sure, but to

be relieved he's gone is something *else*. When I saw his bashed-in face, I was shocked, disgusted, scared—but what followed was a single thought: *I can breathe again.* How is that possible?

Even if we catch Mr. Sandman soon and figure out who is killing us, I'll be excavating these confusing emotions for years.

I look up as Mom walks up to the ambulance, in full work mode. She closes my hands around a paper cup of hot tea.

"You're sure it was Grover?" she asks, wincing. My mind flashes back to looking down at him, his face torn up, mutilated. "He looked rough."

Mr. Sandman has bashed in his victims' faces before. According to the show, authorities believed that when he mutilated a face, he was especially angry with them. Why angry? Well, medical examiners found high levels of salt under the victims' eyes. They'd been crying, and Mr. Sandman can't stomach that. So. Grover died crying, just like he lived, just like he always feared.

"I think I'd recognize him," I say, wrung dry of any emotion. "We dated for two months." Those gray eyes will stay with me forever. But why am I not more upset? Why am I not crying? People will be expecting tears. If I don't cry, it'll only dump gasoline on the suspicion about me and Cole. But no tears come. Hmm.

"I'm so sorry," Mom says, searching my dry eyes. "Are you feeling better?"

"Mom, he was killed like a minute ago."

"No, you fainted. Don't you remember?" I grip the bumper beneath me. *I fainted?* Mom looks at me like she's worried. She pushes the cup of tea toward me. "Drink more, here." She softly tips the bottom of the cup toward my mouth, and I drink the flavorless tea until it's gone.

I don't remember fainting. Why is it that when it comes to these big moments with Grover, my mind starts editing shit out like it's too scandalous for TV?

Mom helps me to my feet. "Let's find Cole. We've got some stuff to go over."

She tightens her arm around my shoulders and guides me through a maze of flashing police cars and ambulances. In the full glare of the stadium lights, the magic of Mooncrest is gone. The arena is just a ring of Astroturf flanked by dusty graves.

Walking is surprisingly easy. Walking past my ex's body is not.

Like ships passing, we crisscross with Grover's stretcher, his body concealed by cloth. Kevin Benetti, the medical examiner and Mom's best friend, walks alongside the men pushing the stretcher like a pallbearer, his handsome face sunken. He's a man who's been shaken out of bed to deal with something wretched. He smiles sadly at me and mouths, "I'm sorry."

I can only blink. Last week, we were all in my living

room, safe and rested, laughing about Kevin's miserable dating history.

Finally, we reach the refreshments tent, where a small group of people huddle around a black minivan parked parallel across from the crime scene. It's a Queer Club reunion: Em, Theo, Mike, Lucy, Benny, and Cole.

The sight of Cole reawakens me from a deep psychological slumber. I race into his arms. There's nothing on Earth like a hug from Cole. It's like medicine.

Benny shuffles away, looking stung.

"I'm sorry I left," Cole whispers.

Everyone else looks too pulverized with sadness and terror to make their usual snide remarks. Sniffling, I let go of Cole and scan the Queer Club faces: no Justin. That coward ran out and is probably already asleep.

I clear my throat and address the group: "Why didn't you all leave with everyone else?"

Unsurprisingly, Theo, Queer Club president and the unelected president of everyone's business, speaks first. "We came to see if Grover was okay."

"Well, he's not," I say.

"We told him and Justin to sit with us," Lucy says, wiping her nose with a tissue. She turns to Theo and Mike for backup. "Right? I kept saying and *saying*. He was being so stubborn, like he didn't want to have anything to do with us!"

Mike rolls his eyes. His furry arms are crossed so tightly

across his chest, it puffs him up like a teddy bear. "He was on a date," he says. "Stop taking it personally."

"Well, now he's dead!" Lucy throws up her arms. "Everyone complains about me being a hovering mom, but sorry about it, none of us should be alone right now!"

Silence falls. Theo and Mike cast angry glares at their feet. Lucy's right—it's way past time we stop trying to live normal lives while Mr. Sandman is out there. We have to be strategic.

"Well, Benny was with me at Stu's Diner," Cole adds a bit too eagerly. He's smart to put his whereabouts out there quickly so nobody starts suggesting it was him who did it.

"Em?" I ask the silver-haired girl. Wrapped in a blanket, she looks like she'd rather be anywhere else. "You weren't sitting with the rest of the Queer Club. You were with your friends. So why are you here with everyone now?"

Her jaw trembles with rage. "Someone's killing queer people. I want to know what's going on."

Finally, someone is talking about the elephant in the room. Four queers are dead now.

Before I can heartily agree, a booming, authoritative voice does it for me. "Frankie, your friend is right," says Agent Double-A, striding toward us. With the iron fence and desert wasteland behind her, she looks like a rancher, with her tan suede jacket and sensible jeans. She appraises the Queer Club with a half smile. "I'm glad you're all motivated to help."

She turns to the crowd. "If you haven't already tried, I want you to text your parents where you are, tell them you're safe, you're with the authorities, and to come get you if you don't have a ride. My team has set up a remote antenna." She gestures to the black minivan, which I suppose is her mobile investigation unit. "That should boost your phone signals enough to get a clear message through."

This, more than anything else that's happened tonight, sets every atom inside me ablaze.

"Where was that antenna before?" I ask. Cole exchanges a sharp, worried glance with Mom, next to Astadourian. My chest heaving angrily, I shake my phone at the crowd. "While you were all dicking around, I was trying to get a signal, trying to help save Grover! So, thanks for the signal boost *now*, but maybe the better time to break that out was"—I whip my phone to the ground—"before the fucking killer showed up!"

The crowd gasps. Benny and Mike cover their mouths. Cole and Mom advance toward me, but Astadourian— dead-eyed—raises her hand to stop them. "It's all right, he's upset."

I laugh bitterly. She has no idea how relieved I am to finally be feeling *something*.

"I've got questions," I say, facing the Queer Club. They

flinch at what is most likely my very twisted expression. "When Ray Fletcher was introducing the movie—when Grover was being killed—where was everyone? Cole, you were getting food with Benny. I was in the parking lot calling my mom to get her down here. I saw Justin running out like he was being chased. On my way back, I ran into Lucy and Mike. That's it, that's everyone I saw. Em, Theo, where were you? Agent Astadourian, where were you? Because we were LOOKING."

No one answers or moves.

Agent Double-A takes a deep breath. "Are you finished?" When I shrug, she advances. "I was right where you left me."

"Watching Leo Townsend?" I ask defiantly. Cole groans, powerless to stop me. Hell with it—Grover's dead. Might as well put it out there.

Startled, my mom warns, "Frankie!"

Astadourian turns to Mom, then back to me. She knows I know, and she knows Mom knows I know. Righteous anger builds in me until I don't care who I'm talking to—all I know is they could've stopped what happened tonight but didn't. "Were you watching Leo or not?" I ask.

"I can't comment," Astadourian says.

"Well, I can." I turn to the Queer Club, who don't dare draw a breath. "Leo Townsend is Ms. Drake's ex-husband. He helps run Mooncrest. He went to St. Obadiah High—"

"That's enough!" Agent Double-A says, but this true crime–loving crowd already knows what I mean. St. Obadiah is the birthplace of Mr. Sandman. Several of them mutter "Holy shit" and "Oh my God" while the rest of them just stare at the storm brewing between me and the FBI.

"It's public information!" I throw my arms up. "He's IN the show!"

Fire is brewing behind Astrid's eyes now, and she glances at Mom, who has gone pale. "I don't know what you think you know," she says to me, "but if you want to find Grover's killer, stop talking."

"He's just trying to help," Cole says.

"Unlike you," Theo scoffs.

All heads turn sharply to the new battle.

"What is your *problem*?" Cole snaps. "This isn't the time for petty Queer Club horseshit."

"It isn't, it's time for you to help the investigation," Theo says, angrily calm. They raise an accusing finger at Cole. "Cole knew Paul, the Tucson victim . . . in, you know, *that* way."

Oh my God, not now.

This is news to only Mom and Astadourian. It's the one time tonight the Queer Club hasn't gasped. Cole stands apart from the group, his eyes no longer furious. He's gone inward, deep in thought, deep in betrayal. He glances at me. "You told Grover?" he asks.

"Never!" I say breathlessly.

He turns on Theo. "Then how did you know?"

Theo doesn't blink. "I have friends at Tucson High," they say. "We talk."

Cole snorts and begins to circle the club. "Looks like you all talk. Looks like you *all* already knew." His shoulders heaving, he turns to Mom and Astadourian. "I was going to tell you—"

Mom shakes her head, looking desperately sad. "Honey, why?" she asks. "It's been a week."

"Because . . ." Cole's chest pumps on each agonized breath. "He wasn't out. We FaceTimed the day Gretchen died—while she was being killed—he was my alibi. But he wasn't out. His family is awful. Telling was gonna ruin everything. So we decided to wait until it was necessary to tell you. But then he died, and I never knew if he wanted his family to know and . . ." Cole's hands close into fists as he glances at Theo. "You're an ASSHOLE. All your high-minded Queer Club crap about how we're all supposed to treat each other, how bad Dearie and I are for the community, and then you just OUT a dead kid in front of everyone?"

Ashen-faced, Theo stammers, "I didn't know he wasn't out."

"Oh, so you just heard the 'Cole's a slut' goss—it's Cole the Hole at it again!—and that was enough for you to spread the story."

Before I can step in the middle, Theo shuffles closer. "You had a responsibility to tell people how those murders were connected."

"Gimme a break," Cole growls. "You could've talked to me about this days ago. While I was SUFFERING losing someone who MATTERED to me. You didn't because all you wanted was to trash-talk with Grover and make me look like a lying monster!"

"You *did* lie!"

A hush falls over the group. Mom moves closer to Astadourian. They haven't intervened yet—probably because they're learning more by listening than through an interrogation.

Cole clicks his tongue, deciding what to say next. He looks beyond Theo at Em. "Hey, Em, do you want to date Theo?"

"What?" she asks, fidgeting inside her blanket. "I, uh, don't really think . . ."

"Hmm, sounds like a no. Well, Theo likes you and wanted to ask you out, but if you have zero interest, that's a no-go." He frowns pathetically at Theo, whose mouth is agape. "I was really hoping a relationship would work out for you, Theo. You know, so you could stop being so obsessed with what I'm doing?"

"All right, that's enough," Agent Astadourian says, stepping into the center of what was about to be the second murder of the evening.

Collecting my cracked phone from the ground, I shuffle over to Cole. "I'm sorry," I say. "I never would've told anyone."

"I shouldn't have questioned you," he says, wrapping his arms around me in apology. Warmth follows. Once again, Benny flashes me a wounded glance.

Besides Cole and me, the surviving members of Queer Club pull away from each other—once again—into separate islands of distrust and pain. Yet Astadourian still commands our attention. "Going forward, I expect honesty," she says. "Whether you think you're doing the right thing or not." She looks us all in the eyes one by one. "You kids aren't scared enough. I've tracked killers before, but whoever this is, he's a ghost. He just finds you."

I clench Cole's arms tighter.

Astadourian steps closer, her dark eyes softening into something desperate. "Until this is over, be cautious. No going off alone together. Check in with your parents multiple times a day. Leave your phone locations on."

"What about Leo?" I ask, remnants of my own anger still lingering.

Astadourian becomes stone-faced. "Just so you don't go pestering that man, know that we were watching him every second. He never left the projection booth."

"That's impossible," I spit, held back by Cole.

"I don't think it's him, bestie," Cole whispers quickly.

I growl impatiently. Leo *has* to be part of this. How could a St. Obadiah graduate who was married to the head of a club full of victims not be? It's too coincidental.

Bzzzzt! Bzzzzt!! Bzzzzzt bzzzzzt!!!

Multiple phones go off at once. We all check, swiping open the message.

Then, the crying begins.

The Queer Club, huddled in a semicircle, stare at their phones in horror. Em covers her mouth with a quaking hand. Mike's lips have turned white. Theo and Lucy look nervously at each other. Benny tugs at his hair. I don't need to look at my phone because I already see the message on Cole's. I raise my phone next to his—kissing cousins—and read the identical message:

YOUR LONELY NIGHTS WILL SOON BE OVER.

Astadourian draws her weapon. "He's here."

"The antenna boost gave everyone signal," Mom says, drawing her own gun. "He knew he could text now."

Cole pulls Benny protectively to his side, clutching both of us tightly. Benny gasps, not expecting this move, but he looks as though he wouldn't let go of Cole for a million dollars. Lucy, Mike, Theo, and Em form a similar huddle. We press our backs to the minivan, hopefully closing off our vulnerable areas of attack.

Astadourian orders her agents to wait with us while she and Mom race forward, out of the safety of the light and into the dark abyss of the desert to find the killer. He must have been watching us this whole time.

"Mom," I squeak, staring into the darkness, my throat closing.

"She'll be okay," Cole whispers into my hair. My heart is making a terrible racket.

CRACK! CRACK! Two shots fire in the dark, and everyone shrieks. The sound echoes across the mesa. Benny and I hunch into tight, tense balls, but Cole squeezes us tighter.

I can't see what's happening.

"MOM!" I scream. "MOM!!!!"

"ASTADOURIAN!" shouts another agent. He shuffles in place, clearly fighting an overwhelming urge to abandon us and rush toward the shots.

But there's no scuffle, no telltale *thud* of a body hitting the ground. The shots didn't land.

My heart twists as I wonder who the hell is out there, if my mom's okay, if they'll find him.

But time moves slowly as we wait with the agents. They murmur on walkies until finally Astadourian's voice comes from the darkness. "He's gone!"

Where's Mom? Is she hurt?

My heart finally relaxes when I hear the unmistakable sound of footsteps coming closer. Seconds later, Mom and

Agent Double-A reenter the protective circle of the stadium lights.

"He was here. We lost him," Astadourian whispers to her team. She's out of breath, looking back out into the darkness. "I don't know how he's seeing anything out there."

I pull free of Cole's grip and run to my mom. Sweating and still catching her breath, she smiles. "I'm okay, Frankie." Then she turns to the agents. "He threw this at me."

In her gloved hands is a bronze mask, shaped like a skull so it can envelop the entire head. Its face is a theatrical tragedy mask.

Mr. Sandman has never been closer.

CHAPTER SIXTEEN
COLE

RETURNING HOME FROM MOONCREST takes some figuring out. No one wants to go alone, but nobody wants to ride with anyone else. Em came with her cheerleader friends, who already left, so her parents pick her up. Her dad is so frantic, he hustles her into the back seat like a bodyguard ushering a celebrity away from the paparazzi. He's a peach compared to Theo's parents, two rich pricks demanding Astadourian's full explanation and suspects list. Typical River Run jerkoffery. Lucy's mom—a night owl guzzling Nitro cold brew—collects her daughter without fanfare.

Besides Dearie, Lucy seems the saddest that Grover is gone. But in the wake of getting a "You're next" message and finding the killer's mask, Grover's mangled corpse has plummeted to third-place news in everyone's minds.

I'm not ready to make judgment leaps yet, but it is . . . interesting Justin blew out of here when he did. The one person who was keeping Grover company left at the precise right moment for Sandman's attack. And as someone who's hooked up with Justin, I can attest that boy knows how to flee a room leaving you unsatisfied. When Justin first moved to Stone Grove sophomore year, I felt sorry for him. New kid. Cute but not cute enough to attract friends without effort. Solid at basketball, but not good enough to beat me or Walker Lane for the key positions. Never able to keep an active social calendar because his needy, divorced dad kept expecting him home to cook and clean. So I threw him a pity fuck. Our hookup was boring, but as soon as I turned down any future invitations, Justin got what he'd always wanted: a new best friend in Grover Kendall. For almost two years, Grover, Gretchen, Justin, and Theo have built a Cole Hate whisper campaign so strong that the moment murders started happening, I was the only suspect in anyone's minds.

Was this on purpose? Did Lonely Justin collect friends just to use them as pawns to dominate the boy who rejected him, both in the bedroom and on the court?

Where was he when the Queer Club was getting a mass text of death threats? I hope he can prove he was at home, not running around this desert.

For the time being, I file this thought away under *H* for "Hmm."

Benny's father shows up next—a salt-of-the-earth man with a giant mustache and bald head that shimmers under the stadium lights. I always marvel at how small, gentle

Benny came out of that tough customer. It's like a daisy sprouting out of a rock quarry. As they drive away, I toss Benny a wave, which he eagerly returns. Is he really that sweet? Outside the diner, I caught a dangerous vibe from our softest Flop, but it was probably just paranoia set off by Leo's meltdown.

In twenty-four hours, we'll see if I was paranoid. Ol' Sandy has never missed a deadline.

But how can he get all of us at once?

I'll worry about that after I sleep.

My moms told me to leave Julieta and let them pick me up, but my babygirl has been through enough today. I don't need coyotes building a den inside her overnight.

Dearie is staying with his mom until she and Astadourian wrap up the crime scene. That just leaves me and Mike Mancini to drive back alone—an idea I'm not in love with. Neither is Mike. He rummages through his messy dorm room of a back seat, making sure nobody's hiding back there with an axe. He looks silly, but then again, checking the back seat might not be a bad idea.

Agent Astadourian orders her agents—all square-jawed tough guys—to accompany Mike and me on our drives home. "Jurgen, stay with me," Astadourian says as she sips coffee wearing blue evidence-handling gloves. Two other agents leap to attention. "Manfredi, go with Mancini. Jackson, you ride with the Mouth." She nods at me, and a

Black, dark-skinned agent nods. "Get them to their doors safely, then taxi to our motel. Don't leave until their parents have them."

With that, there's nothing left to do but hug Dearie good night. He and his mom look exhausted. "Are you okay?" I ask.

Dearie struggles through a shrug. "I'm gonna be."

"Are *you* okay?" Mrs. Dearie asks, petting my arm, not realizing how close she is to the spot where Grover clawed me.

Grinning, I shrug. "I could be the killer, I could be next on the hit list. It's all good!"

"Nothing's gonna happen to you," she says. "It's the weekend. You're all going into lockdown at home."

"I really was gonna tell you about Paul."

A thick silence passes. The wind grows harsher. Finally, Mrs. Dearie admits, "I believe you. Right now, we're gonna focus on keeping you safe. You and Frankie, trust each other. Keep your eye on the others."

Dearie and I exchange glances. What does *that* mean?

Does she know something that indicates the killer is definitely someone from Queer Club?

Too much thinking for the day, Cole. Need sleep.

Trust Dearie and nobody else. That's how I live every day.

Leaving the Dearies, I walk through Mooncrest with my new best friend, the short, muscular Agent Jackson. Evidence of hasty picnic getaways is everywhere: overturned plates, empty wine bottles, blankets and chairs simply abandoned. A charcuterie graveyard.

"Good night, Cole," Ray Fletcher says, waving from the door of his projection booth. He's ditched his suit jacket and undone the top buttons of his dress shirt. A duo of plainclothes officers scurry around his booth, deep in their examination.

"Night, Ray," I say. "Sorry about the mess."

"Worse things happened here tonight."

I try to keep walking, but after a quick glance at Agent Jackson, I risk it all. "Hey, Ray, where's Leo? He doing better?"

Agent Jackson impatiently clears his throat, but I don't blink. Ray will answer—he's always honest with me. Finally, he just shrugs.

Bummer.

Leaving the parking lot, we pass a line of news vans reporting on the night's chaos, but squad cars prevent them from proceeding deeper into Mooncrest. The drive is silent. My hands stay firmly at ten and two. I'm not making a single mistake, not a hint of a guilty conscience they can use to fuel their suspicion. We're minutes from my house when Agent Jackson finally speaks: "So . . . your mom and dad gonna be up? They'll be at the door?"

"You won't have to wait," I say, tapping the wheel. As usual, I do the dance of weighing whether or not to correct people. "It's 'moms.' Two moms."

"My mistake." Agent Jackson throws up his hands. "Must be cool to be gay with gay parents."

"Yeah." I laugh. It wasn't funny, but whatever. "Gay moms. Gay son. Gay dad."

Agent Jackson shifts toward me, crinkling my leather seats. "Dad too?"

"Yep, a dad, but he's in LA. Sperm donor vibes. He and my moms were college friends. They wanted a baby, so he helped out."

"Cool."

"I guess." I laugh again, but it comes out pained. Talking about Dad usually does that. In my eighteen years, he's visited three times. In a way, changing schools to Columbia means I don't end up living minutes away from him in LA. I won't have to face the grim truth behind the long-wondered question, *Does Dad want to see me, or am I annoying him?*

He's a gay party monster, and so am I. Would I want to see my kid all the time if I thought my job as a dad was just doing a bestie a favor and being done with it?

Thankfully, I'm finally home, so I don't have to linger on these thoughts. When I pull into my driveway, my moms are already waiting on the front stoop, side by side, bundled in their bunchy robes. They rush to meet me. My mother Monica (Mami) throws her arms around me (but is only able to reach my chest), and my other mother, Frederica (Ma), shakes Agent Jackson's hand.

"How are you getting back?" she asks him.

Agent Jackson glances around at the darkened suburban streets. "Uber?"

We all scoff—he'd get there faster walking. Ma motions Agent Jackson toward the garage with a jangly set of keys. After I yell at Ma to be careful and check her back seat, Mami and I return inside, where a reheated plate of tonight's dinner of chicken and rice is waiting. I lick the plate clean. Mami sits on our kitchen stool, sips decaf coffee, and watches me eat while I catch her up on the night's horrors, except the most important detail: my text message of doom.

But Mami is like me—she sniffs out when you've skirted around something.

"Mary Dearie called," she says, her hand shaking. "We know about the message."

This is gonna be so much worse than if Mr. Sandman had just jumped out and throttled me.

"I don't want you to worry," I say, pushing back my plate.

"It's him who should worry!" Hopping off her stool, Mami raises herself to her full four-foot-eleven height. "We did a room-by-room, closet-by-closet search of the house." She reaches behind the kitchen island and produces a shiny blue aluminum bat. "It's all clear."

I roar with laughter. "What were you two gonna do if you found somebody? Beat him to death with your Lezzie League bat?"

She lowers the bat until it boops my nose. "I'll do a lot more than that. He threatened you."

Usually, I'd be annoyed, but after a car ride thinking about my hates-to-visit dad, my insides get all soft for them. My moms heard I was in trouble and immediately snapped into action with a horror-movie search of the house.

When it's time for bed, Mami climbs into her big living room chair that faces the front door, bat in one hand, remote in the other, and waits for Ma to return. My room shows signs of motherly interference—the closet doors hang open, and they've snarled a bicycle chain around my second-floor window. Makeshift for now, but a proper barricade is likely forthcoming.

The room has a stillness I don't like.

Astadourian's Mr. Sandman warning—*he just finds you*—rings in my ears.

I tap on my moonglow lamp, fire up a playlist of electronic ambience, change into pajama bottoms, and slide into bed. Mr. Sandman's text sits in my message history. It was frightening when I got it, but now it's just there in my phone, sandwiched between friends and family, as mundane as spam.

Mr. Sandman says I die tomorrow, but we'll just have to see.

I text Dearie that I made it back safely and that I'm sorry for what happened. I am, kind of.

Then I text Benny. u ok?

His reply comes instantly: Yeah! You?

It's weird to have all this happen and then just go
to bed lol.

haha yeah. After another bout of typing, another text comes: can I be honest?

I pull my phone to my nose. No gay alive can resist this question. please!

If I sound like a creep, just ignore this message lol. I'm kind of scared to go to sleep.

A small smile emerges. Me too.

Would it be ok if I called?

In any other circumstance, I'd be repulsed, but with the world ending, I should be honest with myself: I don't want to be alone. I FaceTime Benny. He's in bed with every light on. His smooth, bare chest peeks out from the top of his covers—skin he's kept strategically hidden under endless pop-culture character shirts.

Behind his large glasses, his eyes are pink-kissed and watery. "Hey," he says, sounding plugged up. "Clearly not taking this well."

We laugh sideways into our pillows, and it's nice to forget our traumas for a moment. In fact, when I was with Benny earlier, it was easy to forget everything else. He just has that effect.

Benny sniffs again. "I need to know—in case something happens to me—I need to know I wasn't imagining it. Tonight at the diner, were you serious about taking me out?"

I smile. "I don't lie just to be nice. Survive the weekend, and I'll take you anywhere."

Benny laughs as more tears fall. "Really? Me?"

My smile vanishes. "Yes, you. You're cute. You're chill to get along with. You don't change who you are to please other people. You're always you. That's sexy."

Benny doesn't smile, but he isn't sad anymore either. We simply watch each other, me lying on my left side and Benny lying on his right. We might as well be in bed together.

"People who get that message usually end up dead," he says.

"They were lonely," I say, shrugging. "I don't feel lonely. Do you?"

Benny curls his blanket up to his bare chest. "Not when I'm with you." I hum happily into my pillow. In my mind, I trace my finger over Benny's hips, cup my hand under his thigh, and pull him tight to me.

"Cole? Will you leave your screen on while I go to sleep?"

It's an excellent idea. I pull my rolling desk chair until it's kissing my bed frame, position the phone against it to face me, and crawl back into bed. In that short window of time, Benny has already fallen asleep, his face smashed into his pillow and glasses hanging off his ear. If he was here with me, I'd gently fold them and place them on his night-stand next to a cup of water in case he gets thirsty.

Huh. Now I know what Dearie meant when he said he felt like all he wanted to do was take care of Grover.

The moment sleep begins to take hold, an urge to check the closet wakes me. My closet doors hang open. Inside, darkness. Did my moms check everywhere? What if Mr. Sandman was hiding in the ceiling?

"Who's there?" I whisper to the closet. Nothing.

But I get up, slam my closet doors shut, and drag my night-stand over to barricade it. I return to bed. If Mr. Sandman is in there, he'll have to wait to kill me until the morning.

CHAPTER SEVENTEEN

DEARIE

SATURDAY MORNING, THE COUNTDOWN begins.

Last night at 10:38 p.m., every surviving member of Queer Club received the message. And Mr. Sandman's never late. So the name of the game is to survive until tomorrow.

For safety, we're staying in our separate homes. Mr. Sandman can't attack everyone at once, so the current theory is that he sent all of us the same message to obscure which of us he's really after. "That, or he's going to pick us off one at a time," Benny says on the group Zoom. "It's pretty much how every horror movie goes."

"No," I say. "If this were a horror movie, we'd all get together for one big party, and *then* he'd pick us off one by one."

"Yeah, please, nobody do that," Mom shouts from across the room as she and Astadourian's team secure surveillance equipment onto our mantel. Each Queer Club family is getting the same package, courtesy of the FBI: two officers posted outside, surveillance cameras in every room but bedrooms and bathrooms, door and window sensors, and motion detectors on the ground floor. For the duration of the day, everyone is being quarantined in their bedrooms or second floors.

"If anything moves in your houses," Agent Jackson says, loud enough for everyone on my Zoom to hear, "your phones—and the officers' phones outside and at the station—will make a chime like this." Over Zoom, everyone's phones go off at once: a clanging, unignorable wind chime.

"Cute," Em moans into her hand. In her Zoom window, her bougie, sweater-wearing parents clutch her protectively.

"I have a Min Pin that runs all over," Lucy says, cross-legged on her bed with various tasers and pepper sprays laid out carefully. "What if he sets it off?"

"Yeah, what about Pee Wee?" Mike asks. He sits in his living room, bundled in a thick, cream-colored cable-knit turtleneck—looking very cute, like he's at an Alpine ski lodge. Behind him, an orange-and-white kitty prowls across the top of the sofa. I assume this is Pee Wee.

While Theo and I make little finger grabs toward Pee Wee on the screen, Agent Jackson steps into frame beside me. "Small pets won't set it off," he says. "But I suggest you all lay down some towels and keep your little ones locked in the room with you."

At the mere suggestion that Mr. Sandman would sneak

178

into our homes to slaughter our pets, Mike scoops up Pee Wee and holds the wriggling beast tightly. I can't even see Mike's face, just four scrambling, upset cat legs.

"Thank you, Agent Jackson, we're all very grateful," says Theo's father, a white, Brooks Brothers khaki–clad businessman. He brings a double-barreled shotgun into frame. Benny gasps, but Theo just rolls their eyes.

"Put that *away*," Theo says. "Somebody's gonna accidentally get shot."

"I foolproofed it," he says proudly. "First round is a blank to scare the killer. Second round is rock salt. And if he still keeps coming after that, the third round is live."

"Nobody's impressed, Dad."

Unfortunately, Mike's and Benny's fathers murmur with curious interest.

Agent Jackson chuckles. "Mr. Galligan, that's very clever—but today, lock it up in your room. Your child's right. It's a high stress, high stakes situation. We have manpower outside. We don't need any more variables than what we're already dealing with." He clears his throat. "I'm sure you agree."

"Of course," Theo's dad replies, loosening his collar anxiously. "Just know—I've got this."

As Theo pinches back a headache, I make note of Justin's screen, which is darker than the others. Justin's father, a larger, graying man, slumps at the kitchen table, looking half-dead from stress. Meanwhile, Justin has been walking in and out of frame so much, all I see is a green blur. He's still wearing that ugly green hoodie from last night and moaning about an upset stomach. It's getting annoying.

Beside these petty annoyances, this is actually the first meeting of Queer Club where we're all getting along. In hunting us, Mr. Sandman has brought us closer than ever. Our individual loneliness dissipates as we stop being islands and become a whole continent. That's the power of queer solidarity. The harder you hit us, the stronger we become.

If only Grover could've felt this community's power in time. He always rejected that we could all be friends, distrusted all of it, but maybe he could've had a moment of clarity. Maybe he could have seen how badly he'd hurt Cole and taken steps toward fixing things. We'll never know.

All this security rigmarole has been a much-needed distraction from the reality of Grover's horrific death. How he knew it was coming, and suffered exactly how he thought he would.

I push it out of my mind so my ugly thoughts about Grover stay far away. But like a creeper standing just outside my window, it's as if they're just waiting to be let inside.

As if on cue, Cole's booming voice comes, "Hiyaaa!" as he taps open my front door with his foot. *Tinkletinkle-tinkletinkletinkle*, the wind chime noise from my phone sounds loudly. Dressed in a black tank and gray sweats, my cozy bestie lugs in a suitcase and three Trader Joe's totes overstuffed with snacks. Without thinking, I run from the sofa and throw my arms around him the second he sets his bags down. He kisses my hair and whispers, "How are you holding up?"

"Better now that you're here," I whisper.

Cole follows me to the sofa and plops down—larger than life—in front of my Zoom. I click the chime on my phone off. "Hey, party people," he says. "How's everyone's bladders hanging in there?"

"How come Dearie and Cole get to hang out with each other?" Justin sneers from his open refrigerator.

Cole's eyes brighten. He's been ready to scrap. "Oh heyyyyy, muffin. How's your tum-tum? Still jingle-jangly from fleeing a crime scene?" Justin just grunts, while his dad stares into space. "Anyway, my moms and Dearie's mom have to work, and neither of us should be alone tonight. If that's okay with the rest of you."

Cole's hand finds my leg under the coffee table. Soothing warmth shoots through my body.

"It's nice of you to do that, Cole," Benny says, sadder than I've ever heard him. Lovesick.

While Cole catches up with Agent Jackson (and everyone's distressed parents ask more questions about where they can and can't go in the house), Mom readjusts the motion sensor she placed on the mantel next to Dad's urn. She's readjusted it a million times. I know she doesn't want to leave us here, but since Grover's well-publicized murder, anxiety in the department to find the killer has tripled. Grover was under surveillance—just like we are—and Mr. Sandman still got him.

Across the room, from the kitchen doorway, Kevin Benetti watches me. Although he's wearing a bright, tropical print, his expression is grimmer than I've ever seen. He waves me over. While everyone else is consumed with their final security checks, I easily slip away—even though I know Kevin is going to be yet another person asking how I'm doing, as if I want to think about it.

"I don't have a ton of time," Kevin whispers, peering over my head to make sure the Zoom crowd isn't listening. "Do you remember when we were sitting around here a few weeks ago, and you mentioned wanting to get a tattoo?"

". . . What?" I ask, but somehow, his question has started my palms sweating.

Kevin closes his hand—shockingly powerful—around my arm. "It's important."

"I . . . um . . ."

Like Justin, I'm starting to feel jingle-jangly in my tum-tum, but the memory swims back with terrifying ease. When Grover and I were dating, Mom, Kevin, Grover, and I played a party game on the PS5 in this exact spot in the living room. Mom and Kevin, finally off-duty, made each other rum runners and got silly. Grover was being so affectionate. Kevin started bringing up my future move to LA—information I'd never shared with Grover. I didn't want him thinking I was going to abandon him, so to change the subject, I started talking about the ankle tattoo I wanted—the first subject that popped into my head. I wanted to get a blue rose from my favorite fantasy show.

But somehow, this made Grover more furious than my LA news. He flipped out, saying tattoos were hideous, how he hated how many gay guys had them. It was like he was taking it personally. "You're ruining your body, and when you're eighty, you'll look ridiculous!"

When Kevin said he had four tattoos, Grover . . . laughed. Cruel laughter. He flung his hand at Kevin. "Let me clarify, when you're eighty, *you'll* look ridiculous and *sad*. Like you always do."

My memory blurs from there. A rush of pain strikes my temples, like it's forbidding me from remembering more. It stings. Grover had troubles. He was lonely. He was traumatized. He was scared. He couldn't control his emotions.

Part of me will always care about him, but that memory makes me sick.

A tear trembling in the corner of my eye, I peel Kevin's hand off my arm. "Why would you ask me about that?" I ask, not bothering to lower my voice. "He's dead."

Kevin's eyes soften, but his scowl remains. "You do remember. Grover didn't want you to get any tattoos, right? Did he ever change his mind?"

I sigh angrily. "I don't know. Probably not. He was really bothered by them, but he apologized. Does that answer your question?"

My jaw trembles. Kevin nods and darts a glance away. Then he squeezes my shoulder, as if in apology. "I'm sorry he's gone, but I have to tell you something." He looks anxiously over my shoulder, and then whispers, "Back before . . . everything . . . your mom saw Grover looking at an app on his phone. She couldn't tell for sure, but she thought she saw your info on it. Your texts were in blue, as if it was your phone he had. If that's true, it was a tracker. He knew where you were going and what you were texting."

I shake my head—the pain is growing worse. "I don't want to talk—"

"Listen." Kevin squeezes my shoulder so urgently, it hurts. "Since Grover died, he couldn't have deactivated your tracker." He pauses. "We didn't find Grover's phone on his body. If the killer has it, they know what you're texting and where you are. Understand?"

I can barely breathe.

Before I can speak, Kevin places something small, cold, and heavy in my hand. The feeling sends tingling up my arm as another memory returns:

After I told him we were breaking up, Grover put something in my hand. It was small and heavy.

I can't remember what it was and I don't think I have it anymore, but I know how scared it made me. Not scared— more like frantic. Heartbroken and desperate to make him feel better.

Feeling and memory swirl through my mind. Foggy and frightening.

I shake my head and look down at the burner phone in my hand.

It's just like the ones Mr. Sandman planted in our lockers. Kevin taps my hand. "That's got my number written on the back," he says. "Anything you don't want the killer to know, use *that* to communicate. Texts, calls. Your mom only saw this the other day and didn't want to tell you until she was sure—she knows how you feel about Grover. But I'm her asshole gay bestie, and I say your life is more important than your feelings. And I know you can handle it."

He hugs me, but my limbs are numb.

Grover was tracking me? He was jealous, but was it so bad that he needed to see what I was saying about him? And now this tracker is in the killer's hands.

But why the hell did Kevin want to talk about Grover's tattoo obsession?

There's no time to ask as Kevin pats my shoulder and walks to chat with Mom. Agent Jackson and the rest of Astadourian's team file out of the house with their surveillance crates. Kevin and Mom hug Cole and me good-bye, and the Queer Club say their Zoom goodbyes.

My home's automatic locks whir shut, and Cole and I are alone. "I know it's hard," he says, hugging me.

Coldness fills me like a water bottle. The ugly thoughts I've kept outside all day have finally barged their way in: This isn't hard. Talking to Kevin brought it out of me, what I'd been denying since finding Grover's body. When I broke up with him, I felt free. Now that he's dead, I feel even freer.

This isn't me being numbed by shock. These are my true feelings.

Cole leads me upstairs with his bags of snacks. Once we reach the top landing, I activate the motion sensors. The long countdown to 10:38 p.m. begins.

Tonight's about to get interesting.

CHAPTER EIGHTEEN

COLE

THE GOOD THING ABOUT our Death Watch Lockdown is it forces Dearie and me to hang out at his house all day, like when we were kids having a snow day. We dig his old *Rock Band* game out of the attic and battle each other into the night—me on guitar and him singing, of course. Playing Heart's "Alone" plucks an especially nervy nerve tonight.

But we laugh like weasels. We never get out of our pajamas. Sometimes, we even forget this is happening. We forget Grover died. We forget we could be next. We forget we're eighteen, weeks away from never being this close to each other again. In these sparkling moments, we're twelve years old with blue raspberry Blow Pop–stained tongues and no idea how badly the world outside wants us dead.

Thanks to all of his murderous accusations, Grover's death is easier on me—a relief—but Dearie can't control when he cries. Everything is normal and fun, but then an unknown trigger comes and he falls to pieces. Then the moment passes, and he shifts back to laughter, his mood clearing like rain.

When it's night—closer to the fatal countdown—we ease our mounting anxieties by painting each other's nails and watching Melissa McCarthy movies. Dearie paints mine all black with a lavender accent nail. I paint his silver, and with those elegant hands, fierce eyes, and tendency to wear form-fitting crop-tops, he could be Emma Frost leading the X-Men. Yet he's so cute. Looking at him lying on his stomach, kicking his feet back and forth, I can't fathom the pain and confusion he has to carry.

I'll never love someone else as hard as I love Dearie. Any future boyfriends will just have to accept that as part of the bargain.

So far, Benny is proving himself worthy on that front. Not that he's my boyfriend. Yet. Or, whatever, I don't know. We're all leaving each other's lives in a few weeks. I don't even know what *he* wants or thinks this is, but I make sure to text him back. Like Paul, Benny types as fast as a 1950s secretary, and I'm just hoping to keep up. He's killing his boredom by playing *Dead by Daylight* with his sisters, which I feel is a bit much for a time like this. But, work.

"Remember Tween Pride?" Dearie asks, applying another coat to my nails.

Oh no. Another storm is brewing.

"Are you asking me because of Grover?" I ask carefully, watching him paint.

"I know it's corny, but it's one of my all-time favorite memories."

"It's not corny. You're grieving." It's the most generosity I'm willing to give a happy memory of Grover. Before we were high school enemies, we were friends. Benny wasn't out yet and neither were Mike, Theo, Lucy, or Em. And since Justin only moved here two years ago, Grover, Dearie, and I fancied ourselves a little gay-boy trio back in eighth grade.

"Tell me something nice you remember about Tween Pride," Dearie says.

"Dearie . . ."

"Please."

"Okay." My shoulders tighten. "Summer before freshman year. You and I came out to each other. Grover heard about it, and then he came out too. Always copying." I roll my eyes, but Dearie just laughs dreamily. "I was gonna steal Mami's car and drive us to Tucson Pride, but then you two wussed out, so you made up Tween Pride, which was just the three of us at my house while Moms went to the real Pride." In spite of my anger, I catch myself smiling. "We broke into their liquor and got tanked on watermelon coolers like three no-brain bitches."

Middle School Grover dances in my mind. Taylor Swift's

"Style" plays as he strips off his shirt and twirls until he falls off the arm of my family's sofa. But the Grover who died yesterday wasn't the happy, dancing, watermelon cooler–drunk clown at our three-tween Pride. He was angry and jealous, a boy who went out of his way to hurt me and manipulate Dearie.

"Why'd you make me talk about that?" I ask, sighing. His hand turns cold in mine.

"It's nice," he says. "I'm tired of bad memories. Ugly things."

"You can't put bad memories behind you until you accept them."

His jaw hardens. So does mine. "I've accepted—" Dearie starts, but I interrupt.

"You're still not seeing the whole picture of him."

"I just can't right now," Dearie says. Dropping my hand, he screws the tops back onto the half a dozen bottles of nail polish spread over his bed.

After tolerating so much reminiscing, I can't keep my feelings in anymore. "Dearie, you're not listening. I know you're grieving—"

"I'm really not!" The tense bedroom fills with the unfortunate sounds of broad physical comedy from Ms. McCarthy. But Dearie just continues. "I'm not grieving. I don't feel anything. I feel everything, then nothing."

"That's grief."

"I'm a shitty person! I'm supposed to be crying. He died because of me. He was terrible, but he didn't deserve . . . His whole face was *bashed* in. I have to keep thinking of good times, or I'm gonna fall in a hole."

A familiar saber of dread slices across my belly. Grover taught Dearie well. Even in death, Grover has made Dearie believe he's an awful human being who deserves no love, no laughter, no good sex, and no other friends.

"How are you?" Dearie asks. "With everything? Really."

I shrug. "It's almost as if this murder was perfectly constructed to make both of us feel every nasty emotion at once, with no easy way in or out. It just . . . all sucks. All of it. Honestly, I think I've gotta keep thinking of good times too." I gaze down at my new accent nail, which doesn't look as objectionable as before. "Cute nails! I'm keeping 'em."

Dearie laughs, brushing back a tear as he makes a check mark in the air. "Another masc boy ruined!"

Bzzzzztttt!

Dearie's phone goes off on the other side of the room. We freeze. Horrible, Sandman-ian reality returning to us faster than our minds can process. Slowly, he creeps over to his nightstand and reaches for his phone, flipped facedown.

"Don't," I whisper. His silver fingertips graze the phone but stop. He looks at me. "Don't."

He swallows hard. "What if it's someone who needs help?"

The moment Dearie lifts his phone, I scan the room for blunt, heavy objects: a wicker basket for extra blankets, decorative pillows, rows of slipper shoes. Gah! Dearie, why must you live in such a soft-boy sanctuary?!

"It's Justin," he says, puzzled. "He's FaceTiming."

"This bitch," I groan. "See what he wants!"

As Dearie answers, I glance at his wall clock—10:14 p.m. Oh my God, did we girly-girl the entire night away and not realize it was Mr. Sandman Hour already?

Dearie brings over his phone, but Justin's screen is mostly black. Justin must be shaking the camera because I keep catching glimpses of streetlights from his open window. When Justin finally settles, his father's silhouette is crouched low behind the bed next to him.

"Dearie, my chimes went off," Justin whispers.

Gripping his phone like a life raft, Dearie whispers back, "Are you sure?"

"It was the chimes! Aren't the officers supposed to hear it too? Nobody's coming in!"

"I'm texting my mom now!"

But Dearie doesn't text from his phone. He pulls out a *very* Sandman-like burner, and my eyebrows catapult into the ceiling. "What is that?" I ask.

"I'll tell you later," he hisses. "Justin, hang up with me and FaceTime Cole."

"WHY?" Justin and I say simultaneously.

"Because my phone's not safe! Just do it!"

"I blocked Cole," Justin whispers frantically.

"Well, then unblock me, jerkoff!" I shriek in a whisper. "The killer's in your house!"

TWO YEARS AGO. That's how long it's been since I hooked up with Justin, then said "No thank you" to more. He has kept up a grudge for a shockingly long time. Second only to Grover.

A touchy homo who has done zero self-work. Groundbreaking.

But he *would* have a vested interest in seeing me framed . . .

Justin hangs up while Dearie struggles to text one letter at a time on that ancient burner keypad. My heart thuds. Every second counts, or I'd flick Dearie's earlobe and force him to tell me what that new little phone is all about.

Moments later, a text comes from Justin: omg

I reply: what??

No answer comes. I use my Pilates breathing technique to make sure my light-headedness doesn't lay me out flat. This melodramatic queen better respond. Why isn't he calling?!

When he finally does, it's a link to that camera service the cops set up in each of our homes. This is live surveillance footage from Justin's home. "Dearie!" I stammer, and when he sees what I see, his eyes widen. With a shaking thumb, I open the link and hold my breath.

In Justin's dark kitchen, street light pours in from a row of windows above the sink. Beyond the kitchen, a doorway opens into the pitch-black living room.

Slowly, he emerges.

A man in a dark green maintenance suit. Gloves. Boots. And a frowning, shimmering bronze tragedy mask.

Dearie's nails dig into my forearm. "He's there!" he whimpers and pulls out the burner again. "I'm calling Mom."

In the surveillance footage, I watch as Mr. Sandman scurries out of the kitchen. Through the doorway into the living room. Justin's front door buckles. Shakes. Finally, it bursts open as four armed agents sweep inside, weapons drawn.

Dearie and I clutch our chests at the same time.

"Oh my God," he moans. "He can't get away, right?"

Sweat dripping into my foolish grin, I can't stop laughing. "I think they got him!"

Dearie sinks his arms around me, and I press him tighter than ever. It's over . . .

Tinkletinkletinkletinkletinkletinkletinkletinkle.

Chimes. My body chills at the sound.

"What is that?" Dearie gasps, pulling away from me.

There's someone here? That's impossible. Sandman's halfway across town at Justin's place?

But the chimes aren't coming from Dearie's notifications, they're coming from mine. I close Justin's surveillance link and find a link of my own waiting. "It's my house," I say.

"Your moms?" he asks.

I shake my head. "They'll be at the hospital past midnight."

Gathering another strong Pilates breath, I tap the new link. The well-lit lawns of River Run spill plenty of ambient light inside my darkened great room. There's hardly any secluded corners where someone could hide. Yet the chimes mean a person is moving, so where are they?

In the distance, someone slowly descends my spiral staircase. A gloved hand trails down the banister until a man in a dark green maintenance suit reaches the ground floor.

The killer was upstairs. In my room.

There *was* someone in my closet. Was he hiding there while I slept?

Mr. Sandman's boots clunk toward the camera—toward us, as if he knows exactly what to look for. He's close. The face becomes clear—it's another bronze mask.

Only, this one is upturned in a leering grin. A theatrical comedy mask.

The Smiling Sandman throws a peace sign to the camera. Two fingers.

Two Sandmen.

ON THE NEXT EPISODE OF
YOUR LONELY NIGHTS ARE OVER:
THE SEARCH FOR MR. SANDMAN

STAY TOGETHER.

Mr. Sandman's few witnesses and survivors agreed he wore the infamous tragedy mask, but some also claimed to see a comedy mask. Was it the same person, a copycat, or were there two Mr. Sandmen?

A pair made sense. Why would a killer of lonely people hunt alone?

Investigators could confirm virtually nothing about the killer or killers. This anonymity is what led to Mr. Sandman's infamy. It allowed the terror to spread beyond the borders of his San Diego hunting ground. He became like a virus—a force of nature that would either find you or not. You couldn't prevent it.

The only sure way to survive? Fake your joy. Fake your hope. Insist nothing was wrong.

Continue watching?

PART FOUR
TRAGEDY OR COMEDY?

CHAPTER NINETEEN
DEARIE

You all stayed together. Good for you. You're learning. Enjoy your weekend.

Every member of Queer Club received that text just after midnight from the Mr. Sandman burner number. No one has ever made it past twenty-four hours without being attacked, but we did. Not that any of us can enjoy the moment—or trust it. Somehow, the original Mr. Sandman escaped Justin's house without killing Justin—but also without the swarm of agents discovering him. Not only that, we now have proof of a second Sandman, this one in a comedy mask.

Mr. Sandman and the Smiling Sandman.

After Cole and I give our reports to Mom and Agent Astadourian, the officers agree to remain posted outside everyone's homes through Sunday, in case the two Sandmen are trying to fake us out. Agent Jackson can't explain why Justin's chimes went off for him several minutes before it did for the team outside, but they replaced his equipment anyway.

Questions spin through my head, keeping me awake under the covers. *Who are the killers?* Next to me, Cole—thinking I'm asleep—FaceTimes a boy. He whispers too low for me to make out who it is or what they're saying, but at least he's giggling. At least some parts of my world are still the same. We're still here, and Cole still snaps pictures of himself to send to random guys in the night.

I'll be ready for that again with another boy. Someday.

Cole says good night to the boy, and his bug-zapper-bright phone shuts off.

In the dark, I ask, "Cole?"

"Dearie!" he gasps. "Scared the shit out of me. You're up?"

"Don't worry. I couldn't hear anything."

"It was totally innocent. I promise."

"Yeah, yeah." Chuckling, I clutch my body pillow tighter. "I'm trying to figure something out, Cole Slaw."

"What's up, gumshoe?" I can feel the bass notes of his voice vibrating the mattress.

"Our fingerprints were on those phones in our lockers. How did they get there? Either we touched the phones without knowing it, or the killer got us to touch . . . something where they could move the prints onto the phones. It's the only way he could be sure it would be our prints."

"You sound like you've got a Dearie theory."

I smile—my first real one in forever. "It's definitely someone in the Queer Club."

"Your mom hinted at that. But we were all locked up with motion sensors. The two killers showed up on camera while we were locked in. Everyone had an alibi."

"Yeah." Sighing, I crack my knuckles against the headboard. I'd been turning the moment over and over in my head, searching for anything that seemed weird. Then I realized something about tonight *was* bothering me.

Cole looks at me. "What is it?"

"I've got a bad theory." I pause. "Justin." I lay it out. "I asked him to call you, but then he just sends the motion camera link. Mr. Sandman appears. The police finally hear the chimes and bust in. Sandman escapes. But how?"

Cole looks at me seriously. "You think one of the killers is Justin?"

"It would explain why he said he heard chimes but the officers didn't. What if he was already wearing the mask, but we just couldn't see because his FaceTime was so dark. Maybe when he hung up, he ran downstairs, which set off the sensors for the FIRST time. He sends you the link, gets seen on camera, runs back upstairs, and ditches the mask. All the police see is Justin and his dad in their rooms, no Sandman."

"But why call you, then?"

"Create an alibi. Set a scene."

"So, is his dad in on it?"

"I don't know. He'd have to be."

"Why would Justin be the killer? What's his motive?"

I shrug against my pillow. "He doesn't seem to like you—or any of us—much."

"'Not liking someone' and 'murder' are two different things."

"I haven't worked it out yet—maybe there is no motive, maybe he just likes torturing people—but it's the simplest explanation for *how* Mr. Sandman got in and out so easily. He was already in the house."

"Dearie . . ." Soft fingers brush lovingly against my cheek. I really needed his touch right now. "You gotta be careful. Leo told me the killer is already in our lives. That Smiling Sandman was in my house. They've already killed two people close to us. It's like we're being circled."

"I know," I whisper. "I've got another bad theory. Why send all of us the lonely nights message but then not kill anyone? What if it was to make sure the Queer Club had alibis while both killers were caught on camera?" Beneath the sheets, my hand reaches Cole's bare chest. He's boiling hot, but I need him to feel my touch because I'm about to say something scary. "I think this was another setup to make it seem possible that we're the killers. No one was at my house tonight to vouch for us. My mom set up the equipment, so people can just say I found a way to deactivate the sensors and slip out."

"But Justin FaceTimed us."

"If Justin is the killer, he can say he didn't see us. We could've been anywhere during that call."

Cole lets out a terrified, shuddering breath. "Bestie, that theory really sucks."

"It's the worst," I moan. "Whoever the killers are, one thing's super obvious."

"What?"

"They're obsessed with us."

Cole snorts and kisses my nose. "What else is new?"

CHAPTER TWENTY
COLE

You survived the weekend, mijo, but don't get cocky, Uncle Nando texts as Dearie and I get ready to leave for school Monday morning—which they miraculously haven't canceled yet. Uncle Nando advises me that Agent Astadourian allowed me my space this weekend because of the Sandman lockdown, but the minute school is over, I have to go to the sheriff's station to give my full report on Paul.

Over breakfast, Dearie, his mom, and I catch each other up on our weekend discoveries: Grover had been tracking Dearie's location and messages (classic great boyfriend behavior), the killer now has the tracker, Justin's chimes didn't immediately alert the officers outside his home, and Leo fully melted down with anxiety that the killings had started again.

"People lie," Dearie says with a deadly flatness as he sips coffee.

"Maybe," I agree timidly. "And now that we know there's two killers working together, alibis are out the window." I watch Mrs. Dearie staring deeply into her coffee. "What do you think?"

She shuts her eyes. "I think this might be my last case. I wanted to be a small-town investigator, not Clarice Starling." When she opens her eyes, she reappears with renewed energy. "It's Astadourian's case now. She's building a theory that . . . I don't agree with."

My throat pinches closed. It's me. Astadourian's theory is me.

Mrs. Dearie squeezes my hand. "We're fighting her. I don't want to bring you boys into this any more than you already are, but I need you on your guard. She is ruling out Leo, but I think at the very *least* he knows something he hasn't told us." She pauses for a moment. "Something's bothering me about the first murder. Gretchen. Everyone in your club was conveniently pulled away in different places at the time of the meeting. At the exact time of the murder, Leo called Tabatha Drake five times."

"She was divorcing him, right?" Dearie says, mug pressed to his cheek. "He was probably harassing her."

His mother nods. "Possible. Astadourian thinks so too. But . . ." Dearie and I lean closer. "A few minutes later, she called him back. If he was harassing her, why call back?"

Dearie shrugs. "When your partner's an asshole, sometimes it makes you act weird."

Mrs. Dearie and I exchange quick, pitying glances.

Depression has snatched my bestie by the throat this morning.

"There's one more thing," Mrs. Dearie says. "Between the five unanswered Leo calls and the time she calls him back, Tabatha took a call from her father."

"Ray called her?" I ask. "He said they never talk."

"Well, they did that day. She told us Ray's call was irrelevant. But all of this bothers me because her Leo call took her outside the school. If she hadn't called him back, she would've likely witnessed the murder. Seems important."

As I trace my finger along the rim of my mug, a sick idea comes to me. "Is there a way to check where Leo was when he made those calls? What if he was in the school? That could prove—"

Gathering up our empty plates, Mrs. Dearie shakes her head. "Way ahead of you." She returns from the sink with a pen and notepad and begins to draw. In this crude sketch, she draws a box labeled *Stone Grove High*, one labeled *Downtown*, and another labeled *Mooncrest*. Next to each box, she sketches a triangular metal tower.

"Stone Grove has dozens of cell towers," she says. "But any call you make pings off the closest one and can give you an approximate location of where that call was made, physically. Every call Leo made the day of the murder pinged off the Mooncrest tower. If he had been within a mile of the school, it would've hit this one."

She taps her pen on the tower nearest the school.

As my shoulders slump, Dearie buses his own mug to the sink and says, "So Leo got his ex out of the school while Justin killed Gretchen."

"Justin?" his mom asks, sincerely thrown.

"Dearie," I say, "I know you want to help, but you can't run around throwing out names of people you don't like. Grover did that, and it's been ruining my life."

Wincing back something painful, Dearie musses his hair and says, "I'm sorry. Just thinking out loud." He turns to his mom. "I don't know if it's Justin—it's just . . . Things are weird. And I'm not in the mood to face everyone at school today."

We are in sync on that point. After hugging Dearie, I ask his mom if I can hang on to her doodle. She agrees if I promise to keep it to myself. "I shouldn't have shared this with you," she says, hauling her work bag from the table. "But these killers are targeting you. Fuck my job. I'll do whatever I can to keep you two safe."

It's a relief to be spoken to like an adult. The real question is how long can Mrs. Dearie hold off Agent Astadourian now that she's set her sights on me?

When Dearie and I arrive at school, the other students are taking "stay together" quite literally and moving in amoebic clusters from the lockers to the classrooms. News of the

Queer Club's miraculous two-day survival following our Mr. Sandman threat has spread—staying together is the way out.

Before we split up for our morning classes, Dearie screams. I was staring at my phone, so I don't know what happened, only that he's stumbling into my arms.

I catch him. My phone falls. I look up.

It's him. The man in the tragedy mask stalks toward us. He's only a few feet away. Dearie and I scramble backward, our heels squeaking against the floor as we try to run. The world moves in slow motion. There's no time—he's too close. The killer's laugh is muffled beneath his silver latex mask.

Silver . . . Not bronze like usual.

Then someone else laughs, and Dearie and I glance around at the other, cackling students. The masked man continues snickering as Ms. Drake tears the killer's mask off.

Well, shit.

It's just some giggling, stoner freshman messing around. The kid sprints away so fast, no one can catch him. My racing heart won't slow down.

Ms. Drake is dressed in a black jumpsuit, with dark, skeletal circles under her eyes, her black hair lying messily in wilted split ends. She looks like she's had a bear of a week.

"You two all right?" she asks.

"We're alive," Dearie says, catching his breath against a locker, looking as embarrassed as me.

"I don't have time to talk," Ms. Drake whispers heavily,

casting her hooded eyes around the corridor. "I'm going around to all the Queer Club students. I want to clear the air about something. I wasn't planning on talking to you directly, but you're all being targeted, so you have a right to know."

I take Dearie's hand protectively. He's shaking, but we're paying rapt attention to Ms. Drake.

"Is this about your ex?" Dearie whispers.

"Yes." She massages her temples with a trembling hand. "They won't stop questioning him, but I promise he's innocent. It's just like the last time. They've got it wrong."

My heart drums loudly against my aching chest. Why doesn't she just spit out her news?

Ms. Drake casts a dark look over her shoulder at the east corridor. More students are coming. "I was on the phone with Leo when Gretchen died," she whispers. "It couldn't have been him." As I try to look surprised, she glances sharply at Dearie. "Your mom's *superior* doesn't think it's important, but I saw something funny outside—"

The bell rings. Hordes of students bolt out of classroom doors and surround us.

"Saw what?!" Dearie and I whisper.

As the other students get closer, Ms. Drake's nerves get the better of her. She skitters away, hissing, "Library after school! Bring the Queer Club kids, no one else!"

I've never wanted to talk to bland, frozen grapes–eating Ms. Drake this badly before.

"What did that shit mean?" Dearie asks as students swarm us.

"Why couldn't she just tell us now?"

"Maybe she wanted to tell the Queer Club all at once?"

I roll my eyes. "This Queer Club . . ."

Dearie rolls his. "So dramatic."

"See? We attend ONE meeting. Suddenly, we're suspected killers chasing after Ms. Drake."

Dearie presses a weary hand to his forehead. "Getting dunked on by straight freshmen like we're Flops."

"Exactly! We can't live like this."

"We're not gonna be living at all soon!"

After sputtering with dark laughter, Dearie and I split for our respective classes. Now that I have a date with both Ms. Drake and Agent Astadourian after school, the hours have never passed more slowly. I miss the weekend. Hanging nonstop with Dearie was everything my soul needed, but my body . . . Well, my body has been craving Mr. Benito Prince. Three nights of flirty bedtime FaceTimes have teased me plenty. I haven't even seen a nude yet. Just a bit of chest peeking out from his blanket. Everything else has been disguised under baggy, boyish clothes. A smile behind glasses.

I must corrupt him.

This final era of high school hasn't been boring, I'll give it that. Here I am, sitting in class after class with notebooks covering my lap like I'm some pubescent eighth grader again. Finally, after nearly the entire school day passes, Benny appears at the end of the corridor by the cafeteria.

At least, I think it's him.

Over the weekend, my sweet glasses boy in the ill-fitting Loki shirt has transformed into a vixen. Bare, smooth legs in flip-flops lead up to black shorts with a small inseam, highlighting his curves for the first time in his existence. He wears a gray tank with an unbuttoned, cream-colored shirt hung loosely over it—the material is so sheer, the outline of his delicate shoulders is visible. He's applied a thin coat of lip gloss and conditioned his hair—those dark curls shimmer and bounce as he walks. Most shockingly of all, he's abandoned the glasses.

A shame, but he's cute either way.

Supernatural forces pull me toward Benny. The moment he spots me coming, he smiles coyly. He holds his books across his tummy and stands with one foot planted girlishly over the other. The effect is extremely cute and has me speechless for my usual opening lines.

"Hey, Benny," I say, shifting in my suddenly way-too-heavy bomber jacket. "No glasses?"

"Oh, uh . . ." A wave of shyness crashes over Benny, and he tries to push up glasses that are no longer there. "I put in my contacts. I hate them, but I put them in sometimes . . ."

"When you're dressing up cute?"

He glances up, his chest heaving shallowly on short, anxious breaths. "Guess so."

"Well, I think the glasses were cute too." He gnaws on his lower lip. I chew mine. It's my mating dance—mimic their body language. Your vibes should kiss before your lips do. I lean closer. "Are you sure I have to wait until I take you out before I can kiss you?"

He smirks. "Well . . ."

I wink. "I'm going to the bathroom. Join me?"

His joy fades. "A *bathroom*?"

"For privacy."

"Nasty privacy." Benny glances behind his shoulder, thinking. "Bleachers?"

"Classic."

Seconds later, under the bleachers in our blessedly empty gym, I kiss Benny until I've got him pinned against a row of scaffolding. All my anxieties detonate like fireworks— explosive and then gone.

What if this is my last chance to kiss Benny Prince?

It's not just Mr. Sandman making that a grim possibility. In a few weeks, Benny will graduate like the rest of us. Next year, he's going to community college outside Tucson, so it won't be far when I come home from New York on holidays, but then again, what if I blow up those New York plans? LA with Dearie would be closer. Tucson would be even closer. What if I just blew everything up and cooked dinner for Benny while he studies?

His lip gloss tastes like coconut. The kiss is soft as hell. He grips my bristly cheeks, and I trace my fingers down his back . . .

SLAM.

As soon as my hand makes contact with his ass—as if God is striking me down—two loud senior boys storm inside the gym. Benny jerks in my arms, spasming from terror. I remain in place, frightened of nothing but Mr. Sandman. The boys are tall white thugs in Rattlers jackets. I know them—Walker Lane and Teddy Marks; one is the boy I slapped, and both are future frat-house fartknockers of America.

"Whoa, Cardoso!" Walker hollers, wearing an enormous grin, while Teddy giggles into his hand. "Caught in the act."

I wrap my arm around Benny's shoulder, glower at my teammates, and say, "Get lost."

It only makes Walker howl harder. "Looks like you got yourself a little boyf—"

Now I let go of Benny and march my full height toward them. "You want some more?"

He laughs again, but weaker. Teddy goes quiet. "You can't . . ."

"I've got bigger worries than you, Lane. People think

I'm a serial killer. You really think anyone's gonna blink if I smack you around again?"

My face is stone.

Walker stomps out, and Teddy—as usual—shuffles after him. Most importantly, Benny stops quaking. He isn't in the mood anymore, and neither am I, but at least we weren't chased out of the room like perverts. We're finishing this moment nicely.

I kiss Benny's hair, soft and vanilla-scented, and when he smiles, I know he's okay.

"Walker broke my arm in seventh grade," he says, traces of fear still lingering.

A boy this beautiful deserves no fear. I shake my head and say the truth, the first thing that comes to mind: "I don't remember that." I kiss the tip of his nose. "Someday, you won't either. Walker Lane isn't going to show up in the movie of our lives again. When we get out of this place, you get to be anyone you want to be. Queers get to do that, that's our right."

He smiles. "Yeah?"

"And I have a feeling whoever you're gonna be"—I give him a swift tap on his ass—"is gonna be a real kitten."

A naughty giggle escapes him, but then he looks at me seriously, with an admiration I've never seen from anyone before. "You're not scared of anything, are you?"

Smiling, I draw closer. "I'm scared of lots of things.

The trick is to not let them see. They want your fear—starve them."

To ease Benny's anxiety that Walker and Teddy might rat us out, we separate for the start of free period. I think I sufficiently put a scare into those goons to keep quiet, but you never really know what a Brad Bradleigh Braddington is gonna do, so we play it safe. Back in the hallway, Dearie meets me with a cheeky grin.

"You've got icing on your lips," he says, eyes twinkling.

I dig a spare tissue from my messenger bag, dab my lips, and—yes—pull back a shimmering coat of Benny's coconut gloss. Chuckling, in the deep voice of a 1950s TV dad: "Darling, it's not what it looks like."

"Mm-hmm," Dearie says, following along in a nagging 1950s TV mom voice: "You've been canoodling with your secretary again." He smacks my arm, returning to a normal whisper. "Benny Prince? Is *that* who you've been FaceTiming at night, you bad boy?"

"I just . . ."

He scoffs. "What happened to not dropping our guard around the Flops?"

With Benny's kiss still on my lips, the word *Flop* has a new sting to it. Maybe I shouldn't have been so loose with this *other* f-word while Dearie was seeing Grover. It kind of sucks.

With nothing else to defend my behavior, I shrug. "I'm pretty sure he's innocent."

A devilish gleam flashes through Dearie's eyes. "He's not that—"

"Innocent," we finish together.

Our wicked joy is cut short by the arrival of another Flop: Mike Mancini (it's Mike, so I can say Flop about him). While I'm in a basic white tee and light jacket, and Dearie is cute as a button in his fitted crop, this boy is draped in another bunchy turtleneck. He's wearing his chain on the outside, so he looks like that goofy meme of the Rock.

"Aren't you hot in that?" I ask.

"No," he says defensively. God, this mozzarella stick never chills out. He turns to Dearie. "You ready?"

Now it's my turn to swivel in wide-eyed horror. Not Dearie and Mike! Oh God, babe, just be single for a minute.

Luckily, Dearie quickly explains in a low whisper: "I was talking to Mike last period, and he totally independently brought up my same theory about Justin."

Mike nods vigorously. "It's the only explanation for how that chime went off late *and* how no one can explain why they didn't find Sandman in the house afterward."

A queasy feeling swirls through me. I scoff, "What are you jelly beans planning?"

Dearie dead-eyes me. "He didn't come to school, so we're going over there to see if we can talk to him."

"No, you're not. He'll lasso both your throats in the same razor necklace!"

"Which is why you're driving us."

"What about Ms. Drake? We gotta talk to her, and I've gotta talk to Double-A. I'm booked for detective work today."

"We'll be back by then! This is our free period. We're just three seniors taking a senioritis drive off-property."

Mike beams, his chest all puffed up under his turtleneck, so proud that in this one moment he has more guts than I do. But it's not about fear, I just severely dislike being planned around. Since when are we a trio?

I roll my eyes at Mike. "So, you finally agree I'm not the killer?"

Stiffly, he glances me up and down. "There's two killers."

I lean closer. "Well, what if it's Dearie and me? We could be driving you to kill you."

Mike is sweating, but he doesn't want to flinch in front of his crush. After a moment, he admits, "None of the Sandmen are short. Dearie's little. So, even if it is you, you wouldn't hurt him."

"Finally, we agree on something." I pinch Mike's furry cheek, pull out my keys, and wave them both onward. "Shorties first."

CHAPTER TWENTY-ONE
DEARIE

WE PARK TWO STREETS away so that the officers posted outside Justin's southwestern-style home won't notice bright, showy, CHEATER-emblazoned Julieta. While Mom did tell us several of the people in her department are Team Cole, we don't know who's who. Justin's neighborhood is far from where Cole and I live, which is the wealthier end of town. This part of Stone Grove has seen the worst boom-and-bust. Cheaply built tract homes, one indistinguishable from another, half of them vacant and owned by the bank, and all with rocks and cactus gardens for lawns.

It just *feels* ten degrees hotter here.

Slowly, three f-words creep around the side of Justin's house, our backs flat to the walls. All the window's blinds are drawn, so the only way to see inside is to get inside. Good thing the FBI battered the front door off its hinges and hasn't bothered to rehang it yet. It'll just be a matter of walking right in—which sounded like a simpler plan *before* we were staring at the dark, open chasm of the doorway. Barely an ounce of daylight has penetrated their living room.

Justin and his dad are just sitting in the dark, blinds drawn, without a single lamp? Definitely killer behavior.

Mike brought two pocket-size tasers from Lucy's stash, but Cole thought it was best if the smaller guys took them. "You're sure Justin's home?" Cole whispers.

"He said he was too sad to get out of bed," Mike whispers. "Said he was gonna try to finish the rest of the school year at home."

Cole rolls his eyes for the hundredth time. "Acting like a bigger widow than Dearie. He went on one date with Grover. This is just like when he hooked up with me!"

"Well, it's *bullshit*," I whisper, clutching my taser with both hands.

Cole purses his lips disapprovingly. "You're acting really convinced he's involved, but we don't have a single motive other than 'He's an incel who wants to frame me.'"

I jerk my taser toward Mike. "Mike knows a motive."

Sweating into his earlobes, Mike dabs his forehead with his sweater sleeve. "Well," he whispers, "Justin didn't want to move here. His friends are back in Boston, and he's been acting *so* angry the past year. Touchy about everything. Snapping at people. Depressed. Feeling trapped. The only thing that cheered him up was watching *Lonely Nights*. Maybe the show spoke to him . . ."

Mouth open, Cole turns to me. "Not depressed and touchy! Why didn't you say so earlier, Dearie?" Narrowing his eyes, he whispers, "You're describing every teenage homo in America! That's not suspicious, chickens."

Not blinking, I deliver my killshot. "No, but copying a key to your house *is.*"

Cole goes quiet. Mike's shoulders heave, as if he was hoping he wouldn't have to tell this part. Finally, he admits the truth. "After Dearie broke up with Grover, he texted me and Justin. He told us he was gonna key your car." Cole glowers, but Mike waves him away. "I tried talking him out of it, honest! But Grover and Justin were *hot* to fuck with you. Justin got the idea of escalating pranks on you after the keying, so he asked me to break into your car since I help my dad do that with people who get locked out." Mike's eyes drop with shame. "Grover saw you put your house keys in your glove box once, so they thought they could break into your car, copy your house key, and . . ."

"And WHAT?" Cole whispers.

"And I don't know. I refused to do it. They called me weird and stopped texting."

"Mike, one of the killers got inside my house. My moms could've been there. Why didn't you say something?"

"Because . . ." Losing his nerve, Mike fiddles with the collar of his turtleneck.

"Because?"

Stepping between them, I say, "Because Grover got intensely aggro with people who sided against him. We all know it. Now I think it is *possible* that Justin went ahead with his plan after Grover died. That's cause enough for me."

Cole and Mike appraise each other, and finally, they both soften and nod. The three of us hug the corner behind Justin's home's front wall to stay out of sight of the stake-out vehicle parked down the sidewalk. After Mr. Sandman's threat was over, they downgraded our protection from FBI agents to regular plainclothes officers.

"How do we do this?" I ask. "Let the officers know we're here to check on Justin?"

"That's risky, and it'll take too long," Cole says. "Let's just go in. See what we can see."

Craning my neck around the corner, I see the parked sedan, but it's too far to make out anyone sitting inside. "If we rush through the front door fast enough, they won't notice," I say, securing my taser. Mike secures his, flanks me, and we dash inside.

If it was this easy for us to get inside, how simple would it be for the killers?

Justin's living room is muggy. The air conditioner is running, but with the door left open, it's made no impact. It's like walking through curtains of sweat. The home is depressingly unadorned. A single father and his sporty son live here. The living room features a ratty, stained couch that used to be expensive. Two rusted, folding TV dinner trays sit in front, where a coffee table should be. Flies swarm around the sticky plates of leftovers. There are no chairs—the Saxbys aren't used to company. No art on the wall. No pictures. Just an immaculately set up entertainment center with an eighty-inch screen and multiple gaming systems plugged haphazardly into the back.

"This is *vile*," Cole whispers. I just flare my eyes and wave my taser around the room like it's sage. We're not too deep into the house. Running back out the door is still an easily achievable option. Ahead of us are three hallways—three shadowy, empty pathways where a masked man could suddenly emerge, razor noose in hand . . .

"Maybe we shouldn't go too far inside," I whisper.

"I'm with Dearie," Mike whispers.

A bead of sweat courses down Cole's cheek. He exhales slowly to calm himself before agreeing, "Me three."

As if we were one entity, we retreat to the open door, when a voice moans from the other room—wailing. Cole gasps. I stumble backward into Mike's belly, and his strong, calloused hand stops me from falling.

No one says anything. We wait for the voice to come again.

"I did everything you wanted!" a man's voice begs from the other room. Soft murmuring follows from a second voice. Then the man responds, gripped by terrible anguish, "I need to see him! Please! I did everything . . ."

The man—I think it's Justin's father—descends into racking sobs. Then there's a loud *BANG*. Someone pounding on something hard. Something like wood. Or it could be a person's skull. The thin, cheap walls around us reverberate with another pummeling blow. Then . . . footsteps. Louder. Closer.

"Cole," I whisper.

"Run now!" he whispers back.

We don't look back. In under ten seconds, all three of us backtrack through Justin's living room, across his entryway, and out the door. Quickly but carefully. Each of us knows to leave without a sound. When we finally meet sweet sunshine, we sprint down the sloping sidewalk toward the squad car. Moving like a tornado, Mike reaches the driver's side window first, followed closely by me and Cole.

Yet when we arrive, Mike stares into the car window, his face slack and arms frozen midair.

The car is empty.

The windows are down, and it's been completely abandoned.

"This isn't great," Mike squeaks.

"Are they in the house?" I stammer.

"My car—go!" Cole shouts, tapping Mike and me on our shoulders hard enough to shake us out of our stupor. We run, slapping pavement as we pass one vacant, foreclosed house after another.

No one to help. Nowhere to run but the car.

Mike pulls ahead with Cole close behind him. My chunky Cuban-heeled boots weren't made for fleeing for my life, so perhaps I should rethink my fashion choices now that this fleeing *is* my damn life.

One more street before we reach Julieta.

Against every molecule in my body telling me not to, I turn to look back . . .

Standing on Justin's rocky lawn among the cactus garden, watching us run but not following, is Mr. Sandman—wearing his tragedy mask.

CHAPTER TWENTY-TWO
COLE

DEARIE AND I RETURN to school just after the final bell. My hands are sticky with terror sweat as we pull in. Hundreds of students hurry past the posted officers and news vans choking the front entrance. The straights are leaving clouds of dust behind them running to their cars to get the hell away from these doomed queers.

What the hell happened to Justin? Is he a killer or another victim?

No clue, but I do know every one of us is still in deep shit. I'm getting Benny and the rest of them out of school with expeditious speed. We dropped Mike off at his house with Agents Manfredi and Jurgen outside—and left it to him to report the missing officers and what happened at the Saxby home.

And, oh yeah, that Mr. Sandman—the original—was there.

We went to Justin's house hoping to catch him doing Sandman things—and maybe we did, maybe we didn't, but the killers certainly have a grip on that house. We just need to find out what kind of arrangement Mr. Saxby has with the Sandmen.

"I did everything you wanted!" he screamed. *"I need to see him!"*

See Justin? Is Justin a hostage? Mr. Sandman never took hostages, but then again, this time around is a whole different show.

The remains of the Queer Club congregate in the empty corridor leading to the double-doored library at the end—where Ms. Drake hopefully waits with answers to the mystery she teased earlier about Leo's history with the killings. As Dearie and I walk inside the school, Em, Theo, Lucy, and Benny approach us like timid rabbits. Benny's glasses are back. He must've had enough of those contact lenses (or realized he no longer needed them to command my attention). Lucy hugs Dearie, and Benny buries himself in my egregiously damp tee. Theo and Em stand cautiously outside the hugs, their fingers gently interlaced. Whether this is as friends or would-be lovers, I don't know or care.

The time for "Stay Together" is now.

After Dearie and I quickly catch them up on what happened—Benny tugs me aside. His eyes are wide and furious. "You snooped around a spooky house, killer on the loose, with two white people?" he asks, beside himself. "Are you trying to become dead?!"

Chuckling, I say, "This isn't a movie, bunny."

"Keep laughing." Benny calms himself with short,

adorable bursts of breath. "It's a good thing we're not boy-friends, or I'd tell you that you can't do stuff like that again."

That certainly crooked my eyebrow. I poke his chin. "Who says we're not boyfriends?"

"I say." He purses his lips. "Until I'm satisfied you don't have a death wish."

I smirk. "I'm on probation?"

"That's right."

When we rejoin the Queer Club circle by the lockers, Dearie's explaining his Justin theory to Theo and Em. Em is probably the biggest *Your Lonely Nights Are Over* nerd here, second only to me . . . and probably the killers. Em brushes her silver hair behind her ear as she absorbs the horrific in-formation. Most disturbingly, she's hooked her pinky inside Theo's.

I shake my head. Another cool girl lost to a judgmen-tal Flop.

"It makes sense," Em says, "but then why would Justin's dad be begging to see him? Wouldn't Justin being a killer mean . . . he'd be there?"

"I don't know," Dearie moans into his hands. "But Justin's either the killer or—he's dead."

A shocked silence falls.

We don't have time for theories and emotional scenes.

"Either way, whoever was in that mask saw us leave," I say. "They know we're close to figuring out what's going on." Stepping into the center of the group, I drop into my dad voice. "So let's talk to Ms. Drake and then get back to lockdown."

I motion Benny over to me, and he joins my right side. Dearie hugs my left and throws Benny a friendly nod. Benny returns him a sour *you almost got my man killed* smile and takes my hand. Lucy glances down at our hands, then up to me. She whistles.

As we walk toward the double doors, Theo—dressed in all black with a matching black bow tie—turns to me, their freckled face hanging sadly. "I've been seeing Paul on the news. His parents are a nightmare. I'm really sorry."

Did aliens abduct Theo and replace them with this look-alike who knows how to apologize?

Well, they must've replaced me too because I find apologies racing to my lips as my heart softens: "Don't be. You were right." My chest throbs with a swift, urgent pain. "I kept thinking about Paul like he was still alive. Wherever he is, he doesn't care anymore about coming out."

I can't believe I'm grateful to be surrounded by Flops.

Theo opens the double doors, and we follow them in. The library is dark. No overhead lights on. While the sun continues to rage outside, the multiple drawn shades cast the room in a dim beige glow. Our library is pathetically small. Loose bookstacks, not much taller than me, stand on each side, full of outdated volumes of pure nothingness. The study group table in the middle of the room looks ominous. Underneath is total darkness. Someone could be hiding under there to snatch us by our ankles . . .

"Ms. Drake?" Dearie calls out. No answer.

"Tabatha?" Theo shouts.

"Is she late?" Benny asks.

"She's never late," Lucy says.

"Except to Queer Club that one time," I remind everyone, "which she promised to explain!"

As Theo shushes me, Em fidgets in place before blurting, "She chickened out. I'm doing the same." On a swoosh of silvery-blond hair, Em spins around and bolts to the double doors. She throws them open . . .

But Mr. Sandman is waiting.

The Smiling Sandman—not the one at Justin's house. It's an ambush.

Everyone screams and scatters. There's no time to think.

A shiny flash of razors—a necklace—cuts through the air, toward Em's silvery hair . . .

Dropping Benny's hand, I bound toward Em to pull her away . . .

But before I'm close, she's already spun around, leaping like a cat on top of the study table. Her graceful landing is Olympian. The integrity of the table, not so much. As Em's weight hits, it capsizes, sending her careening backward into a bookstack.

"COME ON!" Theo shrieks as the Smiling Sandman moves. Theo is faster, lunging for Em. They hustle her to her feet, and both vanish behind the bookstacks into the shadows.

"I ONLY WENT TO ONE CLUB MEETING!" Em screams.

Turning back, I face the Smiling Sandman, waiting with his ghoulish smile to see what we'll do next. Thinking of Paul, I accelerate into the killer, ready to tackle him, but the closer I get, the shinier that crown of razors looks. And like he's an opponent on the basketball court, I fake left then peel right toward the bookstacks where Theo and Em vanished.

A sharp *whoosh* cuts through the air. The razors missed.

So much adrenaline surges through my body, my legs move independently from my brain. With a *crack*, my shoulder collides into the metal shelving of the stack along the back wall, sending pain through my back and a pile of books to the floor.

Somewhere behind me, Lucy screams.

When the pain subsides enough to clear my vision, I round the corner of a bookstack to see Lucy by the overturned study table. Small and determined, Lucy faces down the Smiling Sandman as she gathers a pile of books in her arms. One by one, she hurls them like bricks at the killer. They whiz by his mask—he barely flinches. A few make contact but do nothing but annoy him. He advances. Lucy's arms go limp, the pile of books dropping to her feet. She turns to run, but she won't have enough time.

Not unless I do something.

Scooping armfuls of books from the floor, I run back to the center of the room, toward the Smiling Sandman, whose back is to me. I palm the largest book and aim for the shiny dome of the back of his mask.

BOOM. BOOM. BOOM.

I chuck three perfect pitches in a row. Each one is a direct hit.

The killer drops like a bag of cement.

Lucy doesn't stop. She vaults over a library cart and disappears past Ms. Drake's desk and down a shadowy corridor. Where does it go? If I ever bothered to come to the library, I'd know.

My hand trembling, heart in my neck, I try not to breathe as I scan the library for signs of the two most important people to me: Dearie and Benny. *Why* did I let go of Benny? Em clearly could take care of herself. I could've gotten them both out of here.

Not wanting to be the lone person out in the open, I double back behind the bookstacks and crouch to catch my breath. These shelves are the only things separating me from death.

Do I call 911? Dearie's mom?

The killer lies flat on his back, not moving. I doubt he'll stay down long.

There's no sign of Theo or Em either.

Any sound could draw him over. I have to get to the doors. It isn't far. On the opposite end of the library, beyond Ms. Drake's desk, faint whispering echoes through the walls. Soft footsteps. Everyone's still here, trying to reach the same exit.

Dearie, please be with Benny. Please be hiding safely under a desk or something.

I can't leave before finding them.

On my hands and knees, I crawl toward the farthest back wall of windows. I stop to glance up through the book gaps along the bottom shelf. It gives me a clear view of the over-turned study table where the Smiling Sandman fell . . .

But he's not there.

"Christ," I whisper.

He's not here. He's DEFINITELY not standing over me with a spool of razor wire.

After three horrible seconds, I allow myself to look up.

No one. I'm alone.

SLAM. In the distance, the double doors burst open. I can't see from here, but two people run out screaming. Their shoes squeak on the hallway floor. It could be Em and Theo.

I force myself to breathe. Someone will be here soon.

Click-clack. The double doors gently shut on their own.

Another *SLAM.* Far away, a different door bursts open. Down the corridor where Lucy disappeared, a shaft of white-hot light cuts into the library as multiple people run out, and the door shuts again.

Maybe Lucy got Benny out? Her, Benny, and Dearie?

Despite the relief that thought brings, it means I'm alone in the library.

Soon. They'll come back with help soon.

I can't stay in one place. I have to keep moving until Mrs. Dearie or Agent Double-A or someone comes to scare the Smiling Sandman away or finally catch him.

Continuing my crawl, I scan left and right for any signs of movement other than my own. A second later, my forehead smacks against something hard, something that reeks of shoe polish.

A high-heeled boot. Attached to a person. Splayed across the library floor.

A body.

My heart stops as I recognize the heel. "Dearie," I squeak like a little boy. *No, no!* Forgetting the Smiling Sandman, forgetting my own safety, I jump to my knees and throw myself at my best friend's body. What I find instead is a black jumpsuit. It's a woman with sunken, skeletal eyes staring vacantly at the ceiling.

Ms. Drake. She's dead. Razor wire is wrapped around her throat. She lies in a puddle of blackened blood, pooling in a halo beneath her head.

Unlike with Gretchen and Grover, her wounds are no longer gushing. She was already dead when we got here. Next to her head, a sandy-brown card sits tented like a dinner invitation.

YOUR LONELY NIGHTS ARE OVER.

I need to leave *now*.

Brrrrrrinnggggg.

A ringing phone cuts like a harpoon through the silent library. I jerk away so harshly, a spasm of pain shoots through my back.

Brrriiiiinnggggggg. The horrible ringing is close.

It needs to stop, or the Smiling Sandman will come looking. I check my phone, but it's not me. Ms. Drake is clutching her own phone, which remains dark. It's not hers either.

Brrrriiiinnnggggggggggg.

The sound comes again. I glance down at my messenger bag, still somehow locked to my side throughout all this chaos. It rings again. It's coming from my bag. I open the top flap and rifle through notebooks, pens, and my iPad. No phone. When it rings again, I know I'm close. There's two large pouches, sealed with zippers, on the inside of the bag. I pull back one zipper . . .

And pull out a small spool of razor wire. The sharpness sits dangerously against my flesh, but I'm too speechless to let it go. This has been in my bag the whole time?!

Brrrrriiiiiinnnnnnggggggg.

Still holding the wire, I pull open the second zipper. Inside is another burner.

Brrrriiiingggggggggggg.

235

Somehow—*somehow*—one of the killers put these things in my bag. When? How?

Oh my God.

That's why we all got the messages and went into lockdown. That's why the Smiling Sandman was in my house when he knew I wouldn't be there. He was planting evidence.

Just leave, Cole. Drop everything and walk away.

But I have to talk to him. I have to confront him.

Holding my breath, I summon the last drop of courage in my chest and answer the burner.

"Hello," I say.

"Gotcha, Sandman," a woman's voice emanates from both the phone and in front of me. A gun clicks. I look up. Agent Astadourian, in a clean black pantsuit, points her firearm with one hand and holds her iPhone in the other. Three fellow agents flank her.

And I'm still holding the damn murder weapon.

"Holster your weapons," she orders the agents. Their guns still drawn, they hesitate. "NOW." Finally, they listen, and Double-A lowers her own. She smirks. "This one's not going anywhere."

ON THE NEXT EPISODE OF
YOUR LONELY NIGHTS ARE OVER:
THE SEARCH FOR MR. SANDMAN

With forced couplings came new families. What better way than having a baby to prove to the world—and the killer—that you're happy, loved, and thriving?

By the mid-1970s, with Mr. Sandman entering his fourth active year and his identity still a mystery, San Diego witnessed an unexpected phenomenon: Sandman Babies. It was a localized baby boom that resulted from the countless hookups and quickie marriages from people desperate to avoid being next on his list. Relationships that would've—or should've—ended if not for the shadow of Mr. Sandman often turned to a new baby as a visible shrine—an offering—to their lack of loneliness.

Half a century later, where are these children of terror now, and how do they feel about their ghoulish origins?

Continue watching?

PART FIVE
SANDMAN BABIES

CHAPTER TWENTY-THREE
DEARIE

WE'RE BACK IN ROOM 208. The circumstances are eerily similar to the last time I was here, when we were all seated islands away from each other, waiting to answer my mom's questions about Gretchen's murder.

Only this time, there's four of us left.

Gretchen, Grover, and Ms. Drake are dead. Cole is in police custody. Theo was quickly interviewed and whisked away by their parents. Mike is at home. Justin is God-knows-where—either he's one of the killers, he's being held somewhere, or he's dead.

Only me, Benny, Lucy, and Em are left. All four of us are too furious to be sad. Benny got all dressed up special for Cole, but now his eyes burn holes into the carpet, his glossy lips twisted in a permanent scowl. Lucy stares angrily at the wall—through the wall, as if trying to peer into another dimension for answers. Em just gnaws on her pen and stares into space.

Me, I'm beyond rage, like the calm eye of a destructive hurricane.

Ms. Drake wanted to tell the Queer Club something important she saw outside when Gretchen was killed— something the FBI was disregarding. Did the Smiling Sandman know Ms. Drake was secretly gathering us?

He had to—the ambush was too well planned.

It pretty much confirms at least one of the killers is one of us. Justin is the obvious answer, but like Leo Townsend, there's holes in that story. I've learned from Cole's experience to think twice when all the evidence obviously points to one person.

I open Instagram to quiet my mind. I expected a deluge of posts and stories spreading the news of Cole's arrest, but thankfully, it's been kept quiet so far. However, Ms. Drake's murder is everywhere. Memorial posts from students filled with pictures of her (and us) in happier times: her Pride jumpsuit last summer (complete with trans-flag-colored eye makeup), her wincing as she sat on top of a dunk tank for charity, and most painfully, her and Grover.

In this picture from sophomore year, Grover—sporting a baggy hoodie and jawline acne—looks happier than I ever knew him in real life. My fingers turn cold. I keep scrolling. Post after post flies by until I finally see something that isn't about death: that basketball twit Walker Lane and some blond girl announce they're going to prom as an official couple. Straight people acting like proms are engagement rings. Yet two posts later, there's an actual engagement: Michael De

La Rosa and Marina Silva show off a giant diamond rock on her finger.

That's, uh . . . quite a way to end senior year.

Three posts later, there's another engagement: Tracee Manning and Stephen Burns.

Are these people pregnant?

A quick scan confirms my suspicions—every photo was posted within the last hour, after Ms. Drake's body was found. Like placing a protective spell on their homes, these people are shouting, "No loneliness here! Move along, Mr. Sandman!"

So, a straight is finally killed, and everyone starts taking the massacre seriously? Disgusting.

Four posts later, a rock drops on me: Theo hugs Lucy cheek-to-cheek. In the picture, Theo's hair is blond, and Lucy's hair is long—not with a buzzed side like it is now. This is from last year! *Can't wait to spend prom with MY BEST GIRL!!!* Theo wrote. *So happy we're FINALLY TOGETHER!!!!*

Worst of all, the caption ends with an engagement ring emoji.

To paraphrase Ms. Spears, STOP!

If anything, I thought Theo and Em had the connection.

"Hey, congratulations!" I squeal across the room at Lucy. Em and Benny shiver, as if shaken out of a bad dream. Lucy instantly recognizes the picture on my phone and scowls.

"What?" Em asks distantly.

I announce, "Lucy and Theo are getting married, or some unhinged shit like that!"

"Theo asked *me* to do that post together, and I was thinking it was gonna be a date, which I was kinda hoping for, but then it was some fake-ass engagement for 'Don't Kill Me' clout, so I told them no, that's deranged." Em can't stop laughing. "They just went down the line to you, Lucy?"

"We're in love!" Lucy says seriously.

Fed up, Benny slams his hand onto his half-moon desk. "What are you talking about?"

Lucy recoils at our horrified faces. "I don't have to explain my romantic choices to you three, and I think it's really uncool you can't be more open-minded."

I needed that laugh.

"Who the hell are you kidding?" I ask. "You're like all the rest of them!" I hold up my phone and scroll through the multitude of engagements like a prosecutor with damning evidence. "Mr. Sandman can smell loneliness. None of this is going to trick him."

Lucy scoffs. "Why can't it be real? You don't know me."

"Well, I know you," Em says, her face buried in her hands. "And you can't stand Theo."

"We have a *Pride and Prejudice* thing!" Lucy's voice gets so frantically high, her throat clamps tight and stops her from continuing. Not that she needs to—her cornered expression says it all.

"Lucy," I say softly, "we're all scared."

Tears stream down her cheeks, and she fans herself in a vain attempt to stop them. "I promise, it's really real," she squeaks. "Why can't it be real? Benny and Cole got together."

At the mention of Cole, Benny glares evilly.

"But that really happened," I say. "You're saying that in the last hour, when we were running for our lives, Theo took the time to get on one knee and ask Em to marry them? Then, once rejected, asked you and it's love?" Lucy just glares with puffy eyes. "Okay, fine, let's see the ring."

She averts her eyes. "Theo's saving up for one."

Em laughs with pure exhaustion, and Benny pries his face from his desk long enough to roll his eyes. Gently, I say, "Theo owns multiple luxury cars and a motorcycle."

"OKAY," Lucy whispers, strangling the strap on her backpack. "We saw everyone else doing it and just did it. It's smart to protect ourselves! We'll pair up. It can be me and Theo, Benny and Cole, you and Mike, Em and . . . somebody?"

"Em and somebody," Em repeats softly.

"Dating someone just to protect the other person makes you both lonelier," I say, fighting another painful memory of Grover begging me not to leave him. Yet even knowing it would put us in danger, dumping Grover freed my soul. Pity-dating is toxic.

Across the room, Lucy's eyes dim. She knows I'm right.

"Well," Benny finally speaks. He stands and, without warning, kicks his half-moon desk. The effect is muted as he hops up and down on a wounded toe. "Mine wasn't fake! Cole actually means something to me!" Benny grips his head. "He finally noticed me, and I thought, finally he might realize I'm not a Flop." He spins furiously toward me. "We *all* know you call us that. Grover knew, and it *hurts*."

As my shoulders tighten with overwhelming fear and guilt, Lucy's eyes drop. Benny can barely catch his breath.

There's no denying it. We said it. It was Cole and mine's asshole joke, but we never told anyone. It was just one of those things you do between friends to be catty.

But here's what came of that: Pain. Loneliness. And now death.

Without speaking, I crawl from my seat, wincing at the strain in my calf from my day of running around. As I approach, Benny quakes from head to toe. I open my arms and ask, "Is this okay?" He simply shuts his eyes and accepts my hug. It's different from a Cole hug. Benny is my height, and this is not a hug of love but of repair. Strangers with the same trauma. He hugs back tightly, gratefully, until we feel Em's and Lucy's arms wrap around us as well. I unhook one arm from Benny and bring them both in. The four of us put our heads together in solidarity.

"Cole didn't do it," I say to the huddle. "We're gonna get him out."

Benny breaks from the hug first and raises a warning finger. "If there's one person I'm convinced had nothing to do with this, it's Cole. And I will do anything to make sure the world knows it."

I throw Benny a peace sign. "So will I."

"Me too," Em agrees.

The three of us glance at Lucy, who is forced to shrug. "He didn't do it."

I brush on a fresh coat of cherry ChapStick and say, "If we're lucky, Justin's the killer. Everyone went over to his house. He'll be picked up, and Cole will be let go."

"But we're not lucky," Em says.

"No."

"Justin makes sense," Lucy says, tapping her lips. "Hated Cole, terrible attitude, never got close to any of us. Like he was pissed he had to be in the club."

"Self-hating queer-killing queers?" I ask. "That would be depressing."

Lucy and Em nod with exhausted agreement.

"Also, Justin getting picked up wouldn't help Cole," Benny groans. "There's two killers. They'll just think it's Justin *and* Cole."

"Yep," I agree with a sigh. "I just can't help thinking one of them has to be the original."

After a moment deep in thought, Benny lights up. "'Always two there are, a master and an apprentice.'"

Three confused heads turn to him, and he smiles nervously. "Yoda."

"That could make sense," I say. "The original Sandman recruited one of us . . ."

"No," Em says, realizing. "There's no reason the original Mr. Sandman would be this obsessed with us. But . . . maybe someone in Queer Club is. One of *us* watched the show and figured out who the original was. *They* found *him.* It's *their* plan the killers are executing."

We all exchange nervous glances. I assumed if it was one of us, they got roped in by a persuasive, seasoned monster, but . . . to have it be *a student's* idea? It makes it feel more wrong. Darker. Cole told me Leo warned him whoever the killer was, he was already in our lives. Close.

Too close.

"Could it be Justin and Leo?" Lucy asks.

We scan each other warily. No one is sure of anything.

"Break it down," Benny says. "The only way we're gonna figure this out—and save Cole—is to work through the details. Find something. A way forward."

I nod. As sick as this makes me, we've got to do it for Cole.

Over the next twenty minutes, we retrace the case's core details: every victim and piece of evidence; phones with mine and Cole's fingerprints planted in our lockers; today, another phone and a spare razor necklace were found in

Cole's bag. The Smiling Sandman must have placed it there when he broke in.

Did Justin steal and copy Cole's house key? Could that be how he got in, planted the evidence?

And then there's Leo Townsend. Part of the original killing spree, Leo moves to Stone Grove, and fifty years later, the killing starts again—after he goes through a divorce.

We know his calls to Ms. Drake happened at the precise moment needed to draw her away from Gretchen's murder. And Cole said Leo broke down in tears trying to warn him that someone close to us was the killer. What if Leo *is* the original Sandman but isn't killing again? He's being forced to help—blackmailed into assisting a young apprentice?

For a second, I take a breath. It's overwhelming and confusing and Cole is still stuck in a cell while we hash this out. It feels like we're out of time. Benny looks over at me, reaches out his hand, and squeezes mine once. It's affectionate but also carries sternness—*focus, bitch*, his eyes seem to say.

Focus. We're in this together.

"Your fingerprints," Benny tells me. "We need to figure out how they got on those phones."

We spread out on our backs across the carpet. I drum my fingers anxiously across my phone. It's the easiest thing in the world to brush your finger against something and leave a print, especially if someone is trying to get you to do it. But when could we have touched some old-ass burners?

"If we're stumped on the fingerprint thing," Lucy says, staring dreamily upward, "anyone want to guess what Ms. Drake was gonna tell us?"

"It was important enough to kill her over," Benny says.

"I know what it was," Em says. We all sit up like vampires rising from coffins. "I'm just . . . trying to figure out how it's important."

"So's the FBI," I say. "Ms. Drake said they didn't really care."

Em bundles her hair into a ponytail and says, "Ms. Drake told Theo and me. We were talking to her about . . . everything. She told us when Gretchen was killed, she was in the parking lot fighting with Leo on the phone." Em tosses up her hands. "But when she first heard the screams, she noticed a pile of clothes on a bench. She didn't think anything about it at first, but later she went back and found the clothes. It was a janitor's uniform. Since the budget cuts, janitors only come Tuesdays and Thursdays—but Gretchen was killed on Wednesday. And why would the clothes be outside, anyway?"

That terrible day shuffles through my mind like someone quickly flipping through a book. Tension leaves me as clarity rushes in. "Em . . . We saw a janitor that day."

She leaps to attention. "What?"

Benny, Lucy, and Em watch me, rapt, as I take them through the day: "We were waiting for Queer Club to start.

Cole was late. Em, you and I were killing time, and then a boy—that freshman—came in asking if this was the Queer Club. We said yes, but he was so freaked out, he left." I swallow hard. "A janitor was holding the door open for him while he talked to us."

"I remember," Em says, breathless. "*That* was Mr. Sandman?"

Lucy slowly leans forward. "Why was he holding the door?"

"It was weird, that's why I remember!" I say. "The kid was small, but he could reach the door handle. I opened it just fine. Cole came in right after."

Like dawn breaking, Lucy brightens, struck by a beautiful thought. "I know how he got your prints on the phone!" She leaps into the air, applauding herself as enormous energy overtakes her. "Dearie, you said Em was already here when you showed up. Then the janitor held the door for the boy and left. Was he wearing gloves?"

I shrug. "He might've been. I don't remember."

Undaunted, Lucy paces the room, alive with energy. "Cole showed up. Then what?"

"Once Cole got here, we waited a few minutes and left. That's when we found out there'd been an attack."

Em's and Benny's eyes follow us like a tennis match. Lucy yelps with joy and bolts to the door. "Since Gretchen's murder, the club has barely met," she says. "Almost nobody's used this room, so I've been sneaking in here to have my own private study hall. It's been great, except there's this annoying thing facilities won't clean: the door handles are *sticky*!"

With bravura showmanship, Lucy tosses open the doors, and me, Em, and Benny follow her into the empty hall. Lucy hurls herself onto the linoleum so that she's gazing up at 208's door handles. Benny and I crouch to see what she's smiling at: under the handle is a gummy, silvery residue, the kind leftover from duct tape.

"Watch enough murder shows," Lucy says, "you know how well tape can move prints."

"Oh my God . . ." I gasp.

Lucy scrambles upright, her eyes wild with discovery. "Mr. Sandman, dressed as a janitor, put duct tape on the door handles. He was watching who went inside. He knew when Queer Club met, and somehow, he knew most of us weren't coming." Lucy snaps her fingers with another idea. "He had to be wearing gloves or knew exactly where to grab the handle so he wouldn't leave his own prints." She points at me. "Then *you* open the door, boom. Fingerprints. He sees the little freshman coming, and oh no! He carefully opens the door for him. Boy leaves. He sees Cole coming— boom, snags his fingerprints." She slaps her hands together. "While you're all talking, he transfers your prints from the tape to the phones, hides them in your lockers, takes off the janitor getup, and leaves it on the bench, where Ms. Drake found it."

Lucy, surging with adrenaline, mimes explosions as she twirls giddily.

Benny, Em, and I fall silent with shock. That's it. That's how he did it.

"How did he do that *and* kill Gretchen?" Benny asks. "It all happened at once."

"Your master and apprentice," I say. "One of them was killing, the other was framing."

"OKAY!" Lucy shouts, the spirit taking her as she rides an invisible surfboard. Just as suddenly, exhaustion crumples her. "I gotta sit down." She squats on the floor, head between her knees as she nurses her energy back to calm.

Meanwhile, my energy is just getting cooking. I squeeze Benny's hand and tell him, "This is how we get Cole home."

As hope returns to Benny's eyes, I text my mom that we have breaking news.

CHAPTER TWENTY-FOUR
COLE

THE INTERROGATION ROOM IS small, airless, and hot. A two-way mirror hangs on the peeling, water-damaged wall beside me. Behind it, I imagine countless detectives, officers, and FBI agents are watching and listening. I keep glancing over in case it lights up like a *Drag Race* makeup mirror reveal. Surprise! All of this has just been an elaborate prank! Look, in the mirror—there's the infamous queen Monét X Change!

"If you want out of this cell," she says, *"you'll have to beat me in a lip sync to 'This Is My Life' by Dame Shirley Bassey!"*

Ugh, a ballad? I was hoping I could drop-splits and bussy-pop my way out of this.

"Cole, are you listening?" Uncle Nando asks.

Jerking out of my stress hypnosis, I wipe a film of sweat from my forehead. Uncle Nando sits with me at a rickety interrogation room table. I don't know how he's staying so cool; he's in a full suit—tailored, buttoned, and sharply ironed. His black hair—identical to mine before I bleached it—is slicked back but silvering at the temples. Exactly how I want to age if I get out of this alive.

I don't bother lying: "I wasn't paying attention, no."

Frowning, Uncle Nando taps an expensive silver pen against his legal pad. "You bleached that hair of yours down to your brain stem, mijo. You have got to take this seriously."

Oh, no, this man did not just. Today alone, I have been chased *twice* by a serial killer, fallen on top of a dead body, and then gotten shoved in an FBI van.

"I promise I'm taking this seriously," I say, struggling to swallow. "I'm just freaked, so it's hard to, you know, stay present." Tears rise unexpectedly and unwanted. I'm not a crier, and certainly not in front of Uncle Nando, but my body has other plans. "I'm clearly being targeted. I don't know how that phone or that razor thing got in my bag, but I think it was when the killer broke into my house—they were caught on camera. Isn't it obvious?"

The harder I push down my emotions, the harder they push back.

Shifting uncomfortably, Uncle Nando glances away from my tears, which dries my eyes as anger replaces all other emotions. "I'm sorry la fresita is bothering you."

He glances back, looking stung. "Fresa?"

"Abuela's funeral? I was twelve? You told me to stop crying."

"I *never* called you—"

"You told a little kid to stop crying at his grandma's funeral. What's the matter with you?"

Uncle Nando waves me off. If there weren't police watching from the other side of that mirror, I'd jump him right now and show him what happens when your nephew gets bigger than you. Instead, I let anger consume every atom in my body.

"Ask your mother," Uncle Nando says, embarrassed. "I was awful to everyone at that funeral. She was my mother." He shrugs, his scowl softening. "Don't listen to me." He shakes his legal pad. "Unless it's about this, right?"

As close as someone in my family will ever get to getting an apology.

"First thing you gotta know is they'll try to scare you and confuse you more than you already are," Uncle Nando whispers. "Their case isn't airtight, so they'll want to catch you in a lie or contradicting something you said before. So tell the whole truth, even about little things, even if you're scared it'll sound bad or get one of your friends in trouble. They're gonna have to prove everything later, so if you stick to facts as emotionlessly as possible, it makes their job harder."

I nod rapidly, willing Uncle Nando's even-keeled voice to transfer courage into my body. So far, it hasn't stuck. "This really sucks," I say.

His expression doesn't change. "No, it sucks for them

because this is now two times they've messed with you. I'm getting you out. I'm not the guy for hugs or funerals, but I'm the guy for this." His hand inches toward mine but stops. *No touching*, we were warned. "My ass is on the line here too. Do you have any idea what a golden boy you are to this family? When you were born, I tried holding you, and your abuela said, 'Gimme that baby! You'll drop him!' I'll be an outcast if I don't save you."

I smirk. No lies spoken. "I'm glad you're here."

"You better be." As he chuckles, a red light flashes over the door ahead. An alarm blares once, followed by the door's bolt locks sliding back. My heart hammers in my chest. When the door whines open, Agent Astadourian strides in alone—the first time I've seen her since she hauled me out of the library. She flops a green folder of evidence onto the table.

Bring it on, Special Agent. Open that folder, and Nando will dismantle it piece by piece and coolly explain what a travesty your case is.

"Special Agent Astadourian," Uncle Nando says, "all due respect, but I need assurances that your office won't be as sloppy as the department the last time you dragged my star-athlete, honor-student client in here on spurious evidence. Cole's name must be kept out of the press."

Astadourian nods, popping open the plastic lid on her coffee. "Until I charge him?"

Uppercut–pile driver combo to my chest—yet my uncle remains stone-faced. "*Are* you charging him?"

Astadourian smiles, crow's feet cracking around her deep-set eyes. Her beautiful maturity gives off such a powerful aura, I'd be obsessed with her if she wasn't trying to stomp out my life. She opens the green folder. "Let's start with some of that 'spurious' evidence."

Agent Astadourian spreads multiple photographs across the table, each with a fingerprint scan paperclipped to the top. My stomach lurches again, like I'm riding the lift hill on a roller coaster—*click-click, click-click* all the way up—building to something very chaotic.

She taps the first photo—a burner phone. "From February," she says. "Cole's prints on it, which sent a death threat to Grover Kendall, deceased." I hold my breath as she moves to a printed transcript. "Interviews with members of Stone Grove High's Queer Club admitting Cole has a history of verbal and emotional abuse against the victim."

"*Abuse?*" I interrupt hotly.

"Cole," Uncle Nando warns, and I fall silent. This is bullshit. Because Grover and I weren't friends anymore, suddenly I'm his abuser? How many of these claims are just people repeating exaggerated stories from Grover?

"How about 'bullying'?" asks Astadourian. "Is 'bullying' a better word?"

"Do you want me to answer?" I ask coldly. She nods.

"Grover, Dearie, and I were friends freshman year. Then we drifted apart from Grover. He was jealous I stayed so close with Dearie when he didn't because he had a huge crush on him. He was convinced we were a couple."

I take a breath. "Grover acted out, but only when I was alone. *I* was *his* target. I'm a big guy who doesn't get his feelings hurt easily, so bullying me looks different. Nobody noticed or cared. Not even Dearie, because Grover always acted so pathetic. He was a manipulator, and I don't take shit from bullies without saying something back." I lean forward, grateful to finally be letting this out. "I believe Grover methodically turned his friends in Queer Club against me. I'm not surprised you have little notes from people calling *me* an abuser because they couldn't spot real abuse when it was sitting next to them at lunch."

Uncle Nando whistles once, sounding impressed.

Astadourian and I don't break eye contact. After a long moment, she says, "Sounds like you have a lot of anger toward this boy." My jaw trembles, but I command it to remain set. "I'm curious. If it wasn't you sending these death threats, who do you think did?"

"Justin Saxby?"

"We'll get back to him." She flips to the next photograph: the CHEATER scratches on Julieta. "Grover defaced such a fine car." She clicks her tongue and cycles to the next photograph: a black-and-white close-up of a corpse's hand, its fingernails stained brown. *Grover.* "Blood under the victim's nails." She looks up at me. "Yours."

"He scratched me," I mumble, turning over my wrist to show the healed, dull-brown scars.

"Witnesses say it was some fight," Astadourian adds, sliding to the next photograph: cards with the message YOUR LONELY NIGHTS ARE OVER written on them. "Found at the crime scenes of Grover Kendall and Tabatha Drake. Your prints are on both."

"HOW?" The room feels tighter. I turn to Uncle Nando. "I never touched those notes." Those last words come out as a gasp. "The phone and razors in my bag. I had no idea they were there, but clearly during the break-in—"

"Let's jump to that." Unblinking, Astadourian slides over the next photo: another burner. "We recovered a phone from Mooncrest. Earlier in the day, it received these messages: *Grover is finally over. Disband the Queer Club chat before the movie so he won't feel safe texting anyone.*"

Unable to listen to anymore, I try to rub away this throbbing headache.

"We've been looking for the phone that sent these messages," Astadourian says, collecting the photos. "It was in your bag. When your friends ran out to tell me the killer was in the school, I called that number on a hope. You answered. And you had the trademark weapon in your hand."

"Why would he keep any of that on him?" Uncle Nando

260

asks. "The phone or the weapon." He peels off his glasses and wipes them with a microfiber cloth. "Or the other one in his locker. This is all suspiciously easy. Fingerprints on everything. Evidence left for anyone to find it."

Astadourian shuts her folder. "I didn't say he was smart."

Uncle Nando leans across the table, fuming. "This boy is the cleverest son of a bitch I've ever met, and ma'am, I studied at Georgetown. He stole my baseball signed by the '93 Angels roster. It is priceless. No one in our family knows how he stole it or where he hid it."

"It's in your china hutch," I mutter.

"What?"

"There's a false bottom Dearie and I made. It's in there." Nando clutches his chest like a doctor just told him he's gonna live. I shrug. "Payback for Abuela's funeral."

My revelation giving him a new outlook on life, Nando returns to Astadourian with strength. "There's a technique for determining if fingerprints have been moved from one surface to another. I'm assuming you've already done that test before dragging a traumatized child through all this?"

For a moment, Astadourian is speechless. "Mr. De Soto, we are performing those tests now based on new discoveries."

I don't know whether to be relieved or enraged.

Uncle Nando struggles to keep his anger intact behind that clenched jaw. "I think you don't know anything. I think this is another story of a lazy police force, out of ideas, desperate to pin the blame on somebody—bonus points for someone brown—so you can all go home in time for dinner. And you're going to let an innocent child rot in prison based on evidence that's so shaky, your only hope is you get a jury racist enough to believe it. And kids will keep dying."

For the first time since this nightmare began, I feel a deep, abiding strength.

Finally, *someone* has spoken the truth.

Agent Astadourian, as blank as a brick wall, pulls out a large Ziploc bag. Inside is a letter. "One last thing I want your thoughts on," she says. "We found it during a search of your bag."

She slides it to me. Even through the plastic, the letter's pristine handwriting is easy to read:

Dear Cole,

You make me feel young again. When Mark died, I thought everything was over. But after last night, I wrote more pages than I have in years. What a joy to still have surprises in life. You're a beautiful boy. I know what you're going to say. "You just think I'm a beautiful top." While that isn't untrue, you must know what a beautiful soul you have. You're going to have a lovely life in New York. The boys are going to find you! I'm jealous that you are just starting your life. Sometimes I wish I could get a second chance at one. Thank you for loving an old dummy like me.

Yours always, Claude

My heart is beating so fast, it might burst like a water balloon.

Claude Adams, the second victim after Gretchen. Killed in a cabin outside of Mooncrest.

"I've never seen this," I whisper in my smallest voice. "It's fake. I never met Claude . . ."

"So why are your fingerprints on the note?" Astadourian asks coldly.

"I don't know!" I look at Uncle Nando. "Maybe I touched it after Mr. Sandman stuffed it inside my bag along with all the other stuff?"

"Don't go worrying," Nando says, nodding. "You never had any contact with that man. I'm all over this." He turns to Astadourian. "Wait for the fingerprint test. Release Cole home. You're being misled. You have to understand that."

Astadourian takes a deep, angry breath. "We're out of time. Cole, I need you to help me find your partner. Where is Justin Saxby?"

"My partner?" I laugh, briefly forgetting my horrific situation. "What did you find at Justin's house? Were they dead? The officers missing from the car?"

Blank eyes from her as she says, "It'll look better on you if you cooperate." But I've already disappeared into my head, where it's safe. Astadourian leaves, and as she grips the door, she turns back. She almost looks . . . scared.

"Bodies are piling up. If it's not you, if I'm wrong, two killers want you gone. Either way, I'd say the safest place for you right now is a cell."

CHAPTER TWENTY-FIVE
DEARIE

OVER AN HOUR AFTER Lucy's fingerprint discovery, Mom arrived. I thought she would help and listen, but she barely even reacted to the news that we'd had a serious breakthrough in how the killers framed Cole. Instead she just dropped everyone off at their homes, telling each set of parents to keep their kids inside and not let them out under any circumstances. Worst of all, she won't discuss what her people found at Justin's house.

She won't talk about anything.

Mom just texts in silence in the parking lot of Tío Rio's, the family restaurant and karaoke bar run by Benny's dad. With the sun close to setting, the neon sign above the restaurant lights up in hot pink and violet. After a minute of her texting and me staring up at a billboard advertising tonight's musical act—a band called Laceface—I snap:

"MOM."

She flips her phone facedown and looks up, harassed. "Frankie?"

"Why are you mad at me?"

"Because you're trying to catch a pair of serial killers, you don't know what you're doing, and you have snuck off time and time again. Each time, the killers have found you, and each time, you have almost gotten yourself and your friends MURDERED." She blinks, catching herself before she gets too furious. "You're done."

My throat clenches. She's too angry to talk to, but Cole's life is at stake.

"Mom," I say softly, "my boyfriend is dead. My best friend is in jail. You have the wrong suspect. What else am I supposed to do?"

The car is brutally hot. Even through the exposed sides of my top, everything feels sticky. I don't know how Mom is existing in her pantsuit. She glances at her phone and then back to me.

"Lucy's fingerprint theory proves Cole's being framed, right?" I ask. "You're running your tests, and then Astadourian will have to—"

"Agent Astadourian has made up her mind," Mom says with a faraway rage. She knows Cole is innocent. In her face, I see the daily battles she's had with the FBI over this. Battles she's lost.

Mom sends another text, and I can almost see the code swimming past her eyes as she types. "If we're gonna help Cole," she says, "we're gonna need more support from the department. But I need you to trust me—and stay safe. Stop running off on your own." She looks at her phone again, and a new message softens her scowl into a smile. "Kevin is gonna help. I'm going to his place, and we'll brainstorm how to present this new evidence to Agent Astadourian."

Before I can beg her to let me come along, Mom gently rubs her thumb over my palm. Winking, she says, "Every Queer Club kid has been ordered to stay with their parents. Looks like you're coming with me."

Finally, a plan I can get behind.

Twenty minutes later, we finally reach Kevin's place. He lives near downtown, far from the suburban sprawl where Cole and I have suffered. Downtown Stone Grove has a gay nightlife—not that Kevin gets enough free time from his medical examiner duties to enjoy it, or so he says. His apartment complex looks like an old Palm Springs postcard: sunset-colored desert, surrounded by cacti and palms like a pleasant oasis. The building clearly used to be a motel that some ruthless landlord bought and converted. The stucco walls are decorated with sherbet orange–hued mid-century wall installations that look like surfboards.

A splash of queer decadence in a bloodlessly straight town.

Mom buzzes us in through the outer gate because she used to watch Kevin's cat when it was still around. He had that kitty for twenty long years—before I was even born—and she peacefully passed this January. Still, Kevin was a mess. I once heard him crying in our kitchen, telling Mom the cat was the only one who needed him. Even though Mom insisted that she needed (and loved) Kevin, his words stung my queer heart particularly harshly. Kevin is such a beautiful person, we assumed he dated around like Cole does and was happy with his life.

It's hard for Mom to understand queer loneliness. How it hides in the daylight.

Well, now Kevin can add me and Cole to the list of people who need him.

Beyond the gate, we cross the sleepy, motel-like courtyard with a shimmering pool in its center. Kevin told me this building was like a beehive of gays a few years ago, but for one reason or another, the other gays kept moving out and moving on. Another reason why I have to escape to a big city. I don't have it in me to weather small-town gayness.

My head on a swivel, I follow Mom to Kevin's apartment door. She knocks. After a few more tries with no answer, she texts Kevin. I glance behind me at the pool and all the quiet rooms with closed blinds. Spooky.

"He says the door's open," Mom says, putting away her phone and turning the doorknob.

Fear hits my heart like a railroad spike.

"Mom!" I whisper, clutching her wrist. She looks at me like I'm an alien, but I've crept into too many scary rooms today with disastrous results. "Why wouldn't Kevin just open the door?"

She doesn't blink. Her other hand floats soundlessly to her hip holster. She pops the clasp and pulls her service revolver. I want to leap backward, but I'm not leaving her side. Slowly, she returns to the door, weapon ready.

I hope I'm wrong.

Please be wrong.

Except Mr. Sandman has known where we're going to be every step of the way, a moment before we're supposed to be there. Anyone who tries to help us—Paul, Ms. Drake, even Kevin—is in danger.

The door opens with a creak. Everything is dark inside, but the harsh early evening sun illuminates enough to give us some hope that Mr. Sandman isn't waiting in the shadows. Mom enters first, weapon high, scanning the room, her back flush to the door to close off her vulnerabilities. "Stay," she tells me, so I linger in the doorway. Overhead, a rattling wall-unit AC blasts freezing air into the room. From here, I spot the red numbers of a thermostat: sixty-two degrees. Its sputtering white-noise hum prickles my neck hairs.

"Kevin?" Mom asks weakly. Stronger, she adds, "Say something."

His studio apartment is, of course, fabulously detailed. He knows how to feather his nest. Rose gold wall art. Lots of mirrors to expand the visual space. Tropical throw pillows on a beet-red sofa. No . . . Kevin's sofa is cream-colored . . .

"Mom, get out of there," I gasp, willing myself not to scream.

Kevin Benetti—my first crush, Mom's closest friend, and a beautiful, brilliant, and funny yet ultimately lonely man—lies dead on his stomach on the sofa, which has become soaked dark red from the enormous blood loss around his throat.

The razor necklace. A sandy-brown note lies tented on his back.

"No!" Mom squeals in a wounded, heartbroken way I've never heard from her before but will remember until the end of my life. I watch as she aims her revolver at the shadows, holding it steady as she scuttles backward out the door. When she's over the threshold and next to me again, her trembling hand moves to close the door, but I reach forward to do it for her.

"Frankie, stay close to me!" she shouts, and I dutifully cling to her like a barnacle as she shepherds us out of this hellish, lonesome motel and into her car. With one quick sweep, she scans the back seat for someone hiding. I grip the door handle, ready to leap back out if I see even a hint of a mask.

There's nothing. On a pained grunt, she slaps the door locks, and we're sealed inside.

I don't talk or hug her. Her business side rapidly takes

over, even as tears stream into her lap. Once she radios for backup, she returns to her phone and rapidly pulls up Kevin's number in Find My Friends.

She's tracking his phone. Mr. Sandman is the one who's been texting her, not Kevin.

"He's in the building," she says, gazing at the blinking location dot.

I lean closer to Mom's phone as she cycles back to her text chain with Kevin.

The killer is typing.

The bubbles briefly stop, and so does my breath. Finally, a message comes:

I'm done with his phone now. Goodbye, Mary.

CHAPTER TWENTY-SIX
COLE

HOW AM I GONNA tell time in prison? Do they have clocks everywhere? I'm used to checking my phone like it's some old-timey pocket watch, but now I'm stuck in a cell in the bowels of the Stone Grove Sheriff's Station with no phone, no clock, and no window to see if it's day or night. I'm starting to feel a little . . . unsettled.

Why is *this* the worst part of being accused of serial killing?

My cell looks old—everything in this town hasn't been updated since the seventies. This basement is nothing but long rows of iron cages facing each other. My cell has a dingy cot, a sink, a toilet, and a view of the small staircase leading up into the main station. The sounds of life above are comforting—chattering voices, ringing phones, typing keyboards. Even if they are chattering, calling, and typing up my imminent doom.

This ratshit cell is merely a stopover—a brief oasis before I'm sent to The Big Boy Place.

Astadourian is convinced it's me and Justin. He and I

couldn't be lab partners without strangling each other, but sure, we orchestrated this homicidal masterpiece.

No one can even scrounge up a suitable motive for why it's us. Bad attitudes? Please.

While we await the results of the fingerprint testing, Uncle Nando is updating my moms, who ordered a spread of catering for the onslaught of LA and Tucson relatives about to descend on my house to support me. Most importantly, I asked Nando to bring Julieta from the school parking lot to the station and cover it with a tarp. Any minute now, people will find out I'm being held for questioning, and my CHEATER-branded baby will be the first victim of mob justice.

Not on my watch.

"It's up to you," I sing softly to myself, lying on my side on the cot and staring into space. "New York, New York" wormed its way into my brain while I was scrolling through disaster scenarios. It's comforting imagining my life at Columbia.

In my jailhouse hallucination, Dearie gets so fed up with his mom, this town, and our old lives that he ditches LA and comes with me to New York. We'll make a brand-new start!

"It's up to you," I sing blankly on my jail cot. *"It's up to YOU."* As I sit up, a rush of blood to the head tilts the room. *"If I can make it in jail, I'll make it anywhere!"* I stomp the cement floor, building up rhythm and volume. *"Because it's up to ME, New York!"*

I slap the iron bars like drums as a berserk energy overtakes me.

The noise draws the only other person down here to bolt upright from their cot. A white, fortysomething dude with a nasty, unwashed T-shirt and a shaved head. "SHUT UP," he hollers.

I push my nose and lips through the gaps between the bars. "Don't mess with me, man. I'm in here for mass murdering."

He drops back to his cot, muttering, "Damn tweaking kid."

Well, that took care of him. I can handle prison. The guys I can't get tough on, I'll just act like a wacked-out, high-as-hell weirdo, and they'll leave me alone. As long as I don't think about where I am or the fact the real killers are *not* in jail . . . then I'm okay.

God, I need water.

CREAAAAAK. A rusted hinge whines as the door at the top of the stairs opens. From here, all I can see are legs—smooth, long legs in short shorts. Benny—my Benny bunny. I knew that he and Dearie were okay, but the visual proof of it pummels me.

Loopy from isolation, I bounce giddily on my toes like an eighties aerobics instructor as Benny arrives down the stairs. "Hey, Cole," he says with vulnerable, frightened eyes.

"Hey, you," I say. "It's not safe. You should be home."

"I had to see you. Lucy found something that could help. Dearie took it to his mom."

As Benny recounts the tale of the mysterious finger-prints, my brain returns to level flying altitude. That's why Astadourian was suddenly running those tests. If it clears us, the only thing she could nail me on is that fake Claude Adams letter . . .

I can't believe Grover and Theo's "Slutty Cole & Dearie" narrative could make it to a federal trial. Because of them, it's easy for people to believe I'd hook up with a gazillion-year-old man in his writing cabin, butcher him, and then keep his love letter hanging around.

When we're finished trading stories, the quaking, awful silence returns.

There's pain behind Benny's eyes.

"You need to get home," I say.

"Don't tell me what to do." He steps closer, the overhead lights casting deep shadows from his glasses across his round cheeks and full lips. If I were anywhere else with him . . .

I grip the iron bars as realization crashes onto my mind like waves on a rocky shore:

Logic and facts are on my side, but that doesn't always save people in situations like this. I've seen enough true crime, and I've lived enough days in this ugly town. Sometimes, being illogical and irrational just shovels more and more power into your life.

"Please, Benny," I finally say. "I can't lose any more people."

"You're not going to." He steps closer, his expression stiffening. "Don't make fun of me, but I can be psychic sometimes, and I've seen it happen: whoever's doing this, you and me stop them."

My dimples flare. "Crystals tell you all that?"

"I said no making fun!"

"Sorry, I had to!" Unable to stop smiling, I press my face to the bars and gaze at my boy. Is he a boyfriend? Seems like a prospect, but I want to wait to assess something so important until after the danger has passed.

I flap my fingers through the bars. His small, soft hands are so close.

"I really want to touch you," I say.

He smirks. "Plenty of time for that, after we catch the master and apprentice."

Through many unnecessary Sith Lord analogies, Benny takes me through his and Dearie's logical conclusion about the two Sandmen.

"So, it's Leo?" I ask. "Talking to him, he just felt so victimized by all this. He could've been lying, but I don't think so. My radar is never wrong."

Benny frowns. "Ms. Drake was outside on the phone with Leo during the murder."

I nod. "And his calls pinged off the Mooncrest cell tower. He wasn't at the school."

Another dead end.

I pace my cell, thinking of how Leo could be so continually linked to the crimes, but never involved. Like someone was framing him the way they're framing me. Someone close.

"Something else is bugging me," I say. "That fake letter from Claude Adams said I was gonna have a great time in New York."

"New York?" Benny asks with a drop of sadness.

"I might be, sort of, going to film school there in the fall. You know, if I'm not in prison."

"Oh."

I don't look at him. I just keep pacing my cell. My thoughts are spinning too much on the letter and its mysteries to dwell on the fact that this is not how I wanted to bring up New York to Benny.

"I'm sorry I didn't tell you," I say. "That's actually what's bothering me. I didn't tell anyone. Just my family and Dearie. So why is Claude Adams writing to me about New York when Columbia hadn't even accepted me before he was killed?"

Benny bites his thumbnail as he processes these overlapping, unpleasant realities. "So, you're saying Dearie faked that letter?"

I snort. "He would never. But . . . there is one other person I told."

I stop pacing.

A wretched little bug of an idea slithers through my brain. If I'm right—as I so often am—Leo Townsend is innocent.

Two Sandmen. Master and apprentice. Knows the Queer Club. Could get close enough to me to put my prints on almost anything. And then I remember something else—my palms sweating with this awful thought, I march toward the bars—toward Benny. "Benny, run upstairs and call my uncle." He doesn't blink. "Tell him he needs to make Agent Astadourian check Ms. Drake's phone for one more call."

CHAPTER TWENTY-SEVEN

DEARIE

THE BACKUP MOM CALLED for arrives—four officers loyal to her over Agent Astadourian. They promise to give her a head start before alerting the agents about Kevin's murder. Since it looks like Kevin was killed before Cole was jailed, Mom wants to avoid this new murder being pinned on Cole. And if Mom called in Astadourian herself, she'd be stuck following orders, returning to the station.

Mom has other plans.

She and I drive in silence back through the suburbs. All the while, I wait for her tears to return. Some kind of release. I know they're there, like thick storm clouds with no rain.

"Where are we going?" I ask, worrying the strap of my seat belt.

"Mooncrest," she says, dialing a number.

"Are you gonna arrest Leo?"

"I just want to talk to him, with no big police presence around to scare him. Just talk. The last time I was with him, I could tell he wasn't saying everything. Whether or not he's the Sandman, he knows something. Astadourian doesn't want us harassing him anymore, but . . . he'll talk to me."

"Why?"

Mom smiles. "Because I won't be Detective Dearie, I'll be your mom."

My heart lifts. I just want her to quit this goddamn job, like she's always saying.

Please, let this be retirement.

Mom presses her phone to her ear as it rings. "Detective Dearie. Are you still watching Leo Townsend?" Murmuring on the other end. "Good. Collect him. No arrest. Walk softly. If he runs, hold him, but I'd prefer you do it friendly. Bring him somewhere quiet where we can talk." More murmuring, this time sounding surprised. "No, I'm coming to you. Twenty minutes. Whatever you do, don't let him near a phone. No calls, texts, nothing."

Mom hangs up. She holds the phone to her lips, deep in thought.

I reach for her arm. When my touch makes contact, she twitches as if I were the killer, and it makes me jump. After she heaves a sigh of relief, her tears come.

"What is it?" I ask.

"He knew," she cries. "The killer knew Kevin was alone and no one would find him all day."

On a terrible, pained roar, Mom unleashes her fury on her steering wheel. I don't flinch, speak, or move. "He must've been so scared," Mom whimpers as she strangles the steering wheel. "He was having nightmares he'd be next. I promised him . . . Why didn't he *tell* me he got a message? I would've brought him home."

Now I break. The grief is too much. Cole in jail. Grover in the morgue. Kevin. Paul. Gretchen. Ms. Drake. Even Claude Adams. All these people who didn't have someone who loved them enough to save them.

"I made fun of Kevin," I say, my voice shaking. "Jokes about being old and his bad dates and . . . Grover was right. I'm such an asshole."

She squints. "Grover said that?"

"No, um . . ." I continue fiddling with the seat belt and avoiding her mom gaze. "He just—he joked. But he liked Kevin. And I really liked Kevin being around."

Mom's hand finds my leg. "Kevin loved you. He thought of himself as your uncle."

"I thought that too." I pause. "Was he lonely?"

Mom shakes her head softly. "Sometimes. Then other times, no. It's not always easy to see."

I nod, over and over, until the truth rises in me like an elevator. "I'm lonely, Mom."

"I know." Mom reaches across to brush my cheek. "That's why we're gonna pay a visit to Mr. Townsend. It's time for him to tell his story, and maybe we can end this."

Minutes later, the suburbs of Stone Grove sink into our

rearview as the lowering sun splashes brilliant, warm rays across the red mesas. As we soar down Mooncrest Highway toward the cemetery, the shocking fuchsia from cactus blossoms smother the landscape. It's a much different drive from when Cole and I came at night three days ago. That trip was doom-filled, with Mr. Sandman lurking behind every shadow, but now there's nowhere for him to hide in the sunset rays of this beautiful, lonely town I will miss so much.

DEAD AHEAD reads the sign posted to the cactus.

Not anymore. No more death.

Beside me, Mom lowers her window, and our bulleting speed tosses her hair in every direction. Her steel gaze never strays from the road. I lower my window, letting the wind whip my curls and declutter my thoughts.

Mom will question Leo. He'll crack and name the other killer, and if it's not Justin, I'll sexually worship Mike Mancini for a week.

Well. I mean, that wouldn't be the worst thing. Mike *is* cute, and I *am* starving. Anyway, it's time to wrap this up.

We pass beneath the archway into Mooncrest Cemetery. Even though the sun is about to dip below the mesa, the area feels less frightening today. Ray Fletcher's projection booth rises high behind the empty picnic arena like a lifeguard tower. The only part of Mooncrest that feels scarier now is the entrance to the arena, which has been barricaded by yellow police tape.

Pain scrapes against my chest. Grover went in but never came out.

Mom hops out to tear the police tape in half, and then climbs back in to drive us the rest of the way to the projection booth. From the driver's seat, she scans the arena, searching for signs of the officers she ordered to bring Leo.

Instead, we find Ray Fletcher, staggering down the small steps from his booth to the lawn. He looks like he's been partying all night. No spiffy, kindly Tom Hanks gentleman from Friday's screening. This evening, Ray sports a two-day-old silver scruff and a rumpled dress shirt with conspicuous stains. His walk is wobbly as he approaches the car. Mom leaps out.

Oh God. I'd forgotten Cole told me Ms. Drake was his daughter.

He's been all alone out here, getting piss drunk with the news.

"Detective," Ray greets Mom cheerfully, shielding his eyes against the sun.

"Mr. Fletcher," Mom greets him kindly. "I'm looking for the officers I posted. Have you seen them in the last half hour?"

"Yeah, they came 'round," Ray slurs drunkenly, "told my friend to come with them, and frog-marched him past the refreshments tent."

Stumbling as he turns, Ray waves toward the far end of

the perimeter fence, where Grover was found. From this distance, the refreshments tent looks as small as a Monopoly hotel. Mom nods, turns to me in the passenger seat, and says, "Wait here."

As badly as I want to watch Mom put the heat on Leo, it's probably going to yield the best results if she does it alone. Plus, the last place I want to be is behind that goddamn refreshments tent again. Grover's blood is probably still on the sand.

As Mom walks out to meet her officers, Ray barks powerlessly after her, "What about my friend?" The man looks so defeated, I can't just leave him there.

I slip out, leaving the passenger door ajar. Cole is more familiar with Ray than I am, but we're friendly, he just lost his daughter, and he needs someone to talk to.

"Don't suppose you'll be able to illuminate me, Frankie?" Ray asks with a tired laugh. "On what the fuck's going on in this town?"

I return the laugh, hugging my bare arms as the evening cools all around me. "I wish I could explain anything that's happened this year." Ray laughs again. He leans against the hood of Mom's car again but loses his footing. I rush to catch him. "Whoa, uh . . . You okay?"

"No." Ray runs a shaking hand over his forehead. "My daughter's dead."

I feel Ray trembling as I try to help him stand. I can't

believe how many grieving people I've been comforting in one day. "I, uh, I heard. Well, I was there. I'm sorry."

Ray nods, his chin trembling as he tries to speak a terrible truth. "Tabatha and I were just starting to know each other again." He grips his head with a fierce pain. "Now I'll never . . ." He exhales deeply to pull himself together. "I didn't like her marrying my old friend, but you can't get in the way of that kind of thing. Fifty years I've known Leo. I convinced him to move here, you know? My family always visited his in San Diego. It got me out of this dump every once in a while, but then that terrible business with the—"

Brrrriiiiiiiiiinnggggg.

I leap like someone lit a firecracker between my toes. Ray looks around, confused.

The phone rings again—from Mom's car. She left her phone behind. "Sorry," I say, running for the phone. Mom's caller ID strikes me with a gut punch: Agent Astadourian.

Shit. She'll ruin everything.

I ignore it. Mom doesn't want her knowing where we are.

But before I walk back to Ray, my own phone goes off in my back pocket: *Bzzzzzttttt.*

It's Benny.

He wouldn't call unless there's news or trouble—or news and trouble. "You okay, Benny?" I sit down, half in the car and half out.

"Dearie, where are you right now?" Benny asks, sounding frenzied.

"Mooncrest," I say. "My mom said—uh—don't tell anyone."

"Oh my God." Benny shouts to the other people in the room with him.

"Benny, what's going on—?"

"Dearie, we found something!"

Before he can say anymore, a more urgent voice wrestles his phone away: "Frankie, it's Agent Astadourian. Put your mom on."

I pluck at my vinyl seat and pray the truth doesn't ruin things: "She's talking to Leo."

"Frankie, get in the car, find your mother, and get back here."

Outside the car, Ray Fletcher sways dangerously as he tries standing straight.

"What did Benny find?" I ask low, so Ray doesn't hear. "Why is he with you?"

"Your mom's back," Ray slurs. I strain over the dashboard, and Mom is indeed in the distance, a small Monopoly piece on her way back to me. At least she'll be able to take this call, and I don't have to keep being yelled at by Double-A Batteries.

"I'm telling you this because you're in danger," Astadourian says. I don't interrupt—she has my attention.

Something feels wrong. "The day Gretchen was killed, Leo called Tabatha Drake multiple times before she answered. I didn't pursue it because his calls pinged off a cell tower near Mooncrest."

"Oh, that's wild," I say, hoping I sound shocked at this brand-new information.

"Mom looks mad," Ray says outside. I glance above the dashboard again, and sure enough, Mom is closer but still a football stadium away. She's running like a cheetah. My heart drops—what's happened? Another body?

"I overlooked something," Astadourian explains. "Leo wasn't the only one who called Tabatha that day. Ray Fletcher—her father—called. It was his call that convinced her to go outside and talk to Leo. Frankie, we just searched Ray's call, and it pinged off a tower next to the school. He was in the school when Gretchen died."

My phone almost leaves my hand.

I peer over the dashboard. Mom is sprinting toward me—still so far away. Her gun is drawn.

"Frankie," Astadourian pleads, "we lost contact with the officers at Mooncrest fifteen minutes ago. Do not go near Ray Fletcher."

I can't move.

Ray walks around the car toward me, his drunken stumbling suddenly perfectly, soberly smooth. Many dreadful realities crash down on me at once:

It's Ray—Mr. Sandman, the original.

The police are dead.

Leo is dead.

Mom found their bodies, like Grover, stacked behind the refreshments tent.

And one final truth: she won't make it to me in time.

"He's here," I say, just as Mooncrest's friendly grandpa leans down, smiling.

A large, powerful hand snatches the back of my hair as swiftly as a snake bite, and I'm dragged from the car. Pain like nothing I've ever felt before detonates in my skull as he hoists me by my hair to my feet. A blade arrives at my throat the moment Mom does.

"FREEZE!" she screams, aiming her weapon.

Mr. Sandman roars, "MOVE, AND I KILL HIM!"

CHAPTER TWENTY-EIGHT

COLE

FROM MY CELL, ALL I can hear from upstairs is shouting. Something's gotten them whipped up into a big frenzy. I cannot believe that, after all those hours I sank into watching *Your Lonely Nights Are Over*, it was Ray all along. Disturbed by the implications, yet satisfied that I'm right once again, I lie back on my cot and kick off my shoes. What's better, I was able to pick apart Agent Astadourian's weak case against me from inside my literal cage.

All Uncle Nando needs to do is get Columbia to confirm the date they sent my acceptance letter and see how it majorly doesn't match Claude Adams's alive era. That and Lucy's fingerprint theory will cast all of this evidence into question, and we'll be suing the FBI by breakfast tomorrow.

Then, I'll be home free. But my stomach turns thinking about Ray. All the hours I spent with him alone in the projection booth. And all that time I spent watching that show, how could I have known I was becoming friends with one of the world's most infamous monsters?

And I told Ray *everything*. About New York, because I was excited to share my news with a fellow film guy; about my stuff with Dearie, my fight with Grover, my issues with the Queer Club. He had every bit of information he'd ever need to set me up. I was always in his projection booth, touching things, touching papers that probably wound up being Mr. Sandman notes and incriminating letters. He wore white gloves to load the film canisters—protecting his own prints from getting on anything I might touch.

And Ray probably had a lifetime of making sure his old buddy Leo took the heat for him. Leo warned me the killer was already in my life. Did he know then? Did he always suspect his old buddy? And Ray killed his own daughter, Ms. Drake? Why?

Who knows why any of these fuckers do what they do!

I can't help but think about Astadourian's face when I asked about Justin's house. She looked gutted, as if she was thinking about Justin massacring his family. But when we were in there, Justin's dad sounded like he was begging to see his son, like *Justin* was in danger.

What was really going on in there?

I'm on my back, in the middle of whistling and daydreaming about my congratulatory news conference, when the upstairs door opens with a sharp whine. Benny leaps downstairs like he's running from a panther. He reaches my cell, out of breath, and huffs, "You were right."

His lips are shaking.

"What's wrong?" I ask, sitting up. Benny clutches his chest to slow his breathing. He looks at me, shattered eyes behind his glasses, and wants to say something . . . but can't. "Benny, what?"

"Dearie went to Mooncrest. Ray's got him."

DAMMIT, COLE, YOU'VE GOTTA BE RIGHT ALL THE TIME.

I spin around, willing my brain to think of a new plan.

"Everyone's heading out there now," Benny says.

My vision blurs. The vertical bars surrounding me double and blend together.

I reach through the bars, grab Benny by the back of his collar, and bring him to my lips. The kiss is soft, urgent, and quick—and not allowed, but the police should be busy saving Dearie, not minding what I'm doing. I needed to send Benny off with something.

"Go home," I say, my dad voice emerging. "The second killer's still out there."

"What about you?" he asks desperately.

"I'm in a cage. Sandman can't get me. GO!"

Benny leaps onto his tiptoes to kiss me one last time before sprinting away. The basement door shuts behind him, and I'm thrown back into silence.

CHAPTER TWENTY-NINE
DEARIE

THE SUN HAS LEFT us with shocking speed. The moment it dipped beneath the grand mesa bordering Mooncrest, the air became freezing as dark violet twilight swallowed the picnic arena. Ray Fletcher and Mom circle each other between the projection booth tower and the parking lot. Mom has her gun trained on him. She doesn't blink. Ray moves with equal calm, one hand gripping my hair, the other gently pressing a knife to my throat.

America's most infamous living serial killer is currently pushing a blade against my jugular, and I never even wanted to watch that goddamn show. All my body wants to do is take a hit from the vape pen in my pocket, but my brain knows to keep absolutely still or it's all over.

"Where are you gonna go, Ray?" Mom asks. He laughs, and his breath smells like Cherry Coke. That drunken act was a lie to make us think he was grieving the daughter he killed.

Poor Ms. Drake.

"Detective, I'm not going anywhere," Ray says. "My daughter's dead, so it's the end of the line for me."

"I agree." Mom takes a deep breath. "Why don't you let Frankie go, and we'll talk?"

Ray groans. "No, *no*, Detective. This is your son. Your only child. Tell me to let *your son* go."

"That's what I said."

"Say 'let my son go' or he dies." The knife pushes against my neck with another ounce of pressure. I take a sharp breath.

Mom twitches. "Let my son go!"

My mother's plea has hit a button with Ray. He exhales luxuriously, the way I do when I'm vaping with Cole and feeling my oats. GOD, I want my pen so badly.

"The way you've been keeping your emotions out of this, Detective," he says. "You hide them so neatly."

Ray pushes his blade deeper. I feel the first hint of pain. I squeal.

Something about this knife is making me feel delirious. Almost . . . nostalgic somehow?

Ray chuckles. "Detective, the way your emotions flowed into those words: *My son. Let MY SON go.* That's how you beg. I begged my apprentice not to kill my daughter. I said take someone else from the club instead, but you know kids. Never listening." So the second killer *is* a student. Ray snickers again. "But I *can* be moved by begging. You begged well.

Let MY SON go. Do you know what I heard underneath those words? Answer."

"Fear," Mom says without pause.

"It's deeper than fear. I heard time travel. Your mind jumped into your miserable future: Christmases, birthdays, movie nights. And *your son*'s not there."

"Please!" Mom's voice cracks, but her weapon never wavers. Fresh pain shoots through my skull as Ray hoists me by my hair until I'm on tiptoes.

"Detective, call all units down here. Everyone you've got in this rinky-dink town."

"Why would you want that?" she asks cautiously.

"Like you said, I can't run. I want a BIG send-off. I think I've earned it."

"My radio's in the car, and I'm not letting you out of my sight."

"Your phone," I say, my voice strained against the pressure of the blade. "It's right there on my seat. The door's open. Just reach back."

"See?" Ray whispers. "Teamwork. Call now or I kill him."

Slowly, Mom creeps toward her car's open passenger door in small, sideways steps. She searches frantically behind her back, not taking her eyes (or gun) off Ray. Finally, I hear her phone make a soft *bloop* sound.

"Call Agent Astadourian," she says, and the phone obeys.

One ring later, Astadourian's voice comes: *"Mary, where are you? It's Ray! Not Leo—"*

"I know," Mom interrupts, staring at us for a long, dreadful moment. "Ray's got Fr—" She stops herself before correcting. "Ray's got my son."

"Smart girl," Fletcher whispers, impressed. The effect is as intoxicating on me as it is on Mr. Sandman. Every time Mom says *my son*, my death somehow becomes closer. Clearer. Everyone I won't see, everything I won't do. No creative empire. No LA boyfriend. No Cole. I'll never even get to meet the person I was becoming.

"He knows he can't run," Mom says. "He wants all units at Mooncrest for a big send-off."

"*. . . Then he'll get one*," Astadourian replies.

Mom's eyes move as fast as a hummingbird from Ray to me. "Hurry."

With that, Mom drops her phone and creeps toward us under the entry gate. The purple twilight sky darkens to indigo. Night is engulfing us, but without any of the Mooncrest stadium lamps on, there won't be any visibility soon for Mom to take her shot.

Mr. Sandman, however, only has to flick his blade. Darkness gives him an advantage.

Ray clicks his tongue disapprovingly. "Oh, Leo. His family was so hospitable to mine every time we visited San Diego, I hated scapegoating him. But it was too easy.

Everyone was looking for a local. No one ever considered that the killer was simply a bored country boy in town on vacation."

"Why'd it start again, Ray?" Mom asks. "Did you get bored?"

She steps closer, moving in millimeter-short spurts. In the night, I'm starting to lose details of her face.

"My apprentice found me." Ray chuckles. "I was retired. That show started up, and everyone got the bug. My apprentice is so clever. They put it together—what none of you ever could my whole time living here. Ambitious, too. If you want to know, they've done every new kill, except for Leo and your officers. Had to improvise when I was told you were coming. Oh, and Claude Adams. A request from my apprentice: I could pick anyone. They just had to be a gay man. And Claude was so lonely."

The Smiling Sandman. *Justin?* It could be any of the Queer Club kids obsessed with thinking Cole is the reason their lives are miserable.

"Who's your apprentice, Ray?" Mom asks from the enveloping darkness.

He whistles. "That would spoil the surprise. But don't worry—you won't be waiting long. They have a plan. Frankie, I'm just sorry you'll never get to meet them."

"Mom . . ." I whisper. I can't see her face—just an outline in the shadows.

"I'm here, baby," she whispers, no longer able to keep the terror from her voice.

In the dark, my hand closes around the vape pen in my pocket. Ray doesn't move. He didn't see me. I only have one shot, but I'm crafty. Queers know how not to be seen.

Ray steps backward, dragging me away from Mom, the knife still tight against my throat.

Now or never, ho.

As Ray pulls me, I whirl the vape through the air, unnoticed, until its electric blue tip is all Ray Fletcher's left eye will ever see again. The pen drives with such force, it meets with almost no resistance. Foul-smelling liquid splatters onto my neck. The pain must be excruciating because his hand leaves my hair, and his blade leaves my neck. I drop to the ground, trying to get away, but Mr. Sandman swipes the knife through the air and my forearm opens with instant, lacerating pain. I can't see how deep the cut is, but there's no time to look. I open my phone flashlight, shine it on Ray, illuminating his gushing eye. "NOW!" I shout.

A crack erupts through the silent desert as Mom fires.

Ray is thrown off his feet, and he lands powerfully on his back.

"Shine your light!" Mom orders, and I scramble to meet her, blood dripping down my arm as I turn the flashlight toward Ray. He clutches a pooling wound on his shoulder, tapping helplessly at it before looking at us.

"Who's the other killer?" Mom asks, pointing her gun at him.

Ray laughs on the ground. "Are the police coming?"

"Any minute."

"Good." His laughter becomes a coughing fit. "You fell for it."

"Fell for *what*?"

"You'll never stop my apprentice in time," he says. With his good arm, Ray raises his blade and opens his own throat. Mom and I scream for him to stop, but there's no use. As his throat pumps out a river of crimson, his hands flop limply.

"WHAT'S THEIR NAME?" Mom kicks Ray's shoe, but his leg just sways and then stops.

Decades of murderous American history spill into the soil of Mooncrest cemetery. Ray's dead. The original Mr. Sandman.

In the distance, a rhythmic thumping strikes the air—helicopters. Astadourian is close.

Shining my light on my arm, I see it's a shallow wound, painful and leaking—but a bandage is all I'll need. Mom pulls me into the fiercest hug. "Frankie," she gasps into my neck, rubbing my hair over and over. "It was so dark. I couldn't see you."

I try hugging tighter, but my legs are losing strength—and Ray's ghoulish last words still pound through my mind.

"What did he mean, we 'fell for it'?" I ask. "How is that a trap?"

Agent Astadourian rallied the entire station to speed the fifteen miles out here to the middle of nowhere. I can just see the police lights in the distance. They're here.

Ray said we wouldn't stop the Smiling Sandman in time. Stop what?

But then the answer unspools in my mind like a movie: The station is empty. All officers are racing to the desert, miles from town. The Smiling Sandman walks toward their next target with no one to stop them and nowhere for the next victim to run.

It *is* a trap.

I snatch Mom's wrist. "Order your units back to the station."

"Why?" she asks.

"Cole's alone! He's next."

CHAPTER THIRTY
COLE

IN MY CELL, SILENCE crushes me. There's no more bustle of officers and desk clerks upstairs. No shouted phone calls. Just the weak snores of the drunken man three cells over and my own shuddering breath. A nauseated, seasick swell capsizes my stomach, and I lurch forward, holding myself upright against my cage's iron bars. I wince back a barrage of sharp thoughts:

Ray Fletcher has Dearie.

I'm in a cage and can't help.

And there's a lot fewer people in this station than there were a minute ago.

Sweat streams down my cheeks. I press my forehead to the bars to concentrate on organizing my thoughts. Horrific, grisly images from *Your Lonely Nights Are Over* rush to the forefront of my mind. Ray killed them all. The open, perforated throats. He's gotten away with it for decades, and now he has Dearie.

Finally, there's nothing left to do but let the ugliest thought inside: Dearie could already be dead. I spin away from the bars, down becomes up, and I land on my knees against the cement. Before I can stop myself, before I can make it to the bowl, the contents of my stomach spray loudly against the floor.

A few cells over, the drunken man groans sleepily and mutters into his mattress, ". . . What the . . . ? 'M tryin' to sleep this off, kid . . ."

The sour stench is everywhere.

Unfortunately, clearing out my guts doesn't clear my head. I spit onto the floor until my mouth is clean, crawl onto my cot, curl into a ball, and tremble. No strategies come. No thoughts about the second killer's identity, reasons, or next steps. Not even grief finds me. Instead, my mind is pummeled with *No, no, no, no, no, no, no, no, no, no, no, no, no* over and over until I'm numb.

The lights go out.

Pitch-darkness swallows the jail. I can barely see the hand in front of my face.

Is it lights-out already? I'd welcome sleep, but it feels too early. Like something's wrong.

In the dark, a foot softly slaps against the floor, as quiet as a raindrop. I sit up. No breathing. I don't make a sound. The foot taps again. Another step. This one is louder. No, not louder—*closer*. Someone is walking toward me. That door at the top of the stairs is creaky as hell, and I didn't hear it open. Whoever this is was already in here.

The Smiling Sandman.

I cover my mouth. My heartbeat plays ping-pong against my rib cage.

Closer steps. He's outside the cell.

He can't get in. It's too dark. He couldn't see even if he could.

Cliiiiiiick. A heavy key slides into the lock three feet behind my head.

No way.

Shiiiiiiiiiiiiink. The cage door rattles as the key turns the massive lock.

No WAY.

Shuuuunk-a-shuuuuunk-a-shuuuuuuuuuunk. My cell opens.

He's inside.

Get up, Cole. NOW.

The Smiling Sandman's foot taps against my cell floor once . . . twice . . . His mask-muffled breath fills my ears. I scramble toward the foot of my cot, but a rubber-grip glove closes around my ankle. Screaming, I flail my other leg until I hit something solid. First, the cot. Then the floor. Then the wall. Finally—a limb.

"*GYAH!*" the killer shouts in a pained cry. My ankle is free.

Nimbly, I shoulder-roll off the mattress and then shuffle underneath the bed.

He won't find me in the dark.

"*GAAAHH!*" he roars as the cot lifts off the ground as easily as a chair before clattering noisily against the wall. He knows where I am.

He's got night vision, and I'm groping around in the dark. Perfect.

Just run, Cole. Your cell is open. Start swinging, he'll back away, and you can make it out!

But what if some cops still think I'm the killer? They'll shoot if they see me escaping.

COLE. IF. YOU. STAY. HERE. YOU. WILL. DIE.

RUN!

I make it a few steps before my throat catches on something rough and thick. My fingers fly to my neck to free myself. It's not a razor necklace—it's a noose.

"NO!" I choke out. "HELP ME! WAKE UP!"

But my intoxicated cellmate's snores continue to fill the jail.

Behind me, the Smiling Sandman lets out a nasally, cruel laugh. My hands close around the killer's wrists, and I pull with my entire wrestler's weight—I'm gonna flip this fucko and pin him like it's just another match and not a fight for my life. But as I hoist, something hard and bony finds my back—his raised knee, most likely. The pain is so sudden and searing, I can only make gurgling noises. Grunting, the killer tries lifting me off the ground as he tightens his noose, but I'm too heavy and wriggling too hard. "*GRRRRRAAAHHH!*" he bellows in frustration, dragging me across the room to get stronger footing.

Turns out, I unwittingly already set a trap for him.

The Smiling Sandman's shoes squeak on something squishy and wet—my stress vomit. He loses his balance, and we're both pulled to the ground. He lands first, and I drop on top of him like a sandbag. Finally, his noose slackens, and wind rushes into my lungs. We both gasp for air, but as soon as I've gulped a hearty swig of oxygen, I drive my elbow into what I hope is his abdomen.

He squeals like an anguished pig.

I start pounding. Now it's not a wrestling match; he's a punching bag. Come on, Sandman, let me show what these arms are for—well, besides catching the eyes of half of Tucson's queer (and bored straight) population. *SLAM. SLAM. SLAM.* Each wild punch I land gives me a clearer idea of where he's at: a shoulder, the mask, an arm, and finally, his rib cage.

POUND. POUND. POUND.

I whale on the same spot on his chest over and over, and with any luck, I'll break his ribs or puncture his lung.

I raise my fist one more time . . .

But the killer's noose, which had been lying slack around my throat, clamps tightly once again. Tighter than ever. His strength has returned. His will to live (or his will to kill me) is greater than my training.

I spit at him. Kick his ankles. Slap at his hands.

But his grip on me stays firm.

Oh, this asshole wants me *dead* dead.

We're in a fight to the grave.

With one last bellowing scream, my strength gives out. He's too aggressive. I fall to my knees, the noose unrelenting.

It's okay. I'll see Dearie soon. An eternity of chilling with Dearie. That doesn't sound so bad.

"*Hey, you!*" I hear my bestie say.

I smile at my deathbed delusion. "Hey, you . . ." I rasp.

Suddenly, black becomes red. The darkness ignites.

I thought I was dreaming. Dying. But this is reality. The Smiling Sandman screeches in agony as a bright-red roadside flare sails out of the darkness through the bars of my cell, belching sparkling clouds all around us. For me, it's the first thing I've been able to see in minutes. For those of us wearing night vision, however, it's a painful disadvantage.

The noose goes slack again, and I descend into ragged coughs.

Looming above me, the Smiling Sandman—that comedy-masked villain in a dark maintenance suit—slaps gloved hands over his goggles to shield himself from the flare's pulsating red flashes. As I lie gasping for breath on the floor, inches from my puddles of sick, weak as a doll, the killer runs out of my open cell.

Sprinting, he takes a sharp right down the hall of cages. To the left, there's only a wall, and ahead of us is the staircase where the flare came from.

But there's still no exit to the right.

A loud clanking echoes through the jail basement. A second later, the lights return.

Everything is a relief. Vision. Safety. Breath, as sweet as candy.

I pull the noose off my neck and glance down the right hall just in time to see the Smiling Sandman's boots vanish into an air vent, and then he's gone. That must be how he snuck in.

Weakly, I turn ahead toward the stairs leading up to the main station. Cuban-heeled boots clomp down toward me. It's Dearie! His chest heaves breathlessly beneath his cropped tank as he grips a bulky orange flare gun. His arm is wrapped in a bloodied bandage, and more dried blood is splattered across his smiling cheeks.

But he's alive—and so am I.

Those beautiful, bitchy besties, Cole and Dearie, have made it out of another sticky bucket of syrup. Love us.

A moment later, another boy follows him down the stairs. Benny. He didn't go home like I TOLD HIM TO. He's standing shoulder-to-shoulder with Dearie, desperately gripping a loose fire extinguisher like a weapon.

My Grinch heart grows three sizes. My boys.

ON THE FINAL EPISODE OF
YOUR LONELY NIGHTS ARE OVER:
THE SEARCH FOR MR. SANDMAN

It was the breakup no one saw coming. On Valentine's Day 1975—four years to the date after the killings began—Mr. Sandman took a final victim, and with that, the tragedy mask was never seen again. Why did it end there? And more importantly, where did he go?

By leaving so suddenly and mysteriously, Mr. Sandman denied us closure. But what is closure? It can be many things to many people.

It can be clarity—**this is definitely over.**

It can be meaning—**this is over, but here's why it's important you went through this.**

It can be justice—**this is over, and I'm sorry I hurt you.**

Sometimes, it can just be a wake-up call—**this is over. I am not who you thought I was, and you were right to doubt me.**

Mr. Sandman left us with no clarity, no meaning, and no justice, but there was a wake-up call: staying together isn't always a happy ending.

Continue watching?

PART SIX
LEAVE ME LONELY

CHAPTER THIRTY-ONE

DEARIE

COLE AND I NARROWLY surviving being murdered by the Sandmen should have been the end of a long day, but sadly, it's the beginning.

Agent Astadourian released Cole with a fairly desperate apology. Whether it was desperate out of sincere regret or fear of how abysmally this looks on her, Cole didn't accept. All he cares about is finding the Smiling Sandman as soon as possible. That means sticking around the station with me so we can plan our next move. His uncle Fernando left Astadourian with a warning that once the killer is caught, they'll settle up ledgers for Cole's abysmal treatment.

Soon after his release, Cole's moms flooded the station with trays of catered sandwiches. Monica, three steps ahead as always, brought Cole a clean change of clothes and checked out the noose bruises on his throat. While she wanted to take him to the hospital as a precaution, Cole insisted that had to wait unless it was something serious. Luckily, Sandman left Cole in no dire medical situation.

As badly as his moms didn't want to leave him, Cole and I needed debriefing, so they went home to calm the dozens of flustered family members who'd just driven in.

Benny also didn't want to leave, but Cole persuaded him anyway: "Your mom is gonna stop being my biggest fan if you don't let her know you're okay ASAP."

Still, Benny needed more convincing, so Cole sent him on an errand: rounding up Flops. For our plan's next phase, Cole and I agreed we needed all the Queer Club members with us. My mom agreed to let them come to the station for a full update on the situation, so one of her officers and Benny headed out to pick up Lucy, Mike, Theo, and Em.

As soon as they leave, Cole and I can finally get off our feet for a damn second.

While Mom, Astadourian, and every surviving agent and officer congregate in the next room to begin the hunt for the Smiling Sandman, Cole and I relax alone in Mom's office. The room is designed head-to-toe in whiskey-colored wood. It overflows with southwestern flourishes—turquoise lamps, enormous cacti, and Indigenous-woven blankets, which are slung over corner leather armchairs surrounding a conference table. Mom's predecessor personally designed the space. It's so hypermasculine it's camp.

Cole and I silently watch different news reports on our phones—both detailing the breaking Mr. Sandman chaos. On Cole's phone, live footage streams from Mooncrest

Cemetery, where Ray Fletcher—now publicly named as the original killer—is hauled away in a body bag. There's a lot more dead bodies to haul once you add in Leo Townsend and the three officers who were watching him. The footage is intercut with black-and-white stills from *Your Lonely Nights Are Over*, a seventies roll call of everyone whose deaths have now been avenged.

One of the first things Mom did once Cole was safe was ask her team to start confirming Ray as the original killer so they could get the news out. Once they knew it was Ray, forensics used the old incomplete shoe print evidence to confirm him as the killer of at least four San Diego victims. A search of his projector booth at Mooncrest turned up the exact shoes that matched. Shoes from when he was a teenager. He kept them. Why? To keep damning evidence close? Then why not burn them?

I think he wanted them to be found. From the minute Mom and I rolled up to Mooncrest, Ray was ready to go. Evidence waiting to finally be collected. To be anonymous for so long, it must've been joyous when Ray's apprentice approached him for the first time.

To be seen. To be known.

His lonely nights were finally over.

Cole doesn't blink as he watches Ray's victims' families sob in news reports. I quietly swirl my hand across his back. Ray was his hero, and Mooncrest was our movie palace, our promise of a bright, beautiful life beyond the desert walls of Stone Grove.

That promise is gone, babes. We may escape this town, but it'll be wounded and separated.

On my phone, unlike the national news networks Cole is watching, the local news focuses on the recent victims of Stone Grove. Ms. Drake, pulled from the stacks of her own library—her innocence now thrown into question because of her parentage. How much did she know? When did she know? Why did the Smiling Sandman kill her? Only Mom and I know that Ray tried (and failed) to stop his apprentice from taking her. Then there's Kevin, found dead in his lonely apartment. Live footage of Kevin's murder scene is intercut with homemade videos of him hosting a local drag queen bingo. Then they move on to other breaking news: Justin Saxby's home was found stacked with bodies. Justin's father and the two missing stakeout officers, all dead. The police and FBI, now united, are seeking Justin instead of Cole as their prime suspect.

So far, the media's narrative has been *"SLAUGHTER! But thank God it's over."*

But the Queer Club knows it's not over.

The Smiling Sandman is on the loose and hunting us.

For very good reason, the news hasn't been allowed to know that just a few hours ago, the Smiling Sandman broke into the sheriff's station, entered through an air vent (that we still have no idea how he accessed), attempted to kill Cole, and then escaped without a trace.

"So, when you jumped into that helicopter at Mooncrest," Cole says, his eyes never drifting from the news, "did you, like, hang off that bottom rung like an action hero or ride sidesaddle out of the open door, like in war movies?"

"Um, I was seated safely and wearing a seat belt," I say, scratching my fresh arm bandage.

Cole moans. "Not as cool."

"I know. But I got to leap out into the parking lot before the chopper completely landed."

"Sick!"

"I know! I was such a little Charlie's Angel, like, I grabbed a flare gun and started running inside in front of all the cops, like '*MY FRIEND!*' Benny was already in there in the dark, whipping around that fire extinguisher. He almost took my head off."

"My short kings saved me." Cole rubs his pinky across mine.

"Yeah." Smiling, I take his hand, both of us tired but wired.

"I'm sorry about Kevin." Cole smiles sadly. "He was the first gay guy I ever knew—my dad doesn't count. I can't believe he was lonely. Growing up, he was such a hoochie daddy."

I chuckle wearily. "Oh, I *know*."

"He was the inspiration." Cole kisses two fingers and

raises them high to honor Kevin, who is hopefully living it up in that great sky club in the clouds.

My momentary joy passes as storm clouds begin to gather in my chest.

"I don't think Kevin's murder was planned," I say, cracking my neck. "If he got a warning message, there's no way he wouldn't tell my mom. In the show, did Mr. Sandman ever kill without a warning?"

Cole drums his fingers along the conference table. "Not really. Ray kept it tight. There was *one* time, a neighbor of another victim who was up and killed. She had a final note pinned to her, but they never tracked down the warning. People think it was because she lived so close to another victim—she saw Mr. Sandman's face, and he had to improvise." He plucks a half sandwich from one of the trays, chomps into it, and then swallows with disgust. "Pickles?! Jesus, this day!"

Cole angrily whips the sandwich back onto the tray. I softly graze my bare midriff, cooling myself with a pleasant thought: "The killer messed up. Kevin's murder is like pickles on a sandwich. It doesn't belong."

"If the killer is Justin, why would he kill Kevin?" Cole asks, spitting a pickle bit into his napkin. "They didn't know each other."

"Kevin's the medical examiner. Maybe he found something he wasn't supposed to."

My last moments with Kevin return to me. While Mom set up surveillance equipment in our living room, Kevin pulled me aside to give me a burner phone. He said the killer had Grover's phone and could be tracking me. "He asked about tattoos," I say, sitting up. "Wanted to know why Grover hated tattoos."

Cole rolls his eyes. "You mean, when he *forbade* you from getting one?"

Fizzing, crackling energy fills my body. The day I broke up with Grover, he put something in my hand. It was small, heavy, and cold. I can't remember what it was, but it feels important. It feels *essential* to why he died.

"Grover was . . ." But then my words stop, like my brain closed up shop for the night. "He wasn't a good boyfriend." I breathe. "Or a good person, especially not to you."

When I look at Cole, he smiles like he's been waiting years to hear me say this. I wasn't ready. I'd been protecting Grover, feeling guilty that I left him and then guilty that he died. But I can't shut out reality anymore—Grover's smears against Cole were charged with sadistic violence. They led him to jail, and it's a miracle he survived.

"I should've listened to you a long time ago," I say.

Cole's eyes glisten. "Don't worry. Everyone listens to me in the end."

The office door opens and all at once, every surviving, not-at-large member of the Queer Club enters Mom's office: Benny, Mike, Lucy, Em, and Theo.

Mom and Astadourian are having their meeting about finding the second killer.

And we're gonna have ours.

The reunion instantly becomes a land rush of hugging, gasping, and catching up. Mike beams at me, his cheeks red beneath his patchy fur and bunchy turtleneck. "Hey."

I smile back. "Hey. Are you okay?"

"Are *you* okay? Benny texted us you were at Mooncrest! We thought you were gonna die."

I try to laugh it off, but the phantom pain of Ray's knife against my throat stops me. "It was close. But we got him."

Mike whistles with relief, his eyes twinkling. "AND you saved Cole. You're, like, amazing."

I smile, but my heart's not in it. "I'll feel better when we end it."

Too many amazing people are dead because of me.

"So, he could still be up there in the vents?" Lucy asks, eyes cast to the ceiling as if the Smiling Sandman could leap down on us at any moment.

"He's gone," Cole says, shaking his head. "They found a trail of my dried vom leading out into the parking lot." Benny grazes Cole's lower back as Cole lowers a quick kiss onto the top of his head. It's shocking seeing Cole act couple-y with anyone, much less tiny, shy Benny.

"Well, I'm happy you miraculously survived," Theo says, their hands clasped like a preacher.

Cole arches his eyebrow. "Are you?"

"I am, but it does sound pretty miraculous. I've got questions."

The entire room hurls *boo*s at them, but Cole just laughs. "What kind of 4D chess do you think I'm playing? I've been attacked, thrown in jail, I GAVE the police the clue that found Ray, and then got strangled in my cell. If I was really Mr. Sandman, it would've been easier just to kill you all!"

With that awkward silence, Cole and I gesture to the sandwich trays, and everyone digs in. Benny scoops four half sandwiches onto his plate and, without prompting, performs a necessary surgery: he opens them, discards an array of pickle slices stuck between the cheese and cold cuts, and then slides the depickled plate over to Cole.

Son of a bitch, this Flop might be his soulmate.

Grinning ear to ear, Cole bites his lower lip, playfully punches Benny in the shoulder, and devours the sandwiches like Cookie Monster. As Benny shines proudly, Lucy and I exchange a knowing eyebrow raise, both of us united in thought: *Oh, this boy has his eye on an endgame with Cole.*

Once everyone's eaten, we corral together everything we've learned so far about the day Gretchen died and how it could help make sense of where to go next. Ray told me his apprentice murdered each victim except Claude Adams, Leo, and the police officers guarding him. Ray could've been lying, but I don't know what he'd have to gain by confusing us.

That means whoever killed Gretchen was a student in the school while Ray was busy lifting mine and Cole's prints.

"Soooo, the police now think it's Justin?" Lucy says. "Mike, wasn't he with you when Gretchen was killed?"

Mike nods, turning to me. "Him and me were together nonstop. He went to the bathroom once, but it was so fast. I don't think he could've snuck off or anything."

I don't respond. I stroke the bandage wrapped tightly around my arm wound and replay the geography of the school in my mind—where everyone was, where Gretchen was, the order in which things occurred.

While I replay, Theo stress-musses their choppy hair and leans over to Mike. "Justin couldn't have . . . attacked Gretchen and Grover *before* and then met you?"

Cole rolls his eyes. "Without a trace of blood on him? Gretchen dead, Grover bleeding out of his neck for twenty minutes before anyone found them?"

As Theo glowers and shrinks away, Cole covers his face in exhaustion.

Tapping my wound, I reach the same frustrating conclusion everyone else has: there was close to zero opportunity for Justin Saxby to have murdered Gretchen, wounded Grover, and then met up with Mike without being seen.

"Has anyone ever asked *why* Justin would want to kill us?" Em asks.

I look over at Cole, then at everyone else. "Ray said his

apprentice figured out who he was by watching the show, something no one else has done. Was Justin obsessed with the show?"

Em shrugs. "Everyone is."

"Well, why would he want to do this?" Lucy says. "I didn't think Justin was like that."

"Serial killers don't need a damn reason," Benny says.

"Sure they do," Cole says, winking. "Like I've always said: attention. And Justin craved it."

We all pause, thinking about Justin: the tall blond transfer boy from the East Coast, as Irish-pride as anyone can get, from the green tracksuits to his shamrock tattoo. Always grouchy. Never quite gelled with anyone. Already a bitter homo at eighteen.

If Justin is the killer, he worked quickly, but he would've been motivated by finally feeling like a star. No one else in the world could figure out the identity of Mr. Sandman, but the apprentice did. Justin, rejected by Cole and unable to feel at home in Stone Grove, would've adored being told that *he alone* was smart enough to solve the mystery.

Loneliness isn't always about romance. It can have a lot to do with self-worth.

It's possible but still a leap.

"Maybe it isn't Justin," I suggest. "Ray said he killed Claude Adams because his apprentice needed the victim to be a gay man."

Cole nods. "So they could frame me with that bullshit letter that said we were fucking."

"Everyone who's died has either been queer or trying to help queers. Maybe the motive doesn't need to be complicated, maybe this is the work of our old friend the Bigot Tree."

"Hate that tree," Theo mutters into their fist. Em elbow-nudges them, and they both giggle together as if it's a private joke. Interesting. If Theo keeps lightening up, maybe they'll get a date with Em after all.

"It could be Walker Lane," Benny says.

With an entire sandwich stuffed in his mouth, Cole argues, "Walker Lane under no circumstances watched that show and did the mental physics of figuring out it was Ray."

A chorus of murmured agreements pass through the room before Em starts chewing her pen again. "That's what's been so creepy about this time around," she says. "In the seventies, Ray killed anybody. That's what got the country so scared. This time, it's only been queer people . . . It made it lonelier because we were alone. *I've* felt it. You've all felt it."

Instinctively, as if to banish loneliness from the room, we reach for each other. Cole pulls Benny close. Em takes Theo's hand, who takes Lucy's hand. And then there's Mike and me. Not really loved ones, but queer loneliness breeds intimacy. I hook my arm under his and swirl my hand across his back. He smiles weakly, as if he's terrified to ask what this means.

"It doesn't matter who the killer is," Cole says, cutting through the quiet. "It doesn't matter what they want. Because while the cops in that room—who've been getting it wrong, wrong, wrong this whole time—investigate with their usual tactics, we're going to trap this asshole ourselves."

Em's and Theo's eyes pop. Mike and Lucy look at each other, baffled.

Smoothing back my hair, I stand and stretch, the frayed hem of my top exposing more than a peek of midriff, which Mike Mancini does not miss. Holding the room's attention, I announce, "We're going to throw a memorial party for the victims. Tonight." I spin toward Theo. "And we're gonna need your house."

CHAPTER THIRTY-TWO
COLE

THE QUEER CLUB DIVIDES into two teams. Benny and I remain at the station while Dearie leads Mike, Lucy, Em, and Theo over to Theo's house in River Run. Convincing their parents to host the memorial party was shockingly easy. The investigators divided as well: Mrs. Dearie stays with me, while Astadourian and her team go to River Run to watch over the trap. The remaining agents and officers spread out across town on their manhunt for Justin.

Not that I think they'll find him.

The Smiling Sandman isn't going to sit around waiting for Astadourian's sweepers to come calling. They want Dearie, I'm almost positive of it.

Thankfully, Mrs. Dearie believes our theory that Kevin's murder is a bizarre outlier that requires looking into. Benny and I are following her to Kevin's office to investigate. If one of the members of Queer Club is the killer, we might be the only ones who can spot the right clues.

"I think Kevin found something the killer didn't want

him to see," she says as we approach an elevator in the back of the sheriff's station. "You've got good instincts, Cole. And you both know your classmates. If you find anything strange, tell me."

Down in the basement, we'll find the identity of the Smiling Sandman. I know it.

I just need to prove it.

Mrs. Dearie, Benny, and I approach the sheriff's station elevator. Answers lie below.

I elbow Benny, who is so tense, he startles at my touch. "Sure you wouldn't rather be at the party than digging around a basement with me?" I ask.

Laughing bitterly, Benny waves me off. "Oh, please. That death trap is the last place I want to be." He glances at Mrs. Dearie, who's just peered up anxiously from her phone. Benny smiles. "They're all gonna be fine."

While we wait for the elevator, a notification buzzes on my phone: FrankieDearie is going live.

"It's Dearie," I say, and Benny and Mrs. Dearie swarm to my shoulders to watch the stream.

In the video, Dearie and Mike laugh wildly in the back seat of a car, whooping obnoxiously like they're on their way to Vegas. Dearie nuzzles Mike's scruffy cheek and addresses the hundreds of people already watching: *"Absolutely the best feeling in the world. We got him!"*

"*YOU got him,*" Mike says, nuzzling him back.

"Okay, okay, well, my mom did." Dearie winks. *"But I jammed my vape into his eye."*

Mike shrieks with glee. *"You are so sexy."* Mike cuddles Dearie closer and bites at the air around his ear like a snapping turtle, causing my bestie to launch into a giggle fit.

"Miiiiike, stop iiiit."

Benny winces, and I feel like I'm ready for round two of vomiting. Dearie and Mike's behavior is an act to lure the killer, but if those two end up getting together for real, this better not be how they conduct themselves, or we're gonna have a PDA lesson. Gay, straight, bi, pan, nobody wants to see that shit.

"We're on our way to Theo's engagement-party-slash-memorial for the victims," Dearie says. *"Guess it's also a victory party AND a way to show off my new boyfriend, Mike Mancini. Such a sweetie."*

Mike sucks his lower lip in thought. *"We should have a combo name."*

"Shut UP. I was thinking that!" Dearie, all smiles, smacks his shoulder. *"Mancearie?"*

"Francini?"

Dearie snorts. *"Well, as long as I can call you my boyfriend."* They kiss.

Beside me, Benny groans painfully. I chuckle. "It's just an act."

He glances over, hardened. "Not for Mike, it's not."

The tips of my ears pulse with hot embarrassment. "I mean, Dearie does think he's cute."

"Really?" Mrs. Dearie asks hopefully.

"He told me right after Mike came out," I say. "Grover's attack kind of complicated who he was interested in . . . and who he probably should've been with instead."

Mrs. Dearie nods with grim understanding. I think she was as ready as I was for Grover to be out of her son's life.

Is Mike boyfriend material? Unlike Grover, he seems to appreciate boundaries.

Dearie wraps up his stream as they drive past familiar signs for River Run: *"Be safe out there, everybody, because there's one more Sandman. But I have a message for you, killer. I know who you are."* He kisses the camera. *"Tonight, there'll be another stream from me during the party, and all will be revealed."*

I close the video as Mike hollers excitedly, returning the station to pin-drop silence as our elevator finally arrives and we descend to the morgue.

"We're really doing the horror movie thing of gathering everyone at one big party?" Benny asks, anxiously watching the elevator's digital numbers get closer to *M.*

I tickle the small of his back. "Dearie remembered your idea. It's a good way to make the killer show up."

Mrs. Dearie sighs, irritated. "Yeah, well, let's wrap up here quickly and get to the party."

As the elevator reaches the basement, she pulls her

weapon. The doors slide open onto a dark, empty hallway. A dank chill strikes the air. Mrs. Dearie steps out first, scanning for signs of unexpected movement. So far, nothing. Just a shaft of fluorescent light cutting across the hall. Covering herself, she uses her elbow to throw a series of wall switches, bathing us in sweet, swaddling light.

I gently grip Benny's side as we follow Mrs. Dearie down the vacant corridors, past windows of darkened laboratories, the fluorescent blue of the morgue, and finally, the medical examiner's office. Kevin's room is tidy, yet splashes of his personality peek through: a framed picture of him, beautiful and happy, in a snowy mountain lodge, relaxing by a fire with four handsome friends; an old cat toy belonging to his best babygirl; and a hurricane glass filled with hot-pink sand.

Mrs. Dearie pulls on a pair of blue surgical gloves and picks up the hurricane glass with extreme care. "We took our PTO together in Aruba," she says, lost in a memory. "I can't believe he kept this. It was six years ago. I haven't been down here in that long, I guess?"

"Is it a clue?" Benny asks.

"What?"

"You put on gloves."

"Oh." Sobering, she sets down the glass and tosses each of us a pair of gloves. "Just don't want us touching anything. We haven't had time to seal the room yet."

I stretch a set of gloves over my sweat-slicked hands and scan what is otherwise an ordinary office. I thought there would be more doctor-y things in here, like evidence jars or bags of suspicious items.

"Where can we find Kevin's medical reports on the victims?" I ask.

"In the lab," Mrs. Dearie says. "I saw the autopsy reports on the table as we passed."

"Did Kevin usually leave important stuff out like that for anyone to see?"

"Never. Whatever happened to him, he left in a hurry."

"But you said he was killed on his couch?"

"We *found* him on his couch."

"Do you have his phone?"

She shakes her head. "The killer took it. It hasn't been recovered."

I jerk my thumb toward his iMac. "We need to see his texts. You have the password for that thing?"

"Yes, unless he changed it in the past few days, but we only switch them on Tuesdays." She crosses to his desk, types a very long password, and grins as the soft purple glow from the desktop welcomes her. Steel returns to my veins. We could be only a few minutes away from getting to the bottom of this.

Benny and I circle around the desk to Mrs. Dearie, but she's already scanning through Kevin's recent iMessages.

Kevin's computer is still softly playing a looping playlist of nineties R&B.

"It'll be from an unknown number," she says.

"Unknown numbers could be hookups." My voice catches a hint of singsong.

"I know that." She cranes back with a judgmental eyebrow. "How do *you* know that?" I just look at her like I'm glaring over invisible glasses. "Has Frankie ever done hookups . . . ?"

My entire body rejects this conversation like I've been force-fed Kryptonite. "*Done the hookups,*" I repeat in a hyper-white, middle-aged voice. She frowns. "Mary, how many people did you have sex with in high school? Did your mom know about every one of them?"

"Fine, I'll shut up!" she growls, returning to Kevin's texts.

I lean close to look, but Mrs. Dearie has already found what we're looking for: an unknown number, the last person to text Kevin besides her. Instantly, Benny and I look over our shoulders. As if someone's behind us watching. But there's nothing but a large cabinet—big enough for a man to hide in. My fingertips buzz as Mrs. Dearie opens the chat window.

Kevin's message history with Mr. Sandman is brief, but longer than any other victim's:

Unknown: Your lonely nights will soon be over.

Kevin: I know who you are.

Unknown: I'm scared, Kevin. He's making me do it. I thought we were just gonna mess with people, but then he said he'd kill me if I didn't help.

Kevin: You need to leave Frankie and Cole alone.

Unknown: I'm trying, but he says I don't have a choice.

Kevin: You always have a choice.

Unknown: I'm so scared.

Kevin: Come to the station. We can protect you.

Unknown: Not from him.

Kevin: Trust me. It'll be okay.

Unknown: Oh, I know it will. I was just stalling for time.

Kevin: What?

Unknown: Behind you.

The messages stop there. The Smiling Sandman was already waiting to ambush Kevin. He knew he was close to finding out who he was.

"Kevin," Mrs. Dearie whispers, barely breathing.

"He knew him," Benny says, reading the messages over my shoulder. "He was trying to *help* the killer."

An ugly idea is forming.

"Hey, Benny bunny?" I ask. After this much prolonged suspense, my sweet glasses boy looks like he's desperate to be anywhere else, even the trap party. "Come with me to the morgue?"

CHAPTER THIRTY-THREE

DEARIE

AT LEAST ONCE A year since we started high school, Theo Galligan has thrown a party at their house, and as obnoxious as many of us find them, we all show up so we can feel rich for a night. It's a mutually beneficial fake-bitch arrangement. As much as Theo turned against Cole and me after we departed Queer Club, any queer student has a guaranteed invite.

Tonight, they're throwing a Sandman trap.

The good thing about assigning such a party to a stubborn, appearance-obsessed person like Theo is they could be a mess of raw nerves and I'd never have to know. Here they are, all smiles, in their enormous great room, raising a glass of sparkling cider like it's New Year's Eve. They're in their all-black formal wear (suspenders with no jacket), only the bow tie is now a sequined silver one. Lucy hangs off Theo's arm, laughing at every joke and otherwise being as silently supportive as a First Lady. She's changed into a shimmering, champagne-colored midriff top.

The Mom Friend shines up nicely!

They toast to a captive audience of a dozen other students, many of whom saw our stream and invited themselves along. Among the gathering of vaguely familiar juniors and seniors are Em in jeans and a skintight tropical top, looking gorgeous despite her tense, frozen smile; Mike, cute and cuddly as usual in his weather-inappropriate turtleneck; Agent Astadourian, in her usual cool-aunt suede jacket. Her expression is so sullen and watchful, people keep glancing at her like she's an ominous raven.

Just what everyone needs to calm down, a conspicuous FBI presence.

I think she thought there'd be a larger crowd for her to blend into, but the vibes so far are less "teen rager" and more "thank you for coming to my political fundraiser."

At the front of the crowd, the Galligans—Theo's red-headed, khaki-loving parents—listen to their child's bizarre engagement toast with a mixture of pride and unease. "Yes, it's sudden, and yes, we're young," Theo crows. Lucy, always an energetic performer, pokes her forehead to Theo's ear. "But I was always ahead of my time."

Theo and Lucy mumble, "I love you," "No, I love YOU," before kissing, drawing whoops from most of the crowd, including Theo's mom, who keeps dabbing her mascara. I wish Cole were here, so I'd have somebody to groan at. Hopefully, the killer shows up soon, so Astadourian can arrest him and let Lucy be free of this carnival.

Soon. My live stream with Mike was Oscar-worthy nonsense, but I know my tease of a killer reveal will guarantee he shows.

Kissing Mike was strange. It was something I'd thought about doing for real before, but to do it as an act felt . . . wrong, like I was just humoring another poor Flop like I did with Grover.

"*Are you mine?*" Grover asked me sweetly, minutes before I broke up with him.

We were nose-to-nose on my bed. The stress of knowing I was going to break up with him was so severe, I can only recall fragments of our conversation. In that moment, my overwhelming desire was to reassure him. Make him feel safe.

But then I dumped him, and he placed the mystery item in my hand. Then I blocked it out.

The missing detail tugs at me. Something I can't recover no matter how hard I try to see through the fog. Then Mike nudges me and I'm back to the present.

This time, I won't let anything bad happen. I lace my fingers inside Mike's. He jumps slightly but then smiles. I raise his hand to kiss his furry knuckles.

"Oh," he whispers, "nice touch."

His cheeks redden beneath his spotty boy beard, and it warms my chest to make someone feel good. To give them what they've wanted. I'm not an asshole. Even after we catch the Smiling Sandman, I'm going to be a good person who makes people happy.

As Theo's speech grows solemn, commemorating Gretchen, Grover, Ms. Drake, "and the rest," everyone lowers their heads in silent reflection. But my mind isn't silent. It clatters so loudly, my consciousness begins to tilt. The great room spins, and I have to clutch Mike's hand harder to stay upright. Luckily, Theo's father summons me back to reality by dinging a butter knife against his champagne flute.

"None of us would feel safe tonight if it weren't for some of the people here," he says, raising his glass. "Special Agent Astadourian—we're honored to have you." Double-A nods uncomfortably, as if she'd been praying for this man not to call attention to her. "And Frankie Dearie—you and your mom stopped a killer who's been famous since before Olivia and I were gleams in our mothers' eyes." Polite laughter spreads through the crowd. "To Dearie!"

"TO DEARIE," the room cheers. Em squeezes my shoulder, and even Double-A can't hide her smile. So, why do I suddenly want to sink beneath the crust of the earth? Because Cole has suffered worse than I have and isn't getting any toasts. Because Kevin Benetti deserves a commemoration too.

Like always, I didn't do anything except weasel out of another predicament while everyone else around me pays a higher cost.

They're acting like it's over, but this is only the eye of the storm, and the Smiling Sandman is fitter, stronger, and crueler than his master. He almost killed Cole in the middle of a police station, and he still hasn't been caught.

We aren't safe here. What the hell was I thinking?

"We're not out of the woods yet," Mr. Galligan says, as if reading my thoughts. "Apart from Agent Astadourian, there's more agents posted outside. River Run's gates have extra security. And best of all . . ." Chortling, he shows off a security app on his phone, its screen filled with large blue buttons. He taps one. That moment, multiple doors seal shut behind us, in front of us, and upstairs.

"*ARMED*," a soothing electronic female voice says from the front door.

Mr. Galligan smiles cheekily. "Sorry to keep the party inside, but that's house rules tonight. Doors are locked from the inside, so no one's coming in. But if you're going out, if the system isn't shut off in thirty seconds, police will be here in minutes." Winking, he pockets the phone. "And I'm the only one who can turn it off."

Famous last words.

"Have fun!" Mrs. Galligan hollers before yanking Theo and Lucy into a hug. "We'll be upstairs in the library if you need anything!"

The lights dim. Each lamp in the house morphs into an artificial starry twilight as raucous mid-century jazz and swing beats start the party. The great room's furniture has been cleared to create a makeshift dance floor. Directly in front of the tiled entrance hall is a grand staircase with iron railings leading to a second-story landing that overlooks the entire great room.

"Like the Cheesecake Factory," Mike says, sending me into giggles. His smile becomes strained again.

At the upstairs landing, Theo's parents disappear behind sliding double doors. While the doors are briefly open, floor-to-ceiling bookshelves can be seen. They wave to us one last time, and the doors shut.

In the kitchen, Astadourian and the Queer Club gather around a banquet of dips, charcuterie, and tiny pickles. Cole would be in hell. Behind the island is a breakfast nook table with an expansive view of the backyard: a wide, stone patio with half a dozen deck chairs surrounding a firepit; beyond that, an Olympic-size pool, its lights reflecting a serene blue glow onto the many trees that disguise the iron perimeter fence; and to the left of the pool is Mr. Galligan's crown jewel: a massive, ten-car garage filled with vintage collectible autos.

"My dad would freak out," Mike says, awestruck, as he's newly out and a stranger to the Galligan home. "Could I take pics—?"

His hand falls on the patio door handle, and Theo, Lucy, and Astadourian whisper, "THE ALARM."

Mike jerks his hand away as if he touched a snake. "Sorry . . ."

Em and I exchange glances as we sip the kiddie champagne. Yeah, I feel *real* safe.

Over snacks and sips, Lucy, enjoying being yards away from Theo, asks me, "So, you think he'll show up?"

Theo shrugs. "Well, that was Dearie's plan, right?"

I roll my eyes. Theo just can't help themself—always ratting us out to the feds.

Many eyes dart quickly around the kitchen. I glance at Astadourian. She shrugs. "I assumed you were up to something like that," she admits diplomatically. "I can't trust you, Frankie, but I can trust you to be you."

Silence falls. Our masks of confidence fall with it.

Each of us has escaped death multiple times today, and suddenly, congregating in a big, locked room feels like a trap for us, not the killer, which sounded better on paper when I was forming it.

"Very *Masque of the Red Death*," Theo says. Blank, blinking eyes fall on them, and self-consciously, they add, "Rich people party inside while death ravages outside."

Lucy doesn't blink. "Whoever's rich house this is just got real burned."

Theo pouts. The honeymoon is over.

At least they've got Em pulling them into a side hug. Not a total loss.

"We're all stressed," I say, scanning the miserable-looking group. "But there's no safe way out of this. We've all been targeted. This party *is* a trap. It's going to be risky. But a lot of people are dead, and I think we're the only ones who can stop it."

All around me, their expressions strengthen with resolve.

Within minutes, the Queer Club returns to the great room to shred the dance floor, and our bodies—flooded with adrenaline and fear—release weeks of pent-up energy. It's a frenzy of limbs. Theo and Em, finally paired, spin each other like professional swing dancers. They kiss, far more passionately than Theo and Lucy's staged engagement kiss. Lucy, meanwhile, dances—happily, merrily—alone, her eyes shut as she sways with a drink in hand. Astadourian tends to a small, sensible plate of cheese just outside the room—her only job is to keep us in view.

Mike, however, is the surprise master of moves. While high-tempo jazz plays, he takes both my hands, assumes lead, and swings me away from him, then toward him. Away, toward. His strength is so confident. His feet are so nimble. Sweat plasters his hair to his forehead, and I wonder again what made him choose to wear a winter turtleneck. Either way, it's not slowing him down.

He spins me faster. Away. Close. Away. Close.

"I don't know what I'm doing!" I shout the next time he swings me away.

When he brings me close, he puts his lips to my ear. "I've got you, follow me."

I follow, and—briefly—the killer leaves my mind. My entire past leaves me. Every ugly, complicated memory flies away, as if it had happened to someone else.

Mike is new. I'm dancing with him, and it has nothing to do with the murders, my ex, or my guilt . . . In this moment, a future without death materializes in my soul.

I can feel it. And the feeling is so powerful, I'm terrified to let it go.

As the song ends, Mike swings me toward him one last time, and I don't miss my shot. I clutch his bearded cheeks, pull him tight, and kiss him. It's real. The feeling is night-and-day different from our live stream. I kiss him again, deeper, and my hand presses against his back, his clothes divinely damp. I squeeze my fingers into his soft lower back . . .

He lets out a small gasp and pulls away.

Around us, a new up-tempo song takes over and people continue dancing, not recognizing that Mike and I have stopped. The violet Hue lights reflect in his large, glossy eyes.

"What was that?" he asks.

"Kissing you?" I ask.

"Was it . . . for real?"

My smile dawns slowly. "Yeah."

Mike's mouth hangs open for a moment before he moans

something he doesn't mean to say: "I love you." Without any control over my face, I blink several times. Somehow, a spell has been broken. I didn't mean for it to, but Mike knows something has shifted because he looks afraid. Like he just appeared somewhere naked. "Just kidding, I . . ."

"Mike . . ."

"Shit." Terror floods his eyes. "Excuse me."

"Wait!"

Mike vanishes in a cartoon puff of smoke. Pushing his way through the dancers, he grabs Theo—who is hip-thrusting with Em—and asks, "Where's the bathroom?"

"Upstairs, left," Theo says, hypnotized.

Mike isn't only fast on the dance floor. Before I can even make it to Theo, he's on his way up the Cheesecake Factory stairs. "Mike, wait!" I shout over the music and shuffle upstairs after him.

I can't let him go anywhere alone.

"Frankie, don't split up!" Astadourian shouts from somewhere below. I know I shouldn't run off alone, but I have to bring Mike back. He and I reach the landing at the same time. I grab a fistful of his damp sweater. He's already crying.

"Just let me go," he begs.

"Not alone!" I say.

Mike jerks his arm free. On great, heaving moans, he confesses, "I shouldn't have said that. I didn't know what I was saying! I'm just a newbie. I don't know what to say when it's a guy. Please just forget I said that."

"I like you! Mike, please, come back with me and let's talk. I *really* like you."

His frantic breathing normalizes. He tries to smile. I think I've got him.

Then his smile fades. "Dearie . . . ?"

I follow what he's looking at: the sliding double doors of the library where the Galligans tucked themselves away. A thick length of rope—strong enough to fasten a boat to a dock—has been tied around the door handles.

Who did this?

We walk up the rest of the stairs as if in a trance. Mike reaches down to touch the rope as I realize we're just out of sight of everyone downstairs. And we're alone.

The door behind Mike opens with a slam.

The Smiling Sandman marches out at full speed with a spool of barbed wire in his gloved hands, and before either of us can make a sound, he wraps the wire around Mike's throat. "NO!" I scream as the Smiling Sandman tightens the razor necklace. Mike slaps at it, but the killer—using only the leverage of the necklace—hoists the wriggling boy into the air. Mike's feet kick wildly as he squeals and screams.

"NO!!! MIKE!!!" I shriek, lunging. I beat at the killer's arms, wrists, and mask until he drops Mike onto the floor. With a horrifying thud, my boy lands facedown with a stillness.

Mike's lonely nights are over.

CHAPTER THIRTY-FOUR

COLE

IF *YOUR LONELY NIGHTS ARE OVER* has taught me anything, it's that Mr. Sandman leaves no evidence behind that he doesn't want you to consider.

Everything we've found is because he wanted us to find it. That's how Ray operated. We have to accept that his apprentice operates the same way. The only way to unmask the Smiling Sandman is to step outside the picture being painted. That's how I stumbled onto Ray's identity: I was supposed to be swallowed up in Claude's letter, how I was being framed, how I was being intimidated by the FBI, and how being sex-shamed had led me here.

All I needed was to realize I hadn't been accepted to Columbia yet when Claude was killed.

The picture currently being painted is that the apprentice is Justin. While framing me, the Smiling Sandman has been quietly pushing the Queer Club—Dearie and me included—toward him. After all, Justin was the last one seen with Grover, he ran off before the body was found, he wasn't in the Mooncrest circle with us when we were texted, he acted super creepy during lockdown, and everyone else in his house has been slaughtered. Not only that, ever since I stopped hooking up with Justin, he's been running a silent vendetta against me. Whoever the Smiling Sandman is, they want me locked up as badly as they want the Queer Club dead.

But like Leo told me, *It's never the one they say it is.*

The suspect—the one Mr. Sandman wants us to see—is Justin. That's why I don't trust it.

Kevin didn't either, which is why he's dead—and why the answers have to be in the morgue.

Under these dreadful fluorescent bulbs, Mrs. Dearie sifts through postmortem photographs of Gretchen and Grover, and living photographs of Grover from his first attack. Fingers, throats, wounds, cold bodies, and bloodied faces. Whoever the apprentice is, they've got a powerfully steady hand to keep up this rampage. And steady killing hands imply an empty soul.

Another clue to support my burgeoning theory.

Benny handles a vial of blood scrapings—probably mine, from when Grover and Justin attacked me during the movies. They were found under Grover's fingernails. Astadourian was using them in her case against me. Irrelevant.

Or are they?

As I leaf through Kevin's discarded exams, Mrs. Dearie

engulfs herself in a frenzy of texting, probably to Astadourian. I hop onto a stool next to Benny at a table filled with more vials. Sighing, he puts the blood scrapings back where he found them and rests his curls on my shoulder. I kiss his head. I'm so lucky to have so many curly-haired boys in my life eager to swap affection.

"So sad about Kevin," Benny says. "No one found him for so long. I always get scared that's gonna be me in some sad apartment . . ."

Before I can reassure this cutie he's going to live a long life surrounded by fabulous people, Mrs. Dearie turns sharply. She ducks beneath an overhead lamp to meet our eyes. "His apartment wasn't sad," she says. "It was only sad because there was a dead man in it. I've been in that apartment hundreds of times. Game nights. Double dates. Halloweens. Laughing, laughing, laughing." She emphasizes each word. "He had lonely nights, but we all do. It does not make us sad people." She shakes her head. "It's projection. People see a single man, a gay man who—despite everyone's jokes—was very young and happy, and their biases, or cultural crap, or their own fears fill in the holes to make up a story about him that's bullshit. We're all lonely. And we're all not lonely." With burning strength behind her eyes, she gazes at Benny. "You will be okay."

That even made me feel better.

I've missed stanning Mary.

She's right. This *is* bullshit. Why does Mr. Sandman get to decide who's lonely? Two loudmouthed Flops, a widower, a closeted hottie, a happily divorced librarian, a handsome bachelor, and Justin's father, who might be lonely, but I doubt that's why he's in the morgue.

Everything started with Grover and Gretchen getting those messages. Why? After fifty years of nothing, why suddenly these two? Back when Dearie and I were accused of sending death threats, I thought it was faked for attention. It sucked being proved wrong and watching the real Sandman come back, but perhaps I've overlooked a vital detail: I'm Cole Cardoso, and I am never wrong.

The stool squeaks against the lab floor as I leap off it to meet Mrs. Dearie. "Are all the victims' bodies still here?" I ask.

She studies me carefully, unblinking, as if knowing I've figured something out. "All of them but Gretchen, Claude, and Paul. They were buried."

"Grover's still here?"

"Yeah."

"Show me."

CHAPTER THIRTY-FIVE
DEARIE

MIKE IS DEAD ON the upstairs landing. There's nowhere to run.

The Smiling Sandman snatches me by my shoulders and brings the force of his grinning mask down, headbutting me. My skull fizzles like freshly poured soda, splitting my vision into starry fragments. I try to run, but a deep pain slices across my back like I'm a cut of beef.

He cut me. Bad.

There isn't even time to gasp before he hurls me backward into the landing's iron railing. My spine strikes the metal hard and pain explodes throughout my nervous system. The killer advances, and with my last pocket of strength, I do the little man's best attack:

Sweep the legs.

Surprised more than hurt, the masked man collapses, and my own legs give out beneath me. Panting on the carpet, feet away from Mike's body and the killer, I gather the strength to scream, "ASTADOURIAN! HE'S HERE!"

Footsteps storm the staircase from below.

My vision clears long enough to catch Astadourian halting at the top of the stairs. She gasps, "Frankie!" as the killer climbs to his feet and rushes her. She aims . . .

Behind us, the library doors bang loudly, straining against the rope trapping the Galligans inside. The sound is enough to startle Astadourian before she can get off her shot. The Smiling Sandman snatches her by the throat with one hand. In his other, he grabs her gun hand by the wrist, forcing her to aim toward the ceiling as she fires. Plaster and dust rain down on them.

Down below, the previously clueless guests scream and flood out the front door. Within seconds, the stampede flees into the night air of River Run. In thirty seconds, the alarm will sound, and Mom will know we're in trouble.

But that'll be too late.

"OPEN THE DOOR!" Mr. Galligan hollers from inside the library. Their pounding against the doors makes enough racket to draw Theo upstairs like a bullet.

"Mom! Dad!" they shriek.

Theo, dance-drunk only moments earlier, realizes too late what's happening. They find Astadourian struggling within the Smiling Sandman's grip. With one terrible push, he hurls her backward, battering into Theo, and they both crash down the stairs one step at a time.

At the top of the stairs, the killer watches them fall.

Neither makes a sound.

Throughout the house, the electronic security voice counts down to the alarm: *"Twenty-seven, twenty-six, twenty-five..."*

As I writhe on the floor, pain spreads like a map across my back. I can feel wetness spilling from the wound. I don't know if it's the deep cut or my damaged spine from when I struck the railing, but energy is leaving me.

Other than the anguished cries from behind the library door, the house is silent except for the jazz playlist, which has shifted to smoother love songs from the sixties and seventies. "You'll Never Find Another Love Like Mine" by Lou Rawls. The gentle, elevator-like music echoes hauntingly through the house.

The Smiling Sandman continues to stare at Astadourian and Theo from the top of the stairs.

He's distracted.

I'm going to stop this shit—right now.

On a rush of adrenaline, I forget my pain and charge the Smiling Sandman, who turns as I tackle him by his waist. He pounds his fist against my shoulders, but pain doesn't find me. There's only one chance.

I roar, lift, and gravity does the rest.

The killer topples over the railing, his feet in the air, before plummeting over the side. Strength leaves me quickly, and I drop back to the floor.

I didn't see where he landed—but I heard it. A crunch. A

howl of agony. Then a thud against the ground. He must've landed hard, slamming against the back of the sofa.

"*Seventeen . . . sixteen . . .*" counts the security voice.

Survival mode kicks in. I don't check on Mike—I can't help him anymore. I don't think about untying the Galligans—they're only going to get in the way. I only think about one thing:

Astadourian's gun.

"*Thirteen . . . twelve . . .*"

My back rigid with pain, I drag myself to the staircase, gripping the banister with limp arms, and then descend the Cheesecake Factory stairs in a rapid crawl.

"*Ten . . . nine . . .*"

At the bottom of the stairs, Astadourian and Theo lie in a tangle of limbs. They come closer into view until I reach the bottom and slump beside them. Theo, pinned beneath Astadourian, gasps painfully, their front teeth bloodied. "Can't . . . move . . ."

"*Six . . . five . . .*"

"Frankie . . ." Astadourian moans, her wrist bent at the wrong angle. I don't have time to be relieved they're both alive. I search the ground around them—no weapon.

"Your gun," I whisper. "Where is it?"

Astadourian wails as she tries to move, and then she goes slack. "He . . . got it."

"*Two . . . one . . .*"

Warning lights strobe above the doors as high-pitched alarms split the air, drowning out Lou Rawls. Everything makes the pain worse. Out of the shadows behind the staircase, the Smiling Sandman emerges, dragging a limp left leg . . . and aiming Astadourian's gun at my head.

If he was going to pull the trigger, I'll never know.

Behind him, Em and Lucy pounce with a fireplace poker and coal shovel. Whirlwinds of silver and black hair fly as the girls beat the Smiling Sandman with iron. He hisses and scrambles away as he tries to aim the gun, but Em lands a fierce blow against his wrist. The gun falls. Lucy brings her shovel down onto his bronze skull mask with a *crack*.

The Smiling Sandman stumbles backward and collapses against the stairs.

"Get the gun!" Lucy shouts.

But it's so close to the Sandman's hand, and he's already stirring.

"No time! Run!" I say, and Em and Lucy help me to my feet. Now that I'm upright, running starts to feel possible again. The three of us dash out the front door and onto the Galligans' front lawn.

A shot rings out.

We duck. Glass shatters.

No one was hit.

The front lawn is framed by a cobblestone walkway, which leads one way to the backyard pool and the other way to the driveway for a ten-car garage. Lights are on in every home in River Run, but no one has come outside. These aren't the kinds of people who investigate sounds of screaming and gunfire. Parked along the sidewalk is the FBI's black minivan, where Agents Jurgen and Manfredi have been keeping guard.

"FBI in there," I wince, hurrying toward the van. "They've got guns."

Lucy and Em make it there before I do. I'm a few steps away when Lucy smashes her palm against the van's dark windows. "Sandman's in the house!" she shrieks.

Em groans, "Open the goddamn door!" and hurls open the van as I reach them.

Two FBI men—Jurgen and Manfredi—tumble out onto the curb. They both land faceup, eyes vacant, throats gushing.

OH, AMAZING!

Em and Lucy practically tear their lungs in half screaming as they scamper backward from the mangled victims. I don't have the time, energy, or brain capacity to scream. I know the Smiling Sandman is behind us. He'll be here soon.

"Get in the van!" I whisper, shoving Em and Lucy toward the open door. Their legs stubbornly refuse to budge toward the FBI agents' corpses. "Get in now and lock the doors!"

"What?!" Lucy asks.

Each breath exacerbating the knife wound, I spit out,

"Get in the van and LOCK THE DOOR. Find a gun or keys. Call my mom. Call ambulances, just get out of here!"

We have seconds to act.

"Christ," Em says, trembling as she climbs over Jurgen's body into the van. Lucy gives me one last desperate look before following her inside. Em is mid-dial when Lucy pushes Jurgen's lifeless feet out of the van and closes the door.

I'm alone.

Good.

No one else will get hurt. Except me, but what else is new?

The only way to make sure no one else gets hurt is to trap the Smiling Sandman. Mike's sweet face appears in my mind. *"I love you."* Would it have been such a crime to just say it back? He'd be alive. All that boy wanted was . . .

But then my heart stops. I know where to go.

The garage.

I lurch down the cobblestone pathway toward Theo's backyard pool. As I reach the gate, out of the corner of my eye the killer appears in the doorway. The bronze comedy mask glints in the soft light.

Good. Follow me, bitch.

I hustle, faster and faster. I cross the stone patio and the firepit. The enormous pool lies ahead. Maybe I could pull him underwater and drown him.

No. I want to talk to him. I want to know who this is.

The garage looms ahead. It's a darkened, miniature hangar with a domed roof, almost the height of the Galligans' attic. In under thirty seconds, I'll be inside. That's where my date with the final Sandman will begin. Amid the sounds of my own panting and grunting, I can't tell which footsteps are mine and which are his.

He's close. Dragging a wounded leg, bruised and battered by his fall, by me, Em, and Lucy, but he's close.

Finally reaching the garage, I hurl myself at the rear door. Motion sensor lights flicker on and fill the space with a soft, warm light. Rows of luxury vehicles illuminate under individual spotlights. Vintage racers. Motorcycles. To my grim delight, Theo's dad even has a Batmobile—the convertible from the old sixties show.

I can't believe one of my last thoughts will be, *Is that the real Batmobile?*

As I walk past, my hip collides with the hood of a white Dodge Charger. With a sick nostalgia, I recognize it from *Vanishing Point*, a seventies thriller Cole and I watched once at Mooncrest. I slap my hand against the car as my knees buckle and I strike the concrete. I've lost too much blood. The adrenaline is leaving me. What do I have left?

As I slump to the ground, the garage's front door slides open to reveal the Galligans' long driveway—I'm maybe six or seven cars away from it. At one of Theo's summer block parties, their dad boasted that whenever he felt like it, he'd have the street leading into his driveway cleared so he could race his cars. The driveway is very long and leads directly into the street. He can fly any of these cars out on a straight shot or enter the garage at full speed. Cole thought it was so cool.

But who opened the garage door?

"Think you can make it?" a mask-muffled voice asks behind me.

Laughter bubbles out of me. "No, I'm done."

Crawling backward on my ass, I rest my bleeding back against the Charger and place my phone propped beside me on the grille. I wish I had time to call Cole . . . or Mom . . . But I know what I have to do.

The Smiling Sandman limps closer, his leg twitching as he moves. The grotesque comedy mask leers down at me.

"Show your face," I say.

"Aw, face pics so soon?" he asks, giggling. "Don't you know who I am by now?"

"I have a hunch," I say, though the truth, if it is the truth, batters away at my soul, makes my mind and heart race. "But still, let's get a look at you."

Throughout this ordeal, from the moment it began, from Gretchen's and Grover's messages all the way to this very minute, I've been surrounded by carnage designed to get me all alone . . .

The truth arrives in my mind, but my ability to trust my

356

own instincts has been damaged. Cole can follow hunches and feel empowered to stand by them. Me, I've become a second-guessing Flop. There's no way I can name the Smiling Sandman without seeing his face. I know that much.

The killer reaches for a clasp at the neck of his mask, and it falls at my feet.

Oh God. I was right.

CHAPTER THIRTY-SIX
COLE

RIDDLE ME THIS: WHEN is a mystery not a mystery?

When you don't want to know the truth.

The mind can perform many magic tricks to protect you from awful truths. For a long time, probably since Leo Townsend's meltdown, I've suspected the Smiling Sandman is one of us. Not just anyone in the club. Someone close. Someone we liked—maybe even loved—and I worry that facing the truth about our old friend will be a lot harder than surviving them.

Mrs. Dearie glides along a wall of morgue lockers, twelve total, each one containing a Sandman victim. If this doesn't stop soon, they're gonna need a bigger morgue. Mrs. Dearie follows Kevin's notes to locate the one containing Grover's body. Her hand stops on the handle.

"You're sure you want to do this?" she asks. "He looks pretty bad."

"If Cole says he can solve this, then let's go," Benny says, almost somersaulting with anxiety. He charges ahead and pulls open Grover's morgue shelf with a determined glint in his eye. The tray slides out like an oven rack, a black body bag resting on top like a baked potato in foil.

Mrs. Dearie sighs. "Or just open it."

I place a comforting hand on Benny's back as Mrs. Dearie slowly unzips the body bag. We lean over and find my bully, his throat shredded, his cheeks, teeth, and jaw pummeled, and his blond hair matted with dried blood. I scan Grover's body down to his legs. Instantly, I spot what I'm looking for, and it confirms my theory.

The thing Kevin found that got him killed.

Surprisingly, realizing the true identity of the Smiling Sandman doesn't devastate me. My heart rate remains calm. I am activated. Being proven right has always had that effect.

"No autopsy," I say, looking at the body's clean chest. No Y incision has been made.

"Kevin was going to do it yesterday," Mrs. Dearie says.

"But the killer found him first." I motion Benny toward Grover's legs. "See anything?"

Both Benny and Mrs. Dearie lean in closer to inspect. Within seconds, Benny finds what I found. His eyes flare, and he turns, too frightened to speak. "Cole . . ."

"What is it?" Mrs. Dearie asks quickly.

Adrenaline rips through my chest like I'm permanently in the final ten seconds of a tight game. "We need to get to

Dearie right now," I say. "You're wasting time looking for Justin."

She doesn't blink. "Justin's not the killer?"

I shake my head and chuckle miserably. I look down at the body, at our classmate. "When Astadourian was threatening to take my life away on bullshit testimony, I told her some people couldn't spot real abuse when it was sitting right next to them."

Her face, while tanned, turns bloodlessly pale. "What do you mean?"

I take Mary's hand—freezing even through her surgical glove. "Every single murder has been designed to keep me away from Dearie. He's in trouble. He's been in trouble for a long time. You know what I'm talking about, right?"

A tear pools in her eye.

The room becomes so still, dust particles freeze in mid-air. Everyone is waiting for me to turn over my final card. No more suspense. No more running from awful truths.

"There's only one person still alive who could have been present for every murder," I say. "Who could've surprised Gretchen in the hallway. Who could've been at the movies with Grover. Who knew I was fooling around with Paul. Who wasn't at school, so they could easily kill Kevin, Ms. Drake, and Justin's dad." Tears start to rise in me as well, but I have to stay clearheaded for Dearie. "There's only one person willing to do all that just to isolate Dearie from the people who love him and could protect him. To get me *killed.*"

"Who?" Mrs. Dearie asks desperately.

"Benny, show her."

Benny, his hand clutched to his chest, taps the corpse's thigh, which is white, hairless . . . and tattooed with a green shamrock.

"This is Justin's body," he says.

CHAPTER THIRTY-SEVEN
DEARIE

IT'S GROVER. HE'S ALIVE.

The killer under the comedy mask was always Grover. His hay-colored hair wilted under his mask. Bruises mark his sharp, high cheekbones. I have no idea if it's from Cole pummeling him or from me dropping him over the banister. He's handsome, but . . . not warmly anymore. His features have a cold, frightening beauty in the harsh light of the garage.

Of course he's still alive. It was probably obvious to everyone except me.

Am I the last to know? Has this entire investigation been a ruse for my benefit to get me to see the truth? That Grover is an abuser. That my ex killed people, and I ignored the signs.

Maybe if I had been strong enough to face this fact, a lot of people would still be alive.

In Theo's garage, under the unforgiving spotlights, my ex's face makes me remember. All those shards of memories of our breakup, splintered and out of order, finally pull together into a single, clear image of our miserable lives together.

"Are you mine?" he asked sweetly.

No. No, that's not how he asked.

I think back . . . We were in my bed, cuddling. I'd just gotten into a fight with Cole about New York. My best friend was leaving and didn't tell me. In my two months of dating Grover, I'd learned not to mention Cole's name in front of him, but I was upset. It slipped out. Grover's transformation was instant. My sweet, doting boyfriend became a frightening creature.

"You're MINE," he growled.

"I'm yours," I said, eager to reassure him.

"You're NOT his. I don't want to hear his name again. He could've killed me!"

"He didn't do that—"

"You NEVER believe me! You always take his side against me—your BOYFRIEND!"

SMASH. Grover shattered his phone against my dresser. My head ducked into my shoulders like a turtle. Grover's violence was never directed at me, but it was always close. So close.

"He doesn't even love you!" Grover shrieked loud enough to tear his vocal cords. "I LOVE YOU! ME! Cole didn't get your attention for five seconds, so he abandons you—his 'BEST FRIEND'—to go to New York! Do you have ANY idea how PATHETIC you sound defending him?! DO YOU?"

I was crying too hard to answer.

"It's okay," Grover said, pulling me to his chest. As furious as he was moments ago, his heart wasn't racing. He was calm. For some reason, this made me sob harder. "It's okay, Dearie . . . Dearie, Dearie . . ." He pressed his lips to my ear, and I wanted to scream for my mom downstairs, but he'd get angrier. And he was finally holding me nicely again. Maybe he just lost his temper. "Dearie, Cole is not your friend. He's a whore. And a bully. He's everything wrong with this community, and every time we take a step forward, people like Cole drag us back. He attacked me. I think the universe's purpose for that was so I could open your eyes to how he's hurting you too."

"I . . ." I tried saying something, but the only things that raced to my lips were defenses of Cole. As true as those would be, I couldn't say them without summoning the Other Grover.

"You're finally becoming a good person, Dearie," he said, bouncing me to cheer me up. "Whenever you're with Cole, you're an asshole, but that's finally changing the more you're with me. You'll see. We'll graduate. Cole will go to New York and forget you. He'll get into drugs and get a disease—"

"Stop." I pushed him off me. His eyes shifted so quickly from sweet to furious, then back to wounded. An air pocket of courage found me, and I knew if I didn't act immediately, I'd never do it. "I'm breaking up with you."

He smiled. Why did he smile?

Did he know this would kick off his rampage? Was he hoping I'd do this?

"Breaking up with me, that's REAL nice," Grover said. "That'll make you and Cole look great. Who is gonna take your side? People actually LIKE me. I'm the golden retriever here. And you're just a bitch-faced cunt. Who would miss you besides your mom and her pathetic old queen friend?"

Grover had been making so much noise. Why didn't my mom hear? Why didn't she come get me?

His knife appeared from nowhere. I didn't even know he had one. The blade was short. The handle was wooden. He didn't threaten me with it—he placed it gently in my palm and closed my fingers around it. It was small and heavy. Gripping my wrist, he brought the blade to his own throat, to the scars he loved so much. "Kill me," he said. "If you leave me, Mr. Sandman will get me, and he won't be nice about it. If I'm gonna be killed, I want some-one I love to do it."

"Grover . . ." I said, trying not to sob.

"Stop whining, and DO IT!" He held my struggling wrist in place.

"You're not gonna die!" I choked out between tears, wrestling my arm free and throwing the knife to my bed.

Grover didn't yell again. He gathered his knife and broken phone, shook his head, and asked, "Are you happy? You have no idea what you just started."

I might be the last person to know Grover is the killer, but in a way, I was also the first.

These memories were so ugly, so alien to what I believed

was possible, that my brain stuffed them into shadowy corners like irrelevant clutter.

But they have returned.

In Theo's garage, I sit on the chilly concrete, my bruised and cut-up back resting against the white, vintage Dodge Charger. Grover looms overhead, dressed in a hunter-green jumpsuit and heavy boots with filthy soles, with a calm, sly grin on his face. His blond peach-fuzz beard shimmers unattractively under the lights.

"Hi, babe," he says, wincing. "Are you mad?"

My first, abused impulse is to say something calming and pleasing like, "Oh my God, no!" Instead, I suck in a long, wounded breath. I have to keep him talking as long as possible.

"I'm . . . disappointed," I say.

"When did you know it was me?"

Days, weeks, and months of brain fog dissolve, dropping clarity on me like a spring rain.

"The breakup," I admit. "Or right now. Or before. Later. I don't know. You were dead, and I still suspected you. But it's all obvious now." My chest pumps with hot, furious breaths. "I should've known you were a manipulative liar." I laugh to myself. "I should've listened to Cole. I should've asked out Mike—"

"The *late* Mike Mancini," Grover corrects. I push away the thought of that sweet boy.

"Everyone thought it was coincidence or bad luck that every other Queer Club member didn't make it to the meeting on time. But it was your design.

"You asked Mike and Justin to meet you in the cafeteria. You made sure Benny overheard you leaving him out, so he'd blow off the meeting entirely. Then Gretchen sent a text that got Lucy and Theo out of there. Your idea?" He nods. "Em was new to the meetings. That's why she was the only other one there besides me and Cole. So, with everyone gone, Ray collected our fingerprints, and you met Gretchen and killed her. Was she surprised?"

"Yes, but I told her it was for a good cause," he says cheerfully. "You."

"Then you choked yourself with your own razor necklace. How'd you know it wouldn't kill you?"

"Practice. Every time I went to Mooncrest, I tested on a dummy with Ray."

"You're lucky Cole's mom is a great surgeon." I lean heavily on Cole's name. Grover's upper lip curls like a rabid dog's. "Did you know I'd break up with you?"

He scratches the back of his neck. "I knew as long as Cole was around, it would happen eventually. So you needed another reminder of why I mattered."

"You thought of everything." My vision is blurring. I rest my head against the grille, but I'm careful not to move too much. I know what's at stake. "And faking your own death, that was a sexy idea to you because you knew how guilty and miserable it would make me."

He smiles. "I couldn't resist seeing how you'd mourn."

"Were you satisfied?"

He smirks. "You really do care about me."

"So you picked a big, public fight with Cole. You and Justin *both* scratched him, so you both had his blood under your nails. Did you order Justin to do that too? He'd do anything you wanted, wouldn't he? He just wanted someone to need him. And he had access to Cole that you didn't." My mind turns, remembering when the Smiling Sandman broke into Cole's house to plant evidence. "Justin got you his house key."

Grover nods.

My stomach twists facing it all, but I have to keep him talking. "So when I left you at Mooncrest, you ran off and Justin followed you to help. Where you killed him."

Grover sighs wistfully. "Justin was a much bigger fish to wrangle than Gretchen. Took him a while to die."

"You switched clothes, ran through the parking lot to his car so I'd see you thinking it was him, and then where'd you drive? In a circle?"

"Back behind the refreshments tent. I bashed his teeth in with a rock so people couldn't tell that it wasn't me. As Cole would rudely put it, just another tall, blond, white gay. I saw you and the others coming toward the tent. Your scream was so nice. Full of so much love."

I bite my lip again to stop any tears. All of it was for attention—mine.

Sighing, my ex pulls out Astadourian's gun. I hold my breath, but he keeps it limply at his side. For now. "You all ran to get help," he says, "and I threw on the Sandman mask and waited in the shadows until everyone arrived. Justin was unrecognizable. And that sad old queen Kevin got to him first and didn't notice a thing."

"Kevin wasn't a sad old queen," I spit.

"He was *pathetic*! Always bumming us out about how he never had a high school boyfriend. PLEASE. Same thing is gonna happen to Cole. Young SLUTS turn into lonely OLDS. You should be thanking me for saving you from that life. I offered you something PURE and LASTING." He winces with a painful memory. "Before I got with you, every week I'd have to hear from Theo about the newest Tucson boy you drove over to blow or sent pics to. Fucking sick. I had to do something to stop you."

My breaths quicken as my rage comes to a boil. "My body is MINE," I growl. "It doesn't belong to you, Grover."

"The things I could do if I was beautiful like you." Grover's lip trembles. "You're a waste!"

I want to lunge at him, but I'll be shot dead, and I'm so close. Keep. Him. Talking. "Kevin found out about Justin, didn't he?"

Grover laughs at himself. "Me and my tattoo hang-up.

As soon as he saw Justin's ugly shamrock, he knew we had the wrong boy."

"Don't ever get a tattoo," Grover used to say. *"Or I won't be able to look at your body the same way."* He always knew he went too far because he'd immediately soften. *"You're just so perfect without it."*

Complete control of my body, that's always been Grover's primary goal.

Rage churns in my heart. "You did all this just for me?" I ask.

Grover smiles warmly. "Cole has shredded your self-esteem. Yes, *you.* Don't you think you're worth this?"

I want to stand, reach for my phone, but I remind myself not to move. "Killing queer people? Terrorizing everyone? Making us think we were dying *because* we were queer? No, I am not worth that!"

Grover nods with a hint of sadness. "I'm gonna have to build up your confidence more."

I keep slipping lower against the Charger's grille. Every time I straighten myself, pain rockets down my spine. "What's the plan now, babe?" I ask, fighting through agony. "Your old plan was for Ray and Cole to die and go down in history as the killers. Then what? I fall in love with you? We're together forever?"

Grover snorts, calmly explaining as if I'm a silly child: "That's really reductive, but yes."

Reductive.

I almost laugh. All this death, and here I go minimizing. "What NUANCES am I missing?!"

Grover kneels down to me, bringing us almost nose-to-nose. Up close, I was expecting his face to be frightening, different—like I'd recognize something new and terrible, but disturbingly, he looks like the old Grover again. The same cute, smiley Grover—only now, he's saying one inhuman thing after another.

"Come with me," he whispers. "Our lives were going to change after graduation anyway. You were losing Cole anyway. We'll go anywhere in the world you want, babe. We can be anyone. Do anything. Together." He kisses me. His saliva tastes like sour milk, and I bite back the urge to spit.

He pulls back, hardened—feeling my disgust.

"If you don't come with me, I'll kill Cole," he says. "I'll kill your mom. I won't even be cute about it with the razors and the notes, they will just die, boom boom boom." He smiles. "You can save them, but if you're too selfish, if you're too hung up on what you want instead of opening yourself to the possibility of a life with me, then . . . Everyone dies for nothing."

I shake my head as Grover looks down at me.

Grover almost got away with it—shifting all responsibility for these deaths onto me for being a selfish prick who never loved him enough, or in the right way. As Cole always said, bullshit.

Grover is a lying abuser, and nothing he says can be trusted.

His face twists with anger. "No one's seen me alive but you—they can't stop me."

"You're right," I say, smiling. He smiles back. "But you're not *totally* right."

"Yeah?" He bites his lip adorably, so curious what this silly baby is talking about. Well, this silly baby has one big fucker of a surprise waiting for him.

"Check your notifications."

Grover's eyes narrow. As if sensing a trap, he scuttles backward and lifts his phone. He's been tracking us all so effortlessly through social media—tracking me from the beginning—I knew he'd have it on him. He gazes at his phone, and his eyes widen. I know exactly what he's reading: FrankieDearie is going live.

Five minutes ago, I propped my phone—camera out—on the grille of the Charger, began my stream, and used my head to hide it from Grover.

His eyes dart up. I scoot to the right, finally revealing a live stream with tons of viewers.

He stares right into the lens.

"*Everyone* has seen you alive," I say. As Grover quakes with rage, an all-too-familiar beast taking over his body, I harden my resolve and stand. "Ladies, gentlemen, and all the rest of us, I promised you a killer reveal. Here he is, Grover Kendall—live and alive. Hope a few of you save this video confession as a keepsake." My ex and I lock eyes, a long-brewing battle about to begin. "I want something for Grover to remember me by."

Heartbreak and homicide pinwheel through his face. Just as suddenly, his cool demeanor returns. Calm and scary.

When Grover gets calm, that's when the trouble starts.

"Hey, everybody!" he says, not looking away from me. "Don't close the stream just yet because I've got one more surprise." He raises Astadourian's gun. "You're all gonna watch me kill Dearie."

CHAPTER THIRTY-EIGHT
COLE

I RACE JULIETA TOWARD River Run. Mrs. Dearie is close behind me. She tried radioing Double-A or any of the agents at the Galligan house. No one answered. We are *very* late, I fear.

I don't let that thought inside because I'm driving too recklessly to take my mind off the road for even a moment. We alerted all the outlying cars to redirect their Justin search toward River Run, but everyone is far, much too far. It's up to Mrs. Dearie, Benny, and me, if anything can be done at all.

We'll know soon enough. We're both seconds away from reaching Theo's house—but then what? Grover has Dearie hostage, and I have no idea how we're gonna keep him safe.

Beside me, buckled in so tightly he's cut off circulation, Benny clutches two phones in each terror-sweating hand: mine, which has Mrs. Dearie on speakerphone; and his, which plays the live stream of Grover's unmasking.

I don't know how Dearie figured out Grover's secret on his own, but I couldn't be more proud of him finally facing the ugliest truth.

Mostly, I can't believe how easily Grover is spilling his guts. But then I remember Flops are powerless to the lure of attention—which is how I *knew* Grover sent those Sandman texts to himself for sick, Floppy attention. When I'm right, I'm right, and I am *always* right.

But now he's got Dearie at gunpoint. And there's no way I'm losing my bestie tonight, not to Grover, not for any reason.

My heart is racing right alongside my engine, but calm assurance fills my head. Assurance that I will reach Dearie in time.

And I am what? Always right.

As I pummel pavement down the tree-lined, lamplit neighborhood street, cars swerve to avoid us. They'll gladly move for Mrs. Dearie's police siren, but not a teenager's cherry-red BitchMobile. Multiple people lay on their horns, especially as we approach the entrance to River Run, my lovely upper-crust community. River Run's entrance screams "Us vs. Them"—a multilayered barrier of brick walls, iron gates, and manned security outposts. I'm absolutely thrilled to be bringing this chaotic hell down upon my country club neighbors.

The security guard must've heard the siren approaching because he's already opened the eastern gate so we can enter at speed. I decelerate just enough that I don't bottom out on the incline leading the mini-mansion sprawl of River Run.

In the center of the community is a park, and homes radiate outward like spokes on a wheel. The farther out and north you go, the richer you are. I live near the park, but Theo lives in the crown jewel—the northern edge, which borders a vast country club. Many Theo parties ago, I became obsessed with their father's runway-like driveway, and now I can picture the garage clearly in my mind: four streets north, at the end of a long street, fifteen houses deep, dead-ending at Theo's garage . . .

Where Dearie's life is in limbo.

Mrs. Dearie idles beside me and cuts her siren. I don't want to push deeper toward Theo's house until she says so. It's her son. It's her call.

"We have to get close to the house," Mrs. Dearie says from the speakerphone in Benny's trembling hand. *"We can't wait for backup. The main garage is open, so I could sneak up and get Grover in my sights."*

I shake my head. "You really think you could get close enough before he got off a shot at Dearie?"

She sighs, quivering. *"There's no other way. I have to assume the agents are down. Frankie has him distracted talking, so maybe we could surprise him."*

A surprise.

I tap my chin, cold with sweat. *Think, you gay baby.* Like in so many close-to-the-buzzer Rattlers games before, different paths to victory cycle through my brain. Each of them

376

will catch Grover, but none of them are foolproof to save Dearie.

Then, a very bad (yet very sexy) idea floats into my thoughts, making my stomach moan.

Y'all wanted a twist, eh?

I glance at Benny, that saucer-eyed sweetie holding two phones flat in his hands like a diner waitress. His usually glossy lips look chapped and dry with fear. He's trying so hard to keep it cool—but I need to upset him one more time.

"If Grover finds out he's being recorded, he'll be expecting cops," I whisper. "But he's not expecting me."

"You have a plan?" Benny asks, trapped midway between panic and relief.

"Unfortunately, I do." I lean over, grasp him by the back of his hair, and kiss him. We both smile, and I tap his cheek. "Do you trust me?"

His lower lip trembling, he squeaks, "Unfortunately, I do."

"*Oh my God,*" Mary's speakerphone voice interrupts. Benny jumps. We don't have to wonder what she's referring to for long because on Benny's phone—Dearie's live stream—Grover's face is suddenly filling the frame. He stares directly into the camera. His eyes pulse with hate.

He knows we're watching. He knows Dearie tricked him.

Grover raises a gun. *"You're all gonna watch me kill Dearie."*

Breath catches in my throat. We don't have minutes, we have seconds.

A shadow passes in the background of cars behind Grover, but he doesn't turn. He doesn't see them approach. "Who's that?" Benny asks.

That's when the shadow—a third person—catapults themselves toward the killer.

CHAPTER THIRTY-NINE
DEARIE

"DROP THAT GUN!" SOMEONE screams from the shadows behind a bright blue Corvette.

The next moment—the moment I thought a bullet was going to shred my heart in pieces—a person in black tackles Grover. A boy in a . . . turtleneck. I smile, hopeful and frightened, as Mike Mancini—somehow alive—pummels Grover. My ex is taller and stronger, however, and he easily hurls Mike off him.

My savior lands on the cold garage floor with a thud, but he won't be stopped. Fueled by animalistic rage, he lunges again for Grover. The cavernous garage is so dark—and Mike is giving off such unhinged energy—Grover reacts too late.

He aims his gun . . .

I sprint toward them with pained steps . . .

But Mike tackles him again before he can get a shot off. On a swell of pain through my back, I'm forced to my knees, my hip knocking against the hood of the vintage Batmobile. Mike is a frenzy of limbs punching and slapping Grover, but on a terrifying roar, Grover backhands Mike hard across his jaw. In the half second Mike is stunned, Grover's large hands find his throat.

"How the HELL are you alive?!" he seethes. I'm also curious. That razor wire wrapped around Mike so tightly Grover could hoist him into the air. But there isn't a speck of blood on him.

Our answer comes quickly—Grover pulls down Mike's turtleneck to expose his throat.

"Oh my God," Grover and I both say simultaneously.

Underneath Mike's bunchy turtleneck, which he's been wearing all day, is a wide strip of brown, leathery hide fastened into a collar. *Whoa.* My boy took precautions.

"You WEINER." Grover gasps with laughter. "You are such a DORK."

"Leave Frankie alone!" Mike hisses, wild out of his mind.

Grover laughs cruelly. "You wore a collar on your date with *my* boyfriend. You kinky slut!" A hammer click rings through the garage. "Down, boy."

BANG!

"MIKE!" I scream as he howls in pain.

Grover rolls Mike off him, who lands with a limp plop. Clutching a bleeding wound on his hip, Mike rocks back and forth, gasping and whining.

Long past caring about my own safety, I scramble from

my hiding place behind the Batmobile to reach Mike. I place my hand over his as he clutches his wound. We'll stop the bleeding. He smiles weakly as I whimper, "I can't believe you're okay."

"Not for long," Grover says. Another hammer click rattles through the high metal walls of the garage. Mike and I freeze. Then slowly, I turn. My ex, ready to kill, aims at me. He stands astride the white Charger, his back to the open garage door.

"Hey, guys, I hope you're still watching," Grover announces, sweating and huffing, to my still-running live stream. "I am the new Mr. Sandman, and I have come to claim Frankie Dearie—the loneliest person in the world."

Behind Grover, and his gun, I see at the foot of the long driveway . . . Mom.

I don't have space for hope. My only thought is how sorry I am that she has to watch this.

While I press down on Mike's wound, I know the truth. She's too late.

From the ground, Mike weakly strokes my hand with his pinky. I'm not alone.

I close my eyes.

"Grover!" Mom calls from the street. I wait for the shot, but it doesn't come. I open my eyes to see Grover abandoning us, walking toward the open garage. At the end of the driveway, Mom waits alone, with no backup.

Terror stabs my heart. He's gonna shoot her, then me. He's relentless.

For a moment, Grover looks back, pointing his gun and smiling. "If you reach for your weapon, I shoot your son."

"I understand," Mom says calmly, hands up. "I'm getting lots of practice watching my son be taken hostage today."

Grover snorts. "I'm sorry I missed the first time with Ray, but I had other plans."

Mike's blood pools around our fingers. If Mom is trying to reason with Grover, good luck. But at least she's bought us a vital moment.

"Can you move?" I whisper to Mike. Nodding, he whimpers into his sleeve as I help him to his feet. He hops with me toward the row of cars.

Can we make it behind them before Grover notices? My heart doesn't even dare to beat.

"So, what is this?" Grover shouts at my mom. "You gonna bargain for Dearie's life?"

"If you're open to that," she says.

Grover laughs, and my stomach sinks. She's really rolling the dice—but even to save me, she can't let him go!

Only a few more hops, and Mike and I will be back behind the Batmobile. Finally, we reach the shadows behind the car when Mike's strength gives out. I guide him to the floor as quietly as a cotton ball.

It won't save us more than a few seconds if Grover really

wants to shoot us, but maybe Mom could charge in fast enough to help.

"Okay," Mom says, "let's talk about a solution where we all walk out of this alive."

Beneath the wheels of the Batmobile, Mike and I glance at each other, both of us caked in sweat. Grover groans. "Mary, you don't know your son at ALL. After I kill him, I want you to remember this: he was a bitch. A mean asshole who didn't care about anybody."

I bite the inside of my cheek to stop the flood of tears that's building. It's a lie. He wanted me to believe I'm awful so I'd date him as penance. I'm a good person, and I *always* have been!

"He cared about you," Mom says.

"Because I made him!" Grover shrieks. "Did it ever occur to you that I didn't go through all this trouble to make Dearie like me, but that I *had* to go through all this just to get through to a boy who is impossible?!"

Why is Mom promising no guns? Just take him out already. He tried to kill me and Cole. He killed Kevin. He killed Paul, Justin, and Ms. Drake. He killed Gretchen, who thought he was her best friend, all so he could get me to go out with him. He is beyond saving. I am tired of listening to his delusions!

"You're not going to kill Frankie," Mom says, with anger around the edges of her calm.

"Oh?" Grover spits. "And why not?"

"Because Cole has something to say to you."

CHAPTER FORTY
COLE

"COLE HAS SOMETHING TO SAY TO YOU."

That's the signal. Dearie is safely out of range from Grover. My foot slams the gas, my parking brake engaged as Julieta builds up speed. Ever since I got Julieta for my sixteenth birthday, I've been daydreaming of racing her down this street.

Today, I get my wish.

Mrs. Dearie is standing at the bottom of the driveway—but to the side, so there's nothing blocking my entrance into the garage. My shot is clear.

Julieta's engine rumbles like thunder through the empty subdivision. *My babygirl, I don't know if you're going to make it through this, but we have an important job to do for the Bestie.*

Next to me, Benny grips his seat and barely contains his hyperventilation.

"Last chance to bail out," I say.

"No way, Mama," he gasps. "I told you my vision—we stop him together."

My eyes flare wide, briefly stunned remembering that, oh my God, Benny *did* predict that he and I would nab the killer together. I shall process this later.

"Three, two—" The speedometer hits my point of no return.

Benny shuts his eyes. I release the brake, and Julieta takes off like a big-game cat.

Homes whoosh past as Theo's house advances, closer and closer. The growling engine shoves out all other sounds but my breath. I keep my beams off for the surprise. This is going to be a very tight squeeze. I have to nail it.

Benny slaps his hands over his eyes. "I'm gonna die saving this white gay!"

Laughter explodes out from my chest. "Don't think of it as saving a white gay," I shout over the roar. "Think of it as killing *another* white gay!"

"THAT HELPS!"

Benny and I scream together, but mine morphs into a whooping battle cry.

The house is close. Everything is moving too fast, but the adrenaline pushes me harder, and the moment we reach the long, straight driveway, I have only one final thought: Dearie.

My bestie. My schemer. Our Blow Pop–painted tongues. Our go-karts. Our Tween Pride. Dearie saving my life. And all the memories we're still going to make.

Over Mary's radio, Grover's derisive voice floats up: *"You think I'm gonna talk to* Cole? *Wrong! I have nothing to say to that bi—"*

Say hi to this, bitch. I throw on my high beams.

We're already halfway up Theo's driveway. Grover appears in the night, standing dead center in the middle of the open garage, surrounded by shimmering cars. He shields his face from my light.

But no one escapes my light.

We collide with Grover, no different than roadkill. His body pinwheels in the air, his ass striking the windshield, which splinters into thousands of cracks. I throw the parking brake again.

Whirls and blurs follow. We spin. Right is left, left is right, but we don't flip—and we don't hit another car. Theo's dad made sure his beauties could be protected whenever he performed his stunts. For a second, soundlessness fills Julieta's cabin. Benny and I twirl silently, the constant spinning forcing us backward in our seats like astronauts.

When sound finally returns, it's squealing, smashing, and screaming.

Then stillness.

CHAPTER FORTY-ONE
DEARIE

IN UNDER FIFTEEN MINUTES, River Run has become a sea of squad cars and ambulances. Satisfied the danger is over, Cole and Theo's country club neighbors emerge onto their lawns to gawk and record the chaos. The most dire cases are taken first: Theo and Agent Astadourian, thankfully both conscious, are loaded onto stretchers and airlifted to the hospital. Helicopter blowback hits people's lawns like a tornado, tossing KEEP OFF OUR LAWN signs and sending IT'S A GIRL! paper storks flying from their pegs.

At the same time, Mike's bleeding is brought under control, and he's loaded into an ambulance. They cut off his leather collar, revealing a ring of deep-purple bruises around his throat. When Grover lifted him in the air, there was still enormous pressure on his windpipe. A breathing mask is lowered over his mouth, and I follow his stretcher, my fingers still interlaced with his until they shut the doors.

Every second passes like a dream—unreal and slow.

I'm miles from my body. My physical traumas go

dancing with my emotional ones, which have been present for so long but held back while I had a job to do. The job of unmasking and stopping Mr. Sandman. My ex-boyfriend. Thank God I recorded my confrontation with Grover. It will be important to remember how things really happened, how it really unfolded, and how he really made me feel. Because sometimes—as Cole would agree—whenever I think badly of Grover, my mind boomerangs and forces me to say something nice.

I can't always trust my memory, but I'll always be able to trust this recording.

At the foot of the long driveway, Benny perches on the back of an ambulance, still looking precious in his short shorts and big glasses. An EMT makes Benny follow his finger. He must be okay because the man gives him a swift tap on the shoulder and leaves. Lucy and Em approach him, and the three friends pull each other into a group hug.

In my mind, so far away, I'm crushed with relief that they made it out of this okay.

"Frankie, come here . . ." my mom's garbled voice calls, sounding underwater even though she's standing beside me. She gently grazes the cuts and sore spots on my back, brushing the spot where Grover threw me into the railing. Pain rises quickly, and my arm jerks. She pulls me toward the row of EMTs lined along the sidewalk, but I dig my feet into the blacktop.

"I need to see him!" I say, turning.

Reluctantly, Mom walks me back into the garage of death, which is an active crime scene, buzzing with officers, EMTs, and agents milling around the priceless autos. Cole finally got the chance to hot-rod inside here, and he did so exquisitely. Every collectible car remains untouched. Julieta was less fortunate. Her grille lies in blood-drenched pieces as a small pillar of steam rises from her crumpled hood. Her windshield is pulverized.

Grover's body did all that.

Agent Jackson kneels at an evidence site by the Batmobile, feet from Julieta's wreckage. Using tongs, he lifts the comedic Sandman mask and places it in a bag, probably to be sealed away in an FBI evidence locker until it "goes missing" and resurfaces on eBay.

At the back of the garage, four EMTs attempt the impossible task of loading Grover onto a stretcher. Somehow, he's still alive. As they set him onto the gurney, he doesn't cry out. He stares upward, blinking softly, as if he's still trying to process what that odd light was. Next to Grover, seated on the hood of a yellow-and-black 1960s Lotus 7 racing car, is Cole. His forehead is bleeding, but he's 100 percent focused on watching Grover, like he's standing guard.

My bestie.

We notice each other—and smile—at the same moment. He opens his wide wingspan and accepts me into his gentle, immovable grip. It is so nice to be held by someone I trust. Slowly, my faraway mind descends from the stars and reenters my body. Returning to reality will be agony, but at this moment, my only reality is Cole's hug.

"I should've known it was him," I whisper. "It's my fault . . ."

Cole doesn't say anything. He just gently shushes me as he combs his fingers through my hair. Moments later, Mom, Cole, and I advance toward the EMTs hovering above Grover. He can only twitch. Even if he is alive, he can't hurt me or anyone else anymore. One of the EMTs pulls Mom aside and whispers, "His pulse is very weak."

"Do what you can," Mom whispers.

"He won't make it down the driveway."

Grover is going to die any second.

I rest my head on Cole's sweat-dampened shoulder, and we smile at Grover. He watches us, tears spilling quietly down his cheeks. Good—I'm glad the two of us will be the last thing he sees.

"Hey, Flop," Cole greets him. "I know you really wanted to kill us, but looks like that didn't happen. The Floppitude of it all. I know you're embarrassed." Grover moans. Cole presses a finger to his lips. "No, no. Save your strength."

"Grover," I say, grinning, "you were right about something else: you *are* gonna convince the whole world that

Cole killed you." A wheezing laugh takes over Cole. "We're such bullies."

"Much bullies," Cole agrees.

"Guys, some space," an EMT says, motioning us away as she straps belts over Grover's arms. We oblige with a step back and to the left, putting us closer to his face. Yet something has changed—he's smiling.

"What's so funny?" I ask.

Grover winces. We lean closer. Finally, he speaks in a coughing, strained voice: "I win . . ."

"How?"

His bloodshot, hateful eyes fall on me. "You'll . . . never forget me . . ."

Everything becomes cold. Leave it to Grover—he always knows what to say to twist my brain like spaghetti around a fork. With one last cough, Grover's legs begin to seize uncontrollably. We all retreat as the EMTs swarm him. His entire body seizes for another few seconds . . .

And then stillness.

My legs give out. Cole and Mom catch me like I've plummeted from a high wire into a net. I need a doctor. Why didn't I go to an ambulance? Why did I have to come back here to watch him die? To hear one final taunt? What is wrong with me?

What is WRONG with me?

"He hurt me," I whimper in their arms.

"I know," they both say.

My boyfriend killed people. He manipulated me, abused me, separated me from my friends, and then when none of that was enough to keep me, he tried to kill me.

It's the truth I've been running from for weeks.

Well, no more running. My strength is gone.

But to paraphrase Ms. Spears, I'll be stronger tomorrow.

COMING SOON, THE STARTLING SEQUEL
NO ONE COULD'VE PREDICTED—

YOUR LONELY NIGHTS ARE FINALLY OVER:
THE RETURN AND FALL OF MR. SANDMAN

An unflinching follow-up to this year's hottest docuseries with new footage and exclusive interviews!
True crime legend Peggy Jennings emerges from
retirement to trace the shocking, devastating
final days of real-life Mr. Sandman Ray Fletcher,
his young protégé Grover Kendall, and the brave
victims who finally stopped their cold-blooded,
multigenerational rampage.
Was it Ray who recruited Grover? Or was it the other
way around? How did a troubled boy figure out this
friendly neighborhood man was the monster from TV?
One thing is certain—it's safe to be single again.

EPILOGUE, PART I
COLE

BACK IN ROOM 208 for the last time. Three weeks ago, the world found out what I've known for years—Grover Kendall was a one-in-a-million asshole. Since the Mr. Sandman scourge is finally over, the superintendent reinstated an in-person graduation and prom, which is currently thumping in the gymnasium four rooms away. Bass-y pop bleeds through the walls, only a hint of its merriment finding us, which is how joy feels lately. It's there, but just a flavor.

When the semester began, the Queer Club had ten members. Now, we are seven.

Seven spiked punch cups meet with a plastic-y *clink*.

Em—in a clinging silver gown the color of her hair— came with Theo, who will use a wheelchair while they recuperate from their fall. Theo's suit is black with flashes of silver to match Em's dress. A silver bow tie lies casually undone around their neck.

Agent Astadourian survived with similar fractures to Theo's on her wrist, collarbone, shin, tibia, and two vertebrae. Double-A Batteries was happy to see the back of this town.

Going stag, Lucy wowed everyone in a burgundy flapper dress and matching feather fascinator. My date, Benny, wore his grandfather's wedding suit, and the boy is pulling it off: head-to-toe baby blue, pearly-white shoes, ruffled undershirt, and a bolo tie with a large sapphire-stone clip. Not to be outshone, I picked up faux alligator boots, a tailored red suit with no undershirt, and a dozen turquoise necklaces draped over my bare chest. Thanks to physical therapy (and Grover only shooting the juiciest part of his hip), Mike's wounds have healed. He wears a traditional suit, black-on-black, but for a touch of queer panache, he added a black sequined collar. His voice is still scratchy, but his throat bruises have faded. His date, Dearie, matches Mike's black theme, wearing a black blazer with a large, golden tiger lily on the breast; a skintight black sports bra in lieu of an undershirt, women's slacks with wide ankles; dark blue eyeshadow; and silver skull rings on each finger.

All in all, we're serving.

And bizarrely, I'm the one who called everyone in from the party. Me, the one who would've happily seen this dysfunctional club flushed down the toilet months ago. Only I understand now, when it's too late, that it wasn't the club. It was how Grover had already manipulated everyone. Grover's abuse divided us. He wanted us to be islands apart, distrusting each other. It's how he felt about himself, and it was how he was convinced he'd bring beautiful, daring Dearie into his life.

Queer loneliness is healed by queer community, so if Grover's plan was to get Dearie alone, the community had to go.

But he flopped on that too, as all efforts to divide queers eventually do.

I hold out my glass. We've already saluted Gretchen, Justin, Ms. Drake, Paul, Claude, Kevin, and all of Ray and Grover's victims. But I called for one last toast. "I, uh, enjoy talking, but this is hard to say."

My heavy voice cracks. This horrible thought has been building in me the whole night—my era with Dearie is ending. Why can't there be time machines? I need more time. I jump around to everyone's eyes, never staying with one person longer than a few seconds, because if I do, I'll think about how I'll never see them again and lose it.

"I'm just . . ." I say, another frog in my throat. "I'm just sorry."

"What are you sorry for?" Benny asks, petting my free hand.

I land on Dearie for a moment too long. Shit. It's coming.

Friends forever. Friends forever. Nothing will come between us. Friends forever.

"We're out of time," I say, blinking back tears. Theo

looks at me gentler than they've ever done before. Em grips her collar and fights back a slew of tears herself. I'll never get to know them better. I missed out. Finally, the tears leak like a broken shower pipe. "Ah shit, I don't want to be that guy, but I'm gonna steal a movie line for this moment because that's how I do it." I collect a large breath. "I am sorry because this whole time . . ." My chin trembles. "This whole time, we could've been friends."

I crack. Luckily, everyone is right there with me. Six other faces fall at once. No, not fall—*fill* with, well, maybe not love, but affection. We bring the circle tighter, expanded just enough for Theo's chair to enter, and we breathe in each other's presences. These Flops worked their Floppy magic on me. I can't stand these fools!

We're united by Grover's abuse but not defined by it. He was right—we won't forget him, but that's the point. Grover was our warning to keep our community tight and pay tender attention to when a weed is attacking the garden.

In this moment, seven hearts banish any trace of loneliness they've ever felt.

One by one, the others return to the party, until it's just me and Dearie left. *Friends forever, friends forever.* He grins at my wet, Feelings Beast face—and then flicks my nipple. On a jolt of pain, I jump backward, hissing, but it cleared my head.

"You softie," he says.

I groan. "RELAX. It's the schnapps."

"You love these Flops, don't you?" I suck my teeth and roll my eyes. Dearie approaches, more beautiful and peaceful than I've ever seen, and pulls me to him. We hold each other's eyes—eyes I know better than my own. "These tears, are they about me?" I look away, stung. When I look back, Dearie hasn't blinked. "You know we're still gonna talk every day."

Goddammit, how much is one heart supposed to take?

Sniffing, I say, "He stole our last time together. And I *hate* him for that."

Dearie nods, biting back emotion. "Yeah. I hate him too. But we're going to make new memories, us together, us with other people." He socks me in the shoulder. "And cheer up—you killed the shit out of him."

"Oh!" My eyes shut, savoring the memory. "I killed hiiiiiiim."

As our laughter fades, the party calls.

"Our dates are waiting," I say, offering my arm to Dearie, which he hooks.

"Are you and Benny gonna try . . . ?"

"Long distance? Nah. I offered, but turns out, dating me is stressful?"

Dearie fake gasps. "No!"

I shrug. "We're gonna stay close and see what happens, but for now, Benny's got a *ho* new world to explore." Dearie snorts and leans into me as we walk into the darkened hall. Dance pop grows louder. "I'm serious! People better watch out. He's gonna be the Wolf of Tucson."

Dearie sighs. "Yeah, Mike and I will be short-lived too."

I nod. "You okay with that?"

"I am. I'm just . . . gonna need time before I see anybody seriously. I've got stuff to sort out, and Mike and I talked about it. If we kept things long distance, he'd get lonely, and I'd get people-pleasey and just make all the same bad decisions."

"That sounds like a lot of smart words. But we still gotta get you D at some point."

Dearie grins. "Oh, Mike and I are still having sex until I go."

"That's my girl!" He gets the world's biggest squeeze. Interlacing our fingers, Dearie and I sway our arms quietly down the hall—*friends forever, friends forever*—for perhaps the last time. As we throw open the gymnasium doors, we're met by our dates, our friends, and a tidal wave of joyous music. Not a bad closer for our Stone Grove era.

We both lost someone close—Ray for me, Grover for him—people who mattered to us, but our lives literally couldn't move on until we unmasked their destructive influence and purged them. It's been painful, grieving for these killers. Grieving the people we *thought* they were. Grieving the trusting people we used to be.

But tonight, there's nothing in our lives but dancing.

Dearie and I even snatch the Prom King crowns, so even though this is the end, we get a victorious last dance. Holding him on the dance floor, I let the world slip away and beg the universe to make this feeling last forever.

The universe responds, *It's up to you, New York.*

EPILOGUE, PART 2
DEARIE

GRADUATION PASSES IN A blur, as does the summer. We were all so focused on the end of the school year, we forgot there was a whole two months after that before we went our separate ways. Two months of listening to thunderstorms under Mike's covers. Two months of watching Cole race around River Run in Theo's dad's Batmobile. Two months of stealing glances at Benny opening windows into Cole I haven't been able to pry loose with a crowbar my whole time knowing him. Seeing Cole be tender with a boy other than me, playing with his hair . . .

It's bittersweet, but it needed to happen. Cole has so much love to give.

In July, Mom turns in her badge for good. The search for Mr. Sandman brought her to dark precipices she never wants to approach again. It was the push she needed to start over. After Dad, after Kevin, it was time for a new chapter. She flies Kevin's family out from California—a group of bearish friends—to memorialize him and clean out his apartment. He had no will or next of kin, so Mom and his friends divide up his belongings for keepsakes. In the end, she keeps his games, wineglasses, and the urn of his cat's remains, which now sits next to Kevin's and Dad's urns on our mantel. He'll always be home.

In late August, we say goodbye to Theo, who leaves for Stanford, but not before "bequeathing" presidency of the Queer Club to Em, who will be a junior. She's flattered but deeply uninterested. Let the old club die. The next generation of lonely queers at Stone Grove High will find each other, and community will naturally spring from there. Hopefully, this time in a healthier way. The following week, Lucy leaves for the University of Austin, where she'll study engineering and hopefully have her delightfully weird energy embraced on a larger scale.

Later that week, Cole and I move our "sort-of" boyfriends, Benny and Mike, into their rented house near the community college outside Tucson.

Maybe our exes will hook up. School is over, it's the Wild West, and anything's possible.

The four of us spend one last sexy (but super-sad) night in their house before it's time for us to part ways.

When I finally go to Cole's house to say goodbye, his moms tell me he's not feeling well. He isn't coming out. They hand me a sealed envelope labeled DEARIE—a goodbye letter—and I leave, numb, even though I know Cole is doing the best he can.

My train to LA is today. His flight to New York is tomorrow.

I opted for the train, as I want to savor these rust-colored mesas one last time as a local.

With no big fanfare like the others had, I drive to the station with my mom. Retirement is suiting her—a white A-frame tank top and khaki slacks, like a real nineties action-movie gal. We've already said goodbye a million times today: over breakfast, packing the car, getting out of the car, walking up to the ticket booth. This one feels like it's for good, though. She hugs me on the platform. I catch her smelling my hair.

"Frankie," she says, still hugging me, "you are going to find the right person in the right place at the right time." I nod into her shoulder, missing Mike's hands so badly. Missing Cole's arms even worse. Mom, peaceful and pretty, looks at me. "You're still finding you. I know you're gonna find you out there." She points down the platform, past the waiting train, beyond the mesas, to my destiny. "And who-ever they are, they're waiting for you."

We exchange goodbyes and "I love you"s.

I face the train, a steel bullet burning in the summer sun. My shoulders slump. "I just thought . . ." I whisper. "I thought he'd be here at the end."

Mom smiles, squeezing my shoulder. "You know Cole."

I nod. I do. It was hard enough for him to open up at prom.

After boarding and stowing my luggage, I settle into a half-filled carriage by the window. Mom waves from the platform as we begin to move, faster and faster, until she slips away. Then the station slips away. Then Stone Grove slips away. All around us are mighty mesas and pristine desert. I'm leaving Grover here. He'll still be with me, but his voice will be so distant, I'll barely hear it.

He's where he belongs—the shadows.

On the train, loneliness finds me, but I'm not afraid. I greet it like a bestie. It's nothing to be scared of; it's just me looking at my own reflection. And I'm liking it more and more.

After a few minutes, I'm ready to read Cole's card: DEARIE. My fingers shake so hard, I almost drop it. I peel open the envelope, pull out the plain white card, and read Cole's last, handwritten words to me:

Hey, Bestie.

That's it? I flip the card over—blank. That's all he has to say?

Anger rises in my chest. I thought Benny opened up that masc-head! I thought Cole would make a bigger moment of this. I thought he'd—

But then Cole Cardoso, in all his maroon-jacket glory, plops into the open seat next to me—his hair returned to its natural jet-black. "I suck at writing notes," he says. "But I'm great at talking, so here I am."

My mouth hangs open, speechless, most likely spewing out the infinite stream of purple and pink heart bubbles currently detonating through my body. "What about Columbia?" I ask breathlessly, hoping his response is something like *idk, bestie, the place burned down in a fire.*

He shrugs. "Meh."

"You're coming with? What are you gonna do there?"

"Same thing I always do. Thrive." He winks.

I roll my eyes. "Dork farmer, I mean, what . . . What? Like, what?"

He searches his hands through the air, as if to catch the right words. "UCLA let me back in—you know, star slayer of Mr. Sandman—"

"You killed one, I killed the other."

"Dream team! Anyway, I can officially join in the spring, but I talked them into letting me audit for the fall. Until then, I'm gonna crash with my dad and just, I don't know, start filming shit." He smiles again, but vulnerably this time. "With . . . you as my lead?"

All I can do is smile. "Cole . . ."

"You're on your own new journey! I stand by all of what we agreed to about forging new paths, making our own lives apart."

"Just not too far apart." We interlace our fingers on the train's armrest. I squeeze, flush with a wonderful thought. "Do you know who would *hate* that you did this?"

"GROVER," we say simultaneously. He scrunches his face wickedly. "I just couldn't let him win by keeping us apart." His eyes alight, Cole smacks me. "Know what the first thing we should do in LA is?"

"What?"

"Tattoos."

Gasping, I clutch his forearm like I'm a falcon perched on a glove. "I would LOVE that, and Grover would HATE that."

"I know!" Cole digs into his jacket pocket for a small spiral notebook and two pens. "Let's draw the tattoos we want, and then tape them to the seats in front of us."

"Why tape them?"

"So we can get used to looking at them. We'll be wearing them the rest of our lives."

If only this moment could be a tattoo. I want to look at it forever.

At long, long, *long* last, Cole and I finally shut the hell up.

As we leave the mesas behind, we doodle and laugh our way toward our destinies together, to a place of no more lonely nights.

ACKNOWLEDGMENTS

This book—originally titled *Dearie*—has had almost as long of a journey reaching bookshelves as my first thriller, *Surrender Your Sons*, did. In fact, I began writing this to distract myself from the hellish submission process of selling my debut. At first, I didn't even know what *Dearie* was going to be. Just a mood. Two friends, as close as boyfriends, driving along a desert road toward a movie theater in a graveyard, smoking and chatting about life, sex, death, and social status.

You know, gay stuff.

I didn't even have a story yet—I just knew that by the end of the night, they'd discover a body. While I waited (and waited and waited) to sell that first book, I immersed myself in a dark, vibey, Lynchian world that was modern but channeling 1950s Americana cool. Looking cute and feeling flip in the face of unknowable terror.

Very today.

A book doesn't "just" go from a moody vibe piece to finished work that's worth someone's twenty dollars. Help is needed, and throughout the years, the following people helped, either creatively or personally.

First, to Eric Smith, who signed me and *Surrender Your Sons*, not knowing what he was getting into with this creepy, unfinished desert quasi-noir, thank you for shepherding my characters to the right place! To my editor, Kelsey Murphy, thank you for being the right place! Dearie and Cole went through several iterations and tweaks before the story clicked into place, but once they did, they really flew. To Michael Bourret, thank you for hitting the ground running in the middle of this project. To Monica Loya and Kaitlin Yang, thank you for illustrating and designing (respectively) a beautiful cover that plunges readers immediately into this dark world.

To my authenticity readers, David Nino, Rick Capone, Russell Falcon, and Terry J. Benton-Walker, thank you for trusting me and for offering your insights on Cole and Benny to help shape *Your Lonely Nights Are Over* into a book that's worth POC readers' time and safe enough so every potential reader could sit back and have a scream-filled, slasher-ific ride. To David, I hope you trust me even more now that I kept my promise to make sure Benny survived! To Russell, thank you for getting me to ditch fast fashion and for always encouraging me to be a cat, not a mouse. To Terry, what can I say that hasn't already been said—but I'll say it again. Thank you for your presence in my life. I've had several Coles in my years, but you're the Cole who got on the train.

To my early readers, Caleb Roehrig, Tom Ryan, Kevin Savoie, Phil Stamper, and Ian Carlos Crawford, thank you for lending me your razor-sharp minds to make this book as taut as possible. Caleb, I appreciate our many talks about being ~queer elders~ and many of these debates trickled down into the Queer Club. Tom, you taught me the Spielberg method of setting a scene in prose, and my work has never been better.

To my dearest, oldest friends, Cat Griffith and Rebecca Kirsch: Becky, it's all for you, Damien! This whole circus began with movies in the cemetery, and my love of them is all thanks to our many years enjoying Hollywood Forever—whether it's a movie picnic or a weekend stroll among the stones, this book is spooky because of you! Cat, my bravest friend: thank you for sharing your toughest moments (and your home) with me while I finished writing. *Lonely Nights* takes best friends to the brink of darkness and lets them laugh at the abyss. That's you and me, frienddddddd.

To my family, thank you for supporting my love of movies from an early age. I never had to sneak around your backs to catch the R-rated suspense films and slashers that inspired this book because you trusted me to understand them. Finally, to my husband, Michael Russo-Sass, and our babies, Marty and Malibu, thank you for always being the warm, safe light I come home to—since the day I met you all, I've never had a lonely night.